THE LINDEN TREE

Kate Brooks had helped the Fitzwarrens create showpiece gardens at a large old house in Somerset. When her elderly employers die, Kate finds that Whitsun Gate house has been left jointly to her and the Fitzwarrens' nephew Smithy, on condition they run the public gardens for two years. Kate has good reason to be wary of men and Smithy, recovering from a car crash and a failed marriage, is equally wary of women. It is clear the Fitzwarrens had hoped these two damaged people would heal each other, and they might—if they don't kill each other first ...

THE LINDEN TREE

THE LINDEN TREE

by
Anna Barrie

Magna Large Print Books
Long Preston, North Yorkshire,
England.

British Library Cataloguing in Publication Data.

Barrie, Anna
  The linden tree.

  A catalogue record for this book is
  available from the British Library

  ISBN 0-7505-1364-0

First published in Great Britain by Judy Piatkus (Publishers) Ltd., 1997

Copyright © 1997 by Anna Barrie

Cover illustration © Len Thurston by arrangement with P.W.A. International Ltd.

The moral right of the author has been asserted

Published in Large Print 1999 by arrangement with Piatkus Books Ltd.

Magna Large Print is an imprint of
Library Magna Books Ltd.
Printed and bound in Great Britain by
T.J. International Ltd., Cornwall, PL28 8RW.

For my sister, Marianne Edwards,
with love.

Chapter One

They'd brought Smithy the tall carver chair from the dining room and plonked it down in a corner, where he could see the others without giving them the trouble of seeing him. He'd been out of hospital barely a week and, although he'd grown accustomed to the rearrangements of his face, legs and other anatomical particulars, his family—such as they were—had not. He quite saw their point. When a man changes his condition from 'one hundred per cent fit' to 'ninety per cent wrecked' and from 'ninety per cent happy' to 'one hundred per cent miserable', he requires a major character reassessment. They hadn't found time for it yet—and, with poor old Mags snuffing it so suddenly—they were evidently finding it easier to pretend he wasn't there.

It was different for him. He couldn't pretend. He'd never got the hang of it, somehow: that funny little trick most people had of changing the facts to suit their fantasies—or to subdue their fears. But it was a trick he wanted to learn, all of a sudden. He'd never been this scared before. He'd never felt so *alone*. He couldn't believe Mags was dead. He'd just been to her funeral, yet still couldn't believe it. Neither could he believe that the rest of her family were taking it so calmly. Pretending again? Or did they really not care?

Fiona looked bored stiff, as usual, and Michael embarrassed, much as usual. Pamela was as ever: affecting to be cool and self-contained when in fact she was neither. And beyond them, misted over by the dirt on the windows, seven acres of a garden so beautiful it could bring tears even to Smithy's eyes. Whitsun Gate, the love of Mags' and Billy's lives ...

Yet to the family at large Whitsun Gate was just a blot on the landscape. The gardens meant nothing to them. Perhaps they meant something to their daughter Pamela, but only as a symbol of her own failure. Or maybe ... Smithy didn't know. Whatever it was, Pamela kept it well hidden, disguised by the games she played.

And then there was Kate. Kate wasn't family, of course, and even if she had been, she'd have remained an enigma. She and Pamela's daughter, Fiona, were much the same age—twenty, twenty-oneish—and as different as chalk from cheese. Fiona looked about thirty, Kate about twelve. Fiona was into power-dressing, Kate into school uniform: little grey kilt, black tights, sensible shoes. Smithy had known her, off and on, since she was sixteen, and had only set eyes on her legs twice: last year for Billy's funeral (she'd worn the same kilt then) and today for poor old Mags'. Nice legs, too, sweetly rounded in all the right places, if just a touch too thin for perfection. God, she was a pretty girl! The legendary 'English Rose' type, permanently aglow with an old-fashioned excess of fresh air and exercise. Hay-coloured hair, big blue eyes ... Highly fanciable. But off limits. 'Don't even think about it,' Mags had warned him when Kate had first appeared on the scene. 'She's afraid of men, although I'm hoping she'll get over it.'

She hadn't, of course. She probably never would. That sort of thing cut deep.

Pamela said something weary about having to sort through everything. 'Those attics! When will we have *time?*' She directed a pitying glance at her cousin. 'You've gone very quiet, Smithy. Pain-killers wearing off?'

'No.' They were, but he could last another hour if he kept his mind busy. After that, he'd get ratty and ruin everyone's funeral. Not that it would take an hour to give Kate her marching orders. She wasn't daft; she knew the score. It was just a matter of getting the formalities over now.

In the car, on the way over, when Pamela was wondering how—most tactfully—to put it, Fiona had said, 'Hell, Mummy, she's only the *gardener!*' which neatly summed up how much Fiona knew. Not that it mattered. Whitsun Gate was Pamela's now and she'd be turning it into hard cash as fast as she could contrive it. Only the gardener or more than the gardener, Kate would have to go.

Smithy tried not to wonder where she would go and was helped in this endeavour by a slow, cold pain, like a slow, cold blade, that sliced along his thigh to settle icily in his groin. He shifted sideways, very carefully, and as the pain eased heard Pamela saying briskly, 'You'll have plenty of time to find something else, Kate. The will has to go through Probate—that'll take a while—and then it'll be months, probably, before we can find a buyer. You can stay until then, or—'

'In fact,' Michael put in, 'we were rather hoping ... We'll need you to keep the gardens up to scratch, you see. With the house in such a mess ...'

Everyone followed his gaze as he peered at flaking paintwork, peeling wallpaper, and a large dent in one of the door panels which dated from an especially memorable family fight in 1963.

'With the house in such a mess, the garden's the only selling point we have.'

Kate blinked and lowered her eyes. It was a trick she had—quite a clever one, too—for making herself seem shy, vague and harmless, when in fact she was hopping mad. Or terrified. But she covered it so well it was hard to tell one from the other. Smithy watched her for another sign, decided on 'terrified' and thought it over.

'How's she meant to live?' he demanded, scanning their faces as he spoke, checking their reactions. Pamela clearly hadn't understood the question. Michael coloured up and looked at his hands, which meant he'd understood the question but had hoped no one would ask it. But Kate—silly girl—hadn't thought of it at all! Her jaw dropped. She widened her eyes (fabulous eyes: a dark, slatey blue which at times looked almost black) and then squeezed them shut as the implications hit home. She'd been

12

totally dependent on Mags—and now Mags was dead. How was she going to live?

If push came to shove, Smithy could tide her over until she found something else, but he was damned if he would. Pamela stood to make a few hundred thousand when she sold up, perhaps half a million if she was callous enough to sell it for development. The least she could do ...

'You can't ask her to look after the house, keep up the gardens and *starve*, now can you?'

'No one's actually *asking* her,' Fiona informed him coolly. 'Actually, we're *letting* her—'

'Starve,' Smithy repeated. 'How thoroughly Christian of you, darling. Have you thought of becoming a missionary, at all?'

Fiona dealt with, he returned to Pamela. 'Mags was paying Kate thirty pounds a week, all found, which means she'll need fifty a week just to keep her head above water.'

'Fifty *pounds?*' Pamela gasped. 'A *week?* Are you mad?'

'Better mad than mean!' (The pain was developing nicely.) 'Not to mention callous and disloyal! Your mother thought the world of Kate, you know that. How do you suppose *she'd* feel—?'

Kate stood up and muttered something about making coffee. She'd never had much stomach for a fight, poor girl. Now, Smithy, on the other hand ...

Kate closed the door, rolling her eyes in despair. The Fitzwarrens were notorious for fighting among themselves. Mags had always said it was healthy: 'Clears the tubes, darling.' But Kate had never believed in its health-giving properties: there was a dent in the sitting room door where Mags had lobbed a paperweight at Billy's head and missed him by an inch.

'She was *my* bloody mother!' Pamela yelled. 'Not Kate's! And not *yours*, Smithy, so mind your own bloody business, will you?'

God, that'd stir him up! He was actually Billy's nephew's son, but his own mother had died when he was ten and he'd adopted Mags as a spare, much as Kate had. But Smithy had rights. *He* was family. Kate was not.

'Listen to yourself!' he said now. 'And ask yourself who's speaking: you, or the little green-eyed monster? You are forty-three years old, Pamela.'

'Oh, trust *you* to keep count!'

'And Kate's only twenty! She's alone—'

'Liar! She's twenty-one!'

'Ha! Trust *you* to keep count!'

Kate shut herself in the kitchen, where their raised voices were just a muted quacking in the background. Although they quarrelled nearly every time they met, they'd never fought over her before and it felt awful, not just because it was embarrassing but because she felt she should be there, trading insults with the rest of them, if only to show Smithy she appreciated his support. Not that she did appreciate it. Pamela was right: it was none of his business. Whitsun Gate was Pamela's. Kate was nobody's.

She put the kettle on, set cups on a tray

and sat at the kitchen table to gaze out of the window. It was a lovely day out there, probably one of the best days of the year. The best days were always in May ... Or perhaps September ... No, definitely May, with the linden tree in fresh new leaf and the sky so bright and clear a blue it made one think of ... heaven.

Mags was dead. Kate had had almost a week to get accustomed to the idea, but she hadn't, yet. Every time she thought of it her heart sank—or, rather, leapt—with shock and disbelief. And yet she'd expected it ... Mags had been almost eighty and when a woman gets to that sort of age, every day is a bonus. But she'd changed since Billy's death last year; she hadn't really wanted to live without him. If it hadn't been for Smithy's accident, if she hadn't wanted to be there for him, she'd have given up months ago. Mags had adored Smithy. For some reason.

The kettle boiled. Kate opened the door and heard Pamela shout, 'Why should I care about their bloody gardens? They never cared about anything *I* did!'

'Perhaps that's because you never did any-thing!'

Kate shut the door again, sighing. Mags had said Smithy had integrity. 'Honest as the day is long,' she'd said; and that was true enough, but was honesty *always* a virtue? Pamela had just lost her mother, and although she and Mags had never seen eye to eye, she must be sad; she must be grieving. Why did he have to duff her up today of all days? He couldn't change anything!

Actually, Kate doubted that he wanted to change anything; he was just arguing for the sake of it, 'clearing the tubes'. And she supposed he had a good many things to clear: his own grief about Mags probably the least of them. He'd come off his motorcycle in September last year and his life had barely been worth living since then. He'd been invalided out of the Army; his wife had left him (they'd been married scarcely two years) and he still couldn't move without the aid of two walking sticks. So why on earth was Kate wasting sympathy on Pamela? Smithy had lost everything.

So had Kate, of course, but she was accustomed to losing and was getting used to it. Just because she didn't know how she'd survive from now on didn't mean she wouldn't. She was one of the most knowledgeable (Mags had said brilliant) young gardeners in the country, and although she had no qualifications—not even a testimonial—to prove it, she should be able to convince someone she was worth paying. Everyone who was anyone in the gardening world had known Mags and Billy. Everyone who was anyone had heard of Whitsun Gate. Surely *someone* would give her a job?

The immediate future was her worst worry now, although she hadn't even thought of it until Smithy had spoken. How was she going to live until she *did* find something else? After buying a new blouse for the funeral, she had twenty-eight pounds in the bank and less than a fiver in her purse, and although the fruit and vegetable gardens would keep her alive *after* next month ... could she live on cornflakes until then?

Things had gone very quiet in the sitting room. Kate opened the door, listened for a moment and heard Pamela saying, 'Surely you can take some more? Every four hours is only a guide, for heaven's sake,' which seemed to indicate that Smithy was in trouble.

She took in the tray and was greeted by a glum silence. Michael was standing at the window, staring out over the lawn. Fiona was flicking through a magazine, Pamela staring at her feet and Smithy, grey-faced and white-knuckled, had squeezed his eyes shut against a pain Kate couldn't even imagine. He'd been so tough, so fearless ... He was probably still fearless, but he certainly wasn't tough any more. He'd only come out of hospital last week—just in time to hear that Mags had died.

'Coffee, Smithy.'

He opened his eyes, said, 'Thanks,' and shut them again.

'Would you like a glass of water? For your pills?'

His mouth tightened angrily and she turned away, shrugging. He knew best. He always had. Bossy sod. But as she resumed her chair, she found herself watching him, tensely waiting for a sign that the pain had eased. If Pamela hadn't told her 'We'll be bringing Smithy', Kate would never have recognised him. Mags had called him 'her golden boy'—with some justification, since he'd always had a sun-tan—but now he was pale as a lily, with shadows under his eyes and gaunt hollows where his cheeks used to be. The scar on his face didn't help either, but it was neat enough; it would fade. In time ...

'We'll be seeing Mummy's solicitor in the morning,' Pamela said. 'We'll see what he says, Kate. There might be enough to pay you from the estate, and if there isn't ...' She glanced at Michael, who failed to meet her eyes. 'Well', she concluded, 'we'll see.'

They were all staying at the Royal Oak, a few miles down the road. In Kate's experience, Pamela had never stayed at Whitsun Gate and Smithy, who always had, now couldn't manage the stairs. Or even the doorstep. He'd have coped better had he let anyone help him, but his temper—or perhaps just the pain—had got beyond him, and when Michael offered him an arm, he snarled, 'Leave me alone, will you?' and did it the hard way.

Michael had parked his BMW under the linden tree, and as he opened the passenger door for Smithy, discovered the sticky honeydew that had covered the paintwork with a fine, sugary glaze.

'Bloody tree,' he muttered. 'Should have been chopped down years ago.'

Smithy lowered himself to the front seat and reached out to retrieve his walking sticks from Kate. 'Sorry,' he whispered. 'I wasn't a lot of help, was I?'

'Never mind,' she said. 'It cleared the tubes, anyway.'

'Hmm. I'm not so sure about that.' He closed his eyes. 'See you tomorrow,' he murmured.

18

A garden, Mags had always said, was the most demanding lover a woman could have. In return for a few brief moments of bliss, it nagged, bullied and beat her, wore her into the ground in its service and, at the end of the day, always complained: 'You haven't done enough.'

'Men are easy by comparison, Kate. At least we can meet *their* needs lying down.'

'Speak for yourself,' was Kate's answer to that. 'I'd rather shovel three tons of horse manure.'

'Oh, I *am* glad you said that, darling. The stables are delivering tomorrow.'

The joke was over now. Mags was dead and the world, which for the past five years had been all roses and horse manure, was suddenly full of men. Not that Kate actually disliked men. Standing at a distance of five yards behind a thorn hedge and talking about computers, farming, or international politics, men were perfectly all right. In such circumstances Kate had even been known to find them quite attractive: strong shoulders, good legs, nice smile. She never looked at the bits in between and avoided their eyes for fear of discovering that they were looking at *her* 'bits in between', so she could never say what colour a man's eyes were. Even Smithy, whom she'd known—off and on—since she was sixteen, could have green, blue or brown eyes—or even pink—and if a policeman asked for a description of him, she'd have to say, 'It all happened so quickly, officer, I didn't notice.'

At this time of year, she and Mags used to work until it was too dark for them to see what they were doing. You couldn't do much when the visitors were in and the gates were open between eleven and six every day. But that was all over, now. The gates were shut and the gardens ... lonely. Kate did her final tour of inspection just after sunset and then locked up the house and went to bed.

She'd never spent a night alone—in this house or any other—until a week ago, when they'd taken Mags out in her coffin. And Whitsun Gate was an awful house to be alone in: too big, too gloomy, too old and neglected. All its little noises—creaks, tickings, knocking pipes and dripping cisterns—now seemed strange and threatening, louder than usual. But this was what life would be like from now on and she must get used to it.

But how? How was she meant to live? Her mother would lend her money, she supposed. If she asked. But her mother couldn't give her a home: Kate would rather die than spend a single night under the same roof with her stepfather. She'd rather die than set eyes on him again. In fact, just the thought of him made her want to die. Or at least, throw up. He'd ruined her for life.

Had she been any other reasonably good-looking girl of twenty-one, she'd probably have had a boyfriend now, someone to care, to give her some sort of hope for the future. But—not counting a few juvenile crushes when she was twelve or thirteen—Kate had never had a boyfriend. She often fantasised about having someone to love her, someone to care. But her fantasies never went further than comforting hugs and platonic kisses; there was never anything lover-like about him. If there was a man on earth prepared to put up with such a relationship, he was eighty-three and past wanting anything more. Because there couldn't *be* anything more. Ever.

'And to my great-nephew, Courteney Fitzwarren-Smith ...'

The front seat of a Ford taxi-cab wasn't half as cushy as the same spot in Michael's BMW, and as the driver, oblivious to his passenger's discomfort, took a sharp left from the Frome Road into Lower Minden, Smithy gave up thinking about his surprise inheritance and yelled, 'Slow *down*, will you?'

'Oh. Sorry, mate. Didn't hurt you, did I?'

'No, no. I always scream on the corners. So exciting, aren't they? Left after that thatched cottage. *Slowly.*'

Kate was waiting by the gate, pretending to pull weeds, although Smithy knew from the frantic look on her face that she was just waiting. He glanced at his watch. Pamela had said they'd be back at 'about eleven' and it was now half-past twelve. Lord, the state Kate was in, she'd pass out when she heard the news! Better get her inside, sit her down ...

'Smithy! Where's Pamela?'

'Get my sticks, will you? They're on the back seat.'

21

She did that. She offered him her arm and he felt her biceps harden like small rocks as she hauled him, very competently, to his feet. If she'd been any other girl he'd have mentioned her muscles, teased her a bit, made her blush. But Kate was different. He couldn't claim to know her well enough to say *how* different, but until he knew her better ... Softly, softly.

'Why've you come in a taxi?' she asked now. 'Where are the others?'

'Hey, let me get my breath back!'

'Sorry.' She took a few steps backwards, as if afraid he'd start clearing his tubes again.

He smiled, trying to look boyishly rueful. 'They're—um—not coming. I know you'll find this hard to believe, but ... we had a bit of a tiff.'

'Oh, no! *Again?* What about this time?'

He pulled a face.

'Me?' she asked faintly.

'After a fashion.' The taxi sped away and, with his runway cleared for take-off, Smithy set his walking sticks one pace forward. It wasn't wise to break both legs at one go. He had never minded sweating buckets for a morning run up the Brecon Beacons, but considered it a complete waste of sweat for a single doorstep.

'Say if you want a hand,' Kate offered.

'I want some coffee.'

'Right.' She went ahead and disappeared into the kitchen, tactfully leaving him to it. He appreciated the tact—being watched all the time was the most infuriating part of it—but at the same time he was thoroughly peeved she'd gone. He could fall flat on his face for all she cared.

He tried to drag his mind from that thought—the most distressing of many distressing thoughts he regularly entertained—that no one cared. Even Pamela ...

He struggled into the kitchen and found Kate waiting for him, a chair at the ready and firmly braced to keep it from sliding backwards as he sat down. This was only the third time she'd seen him this week, but already she knew all the tricks; not because she cared, but because she couldn't stand being barked at.

'The kettle hasn't boiled,' she said nervously. 'Won't be a minute. Could you—er—tell me what's going on?'

He smiled. 'Could you—er—sit down?' he teased. 'It might come as a bit of a shock.'

The roses in her cheeks faded to white. She blinked and sat down, biting her lip to keep it from trembling. Smithy had the grace to feel ashamed of himself. She was ten years his junior, scarcely more than a child, and no one cared for her, either.

'But not an unpleasant shock,' he amended hastily. 'For one thing, Mags had more capital than anyone had imagined: sixty thousand pounds, to be precise.'

Kate's eyes widened.

'Pamela got thirty thousand, the three grandchildren five thousand apiece ...' he smiled again 'ten for me ... and five for you.'

Kate's mouth widened to match her eyes. 'Five ...?' she whispered. 'P-p-pounds?'

'No, you twit! Five th-th-*thousand* pounds!'

'Oh, my God!'

'But that's not the worst of it,' Smithy added smugly. 'She left Whitsun Gate ... to me.'

Kate's brain had slowed down. She couldn't keep up. Five thousand pounds? For her? Oh, God. She'd been rescued at the last minute, at the last gasp! She could ... She could ... Well, she didn't know what she could actually *do* with five thousand pounds, but at least she knew she wouldn't be homeless, she wouldn't starve!

And what else had he said? Mags had left Whitsun Gate to *him?* Why not Pamela? And what the hell would *he* do with it? He loved it, certainly, but he couldn't even walk, let alone ... Oh, Lord, did he want her to *stay?*

'To you?' she repeated faintly.

'And to you. Jointly. On condition—hold up, there, Kate; if you pass out, you're on your own—on condition that we run the place as she and Billy ran it for a minimum of three years.'

Kate wasn't the sort to show her feelings if she could avoid it, but now she had too many feelings and nowhere to hide them. What does a girl *do* when the world she loves (half of it, anyway) falls into her lap? What does she think? What does she say?

Although she said nothing at all, the thoughts came thick and fast, flickering through her mind like the disjointed frames of a silent movie. Heartfelt gratitude to Mags; sympathy (equally heartfelt) for Pamela, to whom a mere thirty

24

thousand pounds must feel like a slap in the face when she'd expected so much. Mothers and daughters never turned out as they were meant to.

She didn't think of Smithy at all until he said, 'There is one problem.'

Kate looked up. Someone had told her, years ago, that if you looked at a man's mouth, he'd think you were meeting his eyes; he'd think you were frank and fearless, when in fact ... She looked at the scar on his cheek, which had turned his mouth down at one corner, giving him a cynical look he'd never had before. Or maybe he'd become cynical when his wife had left him; or maybe he was just tired ...

She blinked and looked away, feeling a little shaky, totally unequal to coping with anything that had happened, let alone asking about the problem he'd mentioned. But he told her anyway.

'I'm not sure we can work together if you keep prattling on like this. I don't want to hurt your feelings, Kate, but I'm afraid I can't stand women who *yak*.'

Chapter Two

The difficulty with the doorstep at Whitsun Gate was that it was the original: roughly two hundred years old, with a deep hollow in the middle to prove it. The three concrete steps which marked the side entrance to the Seven Stars in Lower Minden were a doddle by comparison. Smithy flew up them in five minutes flat. He even managed a smile while he was doing it, hoping Kate would loosen up a bit when she realised he wasn't *always* in a foul mood. It was true that he didn't greatly like women who talked too much, but he wasn't mad keen on the silent variety either. Especially now. He was so lonely, he'd have paid fifty quid just to have someone open a discussion about the weather. Pathetic. But horribly true. And it was no great comfort to know he'd get over it, 'in time'. Time could be hell when you had too much of it.

Kate held the door open for him. She held a chair for him. She took his sticks and sat down opposite him without saying a word. Had shock silenced her, or was she always like this? He couldn't remember.

She fished in her bag for her purse, holding the latter very tenderly—as she might the Holy Grail—with the fingertips of both hands. Her hands were long and rather bony, with reddened knuckles and short fingernails just on the right side of grubby. Gardener's hands: she'd have to put them in to soak for a week to get them really clean.

'What would you like to drink?' she asked, in the tone of one who is praying he won't ask for a double brandy. He asked for orange juice—alcohol didn't mix with his pills—with difficulty suppressing a grin as she, with just as much difficulty, suppressed a sigh of relief.

He hadn't meant her to pay for anything—*he'd* invited *her* to lunch—but if they were really to be business partners, it was best to start as they meant to go on—with a clear, clean line straight down the middle.

He should also, he supposed, try to forget she was a woman, but that would be harder to achieve. In her tough leather boots, faded denims and over-large sweatshirt, she should have looked as much like a bloke as made no difference, yet the difference was almost startlingly apparent, not just in the obvious ways—hair and eyes, the tender swell of breast and hip—but in the way she turned her head, the way she stood at the bar, waiting for their drinks, with her feet together and her elbows in, as a man—a straight man, at least—would never do.

Two such straight men—from two different tables—had arrived at the bar a few seconds before Kate. They stood more or less together— logically so, since the barman happened to be at that end—but Kate had gone to the other end, as far from them as she could get without ending up in the car park. Yet the barman served her first, speaking to her in the respectful tones normally reserved by his ilk for elderly ladies or retired admirals. She wasn't obviously shy or unfriendly, but there was something about her—a strength, rather than a weakness—which said very clearly, 'Don't mess with me.'

Smithy wasn't the type to mess with anyone; it was against his nature to be anything less than direct and the only diplomatic skill he'd acquired was the rather limited one of keeping his mouth shut. But he'd have to be very careful with Kate. Mags had given them both the gift they most needed—hope for the future—but for at least three years of that future, their lives must travel the same narrow path, and if they didn't travel with care it might well be a total disaster. *Another* total disaster.

He'd been watching Kate returning with their drinks as this thought crossed his mind and now turned away, his mouth tightening, trying to forget it. But the love of a man's life is not easy to forget (especially when he hates her) and, for a moment, before he took a grip on himself, Kate *was* Tess—as cruel, as duplicitous, as selfish—and it was all he could do to thank her for his drink, let alone be charming about it.

Kate let out her breath in a tightly restrained sigh. 'Tablets wearing off?' she asked warily.

'No.' He smiled. 'Just thinking. Have you managed to think yet, Kate, or are you still numb with the shock?'

'A bit of both. I'm not sure I've quite grasped it. Is it really half mine? Whitsun Gate, I mean. Or do you—er—?' She grinned suddenly, disarmingly. 'Is the biggest half yours?'

Smithy was shocked: partly by that lovely little grin, of which nothing had given him warning, but mostly by the tone of her voice, which seemed oddly at variance with the question she'd asked. With any other woman—Tess, especially—he'd have known he'd been challenged, but with Kate he wasn't so sure.

In fact, he was *almost* sure that if he now replied, 'You get half, but I'm the boss,' she'd accept it with another grin, no further questions asked.

'Straight down the middle,' he said firmly. 'Except ...'

She blinked and peered into her glass, looking vague and shy and harmless, and now he understood. She was so accustomed to being the underdog, so unequal to fighting her corner, she'd learned to pretend she didn't care, that it all washed over her, that her mind was on higher things.

'Except that you'll be the senior partner,' he said, 'for a while, at least. I don't know enough about the business to make any sensible decisions just yet and, in my present state of health, I can't do much to help with the actual work. I'll try not to be a *sleeping* partner, exactly, but I'm afraid I'll need to snooze a good bit. Think you can carry me?'

Kate's heart leapt, like a frightened cat in a sack. Carry him? She could hardly hold herself upright, let alone ... But that wasn't the right thing to be thinking; she knew it wasn't, now. Everything had changed, which meant that she must change too. But she didn't know how. Carry him? Make 'sensible decisions', all by herself?

'I think we ought to order lunch,' she said. 'It's getting late.' And before Smithy could agree, she jumped up and made a dash for the bar to fetch the menu. She felt, as Mags would have said, 'all of a twangle', unable to decide if she was happily excited or just plain terrified. In terms of internal chaos there wasn't much to distinguish one from another: pounding heart, knocking knees; all she needed was for her teeth to start chattering and she could perform in the street as a one-man-band.

She was panicking, that was the long and short of it, and since panic invariably meant loss of control, she must stop panicking. *Now.*

While Smithy studied his menu, Kate pretended to study hers while mentally slapping herself back into line. She *could* carry him. She'd been carrying Mags for the past year and, to a lesser extent, both Mags and Billy for the previous two. She'd made nearly all the decisions; the only difference was that she hadn't realised she was making them, because the burden of responsibility had never before been *officially* dumped on her shoulders. Mags had always had the last word. Now Smithy would have the last word—they were equal partners; she couldn't decide anything without him—so nothing much had changed. She *could* cope.

But she couldn't cope with choosing her own lunch. She'd never eaten here before—even the starters were too expensive for a bread-line salary—and when Smithy said, 'Do you think you'd like the salmon?' (the most expensive thing on offer), she swallowed a gasp of amazement and stared at him over the top of her menu, quite forgetting to avoid his eyes. It was too brief a contact for her to establish what colour they were, but not so brief she didn't notice they were laughing at her.

'Mmm,' she murmured—trying to sound thoroughly bored with salmon, although in fact she'd never eaten it, except out of a tin. 'That'll be fine. Thank you.'

While they were waiting for their meal to arrive, Smithy talked about food—mostly to complain that Mags had been the worst cook on the face of the earth and to ask Kate if she was a better one.

'I doubt it,' she confessed. 'Mags taught me.'

'Oh, dear.'

Kate's mouth twitched. 'You're fond of your food, I take it?'

'It never used to bother me, but six months of hospital food—and non-stop television, of course—seems to have awakened the gourmet in me. When you see a chef producing little miracles with tiger prawns and chilli and all you get is a plate of tepid mince, you begin to feel seriously deprived.'

Until her salmon arrived (a luscious grilled cutlet, with a herby lemon sauce) and she began to compare it with the 'tepid mince' she normally ate, Kate didn't understand what he meant. Mags had been of the opinion that food was an infernal nuisance, something she'd gladly do without if only it weren't so useful for keeping body and soul together. It didn't have to taste of anything or look pretty. It certainly wasn't worth talking about!

'Can *you* cook, Smithy?'

He laughed. 'No, not really. I'd like to try my hand at it, but I'm sure it's not as easy

31

as it looks. I'll have to buy a decent cookery book and study the form, won't I?' Do you read much?'

'Cookery books?'

'Any books.'

Since Kate read everything she could lay her hands on, she found herself disputing with him the relative merits of Dickens and Anthony Trollope. He favoured the former, she the latter, and as the discussion warmed she realised that she had relaxed and was beginning to enjoy herself. She'd never done this before—eating lunch, with a man, in a pub. Just like a normal girl! Well, almost. One of the best things about Smithy, of course, was that he wasn't—for the time being at least—a normal *man*. He was too smashed up and in too much pain even to be thinking about sex, let alone doing anything about it; and anyway, he'd never—even when he was well—taken a blind bit of notice of her, so she probably wasn't his type. That was a comfort. It was so great a comfort, in fact, that when he asked if she wanted a pudding, she actually laughed, 'I thought you'd never ask!'

The barman was busy when she went to place the order and while she was waiting she glanced back at Smithy and realised he was in trouble. He'd turned away from her, but she could see his knuckles whitening as he braced himself against the edge of the table, see him stretching and shifting in his seat, trying to find a more comfortable position. He'd mentioned, as soon as he'd sat down, that the chair was too low and she'd forgotten all about it; but now ... if she didn't get him out of it, pronto, they'd have to lift him out with a crane.

She went back to him. 'I've changed my mind,' she said. 'Let's go home.'

He didn't argue. He didn't even speak until they were back in the car and then he said only, 'Thanks.'

'Why didn't you say something?'

'I don't know. Just shy, I guess.'

She laughed as he'd intended she should, but she felt a little ashamed of herself and surprised—very surprised—that he could be so sweet. He'd been barking and snarling all the week so far: never at *her*, admittedly, but enough to give her the impression that he was permanently bad-tempered. Maybe he just didn't like Pamela ...

He snarled a bit as she helped him out of the car, but she didn't mind; his face was as white as the wall and she began to pity him the doorstep before he even reached it.

'Leave me alone, Kate,' he whispered. 'I need ...'

'Coffee,' she said briskly, aware that he meant something else but not daring to wonder what it was. 'I'll put the kettle on.' She hurried indoors, glad to be leaving him behind for a few minutes. She felt tense and disoriented, too muddled to think, yet thinking of so many things she hardly knew one from another. It was partly, she knew, because Smithy was a man. Until today, he'd been like all the others: easy to ignore because she'd known she'd never have to get involved beyond the ordinary polite exchanges. She was quite good at polite exchanges. She could say, 'Hi,' and 'Good drive down?' and 'Fancy a coffee?' almost as if she cared, making it seem as if she fully acknowledged his existence, when in fact ... Well, in fact, men were like ghosts to her: frightening, certainly, but not quite believed in, not quite seen, just shadows darkening the corners of her vision. It was hard to have to meet one face to face like this, hard to admit he was real.

Smithy's pills worked fast and within ten minutes of taking them he was clumping around from room to room, sizing the place up and talking about moving in, in a month or two, when he was better.

The possibility of his moving in had been one of the many thoughts to have flitted through Kate's mind, but she hadn't really grasped it until now. Having lunch with a man one minute and living with him the next? It was normal, all right, but a bit too normal for Kate's liking. Not that there was any option. Whitsun Gate was half Smithy's now, and she didn't think he'd take kindly to being told that his half was the garden shed.

'We could turn it into two flats,' she suggested hopefully.

'Hmm, possibly. But not yet. There's a chance Pamela might challenge the will, and until we know where we are I'm not spending a penny more than I have to. On the other hand,' he mused after a while, 'she probably won't challenge. For one thing, she'd have to be pretty sure she could win and I don't see how ...

anyway, it would cost a mint, and she's as tight as her parents where money's concerned.'

Kate's eyes widened. 'Mags and Billy weren't tight!'

'Oh, no? Then why did they live on an exclusive diet of porridge and parsnips when they had a cool sixty thousand pounds in the bank?'

Rather in spite of herself, Kate laughed. Porridge and parsnips summed it up very nicely and until today she had been bemoaning how little she'd had to show for five years' hard labour.

'Well,' she conceded, 'maybe they were a little ... er ...'

'Careful,' Smithy supplied dryly.

'But only with money. I can't tell you how generous they were to me in other ways.'

'Same here.' He produced a sad little smile. 'But Pamela could tell another tale. You and I have had the best years of her parents' lives—and now the fruits of their labours as well. It's not to be wondered at that she feels a little peeved.'

'I wasn't wondering,' Kate murmured. She turned to gaze out over the gardens, and to the wonderful view beyond, which stretched for miles across beautiful countryside to the glittering perfection of the Westbury White Horse. 'I just don't ...'

'Don't what?'

Kate shrugged. 'I don't understand it. Mags was such a lovely woman, Smithy. Why didn't she and Pamela ...?' She swallowed, wishing she

35

hadn't started something she was incapable of finishing. She wasn't too articulate at the best of times, but when her emotions were involved she seemed to forget every word in her vocabulary, especially the little ones, like 'love'.

'Genes.' Smithy said. 'The wrong mix, that's all. They were too alike in many ways, too different in others. They never understood each other.'

'Or understood each other too well?' Kate murmured. 'Why didn't Mags leave Whitsun Gate to Pamela? Because she knew she'd sell it?'

'Perhaps. But, Kate, she'd always *intended* to leave the place to Pamela. She didn't change the will until after my accident. It might have been coincidence, but I think it more likely—since Pamela's loaded anyway—that she'd decided my need was the greater. And yours, of course,' he added. 'But that was different. She couldn't have managed without you during the past few years. She owed you the chance of a decent future.'

'Nonsense,' Kate said. 'She just wanted to give you a built-in gardener. I can't leave now, can I?'

Smithy's jaw dropped. 'Oh! Did you want to?'

'Well, yes,' Kate said. 'But only if the National Trust offered me Sissinghurst.' She turned away, suppressing a smile. 'And they didn't, so I suppose this will have to do.'

Realising he'd been had, Smithy murmured,

36

'Tragic, ain't it?' and was rewarded rather more than he'd hoped when Kate sent him another of those rare little grins of hers.

'This is better than Sissinghurst,' she said. 'It's mine.'

He hoped she was right. Pamela *had* been in the mood this morning to hire a good lawyer, and there was no knowing what a good lawyer could do—if he was paid enough. But Pamela was like Mags in more ways than one: she didn't bear malice. Blow up, cool down, forgive and forget ... Perhaps this was different, though. Thirty thousand pounds, when she'd been anticipating three *hundred* thousand? And it wasn't just that. In disinheriting her, Mags had rejected her daughter, *finally*. They couldn't kiss and make up any more.

'Take it easy, Kate,' he said. 'Until we know what Pamela's up to, we can't depend on anything.'

He didn't know how true this was until he returned to the Royal Oak and discovered that Pamela had gone back to London without him. It was a rotten thing to do. He wasn't exactly helpless without her, but he was vulnerable and more afraid than he liked to admit. Hospitals did that to you; they softened you up, cocooned you in a world so small, so warm and safe, that when you came out you were as naked and fragile as a baby. But it was his own silly fault. They'd told him he was taking it too fast. They wouldn't have let him out so soon had not Pamela promised to look after him. And now she'd gone ...

For a moment Smithy would have given her Whitsun Gate—and his ten thousand pounds—just to have her hold his hand for a few more weeks. Then he caught sight of himself in the mirror—the very image of a dying duck—and managed to catch the tail end of his pride as it slithered away to hide under the bed.

He could cope. He didn't need Pamela. All he needed ... All he needed was to recall what sort of man he'd been before the accident and be that man again: positive, optimistic, scared of nothing—much. In fact, the only thing he had been scared of was this, although when he'd dreaded it, then, it had been as the result of warfare, not of a stupid road accident. He'd never been afraid of dying, only of being injured so badly he'd wish he was dead. Six months ago, he had wished it. Even yesterday ... but that was over. Mags had given him a new lease on life, and he was damned if he'd let Pamela rob him of it!

Right, then. Decisions. He couldn't stay at the Royal Oak indefinitely, he couldn't go back to London if Pamela wouldn't have him, and he *wouldn't* (even if they'd let him after the fuss he'd made to get out) go back to hospital. So the only alternative was Whitsun Gate. It wasn't going to be easy—the place was a mess—but there was a bedroom and bathroom on the ground floor (Mags and Billy had been sleeping downstairs since Billy's hip-replacement, four years back), and if Kate could be persuaded to give it a quick springclean ...

He rang her. She didn't answer. It was ten past six. She could be anywhere. He tried her again at half-past six and again at quarter to seven. No answer. His heart began to race with panic. His new found optimism began to leak away, like blood from a severed artery. Gritting his teeth, he reached again for the telephone and punched in another number.

He'd been hoping all week that Pamela would make time for him to look up one of his Army chums stationed at Warminster only a few miles cross-country. He couldn't blame her for not making time—she'd been run off her feet one way and another—but he wasn't dependent on Pamela's time any more. If only Phil would answer ...

'Phil!' Relief washed over him, making him laugh. 'It's Smithy!'

He'd had his explanations all prepared, but needed only one of them: 'I'm at the Royal Oak,' to prompt Phil into action.

Two minutes later he was shaving, singing, changing his shirt for the first truly human thing he'd done in months: a night out with the boys!

Five hours' work on the garden had 'untwangled' Kate's nerves as nothing else could have done and she almost waltzed back to the house at half-past nine, ready for her supper (baked beans on toast), a hot bath and bed. She was happy! Happy for the first time in years, happy for almost the first time she could remember. True, there was still a stray root of fear lurking beneath the surface, but Kate couldn't think about it, didn't want to. If Pamela challenged and won? No, she *wouldn't* think about it. It would spoil everything; and even if 'everything' was Kate's for only a few months before it was snatched away again, she wanted to enjoy every minute of it. Whitsun Gate was hers!

And Smithy's, of course, but she needn't worry much about him just yet. He wouldn't be well enough to move in for a while: Whitsun Gate was no place for a man who couldn't look after himself and she certainly couldn't look after him. No time, for one thing; no inclination for another. He'd been sweet for a few hours today, but that didn't mean he'd changed his personality. He was a natural-born soldier: frank, autocratic and aggressive.

And something else: he didn't care if you liked him or you didn't. He made no compromises. Admirable, perhaps, if you could handle it, but Kate couldn't. It made her nervous. Robert hadn't cared if she'd liked him, either. All *he'd* cared about ... But that didn't matter any more.

All that mattered now was Whitsun Gate. It was hers! She could do what she liked with it! If the gardens opened again on Tuesday, as she fully intended they should, she'd be run off her feet for the rest of the summer. She was going to make this the best season ever.

In her imagination halfway up a ladder, tying in the Gloire de Dijon rose to the top of the pergola, she'd actually stepped inside the open back door and closed it behind her, before she remembered—or thought she remembered—that she'd locked it. She *always* locked it! But maybe

... With all of the day's shocks and excitements ... *Could* she have forgotten? No. The keys were in her pocket, just as they should be ...

She clapped a hand to her mouth and in the same instant heard a man's voice issuing from somewhere inside the house. She couldn't hear the actual words, just a low, masculine rumble followed by a derisive bark of laughter. Burglars!

In spite of her terror, it took barely a second for Kate's brain to process all the facts, possibilities and probabilities of the situation. From the direction indicated by their voices, they were in Mags's bedroom, which probably meant they were locals who'd heard of her death, wanted her valuables and knew Kate was alone in the house. Most of the inhabitants of Lower Minden were retired professionals (her grandparents, for instance, had once lived in the thatched cottage which marked the entrance to Whitsun Gate), but the lower element of Lower Minden was very low indeed: never clean, rarely sober and prepared to do anything—perhaps short of murder, but you never knew—for the proverbial 'laugh'. Vandalism, robbery, violence ... *rape?*

Kate had several times read of a marvellous human instinct called the 'flight mechanism' which, in times of danger, sends all the available oxygen to one's heart, lungs and legs, accompanied by the instruction, 'Run like hell!' But it never seemed to work for her. She received the instruction, but the oxygen seemed to receive it, too, making so smartly for the nearest exit she was left breathless and helpless, with legs made of jelly and feet rooted to the spot.

She *couldn't* run. But she could creep, gritting her teeth as she made a slow, painful progress to the door, heart hammering, skin freezing, lungs squeezed so tight she thought she'd never breathe again. Although the noise she'd made when shutting the door hadn't disturbed the burglars, she was certain the noise she'd make opening it again would have them down on her in a moment. Sometimes the latch jammed. Sometimes the hinges creaked. Was it best to make the swiftest exit, however noisy, or to turn the knob a millimetre at a time and just pray it wouldn't stick?

Having opted for the latter method and reached out a violently trembling hand to grasp the door-knob, she heard a man saying clearly, 'We'll clean the place out,' and then, even more clearly—in fact from only a few yards behind her—'*Hey!*'

Kate gasped, whirled on her heel—and came face to face with both burglars at once: a tall one and a short one.

The short one was six foot three.

Chapter Three

Their decisions made, Smithy's friends wandered out into the hall, leaving him to follow at his own pace. He paused for a moment, trying to get a grip on himself, to calm himself down.

He felt almost happy. Happy for the first time in months. Even Tess didn't matter so much at the moment and Pamela hardly at all. He hadn't realised how much he'd missed the Army, being surrounded by people who (unlike some others he could mention) still operated a policy of mutual support.

He'd scarcely downed his first glass of orange juice, scarcely stated his problem, before Phil had begun to solve it. He'd brought Inky Harrison with him and between them—in prospect at least—they'd redecorated and refurnished Mags's bedroom, re-tiled and re-plumbed the bathroom and made Smithy's life—if not quite a doddle—at least *possible* again.

The only problem left was Kate. She hadn't kicked up a fuss when he'd mentioned moving in, but then Kate wasn't a fusser; you had to watch her to make a fair guess at her feelings. Smithy *had* watched—while seeming to look elsewhere—and had not been greatly encouraged. That shy-vague-helpless look wasn't the only one in her armoury. There was also a look which reminded him of doors slamming shut, a withdrawal of sympathy which, although instantly detectable, seemed to have no outward expression. She could smile; she could continue to look interested; yet something—something inside her—broke the contact and left you talking to the wall.

He heaved a sigh. There was nothing to be done about it—Kate was one problem the Army couldn't solve—so he'd have to move in and she'd have to put up with it. He wouldn't

43

impose on her, if he could help it, but there were certain things, certain practicalities ...

Panic returned, giving him a sharp dig in the ribs before he pushed it away, remembering that with Kate, as with any other problem, one step at a time was the only reliable method of getting anywhere.

'*Hey!*'

Smithy stepped out into the hall and found his friends at red alert, staring at something beyond his gaze at the far end of the corridor.

'You've got burglars,' Inky murmured.

'I know.' It was a faint, husky voice, not quite Kate's, yet unmistakably hers: small, proud, *desperate*. 'But there's nothing worth stealing so I think you'd better go.'

'Kate!'

As the Army retreated, Smithy limped into the breach, not daring to laugh, but not knowing what to do instead until he saw her and thanked God he hadn't laughed. She'd jammed herself backwards into the corner by the door, and although he knew she was terrified, she didn't look terrified. She looked furious, wild, high as a kite on blind rage and adrenalin. Yet it lasted only long enough for him to recognise it—and for Kate to recognise him. Then she moaned, slithered to the floor and covered her face with her hands.

'Kate,' he said. 'Oh, Kate, Kate, I'm so sorry! I thought you'd gone out for the evening! I rang you, but—'

He glanced back at his fellow 'burglars', pulling a desperate grimace which they helplessly

44

mimicked, evidently feeling as stymied as he did. He hadn't told them all Mags had told him about Kate; only that she was an unknown quantity who'd need careful handling. The rest was strictly her own business. Yet even had it been otherwise, he probably wouldn't have mentioned it. The subject of sexual abuse wasn't an easy one to address. However decent a man was, however much he'd rather die than do such a thing to a little girl, it made him feel somehow tainted, as if—just by virtue of *being* a man—he'd been tarred with the same brush.

'Kate,' he said gently.

He heard her swallow, saw her shoulders rise as she filled her lungs. 'It's all right,' she said hoarsely. 'I forgot you had a key, that's all. Just ... Just leave me alone for a minute, will you?'

Not daring to speak, the men retreated to the kitchen. Phil made a pot of tea and tried to look motherly. Inky folded his six-foot-six into a kitchen chair and tried to look small. Phil mouthed incredulously, 'That's *Kate?*'

'I thought she was a kid,' Inky whispered. 'Doing the place over.'

'That's what she thought *you* were,' Smithy said.

'But I'm wearing my best suit!'

'It does nothing for you, evidently.'

Phil suddenly produced a tender little smile and proffered a cup to an apparently empty doorway. 'Sweet tea,' he said. 'Good for shock.'

'No, thanks,' Kate said lightly. 'The shock I just had was quite good enough.' She took a few brisk steps into the kitchen, stared straight into

Smithy's eyes—as a nanny might to someone small who'd wet his pants—and sat down very suddenly, her mouth trembling.

'Drink it.' Phil set the tea on the table. 'I'm sorry we scared you, Kate. Wouldn't have done it for the world. Smithy thought—'

'I don't even know who you are.'

'Major Philip Mungo,' Smithy supplied. 'Captain Rupert Harrington. Known in some quarters as Phil and Inky.'

'And in others as the Hole in the Wall Gang,' Inky offered warily.

Kate smiled at last. 'That's all right, then. For a horrible moment I thought you were Bonnie and Clyde.'

The relief was wonderful. Inky said, 'Whew!' and fanned his face. Phil pulled up a chair and began to explain what they'd been doing—or, rather, planning to do—and, before he could blow the whole show, Smithy said quickly, 'Hold on. I haven't told her about Pamela yet.'

Kate froze. 'What about her?'

'She's gone back to London,' Smithy said. 'Left me in the lurch. Which means, I'm afraid ...' He reached out his hand to give Kate's a reassuring pat, but remembered not to and halted the movement an inch clear of her fingertips. 'I'll have to move in, Kate. As soon as possible.'

It was as if a light had been switched off behind her eyes. She went on listening, she nodded and smiled; she even said 'Oh, I see', and, 'Yes, of course'. But she wasn't really there any more. It was as if they were all actors in a play which would end shortly, leaving her life unchanged. And that wasn't true. Her life was about to change fairly drastically and, with Smithy the architect of that change, he had to know she could cope with it. He had to know she could cope with *him*.

'Kate?' he said sharply. 'Is this all right with you? If not, you'd better say so now, because once I move in—'

Although the light—or whatever it was—switched on again, she immediately averted her eyes, blinked a few times and adjusted her watch-strap. 'It's all right with me,' she said faintly. 'But Whitsun Gate is a garden and I'm a gardener. I was hoping to open again on Tuesday.' Her mouth tightened defensively. 'If you agree, of course. But if we do open, I'll be working a sixteen-hour day, six days a week, for the rest of the season. I won't have time ...' She took a quick, shaky little breath and swallowed whatever else she'd meant to say, although Smithy could easily guess the gist of it: she wouldn't have time for *him*.

A phrase he'd heard in hospital—one he'd hated—floated into his mind and squatted there, digging in its claws like a vulture. *I don't want to be a burden ...*

'Look,' he said, 'I know I said you'd have to carry me, but I was talking about the business, Kate, not—'

'Come on, Kate,' Phil coaxed.

'You could throw him a crust of bread now and then,' Inky said softly. 'Couldn't you?'

47

Kate clenched her jaw. Her eyes flashed with sudden rage and although Smithy said calmly, 'Hey, this is Kate's decision, not yours,' he was as almost as frightened as she was. They'd hemmed her in. She couldn't cope. They'd have to leave, with *nothing* decided, *nothing* solved.

But Kate surprised him. She stood up and walked to the window, leaning against the sink with her arms folded. 'You're missing the point,' she said. 'I can *throw* Smithy whatever he needs, within reason, but that's not good enough, is it? He's ill and in pain. He needs—'

'All I need is a *home*, Kate.'

'No.' It both sounded and looked final. Smithy sighed and massaged his leg, wishing he'd kept his mouth shut, given her no option, just bulldozed her into it. He was tired—was usually in bed by this time of night—and knew he hadn't the patience for another round of gentle persuasion. They'd have to quit. She might feel better tomorrow ...

'A home is just a priority,' Kate went on. 'Once you've got it, you'll want a few dozen other things and be miserable because I can't supply them.' She smiled wanly. 'And when *you* get miserable, *everyone* knows it.'

'She's sussed you,' Phil grinned, but Smithy only nodded and stroked his jaw. She was right, especially about the 'few other things' he'd need once his home was secured. She was right about his temper, too, but only up to a point. When it was necessary—and when Pamela wasn't driving him crackers—he *could* control it. Anyway, there was a traditional element to his spats with Pamela; they'd *always* quarrelled, so why stop now? He'd be more careful with Kate: not just because she was vulnerable, but because—somehow—she demanded it.

'You're right,' he said, 'but—'

'But this *is* your home,' she said. 'And you've nowhere else to go. So it's up to you.' She stared at her feet. 'I just wanted to tell you—warn you—that it won't be ... I mean, that *I* won't be ...' She frowned and blinked. 'Well,' she concluded irritably, 'I've never even *seen* a tiger prawn, let alone cooked it in chilli!'

Just as she'd thought food a nuisance, which came in handy for keeping you alive, Mags had thought a house a *sodding* nuisance, which came in handy for keeping the rain off. In all the years they'd lived at Whitsun Gate, she and Billy had never so much as prised open a tin of paint. The decor—the little that was left of it—was exactly as they'd found it in 1955, only six shades browner. Even when she'd changed Billy's study into a bedroom, Mags hadn't bothered to redecorate: just heaved out the desk and a couple of chairs, shoved in a bed and a chest of drawers, rubbed her hands and said, 'That's that done. Now, let's pot up those fuchsia cuttings.'

So when Kate took a last look at the room before the Army invaded it, she thought smugly—and without sparing a thought for Smithy's hotel bills—'Three weeks, at least.'

It took three and a half days. Smithy's friends moved the furniture out, sanded the floor and washed the walls. A complete stranger refitted the bathroom and another turned up to do the painting. There was a remorseless efficiency about the entire thing, which Kate found a little daunting, especially when the painter (another soldier, apparently) called Smithy, *'Suh!'*

It made Kate view him in a different light, realise that there was more to him than she'd ever considered. A few family insults aside, she'd never heard him called anything but Smithy. To Mags and Billy, he'd always been 'the boy', with various frills attached at various times—golden, darling, poor, perishing, bloody awkward—and Kate had accepted their estimation of him and had never thought beyond it. There'd been no need, because whenever he'd come to Whitsun Gate (which hadn't been all that often), she'd always been able to depend on his going away again. Now she was stuck with him, for three years at least—and although she hadn't the slightest desire to get to know him better—the reverse, in fact—good sense informed her that if she didn't begin to see him as a complex human being, rather than as the cardboard cut-out he'd been so far, his hidden depths might suddenly surface and give her the shock of her life.

The first thing she had to do was to stop feeling sorry for him. He couldn't do much to help himself at the moment, but he could certainly organise everyone else into supplying his needs and Kate didn't intend to be organised. She couldn't claim to have very much understanding of herself—every aspect of her personality seemed to be at odds with every other—but one thing was certain: where her own life was concerned, *she* did the organising; *she* took control.

It sounded easy. But it wasn't. Perhaps owing to her many and various internal conflicts, Kate couldn't handle the external variety. In most situations she operated a policy of 'anything for a quiet life', but that had its drawbacks, especially with people like Mags and Smithy who, deprived of a good bust-up, would always push a little harder to see how far you would go. Over the years, Kate had learned to manage Mags, but she wasn't sure she could manage Smithy. Men were different. They were impervious to subtleties. If you didn't come straight out and tell them the precise rules of the game, they'd get you in a flying tackle before you could yell, 'Monopoly!'

Yet with Smithy in his present state of health, even stating the rules seemed like an act of aggression. 'I'm the gardener,' she'd said, meaning to add, 'not your wife, mother, nurse, valet, chief-cook-and-bottle-washer.' But he'd looked so tired, so pale ... And she'd heard Mags whispering, from somewhere far away, 'Take care of him, you little ratbag, or I'll come back to haunt you.'

So ... she'd take care of him. But she'd do it on her own terms, not his; and although she hadn't quite stated the terms (three meals a day, certainly; all of them cheese sandwiches, probably), he'd seemed to get the message. Actually, he'd looked a bit sick, as if she'd kicked his sticks out from under him, but the

51

thing *she* had to remember was that he wouldn't always be helpless. Pamela had said it might take six months, maybe a year, but he *would* get better eventually, and where would Kate be then if she didn't put her foot down now?

While she was re-employing the staff for Tuesday's opening, she found herself discussing Smithy's difficulties with Mavis Mills, who ran the tearooms. Mavis had known Smithy since he was a child and knew three times more about his private life than Kate did. She was three times more sympathetic, too. 'Poor bugger,' she said. 'Whoever woulda thought he'd come to this? Handsomest-looking kid I ever seen, he was. He had these beautiful curls, all over his head. I coulda killed the Army when they cut 'em off. He looked all wrong after; not so cuddly, kinda thing.' She sighed. 'I feels really sorry for him, though, Kate ... Mags seen it comin', o' course. She knowed that girl weren't right for him, but what can you *do*, Kate? What can you *say?* When a man falls in love, see, he do go blind, deaf and as fick as ten Mars bars. It were the same with our Nigel. Exactly. And look what come of *him*, poor dab.'

As far as Kate was aware, Mavis's Nigel was in perfect health, happily married and living three doors down from his mother, so it was hard to imagine what made him exactly the same as Smithy. But she knew better than to ask. Mavis was the type to tell you her entire family history just to explain why she never wore nail varnish. *Well, you remember me telling you about my granny's sister Agnes, what we used*

52

to call the bearded lady, the one what married the sailor …?

'The thing is, Mavis, that Smithy's not very well—'

'Well, he wouldn't be, would he? After all he been through? Six operations, see, Kate. You don't come outa that the same as you went in, see, do you? And it's not just his bones broke, see, it's his poor liddle heart. Mags and Billy gorn, his wife—silly cow! And now Pamela, too. What have he got left, Kate?'

'Well, he's got Whitsun Gate, and Mags left him some money, so—'

'It's not the same, though, Kate, is it? When a man been knocked back as hard as that, he needs—'

'Food,' Kate said hurriedly. 'And I can't cook, so I was wondering …'

'Well, that's no problem,' Mavis said. 'He can have his lunch in the tearooms. Soup, quiche, baked potato, a nice salad, and there's always a bit of cake for afters. No, no, it's not food he needs, bless him, it's—'

Kate could see where Mavis was leading. She read too many romantic novels and thought love was the answer to everything, rather than the unfathomable question it had always seemed to Kate. Why had Mags disinherited her own daughter? Why had Smithy's wife left him when he needed her most? Why had Kate's mother rejected her for a nasty, faithless, dirty-minded little—

'Mavis!' She put love in its place with a

53

delighted squeal. 'You're a genius—I'd forgotten you do lunches!'

Before he moved in finally, Smithy had hoped to spend a few days getting to know Kate a little better. But he scarcely saw her except from a distance, either working in the garden, or hurtling off in Billy's rust-bucket of a Land-Rover to God-knew-where and for God-knew-how-long. He wouldn't have minded so much had he thought she was deliberately avoiding him, but there was nothing deliberate about it; she'd simply forgotten he was there.

He understood and approved—up to a point—her need to get the gardens in apple-pie order before she opened to visitors again. He understood (but found it hard to accept) that he was not her guest, friend, family or—God forbid—lover, and that she owed him nothing; least of all a welcome. Yet he found the absence of a welcome deeply disturbing. He didn't expect her to like him, but surely she should be showing some curiosity, taking *some* interest in the man who—dammit!—would be living with her for the next three years? As his business partner, she couldn't just pretend he didn't exist. Three *years?* After a mere three days it was beginning to feel like a prison sentence. In solitary.

He spent some of his time checking through the books and realising, to his dismay, that the profits were as negligible as Mags had always claimed and that her sixty thousand pounds was probably the tail-end of Billy's starting capital. Whitsun Gate really *had* been providing a porridge-and-parsnips income, but that wasn't enough for Smithy. Love the old place as he did, he'd rather live well in a studio flat than from hand to mouth at Whitsun Gate. Three years? And then sell up for half a million? Or ...

His eyes narrowed. Feeling the lure of a challenge, he hauled himself to his feet and crept to the window, scanning the lawns and borders for a glimpse of his elusive partner. He saw nothing, except three baby sparrows lined up on a stone bench, fluttering their wings for their forty-fifth course of breakfast. A bright green lawn, a chestnut tree in pink-flushed bloom, and a great drift of late, lily-flowered tulips, fluttering in the breeze like a distant flight of flamingoes. Mags had loved pink: not to the exclusion of every other colour in the floral spectrum, but enough to give the impression that Whitsun Gate was a world seen through rose-coloured glasses.

Yet the part he could see was only a fraction of the seven-acre spread. Beyond his range of vision were the Herb Garden, the Scented Garden, the Rose Walk, the Water Garden, the Kitchen Garden and Smithy's favourite, the Bride's Garden, which Mags had created as a wedding present (unappreciated) for Pamela. Tess had loved it. So she'd said. But she'd said she loved Smithy, too ...

He stroked the scar on his face, wishing he could kick something without falling over. You didn't realise how incredibly physical your emotions were until you were robbed of their physical expression and had to swallow them.

It was no wonder he felt sick all the time.

The back door creaked open and clanked shut and Kate's tractor-tyre boots made sparrow-like cheepings on the flagstoned passage. Afraid she'd be gone again before he could nab her, Smithy yelled, 'Kate!' meaning to sound only urgent, but hearing in the lower registers of his voice a throb of rage which, he realised immediately, was not entirely misdirected. He *was* angry with her: selfishly and unjustly no doubt, but angry all the same. 'Steady,' he told himself grimly. 'Early days.'

She'd been shopping and, when he finally reached the passageway, was still standing there, decorated with plastic carrier bags and a wary—but friendly enough—smile. 'Hi. You want coffee? I've just bought some.'

'Ah ...' He'd have to talk to her about that, too. Housekeeping expenses, rates and electricity bills, salaries ...

She turned into the kitchen and he heard a bustle of activity to set against the tap of his walking sticks and the slow drag of his feet. Rush of cold water into kettle. Slam of kettle on to stove. Rattle of crockery and the gun-fire thud of cupboard doors as the groceries hit home. The speed of her movements was a threat and an irritation, and the offer of coffee no guarantee that she'd stick around to share it.

'Actually,' he said, 'it wasn't coffee—not *just* coffee—I wanted. I think it's time to call an urgent meeting of the Whitsun Gate Board of Directors.'

'Oh.' Kate pulled out a chair for him and

firmly braced it. 'And who are they, when they're at home?'

He smiled. 'Oh, no one you'd know. A Courteney Fitzwarren-Smith—can you believe that name?—sounds like a ballet dancer. And some woman.' He tapped his temple. 'Let me think, now. Katherine, is it? Brooks? Brooker? Broke?'

'That's the one.' She took his sticks and propped them in the corner. 'Katherine Stony-Broke, to give her her proper title.'

Smithy nodded. 'We'll fix that. So, can you stay?'

'Stay?'

'For this meeting.'

Her eyes widened in a show of astonishment which, for a moment, completely fooled him. 'Oh!' she said. 'So *you're* this ballet-dancer chap!' She glanced sideways at his walking sticks. 'The Nutcracker, was it?'

Although the mischief in her eyes produced a corresponding twinkle in his, neither of them laughed. It was difficult not to, but Smithy felt he was walking a tight-rope towards her: if he dared laugh, he'd fall. Mags had always said Kate had a surprising sense of humour and although he'd already caught a few hints of it (wondering at the time if she'd been aware of what she was saying), there was no mistaking it now.

'You're on form today,' he approved warily.

'Yes.' The kettle boiled and she turned away to make coffee. 'I've sorted out a few problems that were getting me down. We started doing lunches in the tearooms this season; I'd forgotten, but it means you can have a decent meal every day, at least until October. It'll also mean you'll have company.' She sent him a wry glance and turned away again. 'Mavis, mostly, I'm afraid, and you're in no state to say, "I must dash", but you should be able to eat outside most of the time and, if you're good at eavesdropping, you could do a bit of market research with the visitors. They usually pay compliments to the gardener, which is nice but not all that helpful. I'd like to know the things they say behind my back, too.'

He was amazed. Not only had she not forgotten him, she'd been actively thinking about him! Food, companionship, something useful to do—and market research was the very thing he *needed* to do if they were to make a decent go of the place.

'Also,' she brought the coffee over and sat down opposite him, 'Monday's my only free day, so if you want anything done, tell me about it on Sunday: shopping, laundry, that sort of thing. Because if I can't do it on Monday, it won't get done. You'll need to register with a doctor, and if you want to change your bank, you'll be better off in Radstock than Frome because I can park outside the door.'

She met his eyes as she'd done once or twice before, her gaze so clear, so frank, it seemed a total contradiction of her character. But who was he to judge her character? To say she was vulnerable was like saying a tiger was beautiful: true only so far as it went. How much did he know about her? Only one thing: the thing that made her different from every other woman he'd ever met and which, by a curious paradox, made her totally *invulnerable*. He wouldn't touch her with a barge-pole. Pretty as she was, interesting as she was, alluring as she was (when she lowered her eyes; he found the directness of her gaze oddly unnerving), there was only one thing that turned Smithy on so much that he couldn't resist it.

'So what about this Board Meeting of yours?' Kate demanded.

And that wasn't it!

Chapter Four

The old stable yard behind the house was used for private parking and plant sales. Neither of its functions was filled very satisfactorily, largely owing to the linden tree which overshadowed it all, dripping honeydew on the cars and staining the cobbles with a nasty black mould. Yet it was a lovely tree, producing the sweetest, freshest green of the spring, and the honeydew, as Kate had often reminded Billy when he'd threatened to chop down the tree, was not exactly the linden's fault. Like every other linden tree in the world it was infested with aphids and it was *they* which secreted the honeydew, not the poor old tree.

Still, it was a nuisance. It made everything look

messy and uninviting. Kate was no saleswoman, but even she knew the advantages of good presentation and knew it rather better since her first 'Board Meeting' with Smithy. Until then, she'd thought Whitsun Gate could doddle on as before, but as he had quite reasonably pointed out, 'doddling' was fine for old dears whose lives were behind them. He wanted more—challenge, profit and a decent standard of living—and, if he couldn't find such things at Whitsun Gate, he'd go elsewhere when their three years was up.

He hadn't added, 'So if you want to stay beyond that, you'd better make it worth my while.' He'd left Kate to draw her own conclusions and she'd been drawing them like mad ever since. Oddly, she hadn't found his unvoiced ultimatum at all threatening. Inspiring, rather. And, in a way, quite reassuring. 'Challenge, profit and a decent standard of living' was, after all, not a bad set of objectives to have in mind. It was cool and business-like, at least. She liked that. If he could stay like that—keep his temper and his emotions under wraps—they might stand a real chance of making a go of it.

With this thought in mind, she'd reserved Monday morning for a springclean of the yard, an invitation to the visitors to open their wallets a little wider than usual. She'd hosed down the cobbles, sorted the plants into some kind of order and had begun to relabel them when Smithy arrived in his taxi, soon after ten. He always seemed to get the same driver and the driver was getting used to him, so Kate didn't bother to go and help.

'Right you are, mate, I got you. *Ups*-adaisy! Yer's yer sticks. Got 'em? *Sure?* Mind 'ow you go, now.'

Kate didn't need to look at him to know that Smithy didn't like being treated like an advanced case of senile dementia. Michael had once asked him if he was *sure* he could manage, but since this had produced an immediate scorching sensation in his ears, he hadn't asked the same question twice. Yet, surprisingly, Smithy didn't give the taxi-driver the flame-thrower treatment. He thanked him very nicely and stood to watch him off the premises before slowly turning and taking a few faltering steps across the cobbles.

' 'Morning, Kate.'

' 'Morning. You're in a good mood today.'

'Am I?'

'Or are you planning to kill him later?'

'Who? Oh, him. No. He's doing his best.' Smithy looked a little hurt, as if he thought Kate had misjudged him. 'I don't ask people to do more than that.' He grinned. 'Not often, anyway. What are you doing?'

She almost said, 'My best,' but paused, wondering if it was true. She should have helped him out of the car. It wouldn't have taken more than a minute and would have saved him the batty-old-lady treatment.

'Plant labels,' she said. 'How about you?'

'With any luck, taking delivery of a new bed. They said about eleven, which probably means about three. Also ...' He tipped his head to one side as if to check her mood.

61

'What?'

'Phil's coming over. Bringing his wife. I thought, if it's all right with you, we'd have lunch on the terrace.'

'*Lunch?* Are you crazy? There's nothing ...' Scowling, she made a mental survey of the larder: four tins of baked beans, three eggs, two squashy tomatoes and a loaf of wholemeal, three parts gone.

Smithy laughed. 'Oh, I'm not asking you to *cook* anything. Salad Niçoise, perhaps? Some French bread? Three or four cheeses? Phil's a Gorgonzola man, but any blue will do.'

Kate realised he was joking only when he mentioned the 'three or four cheeses'. He'd seen—and scathingly remarked on—the featureless wastes of the kitchen fridge, and he knew (at least, if he didn't he was stupid) that nothing in the vegetable garden was ready yet. Any blue will do, indeed!

'Would Stilton be all right?' she asked innocently. 'I think there's a bit left over from Christmas. All it needs is a haircut.'

Smithy grinned and turned away. 'They're bringing a picnic,' he said. 'Thank God.'

They also brought Inky, Inky's wife and Inky's wife's sister. Kate was in the Herb Garden when they arrived, keeping watch for Smithy's new bed which, by ten past twelve, still hadn't materialised. She felt an odd little pang as the cars drew up (under the linden tree; *they'd* be sorry) and everyone piled out, talking and laughing as if to finish a joke they'd been telling before they'd left Warminster. They looked like the sort of people who had never known trouble, never been shy, lonely, or stuck for the right thing to say. She envied them. In spite of his troubles she also envied Smithy, just because he knew them and could call them his friends.

None of the women looked much older than Kate—twenty-five at most—but they were clean, neat, prettily dressed (Kate was wearing jeans, as ever) and nicely finished off with impractical little details like varnished toenails (the only time Kate saw her toenails was when she was in the bath) and dangly earrings (if they caught on the roses she'd have dangly ears).

For all its beauties and satisfactions, Kate had often wished she could do something other than gardening: something clean and well-paid; something you could do in a suit and pretty shoes. She'd been planning to go to university, read English or perhaps History ... But it hadn't worked out. Mags had always said that given a certain amount of intelligence you could do anything, everything; *nothing* was impossible. But you had to want it *enough*. If you didn't want it enough you didn't get it and it was no good to blame anyone else; the fault was yours. But it was too late, now. However much Kate wanted to be like Smithy's friends—and, just at this moment, she wanted it *enough*—she was a gardener and stuck with it: grubby hands, grubby jeans, the lot.

Forgetting Smithy's bed, she wandered off into the Rose Walk, scanning the ground for the spiteful green shoots of bindweed which might have sprung up overnight, pretending to be ivy. The whole garden had been infested with it when Mags and Billy had first come to Whitsun Gate and they'd cleared it all, except here, where a few outlaw roots had taken up a siege position under the roses. You didn't dare miss a bit. In a warm spring, it might grow only two inches a day, but give it a chance in June and it would reach the tops of the arches before you could blink. The visitors loved it. Catching a professional gardener with bindweed in the roses was like catching the Queen with her knickers down.

'Gotcha!' Bindweed, a tiny green leaf on a thread-like stem, had her down on her knees to dig it out just as a soft voice behind her murmured, 'Kate? Sorry to interrupt ...'

It was Inky. Considering his rank, his height and physique, he was one of the most apologetic men Kate had ever met. He gave her the idea that he was ashamed of being so large, almost afraid of it. He spoke in a whisper and walked like a cat—softly, carefully—as if terrified the ground would collapse under his weight. Funnily enough, this made Kate more nervous of him than if he'd thumped around like the carthorse he resembled. It seemed unnatural. Carthorses aren't *meant* to creep!

She blushed and stood up, smacking dirt off her knees. 'You aren't interrupting. I was swearing at the bindweed, not saying my prayers.'

He smiled. 'Er—um ... Smithy was ... I mean, *we* were wondering—that is, if you don't mind—whether you'd have time to do a guided tour? Of the gardens, I mean. If you're not too busy, that is?'

'Oh, there's no need for that. You're welcome to walk around on your own.'

He looked at his feet. 'Um ... Well, we thought a guided tour might be more ... We don't actually know much about gardens, you see, and with this being a new venture for Smithy, we'd like to know what he's talking about.' He smiled again and added faintly, 'He's a bit low on morale, just at the moment. Needs a spot of support now and then.'

Kate turned away, feeling a little sick. 'Yes,' she said. 'Give me five minutes and I'll be with you.'

Until he'd reached the part about Smithy's low morale, Kate had been wondering how Inky could lead men into battle. Whether he'd give orders in a whisper. Whether he'd add politely, 'That is, if you aren't too busy?'

And then it had occurred to her: he was afraid of *her*, afraid of rubbing her up the wrong way, perhaps even afraid that if he offended her she'd take her revenge on Smithy. Oh, God ...

The trouble was, she supposed, that she *had* been feeling threatened; not really by Smithy (who'd been very good, considering) but by all the changes, the comings and goings, the fact that Mags was no longer in the background to make everything safe. And when Kate wasn't safe, she was sharp, like a curled-up hedgehog with all is prickles turned outwards. Everyone knew that hedgehogs curled up only when they were scared, but no one knew that about Kate; only Mags had known. And Mags was dead.

I was swearing at the bindweed, not saying my prayers. She needn't have said that. It had been cold and hard, too clever-clever by half. And the same could be said for a dozen other things she'd said, especially to Smithy. No wonder his morale was low ...

Having traced the bindweed root as far back as she could reach, she wandered back to the house, resolving to smile a lot and say as little as possible for the rest of the day.

They were all out on the terrace, talking and laughing, drinking wine. Smithy looked happier than she'd seen him so far; almost as he'd been in the old days, but too thin, too pale. And the scar had spoiled his face. It wasn't bad enough to be called a disfigurement, but it made him look sad and bitter, even when he was laughing.

'Hi, Kate. Come and meet the rest of the Hole in the Wall Gang.'

Shyness misted her eyes, panic clouded her brain. She gathered that their names were Jane, Joanna and Amy, but failed to establish which one was which. All she could manage was to smile a lot. And say as little as possible.

Although the guided tour had been Inky's idea, he stayed with Smithy while the others went off with Kate. 'She's a puzzle,' he murmured thoughtfully. 'You getting her measure yet, Smithy?'

'Mmm.' He rocked his hand. 'Thirty-four,

twenty-two, thirty-four. And about five foot five, I reckon. Why? What's your guess?'

'Well ... um ... I suddenly thought ...'

'Suddenly? You?' Smithy turned the wine bottle and affected to read the label. 'What's in this stuff?'

'I think she's scared.' Inky drummed his fingers on the table. 'Not like she was the other night—any woman would be scared of burglars—I mean generally.' He scratched his ear. 'She never meets your eyes, does she?'

This last point aside, Inky had hit it spot on. As usual. He seemed a bit slow on the uptake at times, but it was only because he was thinking so hard, planning, anticipating, finding solutions to problems that hadn't yet happened. But he was wrong about the eyes. Kate not only met your eyes, she drilled straight through and out the other side!

'She looks at your mouth,' Inky said. 'You don't notice it in close-up, of course. But you watch her when she's looking at someone else. It's too steady, Smithy, too direct. No matter how tough you are, you can't hold another person's eyes for more than a few seconds at a time. You have to blink, look down, change focus. Kate doesn't do that. She holds. But she cheats. So ... what's she scared of?'

Smithy was impressed. 'You tell me.'

'Any family?'

'Mother. Lives in Bath, I think. Father dead. No siblings. Her grandmother used to live in the thatched cottage by the gate; died a few years back. Kate used to stay with her for the school holidays; earn some pocket money helping Mags with the weeding.' He grinned. 'Mags was never one to turn away cheap labour.'

'So you've known her from her cradle?'

'No ... I might have seen her once or twice when she was a child. Must have, I suppose, but I can't remember her being here until she moved in, five years ago.'

There was a long silence. Smithy, who was on tonic water, raised his glass and caught Inky staring at him with narrowed eyes, thinking hard, summing things up, saying—without saying anything—'You've left something out, you bastard.'

Smithy intended to go on leaving it out, partly because he wanted to see how close Inky could get and partly because he'd been told Kate's secret in confidence, without her knowledge. But it was mostly because ... He leaned back in his chair, thinking it over. Protectiveness? Yes, he felt protective towards her, but it was more than that. He didn't want her to be labelled, pigeonholed, written off as damaged goods. She was only a kid. Well, no, she wasn't, of course; but she had a bad case of arrested development and it had lately occurred to Smithy that Mags might be—at least partially—to blame for that.

'Give,' Inky prompted. 'Are you thinking what I'm thinking?'

'I hope not. I've always thought myself an original thinker. A little above the common herd.'

'Hmm. How long have you had these delusions?'

'She's just shy,' Smithy said. 'Been mixing with the wrong crowd, poor kid. She was sixteen when she came here. Mags was seventy-five and still—it pains me to say—in need of cheap labour. Kate's done nothing for the past five years—except gardening, of course. And she's had no company. Mags was a darling, but she was old. She probably didn't think—'

He thought of Pamela and heaved a sigh. Mags hadn't thought of her needs, either. 'Sink or swim' had been her own philosophy. It had never occurred to her that some people might need waterwings to keep them afloat.

'And the village is full of oldies,' he went on. 'Most of the visitors are on the wrong side of fifty. Kate's had no friends, no fun.'

'No stereo,' Inky recited mournfully. 'No drugs, no drink, no—'

'No computer!' Smithy said. 'Can you believe that?'

'No sex,' Inky concluded with a smile.

Smithy sucked in his cheeks and glanced at his watch. It had taken Inky little more than ten minutes.

'She's a peach of a girl, though,' his friend said. 'Do you fancy her?'

Smithy shook his head and stared down the garden, thinking of Tess. Of his ruined marriage. Of his ruined body. 'I've forgotten what it means,' he said.

Kate hadn't been trusted to do guided tours until the few months preceding Billy's death, when Mags had been rushed off her feet looking after him. They'd only ever done tours for experts and enthusiasts, mostly horticultural clubs, colleges and coach-loads of Americans who, passionately keen to discover the secret of the legendary English Garden, found it hard to accept that the answer ('The Weather') couldn't be bought by the hundredweight and shipped home to Illinois. That aside, the average 'guided tourist' never missed a trick and, since Kate missed quite a few, she loathed doing tours and usually began her talk with the words, 'I'm still an apprentice,' which at least kept the worst of them from turning vicious when she slipped up.

Left to her own devices, she could recall the Latin and common names of most plants—at Whitsun Gate and beyond it—but when some uncompromising expert demanded 'What's this?' she could forget her own name, her mother's name and the name of the common lawn daisy, let alone that of *Fritillaria michailovskyi*. But she never felt shy with the experts. They weren't interested in her. They didn't care who or what she was, just so long as she knew her stuff. It was different with Smithy's friends. They were going to test her in every direction, personal and professional, and if they found her wanting, if they thought she was going to let him down ...

This thought crossed her mind just as they reached the Herb Garden, which marked the beginning of the tour. She said, 'Turn left,' glanced to her right as they obeyed her, saw their cars under the linden tree and wailed,

'Oh, my God! Smithy's bed!'

'What?'

'I was meant to be watching for Smithy's bed! It's probably come and gone while I was down the garden!'

'It came,' Phil said kindly. 'But it didn't go. We saw it in safely, didn't we, girls?'

The one with straight blonde hair—Jane, was it?—smiled over her shoulder and added brightly, 'It was meant to be our job, anyway. Smithy only asked you because we were late.'

'Which was Amy's fault,' Phil said, pointing sideways at the accused, who pretended to look ashamed of herself. 'So don't you go taking the blame for it, Kate. She'd be late for her own funeral.'

Encouraged, Kate began her lecture on the Herb Garden which was received in a silence so total it brought her out in a cold sweat. It also brought out *Rosmarinus* "Jackson's Prostrate" ' as *Rosmarinus* "Jackson's Prostate" ' in the clear, ringing tones of a staff nurse on Men's Surgical. Kate checked their faces for suppressed sniggers and found them all in a state verging on trance: glazed eyes, sagging jaws, the very picture of blissful ignorance. They hadn't understood a word of it, poor old Jackson's prostate included.

Kate began again, giving them a potted history of herb gardens: the Romans, the early monasteries, medicinal and culinary uses, herbs for suppressing medieval stinks and herbs for poisoning your enemies. The group's eyes brightened. They listened, laughed and asked questions, the best of which was an awed, 'Kate, you're brilliant! How do you *know* all this?'

It was a huge relief. *Much* nicer than being told she had bindweed in the roses!

The mood warmed and became more friendly as they did the rounds. Kate finally worked out who was who: Jane was Phil's wife, Joanna Inky's wife and Amy Joanna's sister. Phil and Jane asked all the serious questions; the other two just chatted generally, seeming to assume, in their frequent references to Smithy, that Kate was as much his friend as they were. She began to wish she could be. A man who could command such loyalty and concern from his friends couldn't be all bad.

They talked mostly about his accident, of course. Phil had seen him a week afterwards, still in Intensive Care and still barely conscious, bruised and swollen beyond recognition. He was expected to live, but no one was prepared to say, at that point, if his life would ever again be worth living.

'Had Tess seen him by then?' Amy asked.

Phil shook his head. 'We couldn't find her. She turned up about four days later. He was conscious by then, unfortunately. Wide awake, poor sod. He didn't miss a thing.'

Kate had never before heard any of this. In many ways she didn't want to hear it—Smithy's emotional life was dangerous territory; the less she knew, the less it could affect her. She could cope—just about—with his broken legs. His broken heart was his own business.

Joanna, who had walked ahead of the others,

72

confided mournfully, 'It's all my fault, Kate. I introduced them. Well, how was I to know he'd fall for her? He wasn't the *type!'*

'What type?'

'The damn fool type! You'd have thought he'd have seen her coming a mile off! What did *you* think of her?'

Kate shrugged. 'I only met her twice. She seemed all right. I know she was beautiful, but the only detail I can remember is her red hair. I don't think she said very much ...'

'Huh. Still waters run deep. And the hair came out of a bottle. What else do you remember? Come on, Kate, you must have noticed *something!'*

Kate laughed. 'You're asking the wrong person. I'd have noticed if she'd had greenfly, but anything else ... Why? What was wrong with her?'

'How long have we got?' Joanna demanded cynically. 'She's a raving nympho. She was two-timing him even *before* they got married. I know that for a fact.'

'Didn't you tell him?'

Joanna stared at her. 'Would *you?'* she asked hollowly.

The answer to that, of course, was no. Kate hadn't known him well enough to tell him anything at all. But even if she had, she wouldn't have told him Tess was a nymphomaniac. It would be like telling him there were fairies at the bottom of the garden, something neither of them could believe. And yet, she knew it could be true. Some women (they had to be crazy, of course) actually *did* do it for fun. But why didn't she just do it with Smithy?

'So where was she when the accident happened?'

Joanna shrugged. 'Smithy had been away on a training course. When he came home she wasn't there. He hasn't said, but I think he was looking for her when he had the accident. And she *had* been with some bloke. No one we knew, of course. No one who *knew* Smithy would do that to him.'

Kate could believe it. Anyone who knew him would know better than to mess with him. But surely Tess should have known?

'What did he say,' she asked, 'when she came back?'

Joanna laughed. 'Nothing, presumably, with a broken jaw and a tube down his throat. But if looks could kill ... I'm just guessing, of course. I wasn't there.' She heaved a sigh. 'Poor old Smithy.'

Although she was in the wrong company actually to say so, Kate was beginning to think 'poor old Tess', and to wonder if she'd been misunderstood. It happened, as Kate knew to her cost. Some people saw only what they wanted to see, fairies at the bottom of the garden included.

'He loved her,' Joanna went on softly. 'He still does, I'm sure. But he won't *talk* about her! I wish he would, Kate. How can he get well with all *that* festering inside him? It's wearing him out. I was beginning to think he didn't even *want* to get better, but this place ...'

They'd reached the water garden: Billy's special preserve. It had gone over a bit since he'd died—he'd loved doing his gardening waist-deep in cold, muddy water and Kate, somehow, didn't—but it still looked ravishingly pretty, with drifts of iris and primula in riotous bloom along the stream. 'Wow,' Joanna breathed. 'This'll cure him.' She sent Kate a smile. 'Or maybe you will,' she added coyly.

Until that moment, Kate had quite liked Joanna.

Chapter Five

For Smithy, his move to Whitsun Gate felt more like an end than a beginning. While he'd been 'a person of no fixed abode' he had, almost unconsciously, entertained the hope that he'd end up going back to London, back to Tess. Strange, because the facts had never been open to question and Smithy had dealt with them (he'd thought) in the usual way: accept, adjust and act—one step at a time. The trouble was, he supposed, that he'd always, before, been able to take his 'one step at a time' at a certain speed and with a fair level of authority. He'd never had to wait for nature to take its course, or to stand on the sidelines, helplessly watching, while the events of his life unfolded beyond his control. Had Tess left him while he was well, he'd have followed her, not necessarily to ask her to return, but to prove to himself, once and for all, that his marriage was a battle lost.

Without that proof ... Oh, he *knew* it was lost; he knew *now* that it had been lost from the start; yet sometimes he found himself wondering, wishing, indulging in dreams that it had all been a mistake and that she and he—divided only by his inability to follow her—were weeping for each other in separate beds.

Not that he did weep now. Grief had turned to rage and love to hatred some months back, the rage so deep, so all-consuming, he'd begun to think he'd never be rid of it. Yet as soon as he moved into Whitsun Gate, he ceased to feel angry, ceased to feel anything much. Tess, when she passed—too frequently—across his mind's eye, was like a stranger he'd met once, years ago, and never seen again except in his fantasies. And, in a way, that was the truth. He'd met her once, fallen in love and afterwards failed to see her as she was, only as he'd wanted her to be.

The thought depressed him, as did every other thought that crossed his mind. It was as if, since the accident, he'd been living in Cloud-cuckoo Land, telling himself that although everything had changed, it would somehow change back again. Even Mags would pop up, like a toadstool on the lawn, and say something batty to make him laugh. 'Whew, am I glad to be back! It was *hell* down there.'

His first night at Whitsun Gate cured him of all that. Kate, who'd been so cool and distant since the funeral, broke out in a rash of nerves

76

and frightened him silly. Had she been anyone else, he'd have teased her out of it, but a man who teases a woman can't easily avoid his own sexuality, let alone hers, so he had to keep his mouth shut. This wasn't easy. When another person's difficulties created trouble for Smithy, he was more naturally inclined to talk about it, analyse it, offer solutions; but the only solution to Kate's difficulty was trust, and the only way he could gain her trust was to leave her alone for as long as it took.

She made supper—a bastardised version of Spaghetti Bolognese, which would have been perfectly all right if she'd kept her wits about her. In the event, only the salad (strictly speaking) was edible, but since Smithy was very strictly *not* speaking, he ate the lot, trying to keep smiling while Kate tried not to cry. They both made an attempt to rise above it, but it was as if their wings had been weighed down with lead and at every attempt they returned to earth, hopelessly sighing.

The next few weeks took Smithy into a depression deeper than he'd ever before experienced. Everything was an effort. With Phil's help, he'd set himself up to fill every hour of the day with useful occupations: he had a computer, a stereo, an exercise routine and regular sessions with a physiotherapist. For half an hour at a time, the physio managed to concentrate his mind on the prospect of a fairly speedy recovery, but within minutes of leaving him, Smithy entered limbo again and found himself unable to concentrate on anything at all. Ten minutes at the computer, five minutes with a book ... Then he'd slip away into a drearily repetitive exchange with Tess, in which she begged his forgiveness and he said, 'Too late. Go away. I don't care any more.'

It was bad enough (since he couldn't stop saying, 'I don't care,') to know that he *did* care. Worse was the realisation that she would never give him the chance to say anything of the sort, which made his thoughts a complete waste of energy, both exhausting him and boring him rigid: a treadmill he seemed powerless to escape.

On the rare occasions when he wasn't thinking about Tess, he found himself thinking about Pamela, which was almost as maddening. He'd written to her twice since she'd gone back to London, but had found it hard to hit the right tone and thought it likely that his efforts to smooth her down had only ruffled her feathers even more. She hadn't replied, anyway. She'd sent his things down in a large cardboard box—clothes, camera, field-glasses and a small collection of books and music—but no letter. Kate had helped unpack the box and put everything away. It hadn't taken long, which was probably why she'd said at the end of it, 'Is that all?' no doubt meaning, 'Is there anything else you want me to do?' But Smithy had taken it another way: Is this all you possess? Is this all you have to show for thirty-one years of life? Painful.

Kate might have made it easier had she the first idea of what being a 'partner' meant (business or otherwise), but she was in a world of her own—a convent, probably—and he a beggar at the gate to whom she threw the occasional crumb: 'Hi, you all right? See you later.'

He'd thought she'd been exaggerating when she said she'd be working a sixteen-hour day from now on, but it was often longer than that. She started at six most mornings and rarely finished much before bedtime. Her visits to the house, although frequent enough, amounted to ten minutes here, half an hour there. He rarely buttoned her down long enough to talk about anything and, between one meeting and the next, felt a terrible tension growing inside him, a kind of longing to see her again which made no obvious sense. But, yes, it did make sense. He was like a lonely old man, waiting at the window for someone to come along, to pause and smile, to give him an assurance that he still mattered.

It should have been a relief, therefore, when Mavis Mills fell in love with him. But it wasn't. All it achieved was to kill his appetite for lunch.

In her youth, Mavis Mills had been a tall, strapping lass, long of limb and dark of eye, with deep wells of energy which were evident even in her wedding photographs, three of which she'd had framed and kept ever since on the sideboard in her kitchen-diner, clustered around a vase of plastic roses. To Kate, who'd seen those wedding photographs more times than she could count, it had been obvious at first sight that 'Our Jeff', the happy bridegroom, could never—on the wedding night or after it—meet his wife's romantic expectations. He'd work hard, bring home the bacon, dig the allotment and paper the parlour, but if she wanted anything more, Mavis would have to look elsewhere.

She'd spent the next thirty years looking elsewhere (while Jeff dug the allotment), but romantic heroes didn't come six to the pound in Lower Minden. They were thin on the ground even in Frome, and on the brink of extinction in Radstock. Mavis didn't ask much, of course. When she at last found her hero (which she pronounced 'ear-ole') he'd be tall, dark and handsome, well-dressed, well-spoken and as rich as Croesus.

'Well-spoken' aside, Kate wouldn't have given Smithy a snowball's chance of being elected Mavis's ear-ole. He wasn't dark (unless Mavis settled for the mousey variety that had started out blond); he wasn't handsome; he wore track suits and trainers and—until the will went through—hadn't a penny to his name. But Mavis fell for him. She was twenty years his senior and had varicose veins to prove it, but suddenly she was young again. At least, she thought she was.

There was something rather pitiful about Mavis in love. The tall, strapping lass had become much larger and lumpier in middle age and her attempts to look like a young girl made her look more like a young girl's duvet—all flounces and frills and little pink rosebuds. Smithy privately referred to her as the 'HGV', which not only commented on her height, weight and thunderous speed of movement, but was also short for, 'Has she Got a Voice!' She'd be crushed if she knew, although in fact there was little danger of her ever finding out. Reality—in the shape of home and family, money worries and Jeff's bad back—were things she dealt with and then forgot. Life for Mavis was fantasy, not reality.

'Oh, I fink he's lovely, Kate. He've got such a lovely smile, haven't he? And haven't he got beautiful eyes? Like di'monds, sorta.'

After six weeks of looking elsewhere, Kate had—quite by accident—established that Smithy's eyes were blue, but they weren't even remotely like diamonds.

'Colourless, you mean?' she enquired innocently.

'Sparklin',' Mavis breathed mistily.

'Mmm,' Kate said, 'could be hay-fever.'

'I feels so sorry for him, Kate. I wants to cuddle him and make it all better, like.'

'Is cuddling a good cure for hay-fever?'

Mavis laughed shortly. 'Gerroff. He haven't got 'ay-fever. He'm just sad, poor little love. And you're no 'elp.' Her smile sweetened to syrup. 'Don't you fancy him, Kate? Not even a little bit?'

Kate was adding up the tearooms' takings, which gave her an excuse for sounding distracted and off-hand. 'No, not my type.'

'You're mad, then. I'd run away wiv him, if—'

If you could carry him, Kate thought cynically. 'Ninety-five, ninety-six. Ninety-seven pounds forty. Not much for a day's work, is it?'

'He talks so nice, too,' Mavis went on dreamily. 'Says all his ings. Go-*ing*, eat-*ing*, mak-*ing*. Even when he's talk-ing really fast, he says all his ings. Yet you couldn't call him posh, could you, Kate? He've got no side to him at all, have he?'

Kate sighed. 'Can we get back to business, Mavis?'

'What? Oh ... Well, it was quiet, wasn't it? I only done five lunches, not countin' Smiffy's, an' he only had a sandwich, bless 'im. I said to him, you ought to eat more, I said. How you going to get your elf back, I said, if you don't eat proper? But he only laffed. He've got a lovely laff. Always did 'ave. I fink he's really *brave*, Kate, 'cos he've never had a lot to laff about, have he? Poor little soul. Worst thing that can happen to a kid, losin' his ma when he's little. It do leave him with nowhere to turn, see, Kate. When a man's lost his ma, he's lost his best friend. He's on his own, like.'

Kate shrugged and filled in the banking slip, wishing Mavis had sold six lunches, which would at least have given them a few pence profit. Smithy needed the encouragement. He never complained when they had a quiet day, but their occasional busy weekend brightened him up as nothing else could and Kate liked him better when he was smiling and talking

82

as he used to do in the 'old' days. This was odd, because she hadn't liked him at all before Mags had died. His vitality had irritated her then. She'd thought him arrogant and shallow, too pleased with himself by half. Now, for some reason, she wanted him to be pleased with himself. Pleased with something, anyway.

'How's *your* ma?' Mavis asked brightly. 'Seen her lately?'

In a weak moment—or, rather, in the hope of shutting Mavis up—Kate had once told her that she and her mother were not the best of friends. If she'd been told such a thing by anyone else, she'd have kept her mouth shut about it ever after, but Mavis didn't work that way. She thought a question answered was an open door and no matter how often you tried to slam it in her face, she kept her foot in it, always hoping for more. She did it to Smithy, too, but he seemed better able to deal with it. He just laughed.

Kate could laugh at some of Mavis's questions, but the ones about her mother always shocked and confused her, because she knew what she was getting at and knew ... knew she was right. It was a terrible thing to lose one's mother and, when she wasn't even dead as Smithy's was, there seemed no excuse for not finding her again. Yet Kate had *tried* to find her. It wasn't ... Damn it, it *wasn't* all her fault!

Delivering her usual exit line: 'Must dash, Mavis,' Kate made for the door, but—as usual—Mavis failed to take the hint. 'You ought to ask her over, Kate, now it's all yours,

83

like. Show her around, why don't you?'

Kate smiled, waved and departed. Mavis followed her to the door. 'Cook her a nice dinner.' she added loudly. 'Inter-duce her to Smiffy. Invite *me!*'

'You'd be sorry,' Kate muttered.

For the sake of Smithy's health, she'd actually bought a cookery book at last, but it had made no noticeable difference—except to her opinion of Smithy. As Mavis had said, he was really *brave.* Blackened chops, half-cooked potatoes and over-boiled spaghetti: he ploughed through it all without even flinching. Tact and tolerance were the last things she'd expected of him, but—so far—he'd made only one comment about her culinary efforts: 'You make a great salad dressing.' True, he'd said it with a grin which had filled in the blanks for all the other things he *could* have said, but Kate could live with that kind of criticism. It was positive, at least. It made her *want* to do better, if only because he'd made her laugh when she felt more like crying.

She felt like crying now, but that was Mavis's fault, not his. No, not Mavis's fault ... and not Kate's, either!

As she entered the house through the narrow hallway which led to the kitchen, her memory took her to another hallway, much cleaner than this one and thickly carpeted, with Robert reaching past her to close the door. Kate's mother, Laura, had preceded them but was still there, chatting and laughing, making her way to the stairs with her arms full of shopping.

'I'll put it on. The colour's marvellous, Rob ... you'll love it!'

His wife's proximity had never made any difference to Robert. He'd cupped his hand over Kate's breast, pressed flabby wet lips to her mouth and, as she'd frozen with horror, said, 'Mmm, I'll love it more when you take it off.'

He'd always been very clever with double meanings. He'd been talking to Kate, promising more—and worse—while Laura had thought he'd been replying to her. 'Ooh,' she'd giggled (halfway up the stairs by this time), 'you wicked man!' At the landing she'd turned and looked down, but Robert was already yards up the hallway, innocently smiling. 'He's wicked, isn't he, Kate?'

Could Laura be blamed for being blind when Robert had deliberately blinded her? Kate didn't know. She'd never known. Now that she was older, wiser and better informed, she knew that she should have kicked him where it hurt the very first time, not just stood there like a dummy, trying to protect her *mother's* feelings. Because, in the end, her mother hadn't given a damn about Kate's feelings. Only her own ...

'Hey, what's up?'

She'd been so deep in thought, she hadn't even heard Smithy coming and now she blushed like a beetroot, aware that he'd caught her with 'that look' on her face, the one Mags had always said had murder in it. But it wasn't really murder. In spite of all her protests to the contrary, in spite of all the blame she'd heaped on Robert's head—and yet more on Laura's—Kate knew that at least half of it was her *own* fault. She should have had more sense!

'Bad day in the tearooms,' she explained shakily. 'I was just—um—' She smiled and sighed. 'Actually, I was imagining our last stand against the bailiffs.'

Smithy advanced his walking sticks a pace. He bent his head, bowed his shoulders and said in a faint, quavering, old man's voice, 'Don't worry, my dear. I'll protect you.'

It was—as he'd intended—funny enough to make Kate laugh, but funny enough, too, to surprise her into feelings other than humour. He was so much nicer than she'd expected. The notorious Fitzwarren temper hadn't surfaced once since the day of the funeral. He'd never uttered a word of complaint, never criticised, never asked her for anything beyond the basic necessities. He deserved more. He'd *earned* more, just by virtue of never *claiming* more than she could give him.

Yet what more could she give? High summer, in a garden like this, consumed more hours than the clock provided. There were only six hours when Kate could do any serious work on the ground—three at the start of the day before the visitors arrived and three at the end, when they'd gone. All the mowing, digging and planting, all the pruning, watering and tidying up, had to be done in those six hours. Then, when the visitors were in, she took turns with the part-timers to sell tickets at the gate or plants in the yard.

Given that she needed a minimum of seven hours' sleep and that there was money to be added up (and taken to the bank) every evening, that left just two hours for Smithy: a few cups of coffee, a few friendly words, a burnt lamb chop and a 'great' salad dressing.

No, there wasn't time for more. He'd have to wait until October. Then, if his patience held out that long, she might find a minute to play Scrabble within him!

The correct way to answer the telephone was to say 'Whitsun Gate', because most of the calls were for the gardens, not for Smithy. People asking about opening times or guided tours were inclined to gasp, 'Sorry, wrong number.' and hang up if you said the wrong thing, and although Smithy usually remembered to say the right thing, sometimes he didn't, especially when the phone had woken him from a doze, as on this occasion.

'F'swarren-Sm'ff,' he mumbled drowsily.

There was a pause. Then a woman's voice said, 'Billy? Is that Billy? I thought you were dead!'

'No, I'm not,' he said. 'Not Billy, that is. Not dead, either, as far as I know. Who ...?'

'Then who ...? Oh, I know, I know! Don't tell me! It's on the tip of my tongue! Begins with a P, doesn't it? You're Billy's nephew ... Quentin? Cedric? No, it's on the tip of my tongue, but I can't for the life of me ... Didn't you have an accident? Kate told me you were very poorly, but I can't recall ... Weren't you in the Navy? No, wait, it'll come back to me in a minute—'

'Can I help you at all?' Smithy asked dryly. 'I take it you wanted Kate? She's unavailable at the moment, but I can take a message.'

'*Oh!*' Whoever she was, she was either astonished at his ability to take messages, or completely lost for a message to give him. 'Oh, yes, yes, what am I thinking of? Just remind her about lunch next Monday, will you? Thank you so much.'

'What name shall I—?' He widened his eyes as the woman hung up, leaving both their names (Cedric, indeed!) plus a few other things a complete mystery. On the pad beside the telephone, under 'Sharon from Shearton's, *Papaver* 'Indian Chief' not available,' he wrote, 'Some dippy woman reminding you about lunch on Monday'.

So Kate had a friend? A social life? No ... the woman hadn't sounded much like a social life. Older than Kate. Her voice had had the assertive tone typical of the WI and TWG women who rang to ask for guided tours, although they, generally, expected answers to the questions they asked. *What time do you open? No, don't tell me; it's on the tip of my tongue* ... Daft bat.

He dismissed her from his mind, but later, when Kate came in for coffee, he watched the expression on her face as she read the message, and guessed not only that she'd forgotten lunch on Monday, but that she wasn't thrilled to be reminded of it.

'She didn't leave a name,' he said.

'No, so I see.'

'But you aren't too mystified?'

'No. "Some dippy woman" covers it.'

She turned away to put on the kettle, leaving Smithy no wiser but ten times more curious. He had no right to ask who the woman was and Kate had every right to keep the information to herself, but he couldn't resist having just one more dig at it.

'You don't like her, I take it?'

Kate turned to look at him, her face expressing a mixture of bewilderment and pain that made him blink with astonishment. 'I don't have much choice,' she said. 'She's my mother.'

It was a nasty moment for Smithy. Kate had opened the door on her feelings the merest crack—and his taxi was due in ten minutes to take him to the physio. Mags had told him that Kate's relationship with her mother had been destroyed by the funny business with her stepfather, yet his own experience of family matters should have told him that it was never as simple as that.

'Oh,' he said lightly, 'you can choose not to like her. I've chosen not to like my father, but I can't help loving the old bastard, regardless.'

Kate turned away. He thought the subject was closed—no subject stayed open for long with Kate—but as he prepared to walk away, she asked faintly, 'Is he still in Kenya?'

'Yes. He won't come home again now. Thinks he's old. He's only sixty-eight, but ... Well, maybe he *is* old. It's only an attitude of mind, after all. Mags stayed twenty all her life.'

'Is that what you don't like about him? That he thinks he's old?'

'No.' He glanced at the clock on the wall. Only four minutes to go, and he'd need most of that to get outside. 'It's—' He smiled, inclining his head towards the telephone and her mother. 'It's complicated. Tell you about it later.'

At his usual snail's pace, he negotiated the kitchen doorway and the first two flagstones of the hall (he usually counted them to give him an idea he was making progress) before he heard her mutter, 'He's always rushing off somewhere.'

Knowing he'd been meant to hear, Smithy laughed. But he felt like swearing, loud and long. The moment had passed. By the time he saw her again, she'd have closed the door.

He wasn't certain he could explain it, anyway, except perhaps to say that his father was a little like Kate: detached and remote. Uncaring. He'd been a widower barely a month before he'd booted Smithy off to boarding school and, two months after that, he'd telephoned to say he couldn't make Christmas.

Adult emotions need to be spelled out to small boys. If they are not—and Smithy's father's grief never had been—their existence isn't imagined, let alone understood. Mags and Billy, with whom he'd spent that Christmas and almost every other holiday afterwards, had not been the type to spell anything out, and he'd been seventeen before Mags had at last said of his father, 'He's never got over your mother's death, you know.' That had been the first chink of daylight in what had seemed to Smithy an endless night of rejection, but it had been too late by then. Seven years is long enough to build some pretty impenetrable defences. He'd made other arrangements, filled the gaps with substitutes. He couldn't be bothered.

It was bit different now that he had adult griefs of his own to handle. He understood a little better, now. 'Being brave' was the worst part of it: not being able to ask for comfort because there was no one left to give it. No one to whom he could say, 'I'm beaten; for God's sake help me.'

Actually, his physio, Tom Howard, was more help than anyone. In the course of his treatments he'd managed to winkle out virtually everything about Smithy's life. Home, parents, school, adolescent sex, marriage ... He knew about Kate, too. Smithy had actually told him very little, but his choice of words, fired by the helpless anger her reserve seemed to induce in him, had probably given the game away. 'I don't know what it is about her. She makes me feel guilty, ashamed of being myself, afraid to be myself. And that makes me angry. I've never hurt her, for God's sake!'

'But someone has.'

Yes, some bastard had. And instead of making *his* life a misery, Kate was making Smithy's life ... No. No, it wasn't her fault. His life was a misery anyway.

'I used to be happy all the time,' he said now.

'No. You just think you were. But really there

91

was always a fly in the ointment. While you were taking those morning runs up the Brecon Beacons, for instance, what was happiness? Not the thought that you were running up the Brecon Beacons, but the thought of having a hot shower and breakfast when it was over. It's only now, because you *can't* run, that you think happiness was running. In fact it was agony. Just as much agony, in its way, as walking a few yards is now.'

'At least it was healthy agony!'

'So is this. You were getting fitter then and you're getting fitter now. There's no essential difference. Happiness, we think, is always a stage further on. We're always looking forward to breakfast, or Saturday night, or winning the football pools. We hardly ever halt the forward progress to say, "Hey, this is pretty good. If they stopped the world at this precise moment, I'd die happy." '

'I couldn't say it *now*,' Smithy said. 'Not at this precise—'

'Why not? I've been working this knee for five minutes, and you haven't winced once. Just for this moment, you have plenty to be happy about, but you won't pause to appreciate it. You're waiting for something better to turn up.'

'And you don't think it will?'

'Oh, it will. But the chances are you'll miss it. If you always see happiness ahead or behind, it's never *with* you, is it?'

Smithy didn't think he'd always been guilty of seeing happiness ahead or behind, but it was certainly true of him now. And he could see that there was something wrong with it, that it was—to a degree—as false a standard as Tom had implied. 'If it's never now, it's never,' was another way of saying, 'It's now or never; pull your finger out; start living.' After all, a few months ago he'd thought he'd be happy when he got out of hospital. Now he thought he'd be happy when he could walk without his sticks, or drive a car, or when he could get things moving with Kate ...

Bloody Kate.

Chapter Six

Although they met so infrequently, Kate and her mother always ate lunch in the same place, a vegetarian restaurant in Frome which Laura deemed smart enough for her tastes and Kate casual enough for hers. Her 'salary' had more than quadrupled recently, but so had her outgoings, so she was still as broke as ever, although her mother—typically—wouldn't believe it.

'So you're a wealthy woman now, darling! How wonderful! I must say I'm surprised Mrs Fitzwarren even thought of including you in her will, let alone leaving you the lion's share!'

Although Laura had always referred to Mags as Mrs Fitzwarren, it was a mark of dislike, not respect. True, she hadn't known her except, years ago, as her mother-in-law's neighbour, but even then she hadn't liked her. Mags had been too frank for her taste, too colourful in her choice of language. Kate was aware that she'd since found other reasons to dislike and resent her, but as they couldn't be discussed, they were not worth thinking about.

'It's not the lion's share,' Kate said now. 'It's a half-share. I told you, Mother, Smithy—'

'Oh, don't call him that, darling. His name's Courteney, isn't it? I couldn't remember it when I spoke to him the other day, but now that I ... Mmm, an *elegant* name. It has such a ring to it, don't you think, darling?'

'He hates it. Everyone calls him Smithy.'

'Well, I shan't. I'll call him—'

'Cedric,' Kate said dryly. 'That has a ring to it, too. Well, more of clang, really.'

Her mother laughed and changed the subject.

One of the reasons Kate so disliked meeting her was that she was always changing the subject. It was like having a conversation with a kangaroo. This was partly because there were very few subjects they could 'safely' talk about. Kate wasn't interested in clothes, carpets or upholstery cleaners. She certainly wasn't interested in Robert. So that left out the important parts of Laura's life and, since Laura wasn't interested in gardening, it left out most of Kate's, too.

Laura usually ended up talking about people Kate didn't know. She worked two days a week in a charity shop in Bath and always had something to say about her colleagues' families, their clothes, their manners or their hysterectomies. She might sometimes ask about Mavis, or, today, Smithy, but she didn't really want to know. All she wanted was the outline of a picture—the sort of thing that existed in children's colouring books—that she could fill in to suit herself. She'd already 'coloured' Kate a wealthy woman; crossed out Smithy's preferred name and his status as Kate's business partner. She hadn't yet marked him out as Kate's live-in lover, but had received Kate's reference to his broken marriage with the sort of half-smile which meant she was at least thinking of colouring him pink.

She didn't know how Kate felt about men. She hadn't asked. And if, by a miracle, the question should ever arise, she'd run a mile at the first hint of an answer. The last time they'd talked about anything important had been the day Kate had told her about Robert, five years ago. There'd been almost two years, after that, when they hadn't spoken at all. Then, on Kate's eighteenth birthday, Laura had sent a card and suggested their first 'just us girls' lunch. It had been a huge relief to Kate at the time, but things hadn't improved much since then. The business with Robert ached between them like a bruise, too sore to touch. Laura loved him. He was her husband. No matter what else happened, they couldn't get around that.

'Now that you have some money, darling—'

'I don't, I told you. The will hasn't gone through Probate yet, and there's still a chance Pamela might—'

'Couldn't you get yourself some nice clothes for a change? You look very sweet in jeans, of course, but—'

'The only money we've got is the profit from the gardens and that doesn't amount to much. We have to eat and pay the bills and Smithy's forking out a mint every week in taxi fares.'

'Oh! Hasn't he got a car?'

'He can't drive, Mother. His legs—'

'You should teach him, darling. Everyone should know how to drive. I don't know what I'd do without my car, I'm sure. What does he look like, these days? I remember seeing him once or twice when Granny lived at the cottage, but he was just a boy then, of course. Didn't he go to Eton? Or was it Harrow?' She closed her eyes to think it over. 'No, don't tell me. I remember it was one of the two, because ... or was it Winchester?'

Kate sighed and looked at her watch. 'I ought to be going.'

Before she'd finished speaking, Laura was on her feet, ordering more coffee, making sure their lunch would continue for the usual two hours. It was almost as if she enjoyed it, as if their meetings really meant something to her, as if ... But how could you love your daughter and not want to know the first thing about her? Kate didn't understand it. It confused her utterly.

The restaurant was self-service and patronised mostly by people wearing jeans, brown leather and unbleached linen: arty, crafty, grow-your-own-parsley types who thought 'power-dressing' was something you did to a salad. In her crisp

96

pink suit and high-heeled sandals, Laura looked totally out of place: too clean, too neat, too prosperous by half. In her own social circle, she was usually the prettiest woman in sight. Here, she looked like a plastic doll. She wasn't real. She didn't mean anything. She certainly didn't mean 'mother'!

Smithy usually sat outside to eat his lunch. Mavis couldn't leave her place behind the tearoom counter for longer than it took to deliver his tray, but even then she managed to embarrass him ten times faster than he could blush. She asked such terrible questions! Did he hear from Tess, nowadays? Did he want to? Did he still love her? *Could* he, since the accident? (She hadn't phrased it as tactfully as that, of course. 'Any damage to your doin's?' had been the precise phrase.) He wouldn't have minded so much if she'd ever learned to whisper, but she proclaimed the intimate details of his life (and her own) in a voice to wake the dead.

It was going to be hard to convince himself he was happy with Mavis, but it was worth a try. She was a good cook, for one thing. Reliable. Which was more than could be said for Kate. And she was company, of a sort. She made him laugh at least as often as she made him furious. Sometimes, especially when there was a friendly crowd of visitors to share the agony, his lunch hour was the shortest of the day.

But today it was raining and the only other people in the tearooms when Smithy hobbled along were a painfully shy clergyman and his large, aggressive-looking wife. Both looked up when Smithy dragged himself inside. He smiled and sat down at the table in the corner, where there was room to prop his sticks. Mavis yelled, 'Hello, my darlin',' which embarrassed the vicar half to death, outraged his wife and gave Smithy the ghost of an idea.

Actually, it was a fully formed idea, rendered ghostly only because he had *no* idea how he might transfer it from his mind to Mavis's without breaking her heart. True, she had the thick skin of a rhinoceros, but even a rhino has its soft spots, and Smithy didn't dare offend her. In practical terms, she was very good at her job: clean, capable, efficient and—better still—happy to accept a lousy salary and a five-month winter lay-off without any pay at all. Her one big drawback was her voice and manner of speaking. A garden like Whitsun Gate tended to attract the more genteel sections of society: the frail, the aged, the innocent (or sanctimonious), for whom Mavis came as a slap in the face, a violent spoiling of their peaceful day out. But how to tell her that? And what would be the point? Telling Mavis to tone it down a bit would be like telling a dog to bark softly.

The vicar and his lady departed. Mavis narrowed her eyes to watch them out of sight, before saying loudly, 'Miserable old gits!'

'Hmm?' Smithy said. (It was something he said quite often, both with Mavis and Kate, usually after he'd reminded himself to keep his lip buttoned.)

'Well, they comes in 'ere for their lunch, asks what's on and then orders two measly coffees! What's wrong wiv me bloody lunches? I done a lovely carrot soup, and you're the only one what's tried it! I got six kindsa samwidges, three kindsa kitch—'

'Quiche,' Smithy corrected, but under his breath, just to relieve his feelings. In his normal speaking voice, he added truthfully, 'There's nothing wrong with your lunches, Mavis.'

At her usual speed she was crossing the floor with his 'jacket spud and chilly-cum-carny', but she stopped halfway, eyes widening, jaw dropping, her gaze fixed on the wall above Smithy's head. She looked stunned, appalled, as if she'd just seen a ghost.

'What's up?'

'Oh, Gawd,' she said. 'It's *me*, innit, Smiffy? Kate've bin on and on at me about the takin's being' down, but it never even crossed me mind!'

'Hmm?'

Mavis set the tray on the table and sat down, twisting her hands in her lap. 'Look,' she said, 'I'm not saying nuffin against her—don't think I am—but Mags wasn't what you could call a tactful woman, was she, Smiffy? What I mean is, she said what she meant and if you didn't like it, tough. Well, I didn't like it and when she died ... Oh, *Gawd.*'

She covered her face with her hands. Although she was evidently upset, Smithy received the distinct impression that she was enjoying this as much as she enjoyed every other aspect of

99

her life—giving it her all, wringing the best out of it, making mental notes, perhaps, so that she could act it out again for her husband when he asked tonight, 'Had a good day?'

Mavis dropped her hands, took a deep breath—and laughed. 'She said I'd make a great barmaid,' she confessed ruefully. 'And if I didn't mind me manners, I could bloody well go and *be* one.'

Her shoulders slumping, she turned her gaze to the wall. 'Well, *I* couldn't see what she was on about, could I? I done what she said, like, because I never *wanted* to be a bloody barmaid. I likes it here. I likes the hours. I likes the kinda people we gets in. And I ain't what you could call *rude* to 'em, Smiffy. But Mags said I was. She said I asked too many questions. She said I was—what was it she said?—over-familiar! And I ain't. I'm just friendly! Treats 'em like I treats me own family, and what's wrong with that, I ask you?'

Having once seen Mavis hit her husband sideways with a playful dig in the ribs, Smithy thought there was a lot wrong with it.

'Well ...' he began. 'I suppose ...'

'But what could I do? She was the boss, so I didn't have no choice but do what she said. Trouble was ... she used to keep poppin' in to remind me, and when she died I forgot all about it. Until just now. And then ... Well, I—I saw what she was gettin' at and realised it was probably all my fault ...'

Smithy kept his peace, which was harder to do now than it had ever been. He wanted to shout,

'Hallelujah!' He also wanted to say something to comfort the poor woman, but knew he mustn't, yet. He'd discovered in the Army that if people were reassured too soon, they forgave themselves too soon and then made the same mistakes all over again.

'So *you'll* have to remind me,' Mavis went on briskly. 'Trouble wiv you, my love, is you're too soft. Don't fink I don't appreciate it, 'cos I do, but what you got to face up to is this: Whitsun Gate is a business—and you're s'posed to be the boss—so if you don't learn to speak up for yourself, we'll all go down the drain, won't we, my love?'

Smithy blinked.

Mavis sighed and patted his hand. 'Look, I know you're havin'—hav*ing*—a hard time at the moment. I know you're upset about Mags and your accident and your marriage goin' wrong, not to mention losin'—los*ing*—your job. But—' She sighed again and shook her head. 'I sometimes wonder how you managed in the Army, my love. They didn't toughen you up much, did they?'

Too confused to speak, Smithy blinked again. It was the pills; he was sure of it. They were turning his brain!

Although there was rarely a day when Kate's mother did not cross her mind, she had a nasty tendency to move in and make herself at home after one of their 'little lunches'. Kate woke up thinking about her and went to bed thinking about her. She thought about her when she

101

was potting up cuttings, weeding the borders, mowing the lawns. 'Thinking', in fact, was too good a word for it. 'Brooding' would be a better one. She was like a hen sitting on an addled egg, compelled by her nature to keep it warm while knowing, in her heart of hearts, that the damned thing would never hatch. There were so many things she wanted to say to Laura, so many things she wanted Laura to say. While she brooded, they said them all: sometimes calmly, sometimes angrily, but always, always *rationally*, with only one end in view: to make things right again.

There were times—in Kate's imagination, at least—when they almost seemed to reach that end, but it was usually when Laura said, 'You're right, he's a swine,' which was only marginally less likely than Elvis coming back from the dead. So they never reached the end. They always went back to the beginning, where Kate said (for perhaps the tenth time that day), 'I am *not* a liar,' and Laura said, 'I know, I was wrong,' and Kate said, 'Oh, shut up!' (to herself) and ran back to the house to exchange a few, reasonably sane, words with Smithy.

Kate had realised, just recently, how important those few sane words were to her. She'd never been a person who craved company (given the choice of spending the rest of her life alone or with Robert, she'd choose utter solitude every time), but Smithy was different. Just the sound of his voice was a comfort, even when he was saying something boring about his computer or something dismal about their finances. It was a curious voice: slow, warm, almost lazy in tone, but because he pronounced all his consonants (*and* all his ings), he gave the impression of always being in control of himself, which was precisely the comfort Kate most needed from him.

No, not only that. It was just nice to have someone to talk to, someone who was always there, as Mags had been. Kate missed Mags. She missed having someone who knew everything about her, understood most of it and, better than anything, could be trusted never to tell anyone else. Although no one could call her a tactful or sensitive woman, she'd never been a gossip and seemed to know by a kind of instinct the sort of things other people would want to keep private. She'd never told Kate, for instance, that she'd told Mavis she ought to have been a barmaid. It was true, but only so far as it went. Mavis took pride in being 'a respectable married woman' and (with her usual frail grasp on the realities of life) had always yearned to be a respectable married *lady*. 'Tell you what I'd really like, Kate. I'd like to be able to dress up all the time, like I was goin' to a weddin'. Hat, gloves, bag ... matchin' shoes. Cor, that'd be heaven, wouldn't it?'

It sounded nightmarish to Kate—a lot like Laura, in fact—but if it was Mavis's idea of heaven, the barmaid label would have cut her to the heart and Mags would have known it and been very careful not to mention it to anyone else.

Smithy *hadn't* known it, of course. He hadn't

known, either, that Mavis was always much more interested in other people's troubles than in her own. He'd thought she'd been shifting the blame, telling him it was all *his* fault, when in fact she'd just got bored with her own failings, dealt with them (after her fashion) and moved on to a more interesting subject: Smithy.

Kate smiled to herself. She'd never seen him in such a pickle. He'd hardly been able to spit out the words, poor man. 'Hell, Kate, I've very nearly ruptured myself trying to keep ... Keep myself from telling her ... Telling her to ...'

'Keep her trap shut?'

'Right! And then she has the nerve to tell me—! I couldn't believe—! *Me!* Learn to speak up! And I've spent all these months learning not to!'

He'd been laughing throughout, but Kate, although she'd laughed too, had seen that he was genuinely upset about it, bewildered rather than angry, because for all her faults it was well-nigh impossible to be really angry with Mavis. She was more like an over-sized toddler than a grown woman. No matter what trouble she caused, no matter how enormous the clangers she dropped, she did it all in a state of innocence. Mags would probably have said ignorance, but Kate knew the difference. Ignorant people were those who had intelligence enough to understand what they were doing and *chose* not to. Mavis hadn't that intelligence. Laura and Robert, on the other hand ...

'Oh, shut up,' Kate muttered. '*Stop* it, will you?'

She'd spent the dawn-to-daylight hours planting white hyacinths in a corner of the Bride's Garden. After three days of rain the ground was claggy almost to the point of being unworkable and there was now almost as much mud covering her as there was covering the hyacinths. She was squelching her way to the hose-pipe in the yard when she saw the postman, riding his bike out of the village (rather than into it, which was more usual at this time of the morning), which meant that Smithy had probably been staring at his letters on the doormat for a good half hour or more. He couldn't pick them up—couldn't bend that far—but the post had become increasingly important to him just lately. Kate guessed he was waiting for something in particular—news of the will, perhaps—and, rather than keep him waiting, she squelched back to the house and prised off her boots at the door, mud and all.

In fact, the post was mostly rose and seed catalogues, bills and junk mail. Nothing obviously personal. Kate handed Smithy the whole pile, put on the kettle for breakfast and ran upstairs to shower and change her clothes. It didn't take long. She'd never had reason to care much about her appearance and although she liked being clean and was neat more by instinct than intention, she wasted no time at all in trying to look good. Three minutes in the shower, two minutes to drag on a clean shirt and jeans ... By the time she arrived back in the kitchen, Smithy had barely registered that he—he above all men in Lower Minden—had been chosen to compete in the draw that would win him a quarter of a million pounds, plus a ski-ing holiday for two (just what he needed), if he replied within ten days.

Kate put a few eggs on to boil, shoved some bread in the toaster and made coffee. She told him about her muddy morning with the hyacinths, told him she still had a few hundred tulips bulbs to put in and that, if the rain didn't set in on a permanent basis, she was planning to dig out and re-plant the main herbaceous border.

Whitsun Gate had been Smithy's home base for almost as long as Kate had been alive, and he knew as much about it as she did: its layout, its themes, the names and needs of most of its plants. Unlike Mags, his special preference was for blue flowers—delphiniums especially—while Kate preferred white. They both liked Mags's preference for pink and had discussed its advantages many times—a huge range of flowers, an uplifting effect on the visitors and a 'show' which ran from March right through to November—but they'd both said, at one time or another, 'It might be nice to have a change.'

Kate made a space for Smithy's bowl of cornflakes among the litter of his mail. 'It wouldn't be as easy with blue, of course,' she said. 'But I don't see why we shouldn't try it. It would be a challenge, wouldn't it, to find enough blue to fill the late-summer gaps? September's fine: Michaelmas daisies, second-flush delphiniums, agapanthus ... Hurry up with your cornflakes. The eggs are almost done.'

After a mere five months of giving him hard-boiled eggs—which he loathed—Kate had discovered a funny little clock on the stove that went ping (if you remembered to set it) when the necessary three 'soft-boiled' minutes had elapsed. She was aware that this culinary achievement was nothing much to be proud of, but she was proud of it just the same. After all—who knew?—soft-boiled eggs might be the first step on the road to tiger prawns in chilli.

Smithy was staring at the wall. He hadn't touched his cornflakes. 'Smithy,' she prompted.

'Hmm?' He looked up.

'Cornflakes. The eggs—'

Again he looked at the wall. 'I don't think I want anything, thanks.'

Although his tone of voice was the same as usual—soft almost to the point of blandness—Kate suffered a curious sinking of heart, a mild but very definite sensation that something serious was wrong. Something she'd said? Or something the post had brought in?

The clock went *ping*. Smithy just stared at the wall and, because he wasn't looking at her, Kate studied his face: the sharp line of his jaw, the twisted line of his mouth. Did he look angry? Or just sadder than usual?

'Is anything wrong?' she asked.

He drummed his fingers on the table. 'Is anything right?' he murmured.

'The eggs will be, if you eat them now.'

'No, thanks.'

Her heart thudding, Kate pretended not to

care and ate three boiled eggs and four slices of toast, all by herself. She thumbed through one of the seed catalogues while she ate, but made no sense of any of it. Her feet were itching. She wanted to run, to put as wide a space as possible between herself and Smithy's gloom. But her hands were itching, too. She wanted to reach out and touch him, to ask, 'What's up?' and say or do something to help. But he'd probably misinterpret it, think she cared.

Run, then. As usual. She dumped her plate and egg-cup in the sink, returned Smithy's cornflakes to their box, wiped toastcrumbs from the table and said, 'I'd better be—'

'No,' he said coldly. 'I want to talk to you. I want to talk to you now, so ...' He turned to face her, unsmiling. 'Pour some more coffee and sit down. I'll be as quick as I can.'

Kate's heart sank again, much further this time. The old Smithy had come up for air, like Nessie from the loch, bad-tempered and snarling, brooking no arguments. Silently she warned him, 'Watch your step, buster,' but thought she'd better give him the benefit of the doubt before she said anything out loud. She poured the coffee. She sat down.

Smithy sighed and said nothing. He picked up one of the envelopes that had come in the post, scanned his name and address on the front and dropped it again. 'Tess,' he said, 'is asking for a divorce. I've been expecting it, but ...' He sighed again. So did Kate, more with relief than sorrow. It was his wife's fault, not hers. She could handle that.

'But it's made me realise, Kate, I can't ... I'm not ... Oh damn it! What the hell do *you* know? You've never cared for anyone, have you?'

Kate lowered her eyes. She'd never been a fighter. She hadn't the equipment for it, the nerve. Anger made her shake—her hands were shaking now—and, if she gave it rein, it made her cry. People who cried in a fight invariably lost it, so Kate didn't fight. She just departed by the nearest exit and left her erstwhile opponents to fight the empty air. It sounded good. Peaceable, at least. But in fact that was the last thing it was. It made things worse, not better, because she, too, was left to fight empty air. It also had a nasty tendency to leave her homeless, and this was one home she didn't want to lose, didn't dare to lose. So ... maybe she'd fight, this time. But on her own terms, not Smithy's.

She looked up and smiled, quite cheerfully, at the corner of his mouth. 'If you want to quarrel with Tess,' she said mildly, 'the London train leaves from Bath every hour or so. Do you want a lift, or shall I call a taxi?'

Smithy stared at her. She still couldn't meet his eyes, so couldn't tell what he was thinking. She hoped he was thinking how perceptive she was, as well as how brave. (Not that he'd know how brave ...) She hoped he was thinking how unfair he'd been to blame her for his wife's failings.

Smithy scratched his throat. 'You mistake me,' he said. 'I don't want to quarrel with anyone. But I am angry. I'm angry with myself.'

109

'Then maybe you should—'

'And I'm angry with you.'

The itch in Kate's feet informed her that the exit was thataway. But her legs had turned to jelly. She couldn't move.

Chapter Seven

Smithy had to keep reminding himself that Inky was right: it *wasn't* possible for anyone to meet another person's eyes for more than a few seconds at a time. Yet Kate seemed to be doing it, her gaze so cold, so steady and unflinching ... 'Brazen' was the first word to come to mind and Smithy found it hard to believe that the opposite was true. She was afraid of him, which ... Which, now that he thought of it in such terms, was precisely what had upset him. He bloody well didn't deserve it! He'd done nothing to hurt her, while she—and the rest of the world—had done *everything* to hurt him!

And he couldn't stand it any longer. He'd known all along that his patience had limits and ... Hell, all he'd been waiting for was the end of the season, and now the selfish little—!

No, no. It wasn't her fault. He'd known the end of the season was not the end of the work: that 'putting the garden to bed' was even more laborious and time-consuming than keeping the damn thing awake. He'd known there were bulbs and roses to be planted, perennials to be split, mulches and muck to be spread over the ground. But it hadn't really come home to him until she'd mentioned re-planting the main border, actually *making* work—a further excuse, no doubt, for keeping the resident male at arm's length!

'Angry with *me?*' she said now. 'Why? What have I done?'

'Nothing,' he said wearily. 'That's the whole problem. Look, how would you feel about getting a housekeeper?'

Kate's eyes widened and then closed, a deep flush of pink staining her cheeks as she looked furtively around the kitchen. Smithy followed her gaze, realising with annoyance that although he'd said precisely the words he'd intended to say, he'd conveyed entirely the wrong meaning. The place *was* a mess, of course, but it wasn't Kate's fault. Considering how little time she had to spare, she kept everything remarkably tidy and as clean as basic hygiene required. But it would take a few months, a team of decorators and a small (no, make that 'large') fortune to make the place seriously clean. Thirty years of neglect can't be sloshed away with a wet mop.

'I didn't mean—' he began.

'I usually—that is, Mags and I usually did a sort of springclean in the winter. I *was* planning to do that, but—'

'I'm not criticising your housekeeping, Kate. You do a great job, all things considered. It's just ...' He sighed. 'Look ... I really *don't* want to upset you, but if I can't tell you how I feel, sort a few things out, I'm going to have to quit. Go somewhere else. A ground-floor flat in the middle of London, for preference. If you'd rather I did that—'

Kate looked at her hands. It was the sort of thing a man would do when he wanted to guard his thoughts, and since Smithy could imagine only one of Kate's possible thoughts (Thank God, he's going!) he felt hurt all over again.

'Would you rather it?' he demanded. 'Am I more trouble than the place is worth?'

'No.' Although she smiled, doors had closed behind her eyes, shutting him out. 'Not so far. But you've managed to keep your temper so far and I've got a feeling my time's running out in that department.'

Someone who didn't know her would have thought her completely calm, but she'd hidden her hands under the table and Smithy could see the tendons in her arms working as she twisted her fingers in her lap.

'I don't lose my temper,' he said innocently. 'I speak my mind.'

'Oh, right ... Speak up fer yourself, you mean?'

Smithy's smile was genuine, if rather wan. She'd hit the nail on the head. It *was* all Mavis's doing. At least, she'd made him realise—not for the first time, in fact—that suppressing his nature was a big mistake. He should have spoken his mind from the first. He should have taken control. Now that he'd lost it, it was going to be difficult—not to say humiliating—to claw it back.

112

'Don't blame Mavis,' he said. 'And don't blame this.' He indicated the letter from Tess's solicitor. 'All they've done is to underline what I was already feeling.' He took a deep breath, as though to plunge into an icy sea. 'Kate, I'm lonely. I'm scared. And if—' He took another deep breath. 'And if we can't make some kind of change in our arrangements, I'm going to go out of mind with plain, unadulterated bloody *misery.*'

He closed his eyes. He'd done it. He was up to his neck in it. Now ... would she push him under or give him the loan of her water-wings?

Shocked, Kate turned her gaze to the window, trying to understand what he'd said, which wasn't at all what she'd expected. As soon as he'd said 'housekeeper' she'd thought he was going to give her the long-awaited rocket about her cooking. But this ... No, she hadn't expected this. Lonely she understood. But scared? *Smithy* scared? And why was that *her* fault?

'What are you scared of?' she asked faintly.

'You.' Although he'd spoken very softly, his voice was so grim she'd have been shocked even if he'd said something more comprehensible. Merely to check that he meant it, she looked into his eyes and quickly looked away again.

'You're so self-contained,' he said. 'You make me think I'd mean as much to you dead as I do alive. It's blood-chilling, Kate. Soul-destroying. Can't you see that?'

She looked at her hands. Blood-chilling? God,

she hadn't meant to go *that* far!

'Kate, Mags is dead. My marriage is dead. I've lost the Army, my health and most of my confidence, and I've begun to feel—you've made me feel—that I don't exist any more and that it might be better for you if I didn't.'

'That's not true,' she murmured.

'Maybe not, but that's how I feel. This is a big house. When you go upstairs at night, it's just the same for me as if you were going to the next village. If I fell—I'm terrified of falling, by the way—you wouldn't even hear the screams. That can't be avoided, of course. What really grieves me is that the thought has never even crossed your mind. You don't care. And I don't—I *can't*—ask you to care. I'm not your father, your brother or ... Well, anyway, you don't owe me anything. That's why I thought a housekeeper might help. At least *she'd* be obliged to give the occasional damn about me. When the season ends, next week, I won't even have Mavis to give a damn, will I?'

Kate blushed; he must be desperate if he was thinking Mavis's 'damn' a loss he couldn't bear! 'I'm sorry,' she said. 'But look at it from my point of view, will you, Smithy? I hardly know you—'

'I've been living here for five months, damn it!'

'—*except*,' she went on frantically, 'to know that you're a man who speaks his mind. So ... if I haven't known your mind until now—'

'It's because you've never listened! You're never around long enough to listen! The minute

114

I open my mouth to speak, it's: "Gosh, I must dash!" And what the hell am I meant to do about that? Dash after you?'

His temper was failing fast. So was Kate's nerve. (Did she *really* speak in the silly little voice he'd mimicked just now? It sounded just like her mother!) And it was no help at all to know he was right. She *had* taken advantage of his inability to follow her. That was what had made him so safe, of course, that she could walk out on him any time she liked. She could walk out on him now.

But if she did, she'd lose Whitsun Gate. It was beginning to look as if Pamela would leave them alone, but if the will went through unchallenged, there was still the 'three years' clause to get through before they could sell. She might manage to run the place on her own for three years, but she seriously doubted it. Smithy had seen to all the business side of things—tax, insurance, wages, paying the bills—and if, now, he sloped off to London ... No, she couldn't manage without him.

'I haven't wanted to talk about the business,' she said, 'because it felt like tempting fate. There seemed no sense in making plans, making changes, if Pamela could—'

'Less than an hour ago you were planning a new herbaceous border. Wasn't that tempting fate? Tempting bankruptcy, too, unless I've been reading the nursery price-lists upside down. Yet we've never discussed it—'

'We have! You said you like blue flowers and I thought—'

'*You* thought! We're meant to be partners, Kate, which means you should be discussing these things with me, *sharing* them, not swanning around on your own, as if I didn't exist!'

Kate hadn't quite got her tongue around the protest, *That's not fair!* when Smithy said it for her. 'That's not fair. I'm sorry, Kate. You're doing all the work, which means everything's out of balance, anyway. All I mean is that you're making it more out of balance than it need be. You're leaving me out.'

She could say that there had been no time to include him, but there seemed little point because it was not the whole truth. She'd been avoiding this surrender of control (*he* could call it sharing, but *she* called it surrender) right from the beginning, when she'd said, 'It's mine. I can do what I like with it.' She'd shut him out then and had been shutting him out ever since, taking advantage of his patience, until ... Until it snapped.

The first time Kate had 'had words' with Mags it had been about something very similar, a tendency in Kate to make decisions without first talking it over. So she knew she was in the wrong. She knew she'd have to give in and promise to mend her ways. But she didn't want to. It felt dangerous: thin-end-of-the-wedge stuff that would eventually bring her to grief. Smithy was so much stronger than she was: older, more experienced and—worse than anything—actually trained to take command. Maybe she could consult him as a partner should, but what price partnership if she always ended up giving way?

She could feel his eyes on her now, willing her to admit defeat. She had no other choice, but ... She'd do it *her* way. Assume the right tone of voice, first: cheery but casual, make him think he'd made a lot of fuss about nothing. *Yes, fine, no problem. What would you like to discuss?*

She looked up. Smithy's eyes were directed not at her, as she'd supposed, but at the floor—and he looked exactly as he'd said he felt: lonely, miserable, depressed beyond bearing. He'd said 'scared' too, and although that wasn't at all apparent in his expression, Kate suddenly realised what it meant. Until now, he'd never in his life been alone. At boarding school and university, in the Army, he'd been surrounded by people—people who cared about him, talked and laughed with him, listened, loved. And now, just when he was vulnerable and needed them most, they all—with Mags, with Tess, with Pamela—had gone away. Even Phil and Inky rarely came over now. They'd helped him get settled and then gone back to their own lives, their marriages, their regiment, their busy social whirl: all the things Smithy had lost.

Kate had already admitted—to herself, at least—that she'd been wrong to exclude him, but she'd admitted it only because, as her partner, he had a *right* to be included. She'd scarcely thought about his needs as a human being. She hadn't wanted to, because being human made him no less a *man*. The minute she grew warmer, kinder, less 'blood-chilling' (it was odd how much that remark had hurt), he'd push a little further, ask a little more and, although

117

she was afraid of that for her own sake, she was terrified for his. She couldn't even push him away without knocking him down, poor man.

'Smithy, I'm sorry,' she said. 'I expected you ... I *did* expect you to speak your mind and when you didn't ... Well, I suppose I just ... took advantage. I've never been any good at talking things over. Mags used to complain about it, too, so I don't have much excuse. It's just ...'

She tried another smile, determinedly self-mocking. 'I guess I'm just shy.'

Smithy smiled too. 'No,' he said softly, 'that's not the problem.'

'Oh?' Her heart sank. 'So what is?'

He thought about it, opened his mouth, shut it again. He leaned a little towards her. Kate drew back a little. It was automatic, a reflex she couldn't help and hardly thought about; but when Smithy's smile broadened, she thought about it and wished the floor would open to swallow her. What a giveaway!

And he was not one to let it pass. 'The problem is,' he said, 'that you're afraid of me.'

Kate laughed. 'I am not! Why should I be?'

'Mags told me,' he said. 'I know all about it, Kate.'

Although it was very much in Smithy's nature to speak his mind, he rarely said anything without first thinking it through and he'd been thinking this one through for weeks, months. He'd thought of little else for the past few days. He'd been *ready* to speak and, give or

118

take one or two of Kate's responses, had been pretty sure how it would develop. He'd said nothing that wasn't true, but even the truth can be trained—like a pear tree against a wall—to bear the best crop of fruit. The sob-story, the threat, the escape-clause (his housekeeper, so desperate for a job she'd work in *this* hole!), and a few strands of sympathy to limit the damage. Manipulative, yes, but not unfair. After all, he'd tried the patient method—given it a good, long run—and what had she done with it? Taken advantage.

The only thing he had not been prepared for ...

'Kate, oh, Kate, don't cry! I don't want to hurt you! All I want—'

'I don't care what you want! Leave me alone!'

Smithy clenched his teeth, folded his arms, unfolded them, searched his pockets for a handkerchief and tried to find a way of passing it to Kate that wouldn't involve breaking her neck. She'd curled up like a hedgehog. Not easy to do on a small wooden chair. He envied her her suppleness: hands over face, elbows over chest, knees over ears. Even her feet were in there, somewhere. God, it hadn't been like this in the Army ...

Kate uncurled suddenly, leapt to her feet and ran for the door. Smithy closed his eyes, acknowledging defeat. This was it, then. He'd have to go. But where? How? The flat in London was more a fantasy than a reality: a shop on one corner, a pub on the other, a taxi cruising by whenever he needed it. Even if he could find such a place—and manage it on his own—how was he meant to pay for it? If he left now, he'd lose Whitsun Gate. He'd have nothing.

He smiled ruefully. Maybe Pamela had forseen this. Maybe that was why she hadn't challenged the will: because she'd *known* it wouldn't work.

He heard Kate blowing her nose in the hall, sighing, sniffing, blowing again. She'd gone to his bathroom, he supposed, looking for tissues. He knew what she'd do now: slink past the kitchen door and go back to work. He'd be lucky to lay eyes on her again before dark—if at all. One last try, then?

'Kate?'

'Hang on a minute. I need ...'

He widened his eyes.

'I'm trying to get my breath back, but ...'

'No rush.'

But she sped into the kitchen almost as fast as she'd gone out of it. She sat down, put her shoulders back, sniffed once and jabbed her index finger into the table. 'Now, listen to me,' she said. 'If Mags weren't dead, I'd kill her for breaking my confidence! She had no right to tell you.'

'Kate, she only told me because—'

'It makes no difference. A confidence is a confidence and—'

'—I was about to make a pass at you.'

She withdrew her hand from the table. She swallowed, blinked, bit her lip and went on as if

120

he hadn't spoken. 'And, so far as I'm concerned, it's still a confidence. So if you—*ever*—tell anyone—for any reason at all—'

'She just wanted to protect you, Kate. And it worked, didn't it? The whole point of this discussion was to assure you of that: that your—er—' He smiled. 'Your secret is safe with me. *You* are safe. No matter how you take advantage of me and my deathless patience, I will *not* take advantage of you.'

She was silent for a long time. Then, 'Deathless patience?' she murmured at last. 'You haven't let me get a word in yet!'

He laughed. 'What I had to say was more important. You were just sixteen, Kate, and I was just fooling around. I could have hurt you pretty badly, couldn't I?'

She frowned. 'And you stopped? Just because Mags told you to?'

'No. I stopped because she told me you were afraid.'

She was silent again and Smithy was glad of it. He was beginning to feel confused, to lose his way. He had the curious feeling that he wasn't dealing with the same girl any more. She even looked different. She was frowning again, but both hands were relaxed on the table and she was leaning slightly towards him, not away, which meant ... What?

She drew back suddenly, hiding her hands. 'What did you mean? You said the whole *point* of this discussion was to ...?'

He smiled. 'Yes, I did go the long way round, but only because your problem was the cause

121

of mine. Not your fault, of course, but all men are not ogres, Kate, and for those of us who aren't, it comes hard to be blamed for crimes we couldn't commit. And I mean *couldn't,* not wouldn't.'

Even as he said these words, he knew she'd misinterpret them and, sure enough, her gaze strayed to his sticks, which he'd hooked over the corner of an open drawer, near his chair.

'I don't mean physically. I mean emotionally. There are plenty of freaks who take pleasure from hurting women, but I'm not one of them. The thought of it sickens me. It's offensive to me. Do you understand that, Kate?'

She was quiet. Thinking it over.

'And the housekeeper?' she asked at last.

'A housekeeper would be nice,' he said, 'but it's not a real possibility. Who'd come here? It's like living in a field. And, anyway, how would I pay her?'

Kate smiled and looked straight at him, straight into his eyes. At least, he thought she did, because he had the feeling—for the first time since he'd known her—that her eyes had opened not to see him, but to let him see her. And she *was* different. She'd dropped the defensive shield, but in doing so had become more vulnerable, not less. She looked younger, somehow.

She heaved a sigh. 'Yes, it would be nice,' she said wistfully. 'To tell you the honest, I'd like to have someone to look after me, too.' Her smiled faded. 'But I don't have your excuse. I'm fit and healthy, I can come and go as I like ...' She met his eyes again to add ruefully, 'Mostly go.'

She began to pleat the front of her shirt (which, like most of her clothes, was two sizes too big), watching her fingers as they pinched the cloth, released it, pinched again.

'I do care,' she said. 'I just don't want to *seem* to care, in case ...'

'No such case will present itself, Kate. Being afraid of me is like ... like being afraid of earthworms. I'm a lot less horrible than I look.'

He hadn't meant to say that. The ruin of his looks was a subject he had never before mentioned to anyone, not because he was ashamed of his looks, but because he was ashamed of hating them so much. He'd always been of the opinion that looks didn't matter and he was *still* of that opinion. But his reflection in the mirror ... He'd actually wept over it once or twice. He was ashamed of that.

Kate sighed. She smiled.

He tensed himself for the mawkish compliment that such a sigh and such a smile were certain to produce. (Speaking one's mind had always had its black side.)

But she surprised him again. 'I envy you,' she said. 'I'm a lot *more* horrible than I look.'

Kate felt a little shaky for the rest of the day. It was mostly relief, but also a kind of excitement, the sort of excitement she used to feel when the school holidays were approaching and there was nothing to think about but six weeks of freedom. No homework, no uniform, no prefects to jump

123

on you just when you thought you'd got away with it ...

Smithy wouldn't jump on her. She was sure of it. Not because he'd said he wouldn't but because he'd said he *knew.* True, his knowing had made her cry, but that was only because Mags had told him. It had made her think there was no one in the world she could trust. Yet even before Smithy had assured her of Mags's good intentions, she'd realised that it had made everything better, not worse. If he knew she was damaged, if he knew she was frigid, he'd think her a complete turn-off. *Good.*

Curiously, though, it didn't feel so good. It was a relief, but at the same time she was aware that she hadn't wept only for the betrayal of a confidence; she'd wept for shame that Smithy ... That he knew she was ... Well, that he knew she was a dud. A dead loss. A freak.

Yet *why* was she ashamed? It wasn't her fault! She ought by rights to be announcing it from the rooftops, putting the blame where it belonged—on Robert's conscience (if he had one) rather than her own. But she'd tried that once and been called a liar, a trouble-maker. Jealous, spiteful, wicked, cruel ...

Was Kate ashamed of that? She couldn't be, because she hadn't lied; she'd told the truth! Not the whole truth, maybe, but that was because 'cruel' was the last thing she'd wanted to be. All she'd wanted was to remain a virgin while she still had the chance. Well, she'd done that, all right! Now she was a virgin for life. She'd never have a lover, never get married, never have children ... Was she ashamed of that?

She didn't know. And what the hell did it matter? 'What can't be cured must be endured,' as Mags used to say. 'Life must go on, Kate, even if it kills you.'

It seemed much less likely to kill her now. The danger had passed. She was free.

Chapter Eight

The open season had ended with three weeks of rain. The first week of the closed season was as bright as summer. But not as warm. Smithy put on a down-lined parka for his first walk through the gardens. There had been no frosts as yet, but there would be one tonight, which was why—against his better judgement—he had decided to take a comprehensive look around the place before it finally 'went over'.

It had been easier than he'd anticipated. There was some kind of garden bench every hundred yards or so, and although the seat was generally too low to be of use to him, he could prop himself on the arm for long enough to get his breath back. He'd lost his breath, once or twice, more from amazement than from physical effort. The gardens looked wonderful. Better than he'd ever seen them. He hadn't expected it. In spite of Kate's unremitting efforts during the summer, he'd expected Mags's influence (not to mention her labour) to have been missed and for the lack to be evident everywhere.

Yet nothing was missing. The Rose Walk was liberally sprinkled with repeat-flowering varieties, cut back and fed at the appropriate time to produce a brave, if not glorious, late blooming. Pink, white and maroon cosmos filled the gaps: hardy pink geraniums (surely they should be over?) edged the path. 'And what's this? Do I know it?'

'Diascia,' Kate said. 'South Africa. It's not meant to be hardy, but it's survived three winters under a mulch.'

This said, she pinched her mouth shut, like a child told to hold her tongue. She'd begun their tour talking nineteen to the dozen until she'd realized he hadn't the strength to stand and listen to the life-history of every plant in the garden. He was aware of the irony. After five months of wanting her to talk, he'd now told her to shut up. He'd made a joke of it, of course, but the joke now was to observe her frustration at having to keep her enthusiasm under wraps. She was like a mother, denied an admirer for her child's first tooth. Lacking any other outlet, it seemed she'd invested all her emotions here: love and fury, patience, pride and generosity. It was no wonder she had so little to spare for anyone—or anything—else. Even her 'cooking' skills had been diverted into mixing nice, nourishing messes of bonemeal and horse manure for the roses!

The long herbaceous border was a mist of

Michaelmas daisies, pink kaffir lilies, carmine hollyhocks, pink and white Japanese anemones and rusty-red sedum. The last purple flowers of a clematis on the wall found their echos in a near-solid drift of purple heliotrope and, further on, dark, velvety pansies.

Smithy sighed. He felt unequal to making any other comment. Even 'gosh' might inform Kate that he had expected less and he didn't want her to know that. Not until he'd thought it over.

'Tired?' she said. 'Want to quit while you're ahead?'

He smiled. 'No, I'm fine.' The Bride's Garden would be their next port of call and Smithy was certain she couldn't have kept *that* going so late. It wasn't strictly a white garden, but it was mostly white; at its best in May, when a snowy wisteria clothed the walls and white paeonies and poppies filled the borders.

When Mags and Billy had first come to Whitsun Gate, a burnt-out stone barn had stood on the site: only two walls and part of a third still standing. With the help of a wooden mould and a few tons of concrete, Billy had transformed the ruin from 'barn' to 'chapel' and, thirty years on, there was no distinguishing his 'broken' Norman arches from the real thing.

The missing parts of the walls had been filled in with tall yew hedges, completely enclosing the garden, so that, until one stepped under Billy's broken arch, one had no idea what one might find there. Smithy had always loved it: its peacefulness, its seclusion ... And even in midwinter, especially after a hoar frost, it was beautiful. So he wasn't afraid that Kate might have failed ... he was just excited to think she might *not* have.

He hobbled under the arch and then stood still, dumbstruck with admiration. White roses on the walls, white jasmine on the pergola, tiny white cyclamen crowding the path. The silver leaves of senecio, artemisia and iris made a background for it all and the dark green of hellebores and clipped box lent shape and depth. It was perfect. It was also apparent, if only because the little soil he could see was as clean as a whistle, that Kate had recently been working here; but where she'd put her two hundred hyacinth bulbs was a complete mystery.

'There, there, there and just behind you,' she told him. 'But then I overplanted with dianthus and artemisia. Had to. We still had a week to go and you can't let the visitors see earth, now can you? Filthy stuff, earth.'

She could have made the same quip a week ago, accompanied by a similar grin, but everything else was different. If his legs had been equal to the task, Smithy could have kicked himself for not speaking to her sooner. It had changed her so completely she was barely recognisable as the same person. She moved more freely, laughed more readily, spoke more easily. Even her voice had changed. He couldn't honestly say that he'd been aware her voice had had an 'edge' before, but he was very aware, now, that the edge had gone. Everything about her was softer, warmer, more feminine. Yet, for some reason, she wasn't any more a woman than she'd been before. She was more ... She was like a child, let loose for the holidays. And so, in a way, was he, although that was mostly because the will had been proved at last and the way was clear—on all fronts—for making some kind of progress ... Even if, at the moment, it was all uphill.

The kitchen gardens were set on a south-facing slope. A very *slight* slope, highly advantageous to the fruit and vegetables, but scarcely discernible to anyone else. Anyone but Smithy. Had he been going downhill, his knees would have felt it. Going up, his hips and ankles took the strain, creating a sensation which made him think all his bones were grinding together. They weren't. The problems he had now were mostly caused by wasted muscles, and the only way to strengthen them was to keep slogging up Everest ...

To keep 'up' with him, Kate was doing a sort of slow-motion hokey-cokey, which he remembered doing with Billy after his hip-replacement. It was meant to look as if you were enjoying a lazy stroll, but it felt like being tethered to a post, an agony of frustration.

'Don't wait for me,' he said. 'Go on. Do something useful. Make lunch.'

'That's not useful. That's vandalism.'

'True.' He reached another garden seat and sat on its arm, gasping for breath. 'Altitude sickness,' he explained. 'Leave me here for a week or two, while I get acclimatised.'

Kate laughed. 'You climbed in the Himalayas once, didn't you?'

'Twice.' He'd loved it and had been hoping to go again. Just now, however, he never wanted to see another mountain as long as he lived.

Kate walked twice around the garden seat, pulled a few weeds from the path, began a third circuit—and failed to return. Propped as he was, facing downhill, Smithy had no lateral movement at all, could barely turn his head, but the silence behind him was total. Had she gone off and left him? He'd told her to go and at the time had thought he'd meant it. But he hadn't. There was a long way to go yet! Three hundred yards, at least!

He was just hauling himself upright when she said, 'Did you ever see the yeti?'

She was standing quite still, just a few feet behind him, gazing up into the trees at the top of the garden. The 'total silence' he'd felt had been Kate holding her breath. 'No,' he said warily. 'Why?'

'I just saw one. It was wearing a pink jacket. It took one look at you and slunk away, so it definitely wasn't Mavis. One look at you and she's in your lap.'

Smithy imagined it. 'Don't,' he murmured. 'I'm not very well.'

'There!' Kate hissed.

The sun had climbed to its October zenith, creating patterns of radiance and black shadow under the trees. At first he saw only a moving fragment of pink, detached, it seemed, from its wearer, and drifting all alone, like a petal on the wind. And then, suddenly, he knew who it was. 'Pamela!'

She emerged from the trees as he spoke. At the same moment, Kate went sharply into reverse, clutching the back of the garden seat for support.

'What does she want?' she gasped. 'Smithy?'

He was shocked. He'd recognised Pamela with a faint lifting of spirits, which he might have deemed too faint for his attention had not Kate expressed a quite different feeling. She saw Pamela as a threat. He saw her ... for all her faults, he'd never been so glad to see anyone. Anyone related to him, at least.

He barely noticed the uphill slope as he went to meet her. He noticed, however, that Pamela did not come to meet him and that, as he approached, she averted her eyes.

'I went to the house,' she said. 'Thought you'd gone off somewhere.' She looked at his feet. 'You're walking better.'

'Hey, why didn't you ring? We'd have killed the fatted calf.'

'No need,' she said. 'I haven't come to repent.'

'Okay,' Smithy conceded archly. 'Why didn't you ring? We'd have baked a cake.'

Pamela sucked her cheek as if she were sucking lemons. 'I'm on a diet,' she said.

Kate flew back to the house the long way round, panicking on every front. She was trying to decide why the sight of Pamela had shocked her so much, trying to decide what she could do for lunch that would remain edible when she'd finished doing it, trying to conjure a warm 'welcome home' from a number of emotions which, when added up and divided by three, amounted to nothing warmer than, 'Get lost, Pamela.'

Soup, sandwiches, fresh fruit and coffee. She couldn't make too much of a mess of that, could she?

She hurtled into the kitchen, surveyed the contents of the larder, fetched out two tins of soup and one of salmon and opened the drawer to find the tin-opener. The drawer stuck. She swore, gave it an almightly wrench and deposited the entire contents all over the kitchen floor: knives, forks, spoons, fish-slices, bottle-openers, pastry-cutters ... It sobered her up, partly because the job of returning them all to the drawer took time: time to think.

She was *not* afraid of Pamela. Whitsun Gate was safe; Pamela couldn't take it away. Yet, for some reason, that didn't help. She *was* afraid of Pamela. Afraid—or, rather, ashamed—to face her. This was Pamela's home and Kate had robbed her of it, just as Robert had robbed ...

She returned the drawer to its proper place and stood quite still, feeling cold and empty, staring bleakly into the yard where a smart little car was parked under the linden tree. Pamela's car. Kate was no good at identifying car models, but she knew 'top-of-the-range' from 'bottom-of-the-heap', and Pamela's car was of the former variety. She'd never been strapped for cash, never been in need of any of the things *money* could buy ...

No, Kate hadn't robbed Pamela. Even Mags hadn't robbed Pamela; she'd just bestowed her gifts elsewhere, as she had a perfect right to do. Nothing wrong with that. So why did it *feel* so wrong?

The outer door opened. Kate reached again for the tin-opener, listening for Smithy's voice, for Pamela's. All she heard was the rubbery tapping of Smithy's sticks, the weary scrape of his feet on the flagstones. He was worn out. Pamela was probably hanging back at the door, giving him time.

'Hi!' Kate pinned a properly welcoming smile to her face before going out to meet them. But Smithy was alone, miserable and as white as the wall. Surely they hadn't had another fight? He'd been so glad to see her!

'What's wrong?'

'Get my pills, will you, Kate?'

His pills were on the draining board. Beyond the window, under the linden tree, Pamela was opening the tail-gate of her car. She extracted a Harrods carrier bag and drifted away (Pamela always drifted; ordinary walking didn't suit her style) through the archway that led to the tearooms.

'Where's she going?' Kate held Smithy's chair. She took his sticks and gave him his pills. 'Will she be back? I was doing lunch. I thought she'd want—'

Smithy shook his head. 'She's brought the ashes,' he said.

'Ashes?'

'Her mother's ashes!' he snapped irritably. 'What else, for God's sake?'

Kate retreated, turning away to open one tin of soup, not two. He'd walked further today than he had since the accident. It hadn't been easy. He was in pain. But that wasn't all.

'Shouldn't you be with her?' Kate asked softly. 'Mags was your mother, too, in a way.'

Smithy was massaging his thigh with the heel of his hand, rubbing out that pain while revealing another in the dejected slump of his shoulders. Hadn't he enough pain, without Pamela causing more?

'She doesn't want to know that,' he said.

Kate banged the soup tin down. 'Tough.'

She sped around the visitors' route, which took in every significant part of the garden, hoping to make it seem as if, when she found Pamela, she'd come upon her by accident. They'd had a family celebration for the scattering of Billy's ashes: Mags, Pamela, Michael, the three grandchildren, Smithy and Tess. Although she'd hardly ever shown it in her manner towards him, Mags had adored Billy, heart and soul, but *she* hadn't said, 'He's mine!' She hadn't excluded everyone else who'd loved him, even if she'd deemed their love inferior, partial, slight, or, in the case of Tess—who had scarcely known him—non-existent. They'd been celebrating *his* life, not festering in their own, as Pamela now seemed to be doing! It wasn't right. It wasn't fair. Smithy had loved Mags too!

Pamela was standing at the far end of the Rose Walk, looking at her feet, touching her

134

mouth with her fingers. She looked more like a classy American tourist than a menopausal Englishwoman: slim, blonde and immaculately elegant. Although her features closely resembled her mother's, she wasn't a bit like Mags, who'd lumbered around in unmatched tweeds and woollies, most of them picked up at jumble sales. They'd made her look as tough and uncompromising as she was, while Pamela's beautiful pink jacket (cashmere, by the look of it) just made her look vulnerable, fragile ... sad.

The words, 'Smithy loved her, too' were on the tip of Kate's tongue, but just as she began to speak, Pamela's hand touched her cheeks, wiping away tears. Kate didn't consciously rearrange her words; they seemed to change themselves, almost in mid-air, startling her almost as much as they bewildered Pamela. 'Smithy loves you, too, you know.'

Pamela frowned. 'What's that supposed to mean?' she asked dully.

'That your mother loved you—'

'Hmph.'

'—and Smithy loves you too. There's no need for you to do this on your own. Give him an hour to get his breath back and he'll come and hold your hand.'

Pamela's lips wobbled. She turned away. 'Oh, leave me alone. What the hell do *you* know?'

'I know enough.'

'About what?' Pamela's eyes narrowed. 'Have you been talking about me?'

'I don't need to talk to anyone to know how

135

rejection feels. Neither did your mother.'

The thought flickered through Kate's mind, *Neither does* my *mother,* but she let it go, like an autumn leaf blown loose from the heap. Pamela was taking an interest at last.

'You rejected everything she was, everything that meant anything to her,' Kate went on gently. 'You wouldn't even stay in her house, let alone call it home.'

'It's filthy.'

'No. It's shabby and uncomfortable, that's all. But there was always a welcome here for you, Pamela. There still is. Smithy loves you. He needs you.'

Pamela turned her face to the sky. 'He can't stand me,' she said quietly. 'He's like my mother: if you don't play the game by *his* rules—'

'You're wrong. *He* plays the game by his rules, but he expects everyone else to have rules of their own and he wants to know what they are; he wants to *understand* them, Pamela. That's why he argues with you all the time, because he wants to understand you.'

Actually, this was as much news to Kate as it was to Pamela, but she knew it was true, nevertheless. It was as if a door had opened, letting her into a higher plane of understanding. At the same moment, she realised that *she* was actually arguing, for once, and that she wasn't afraid. She felt very calm and ... very kind. She wasn't angry any more.

'Your mother was the same,' she went on softly. 'She wanted to understand you, because

136

... Well, how else can you give people what they need? How can you make them happy if you don't understand them? My mother—'

She broke off, swallowing poison. 'My mother doesn't *want* to understand. She talks to me about the weather.' She looked at her feet. 'And you can take my word for it, there's nothing quite as loveless as the weather.'

Pamela knuckled her mouth, walked in a circle, folded her arms and sighed. 'I've often wondered about you and your mother,' she murmured. 'Mummy never told me what the problem was. Boyfriend trouble?'

Kate swallowed again, realising with dismay that she couldn't sort out Pamela's hang-ups without exposing her own. Yet again. Oh, well ... Shout it from the rooftops. It was Robert's shame, not hers. 'I've never had a boyfriend, Pamela. I never will. My stepfather put me off that idea, once and for all.'

Pamela's eyes widened. 'And your mother—?' she breathed.

'Didn't believe me. She gave me a choice your mother never gave you. Shut up or get out.'

'She didn't believe ... what?'

Kate sighed. 'My father died when I was twelve; she married again when I was thirteen and a half. Her husband wanted ... both of us.'

'My God.'

Kate shrugged. 'My problem, not yours. Look, Pamela, I've stood in the cross-fire of your family fights often enough to know that *your* mother never told you to shut up or get out. When you really *want* to understand someone, harsh words are ...' She flapped her hands, searching for the right word. She knew 'tin-opener' wasn't the right one, but since—for some reason—it was the first to come to mind ... 'They're like a tin-opener,' she said, 'cutting the lid off your feelings, or at least *trying* to. I know I'm never going to reach an understanding with my mother without first having an almighty row with her, but she won't let me. She won't try. She won't take the lid off the ... the *truth!* That was all your mother wanted—to take the lid off, to understand you. It's all Smithy wants, too.'

Her eyes swimming with tears, she turned away, listening to the garden: a blue-tit, *pip-pipping* in a birch tree nearby; a robin claiming its winter territory with a bright waterfall of song; a dry autumn leaf, pattering through the undergrowth as it fell to earth. Pamela said nothing.

'Look,' Kate said. 'Neither of us wanted to take anything from you, Pamela. It might have crossed Smithy's mind that Mags would leave him something, but it didn't cross mine, I promise you. I was just ... I was just parking here, until the traffic warden moved me on. I *have* felt guilty about it. I think Smithy has, too, but—'

'It doesn't matter.'

Kate turned again to face her. 'It does. Of course it does. That's what this is all about, isn't it?'

Pamela heaved a sigh. 'Yes, I suppose. But to tell the truth ... Well, it's hard to explain.

I'm not even sure it's worth explaining.' She stared down at the Harrods carrier bag at her feet. 'Too late.'

'No.'

There was another long silence. Pamela stooped to pick up the bag. She smiled down at it. 'She always reminded me of a bag-lady,' she murmured. She looked up, her smile still in place, wan and sad, but with a trace of warmth in it now. 'Any chance of a cuppa?'

It happened during the weather forecast, somewhere between the high pressure area over southern Britain and the series of lows sweeping in from the Atlantic. Kate said sleepily, 'That gives me two days to get the tulips in,' and Smithy thought, I'm happy. In spite of the rug over his legs, he was also freezing, but that didn't matter. Kate had switched on his electric blanket and, within the next half hour, he'd go to bed and read a book while he warmed up, aware that—if only for a little while—all was right with the world.

His reconciliation with Pamela had been a muted affair. They hadn't said much, but they'd said it very kindly, with no sparks flying on either side. She'd asked for a progress report on his health; he'd asked for news of Michael and the kids. They'd had lunch and then gone outside to do the appropriate thing with the ashes. Soon after that, Pamela had gone back to London, wishing him well, but leaving him with the distinct impression that she would never come here again.

Since then, he'd spent the entire evening arguing with Kate. He hadn't had so much fun in years, and neither—judging from the contented smirk on her face—had she. She'd won, of course. The best thing about it was that he hadn't let her win, she'd done it all by herself, exhibiting (for the first time since he'd known her) the intelligence Mags had always said she had. Mags had been no great intellectual—she'd thought anyone who could spell 'marmalade' pretty bright—but it seemed she'd been right about Kate. As long as she was arguing in someone else's defence—in this case, Pamela's—she seemed to have no hang-ups at all.

'So what?' Kate had asked when he'd said Pamela wouldn't come back. 'She can't stand the place. It's everything she hates combined with everything she wants and can't have. Same as *my* home, in fact.'

'Nonsense. She's never thought of it as her home, Kate.'

'That's the whole point. From what I could gather, she spent her entire childhood wishing Mags and Billy could settle down somewhere, make a home, instead of always moving from one set of Army quarters to another. A home was all she ever wanted.'

'Well? They did it, didn't they? They bought Whitsun Gate!'

'Too late. Pamela was already engaged by then. Anyway, her idea of home wasn't the same as her parents'. They wanted the garden. She wanted ... well, I'm only guessing, but I'd say she wanted everything this house has never offered: warmth, comfort, security. That was why she married so young. That was why, by your standards, she never "did" anything, because by her standards she *was* doing something. Making the home she'd never had.'

Pamela had, in fact, said all of this at one time or another, but she'd never said it quite as Kate had: as if it mattered, as if it meant something.

'She was probably ashamed of it,' Kate said now. 'After all, the garden was a terrific achievement and Mags and Billy weren't the type to let her forget it.'

'Oh, come on!'

'I'm not saying they bragged, but they never stopped talking about it, did they? They certainly never stopped long enough to let *Pamela* talk! Remember when she bought that Persian carpet for her drawing room? She was as proud of it—'

'She's the type to be proud of a new dish-cloth, Kate, just as long as it's the most expensive dish-cloth on the market!'

'No. Not the most expensive, just the best, and that's no different from Mags—or me, for that matter—searching out the rarest plants, the best, the most beautiful. Would Mags ever fork out good money for the same boring old primula everyone else has? Or even buy inferior lawn seed? And what do you do with a lawn? Walk on it. Look at it. Admire the patterns you've made with the roller. Yet when Pamela bought that carpet, Mags said, "Why on earth should

141

you want such a thing? People will only walk on it!" '

Maybe it was at that point that he'd begun to feel happy: when Kate had leaned towards him, her eyes alight, her face glowing, her teeth bared in a grin so mischievous, so lacking in caution, he'd felt more like hugging her than continuing the argument.

'And if your point is that Pamela's a show-off,' she'd said, 'you might remember which one of them opened to the public!'

He'd laughed. It wasn't as simple as that, of course, but he'd laughed anyway, seeing her point, appreciating it, knowing she was right. There *was* no essential difference between a Persian carpet and a carpet of flowers if that was the thing you most wanted—or needed—to define the meaning of your life.

The only thing *he'd* wanted ...

But it wasn't as simple as that, either. No one could say, 'the only thing I want' with any hope of telling the truth. No one wants just *one* thing. No matter what people have, they always want one thing more. *He* wanted his electric blanket, for instance.

'I think I'll turn in, Kate. Have you locked up?'

'Mm-hm.' She turned off the television and went ahead of him to open the door. Her sweatshirt had ridden up slightly and, as she waited for him, leaning against the wall, he caught a glimpse of her stomach—as flat and silky as a freshly planed board—and the shadowy knot of her navel.

She yawned. The sweatshirt slipped back into place. She switched off the light and said goodnight.

Later, as the warmth of his bed soothed the ache in his legs, Smithy took up his book, stared at it for a moment and laid it down again. So far, he'd seen only her face, her neck, her hands, her arms. Now he'd seen her navel and felt as awed by the sight as his great-grandfather might have felt at the glimpse of a woman's ankle. He hadn't seen her ankles yet. He might never see them, covered as they always were by jeans and thick woolly socks. Still, it was something to look forward to ...

He bit his lip. He smiled and leaned back against his pillows, sighing. God, there was *always* one thing more. Trust him to choose the one thing he couldn't have!

Chapter Nine

On the first anniversary of Mags's death, as the gates opened for the day's business, Kate was coming downstairs and paused at the landing window to take a quiet look at her domain. She was not disappointed. Save for a rather disquieting feeling that it was all looking *better* than it had when Mags had been in charge, she had the idea that she'd never been so happy. They'd had a fair few regulars in this spring, most of whom had expressed admiration for the 'big spring show'. The three acres of woodland had been glorious—and so they should have been since Kate had spent most of the winter working there to let in some extra light. They'd had snowdrops, primroses, violets and hellebores in bloom since February. The violets were still going strong, although anemones, bluebells and erythroniums were taking over now, backed by a starry luxuriance of leaf and blossom from the surrounding shrubs and trees.

It was wonderful to be there when certain of the visitors first stepped into the woods. Worn out by the winter, they seemed to stop breathing for a moment before taking a deep breath of scented air and creeping a few yards forward, blinking with wonderment. You could see the tension melting from their limbs, the anxiety from their faces. And if they spoke at all it was usually only to whisper, 'Ahhh ...' as Kate sometimes did when she fell into bed at the end of a tiring day. It was worth being tired for that.

As she turned away from the window, a familiar movement caught her eye and she turned again to watch Smithy, limping towards the ticket office with only one stick to support him. He'd ditched the other one just after Christmas and had managed pretty well without it, although he still couldn't stay on his feet very long. He'd gained some weight (this was partly because *he'd* learned to cook; Kate was still trying, but not very hard!) and had acquired a healthier colour from his newly discovered open-air life. He did two hours at the gate each day, walked around the garden (either chatting to the visitors or telling them off for pinching 'slips'), and spent much of the rest of his time potting up cuttings in the greenhouse.

At the end of last season, when he'd asked her to 'care', Kate had vaguely envisaged herself as his nursemaid, feeding him nourishing homemade soups (fat chance!), warming his slippers and murmuring, 'There, there,' at regularly spaced intervals. She'd known that wasn't what he'd *said* he wanted, but had suspected that that was what he'd *meant* he wanted. She'd been wrong. He'd meant precisely what he'd said: that he wanted to be included, to share and share alike, as partners should. And it had been easy. It had been fun. She couldn't now imagine what life had been like without him.

She ran downstairs, pushing the thought from her mind. Smithy didn't belong to her. He never would. He'd said (rather venomously) that Tess could wait the full two years for a divorce, but Kate doubted very much that *he* could wait that long. He was a man. And men needed ... certain things. Sometimes—most of the time, in fact—Kate could forget about those certain things and think of Smithy as being as sexless as she was. Just a friend. Just a colleague. Just ... what she wanted him to be. But there were other times ...

As she crossed the foot of the drive to pay her morning visit to Mavis, she looked up to smile at him and wave, but it was one of those 'other times'. He was deep in conversation with a nice-looking brunette, smiling at her as he'd never

145

smiled at Kate. *Other* men had smiled at her that way, as if—while seeming to hang on her every word about the difference between acid soil and alkaline—they were actually giving her a thorough medical. They rarely got further than checking her bra-size (she'd brought 'blood-chilling' down to a fine art), but some women liked playing doctors and the gorgeous brunette was one of them. Smile for smile, X-ray for X-ray.

'Mmm, sounds lovely,' Kate heard her say. 'Thanks. See you later.' She raised a slim, very clean hand to wiggle her fingers in coy farewell. 'Bye-ee!'

And now Smithy was admiring her legs as she walked away. He still hadn't noticed Kate.

Smithy enjoyed his turn at gate duty. He liked summing people up as they approached, categorising them first by the clothes they wore (shoes were especially important), then by the remarks they made to each other, and at last by their manner of speaking to him when they bought their tickets. He'd known at first sight that the gorgeous brunette was no gardener. Wrong shoes (low enough, but with small, spiky heels), wrong skirt: white and too short. If she bent down to sniff the flowers ... But she wouldn't. She wasn't the type. He sussed her as a career girl who'd just bought a ground-floor flat with a courtyard the size of a pocket handkerchief.

She walked straight past the Chinese species rose at the gate without even seeing it, although

146

any idiot would know it was special and remark on the fact: there were very few roses that bloomed in early-May and most of the few were yellow, not pink, as this one was.

Smithy thought it his duty (especially to his bank balance) to give the beginners some extra encouragement, which was one of the reasons he summed them up first: to ascertain what kind of encouragement they were most likely to fall for. This one, he guessed, would like to impress her friends. 'Have you been here before? I'm sure you'll enjoy it; it's a *stylish* garden—lots of rare plants and a chance to buy some of them before you leave. Do you have a garden?'

He'd been wrong about the ground-floor flat. It was a mews cottage in Bath, near Great Pultney Street. (You couldn't get much more stylish than that.) But he'd been right about the courtyard. It was south-facing, would bake in summer and she'd probably go off on holiday and leave it unwatered ... But never mind.

He gave her the map of the gardens, marked the Herb Garden and the south-facing beds and told her she'd find all the inspiration she needed there. As she went on her way, he saw Kate, deep in thought, at the foot of the drive, and noticed (not for the first time) how greatly she'd changed since the autumn. He'd thought she'd changed then, but she'd gone on changing ever since, shedding veils like Salome. She wasn't naked yet (she probably never would be), but when she'd bought new clothes, she'd bought them to fit: jeans that hugged her hips, tee-shirts that followed, rather than shrouded, the contours of her body. In spite of being just a touch too thin for perfection, she had very nice contours, yet Smithy suspected that no one else had noticed them. She was often mistaken for a child and while this usually amused her, Smithy found it deeply disturbing.

In many ways she was older than her years (hardly surprising after living so long with Mags and Billy), but emotionally she was still thirteen and likely to stay that way, because now she had no access to the kind of experiences that allow thirteen-year-old girls—and boys—to grow up.

Smithy's first kiss had happened among the dustbins in an alley behind a Chinese restaurant. He'd planned to lose his virginity among the sand-dunes at Weston-super-Mare, but the game had been rained off, like a cricket match, and he'd finally proved his manhood six months later, in a boat, in Poole Harbour, in December. He'd just turned seventeen. Now, fifteen years later, he could still recall the seaweedy whiff of that damp, icy little berth, still hear the sleigh-bells chime of the rigging against the mast and the mockery of gulls' laughter gusting in from the sea. Even at the time he hadn't mistaken it for bliss, but he'd known it was right, that rite of passage. It had taught him all he needed to know, left him with no illusions, but with plenty of hope that it couldn't get worse!

That was what Kate lacked. That was what had been taken from her: the hope—and it applied to everything, not just sex—that things would get better. It was the only thing that kept people trying, learning, growing. And Kate

148

wasn't growing. Inside, where it mattered, she was stuck at thirteen.

But as a gardener, she was pretty good. He'd never noticed how Mags's age had caught up with her until Kate's youth and phenomenal stamina had filled the breach. She'd thinned out the woods and tidied up some of the corners that Mags had allowed to run wild. Smithy hadn't totally approved of this at first. He liked to see a few neglected spots in a garden. He liked to imagine that there was a 'secret' hidden behind a tangle of ivy and rampant clematis: a den, a dell, a forgotten summerhouse ... Kate had been at pains to point out that if you couldn't get through the undergrowth, it made little difference. You had to tidy it up occasionally or risk making a secret of the entire place. True ... but maybe she was a bit *too* tidy. The last thing Smithy wanted was for the garden to be as repressed as the gardener.

The stylish brunette disappeared at the foot of the drive. Kate looked up, raised her hand and flapped her fingers at him, like a child.

'Bye-ee!' she said, and disappeared, smirking, behind the coach house. He hadn't actually noticed the brunette's goodbye and recalled it now only because Kate had mimicked it. Hmm. He raised his eyebrows and lowered them in a scowl. But what did it *mean?*

Kate caught up with the brunette about an hour later. The words 'caught up' actually crossed her mind, but she dismissed them, sufficiently irritated by the thought to pretend someone else had suggested it. After all, it was part of her day's work to do the rounds, talk to people, answer their questions. Even the idiots in mini-skirts had paid to get in and deserved their money's worth. Still, it would be interesting to check this one over, to find out if she had anything special (other than a body) to have caught Smithy's interest.

The 'dark lady' was crouching over the rockery, glancing first at her map, then at the list of plants on the back, then at the plants themselves, her brow furrowed with bewilderment.

'Need any help?'

'Oh, do you work here? Why aren't any of the plants labelled? I can't tell which is which.'

Nearly everyone asked why the plants weren't labelled. Mags had been quite happy to give them the answer: that some so-called garden lovers have a nasty tendency to be light-fingered, stripping plants of their seed pods, stealing cuttings, sometimes even digging up entire plants and carrying them away in their handbags. Anything unusual, difficult to find or expensive to buy was more likely to disappear if it was labelled than if it wasn't, so Mags had decided to label nothing—*and* make the buggers feel guilty for driving her to such extremes. Kate preferred to err on the side of justice, knowing that even the innocent can be made to feel guilty if they're accused with sufficient conviction.

'What would you like to know?' she asked.

'Well, first, why are all the names on this list

in Latin? What's wrong with English? Do you get many Ancient Romans in, these days?'

Kate laughed, acknowledging with a pang of regret that the woman had a nice sense of humour, a cheeky smile and a twinkle in her big brown eyes to charm the birds off the trees. Very nice ... but beyond Kate's powers of imitation. Not that it mattered. *She* didn't want to marry Smithy; she just wanted him to marry someone nice, someone friendly and fun, someone who knew nothing about gardening and would need Kate to stick around to do the work for her. Yes, the dark lady would do very well.

'Latin isn't really a dead language,' she said.

'It is, it is! I killed it myself!'

'It's an international language,' Kate laughed, 'especially in medicine and horticulture. That's partly because horticulture and medicine have always been linked—the majority of drugs are derived from plants—but also because the early apothecaries were monks, who spoke Latin anyway.'

'Oh!' The woman laughed. 'I hadn't thought of that. Quite neat, isn't it?'

'Latin's a neat language. But the most important thing is that it's used all over the world, so that gardeners in Norway, Italy and America all know what the gardener in India is talking about.'

'You mean, I'm the only one who *doesn't*?'

Kate folded her arms. 'Yep.'

Then, 'No,' she conceded, smiling. 'English is full of Latin words, so you actually know more than you think you know. Here, I'll show you.'

151

As they strolled around the garden, analysing the Latin names of the plants, Kate noticed, from the corner of her eye, that two more people had joined them. Another two soon followed and gradually a half dozen more. Every time she paused, someone asked a question. She asked a few questions on her own account and discovered that, although most were beginners, some had been gardening for years without realising that plant names actually *meant* something! And now that they knew, they wanted to know more. She'd been talking for almost an hour and had the feeling she could go on for another hour, if only she had time.

But she was due to take over from Pat Herald, the part-timer in plant sales and, having explained this and said 'Thank you for listening', she walked away, her heart hammering with a curious excitement. She didn't realise the dark lady had followed her until, from a few steps behind, she said, 'Thanks, that was terrific. The man at the gate told me I'd be inspired, but I didn't guess what he meant! You've hooked me!' She pulled a face of utter dismay. 'And my garden's only fifty feet square!'

Kate laughed. Plants were exciting in their own right, but for people who knew nothing about them—or at best very little—a little background information *could* make the difference between their getting 'hooked' or not. A little Latin, a little history ...

'Do you give that talk to everyone? On a regular basis, I mean.'

'No, it just happened.'

'But you do sell books about plant names?'

'Er—no.' (But they should, they should!) 'Not at the moment,' she added. 'But I'll—er—suggest it to the management. Come again, won't you?'

'Try and stop me,' the dark lady said.

Smithy was eating lunch when he saw the brunette again. Deep in conversation with an elderly couple, she walked past his table on the terrace, drawing her hands apart as if to say, 'That big!' She was carrying a few clumps of garden on the spiky heels of her shoes and there was a bright smear of pollen on her skirt. He'd underestimated her, evidently. The average 'length of stay' was two hours, but she'd been here longer than that already, so something must have caught her interest quite early on. The Herb Garden? No, probably the tulips.

Everyone loved the tulips, especially as they were planted here, in drifts of colour that 'ran' (in dozens of species and varieties) from March right through to the beginning of June. The Bride's Garden was now full of lily-flowered tulips, hyacinths and anemones, paeonies, a rampant *Clematis montana* and, of course, the white wisteria, a combination which threatened to drive people mad with the impossibility of finding words to describe it. Most of them just gasped, 'Oh—my—God,' and then were silent, swallowing tears. As the evenings warmed and the scent of the wisteria grew stronger, it sometimes caught Smithy that way, too ...

'Are you the owner?'

It was the dark girl again, detached from her new friends and carrying a tray of Mavis's cooking. Lovely eyes. Wicked smile. She looked as if she'd lost five pence and found a fiver.

'No,' he said. 'I'm only half the owner, but—'

'Can I sit down?' She leaned over him, grinning. 'I'd like to make a complaint.'

'Ah,' Smithy said. 'In that case, you need my partner. Big chap. Name of Mad Mick. Used to be a wrestler.'

She laughed and sat down. She'd bought herself a fairly lavish lunch, but ignored it for long enough to scan the (by now) rather crumpled map of the garden where it said, 'Whitsun Gate' and the names of its two proprietors. 'So you must be Kate,' she said. 'I bet you found that a handicap in the Army!'

He laughed. 'Someone's been talking.' He directed a despairing smile towards Mavis in the tearoom. 'But what's your complaint? Coffee too hot?'

'No. But I have to tell you you're failing to grasp your opportunities. First, you ought to sell books. Then,' she drew an index finger through the air as if ticking things off a list, 'you ought to do regular lecture tours for people like me. People who don't know anything, I mean. You've got a young girl working here: blonde, big blue eyes, A-level in Latin.'

Smithy's eyebrows went up. Kate didn't have an A-level in Latin. Having left school the day she'd left home, she didn't have an A-level in anything—and still deeply resented the

154

fact. So did Smithy, who was of the opinion that education (spliced with a little love) was the answer to everything. Or at least that it gave one *access* to the answer to everything, simply by training one's mind to ask the right questions. Kate rarely asked questions. She was by no means ignorant, but she couldn't process what she knew, couldn't solve problems, didn't have *ideas*.

'She was marvellous!' the dark girl went on through a mouthful of salad. 'I asked one question—it wasn't an especially serious one, either—and the next thing I knew—' She laid down her fork and scowled at him. 'Now, look here, Kate. I can see you're a hard man—you'd have to be with a name like that—'

Smithy let out a yelp of laughter and went on laughing until the tears ran. It was an extraordinary feeling. He hadn't been aware of not laughing during the past year; was certain he *had* laughed in fact, many times. But not like this. He knew it had something to do with the girl, with the light in her eyes, with the lightness of her heart and the fact ... *Was* it a fact? *Did* she fancy him? The feeling wasn't exactly mutual—or hadn't been—but well, why not?

It was a strange thought. He'd felt a few odd stirrings of sexual interest in Kate, of course, but had always pushed them aside, aware that on that route lay madness. But this was different: a feeling that he'd been restored to himself, set free from griefs, restraints and inhibitions he hadn't even realised were there.

On a descending scale of gasps and chuckles,

155

he wiped his eyes, asked, 'What's *your* name?' and at that moment saw Kate, standing in the archway that led from the terrace to the yard. She turned away immediately, but not before he saw the look on her face change from expectation to dismay and then (all in the space of a second) to the shuttered blankness which meant, 'I can't cope with this.'

The dark girl said her name. He heard it without learning it, his thoughts with Kate, who had now gone back to selling plants in the yard. What did she want? The loo, her lunch or an injection of small change for the till? Whatever, she couldn't get away until he finished lunch—which he should have done ten minutes ago. 'Excuse me for a moment,' he said. 'Duty calls.'

He'd hung his walking stick on the back of his chair. He swivelled to reach for it, hauled himself up and limped two steps forward before looking down to add, 'Don't go away.'

But the light in the girl's eyes had gone out, to be replaced by something else: pity, curiosity ... contempt? Whatever it was, Smithy didn't want it.

'Hey, what happened to you?' she asked.

Smithy shrugged. 'Got caught in the rush-hour,' he said. 'See you.'

It was the busiest Sunday they'd had all spring (it was also the sunniest), but business in plant sales had been quiet. People had been trickling in at the gate all day, in ones, twos and family parties, but hardly anyone had gone out again.

Just for something to do, Kate kept strolling towards the tearooms in search of customers, but although Mavis was very busy and there were no free tables on the terrace, everyone was lingering over lunch and looked likely to stay until teatime. Then there'd be an almighty rush. She'd run out of change, run out of plants ... Hell, why couldn't people be *predictable*, for once?

She hadn't noticed Smithy among the crowd until she'd heard him laughing. But then she'd seen who he was with, and something—she wasn't sure what—had shrivelled up inside her and made everything feel wrong. Not jealousy. It couldn't be that. Fear? Yes, maybe. A woman would be a complication and Kate didn't want complications. She wanted things to go on as they were, just the two of them ...

She sighed. Maybe she *was* jealous. But since it could only be the dog-in-the-manger variety (and there was no sense—let alone dignity—in that), she had no choice but to squash it. If he was happy, the best thing Kate could do was be happy for him. And the dark girl was nice. Very nice ...

'Kate?'

She turned, smiling, expecting to see them together, but there was only Smithy.

'Did you want a break?'

'What?'

'I thought you looked a bit desperate. I'll hold the fort here if you like.'

'No, I'm fine. Bored, that's all. No one's buying anything. Go and finish your lunch.'

157

'I have.' He wandered into the coach house, where there was a stool, a potting bench and small metal cash-box for the plant sales takings. 'I hear you did a lecture tour this morning. How did that happen?'

Kate smiled. 'I don't know. It just did.'

He hauled the stool forward. It was a tall, wooden thing, the seat high enough to prop Smithy's behind without putting him to the trouble of actually sitting down. Just as he leaned back, Kate saw that one of the legs was suspended over a hole where one of the floor-tiles was missing. She darted forward just as the whole edifice (of which Smithy was now a part) began to topple, jabbing her leg out to steady the stool, grabbing Smithy around the waist so that, even if she lost the stool, she wouldn't lose him.

He yelled out, but otherwise did what he was meant to do: throwing himself forward, so that for a moment Kate was supporting his entire weight on her shoulders. Her face was squashed against his shirt. She heard the frightened race of his heart, smelled the cold sweat of sudden terror (hers, as well as his) mingling with the bracing scent of coal-tar soap.

Although their bodies were perfectly balanced against one another, Kate had a nasty feeling it wouldn't last. Slim as he was, Smithy was still very much heavier than she and his arm around her neck was threatening to strangle her. So she had to move. She couldn't stay like this forever. And yet she was aware that she wanted to stay like this, holding him close, keeping him safe.

'Okay,' he gasped, loosening his stranglehold. 'I'm okay. Hold the stool steady, will you?'

He leaned back. The stool supported him and Kate was free, wiping tears from her cheeks she hadn't realised she'd shed. White-faced, one hand pressing his heart, Smithy gasped for breath and for self-control. But the shock was still with him, rippling under his skin like the aftermath of nightmare. Kate's first instinct was to cuddle him like a child. Her second was to go away, leave him to get over it as best he could. But she didn't dare leave him now. She didn't dare cuddle him, either.

'It's all right,' she said. 'You didn't fall. You just think you did.'

'Uhh,' he groaned. 'I always did have a lively imagination.' He took another deep breath and pressed a clenched fist to his mouth. 'Oh, God ...'

Kate sighed, her own imagination conjuring his: the bones all broken again, perhaps this time beyond repair. He'd said once that he was held together with 'six-inch nails and paperclips' and, having had an inkling of this sort of thing when Billy had had his hip-replacement, Kate was aware that steel pins could not be replaced *ad infinitum*. If he broke the bones again, he might well spend the rest of his life in a wheelchair.

That was what had frightened him. Not the pain (he was used to that) but the borrowings of despair from a fate he couldn't yet believe he'd escaped. She must try to take his mind off it. Make him think of something else. They'd been talking about something ... but what?

'So anyway,' she said brightly, 'what were we talking about before I swept you off your feet just now?'

He smiled faintly. 'I don't know. It was all so sudden.' He reached out his hand to grasp hers. 'Thanks.'

Kate blushed. She withdrew her hand and stuffed it into her pocket. 'Oh, I know!' she said hurriedly. 'My lecture tour! That woman—the one you were having lunch with—asked me why all the plant names were in Latin and, while I was telling her, a few more people tagged on ...'

A few people chose that moment to browse among the plants, but Kate knew from bitter experience that, although they'd demand attention when they were ready, they preferred to be ignored until then.

'It's all so obvious to me,' she said. 'The Latin, the history. I've never bothered to explain it before, but they were fascinated; they wanted to know if we sold books about it. We could, couldn't we?'

'About what, precisely?'

'About Latin names! They actually want to know that *dicentra* means "two spurs" and that *digitalis* means "thimble". I did Latin at school, of course—'

'Oh, you did?'

'But most people don't, and when they see

160

the Latin names it's all so much gobbledegook to them. They don't even realise most of it is three parts English: *maritimus, elegans, magnifica, pyramidalis* ... And then there are the names of the places, the names of the botanists ...'

'Yes, but most people—'

'—learn as they go along. I know. It's just that some people—quite a lot, in fact—get put off by the Latin before they begin, and there are others—I met a few this morning—who learn the names without realising what they mean. But they loved being *told* what they mean, Smithy. So I was wondering—'

She went on wondering while she took her first customers' money. Then: 'Couldn't we do a plant-names lecture occasionally—just at weekends, say? And sell books as a follow-up?'

'Are there any books? Just of plant names?'

'Yes!'

'Hmm. But books are expensive, Kate. What if they didn't sell?'

She shrugged. She sold another few plants, watching Smithy from the corner of her eye. His colour had come back; he'd stopped gasping and clenching his fists. So he was all right, damn him. And (not for the first time) was rejecting her ideas out of hand. Yet he was always saying they should be thinking of new ways to make money, and this *was* ...

Well, maybe not. One swallow doesn't make a summer and one woman asking for books doesn't make a bookshop. Books *were* expensive, and when people had already paid at the gate, paid for tea and paid for plants, they were unlikely to fork out for any more.

But the interest had been there!

She narrowed her eyes. 'How about a booklet?' she said. 'You could run up a few dozen on your computer. We could sell it at the gate. Then, if it doesn't catch on, we won't lose much, will we?'

Smithy frowned. 'Give me an example. What would it say?'

Kate picked up the first plant that came to hand. '*Allium aflatunense*,' she said, 'means "garlic, this species first collected from Aflatun, in central Asia".'

'Good Lord, does it? I always thought it meant something to do with flatulence!' He grinned. 'Aflatun? How on earth do you know that?'

'I looked it up.'

'When?'

'God, I don't know! Years ago, I suppose. We've always had alliums and I learned all the plants we had the first year I was here.' She frowned. 'What's the use of a gardener who doesn't know her plants?'

Smithy folded his arms. He narrowed his eyes and watched her thoughtfully, a faint smile playing at the corners of his mouth.

'What?' Kate demanded suspiciously.

'Oh, I've just realised something.'

'What?'

His eyes widened and warmed. 'You're brilliant,' he said.

162

Chapter Ten

'You're a fool,' Inky said. 'You just don't listen, do you?'

He was laughing, but Smithy was aware that he meant it and knew he was right.

'Mags told you Kate was brilliant—'

'Yes, but—'

'Joanna told you she was brilliant—'

'Well, you can hardly say Joanna's opinion was informed! She didn't know a dandelion from a dahlia before Kate—'

'Quite. She knows a dandelion from a dahlia *now*, which means Kate is a good teacher as well as a good gardener. She can infect people with her own enthusiasm, make them interested, make them keen. And that's precisely what you want in a place like this, Smithy. It brings people back to take another look. And they bring their friends; and their friends bring their maiden aunt, who just happens to be the editor of *Country Gardens* ...'

'Oh, shut up,' Smithy said. 'I know.'

It was Monday. Kate was out, lunching with her mother at last (she'd called off the March and April meetings), and Smithy was giving Inky his first complete tour of the garden at its best. It was unfortunate that Smithy had begun to wax lyrical about Kate's 'big idea' just as they'd entered the Bride's Garden. It had spoiled the impact of its beauty, distracted Inky from the job in hand and given him another—to haul Smithy over the coals.

'It's not like you to be blind to a woman's virtues,' he said now. 'Her faults, perhaps.'

He meant Tess, of course, and Smithy wondered if she had had something to do with his failure to appreciate Kate. Once bitten, twice shy. He'd thought Tess so *wonderful* ... And being wrong had hurt his pride as much as it had hurt his feelings. But there was more to it than that. Worse than that.

'Oh, I don't know,' he sighed. 'I was pretty blind to Pamela's virtues, too. I do seem to judge people by their achievements and I suppose I just overlooked Pamela's until Kate pointed them out. I still find it hard to see a collection of carpets and curtains as an *achievement*, to tell the truth, but I suppose ... Well, Kate is different. Kate is complicated. For one thing, the gardens aren't really *her* achievement: she's just carrying on where Mags left off, and for another—'

Inky chose that moment to bury his face in one of the perfumed blooms of the white wisteria, a sensation on a par—if not as lasting—as getting quietly stoned. Smithy sat on the arm of a bench under the arbour, grateful for the reprieve from what had very nearly been a nasty slip of the tongue. Trouble was, he needed to tell Inky about Kate's fear of men. He needed advice; he needed to find a way around it, not necessarily because he really *wanted* Kate, but because he was beginning to *think* he wanted her just because he couldn't damn well *have* her!

He remembered another moment when he might have broken her confidence—also with Inky—and had refrained, because he hadn't wanted her to be 'written off as damaged goods'. He realised now that for the thought to have crossed his mind at all had been highly suspect, because that was precisely what *he'd* done: written her off, wiped her out, told himself (unconsciously, perhaps, but that was no excuse) that if she didn't exist as a woman, she didn't exist at all. No home, no education, no prospects ... Not worth the bother.

Over the past year, of course, she'd worn down his prejudices until his only recourse had been to keep reminding himself of them, deliberately blinding himself, lying to himself in a way he wouldn't have deemed possible a year ago. Other people lied. Smithy *never* did. Ho-ho.

'You were saying?' Inky sat beside him, still smiling a woozy wisteria smile.

'She'd been carrying Mags for years, of course. I know that now. Actually, I knew it the first time I walked around, last autumn. I was expecting to find that Mags had gone missing—gaps in the planting, themes gone astray—but there was nothing wrong. Nothing at all. It was better than I'd ever seen it.'

He gazed, trance-like, into the perfect bloom of a white paeony, dusted with gold at the heart. 'But I didn't tell her that. I kept thinking, My God, this is marvellous ... But I didn't say a word.'

'Why? Afraid she'd get uppity?'

Smithy blinked, trying to imagine this, but Kate getting uppity was almost a contradiction in terms.

'No,' he said. 'I suppose really it was a kind of self-defence. I didn't want to think she was anything special, because ... Well, once you start admiring a woman, anything can happen. And I guess I've been afraid to complicate things, afraid of getting my feelings involved.'

'Sex, you mean?'

'No! Yes ... But not *just* sex. I'm vulnerable all round. And the trouble is that neither of us has any other significant social life. We've got each other and no one else.'

But this fact—true as it was—hadn't occurred to him until yesterday, when Kate had caught him in her arms and—just for a moment—held him so hard, so safe, it was as if the rest of the world had disappeared. True, he'd been terrified and had had enough experience of terror to know that whoever saves you from such straits is the most important person in the world. Even when you count your friends by the dozen, in *that* moment there's no one else.

'And she's a lovely girl,' Inky mused.

'Mmm.'

'Improving, too. She's not as withdrawn as she used to be, is she?'

'No, not as withdrawn, but ...'

Last night, while they'd discussed her Latin booklet, she'd talked and laughed as if she'd been let out of a box, yet he'd been more aware than ever that something was missing. Missing

166

from her eyes, her smile, her voice?

'She's unlike any woman I've ever known, Inky. She hides her feelings.'

'And her legs,' Inky said dryly. 'I sometimes think she ends at the waist.'

Smithy exhaled suddenly, his eyes widening with amazement at such accuracy. Or maybe it was something all men noticed about Kate. Maybe the thing that was missing was sexual chemistry, the actual turn-on. It wasn't something you analysed while it was happening: the veiled glance, the tilt of the head, the smile that meant, 'Notice me'. But most women did it. Even the elderly ones, with whom Smithy sometimes flirted at the gate, wanted to be noticed. But Kate didn't. Yes, that was what was missing.

'You ever seen her legs, Smithy?'

'Only at funerals, but that's been more of a blessing than you can imagine. Yesterday, when she was telling me about this Latin idea of hers ... I fell. I almost fell, but she caught me. She actually lifted me off my feet for a moment. And I suddenly realised, I've been falling for a long—'

His voice faltered and he swallowed the rest, aware that there was a limit to the confidences he was willing to share, even with Inky.

'Falling in love, you mean?'

'No, you fool! *Out* of it. With Tess. But it's taken so long! I thought I was over it ...'

He'd thought he was over it until that bloody brunette had gone cold on him yesterday. Upon reflection, he knew that 'cold' was an

167

exaggeration so gross it verged upon paranoia, yet with that infinitesimal flicker of rejection she'd brought back all the agony of his last meeting with Tess.

'They say it takes three years,' Inky informed him gently.

'Ha! Everything takes three years.'

'No, no. Life imprisonment takes longer. Count your blessings, Smithy. If you hadn't come off that bike, you'd probably have strangled her and still have ten years left to serve.'

Smithy laughed. 'That's true. I was in for grief whichever way I turned, wasn't I?'

'And Mags could have left all this to Pamela.'

'And Kate could have left me for Sissinghurst.'

'Quite,' Inky said. 'You took the words out of my mouth.'

A short time later, as they were admiring the intricate layout of Kate's decorative vegetable garden, he asked wonderingly, 'Who the hell's Sissinghurst?'

Kate noticed, but did not at first remark, that she and her mother 'rnatched', for once. Kate had decided to smarten herself up a little. *Just* a little. She hated the idea of drawing attention to herself, but—having recently begun to notice other women—had realised that being inappropriately scruffy drew just as much attention as being inappropriately smart. Laura seemed to have drawn the same conclusion and as they met and kissed the air beside each other's ear the thought crossed Kate's mind that no one could doubt they were mother and daughter. Laura was wearing cream pleated trousers and a striped navy jacket, Kate white jeans and a blue silk shirt. They were the same height and roughly the same weight. The only real differences between them were twenty-one years—and Robert.

'Darling, you look marvellous!'

Kate smiled stiffly. 'I look like you,' she said.

Laura took this as a compliment, which was fortunate, because the effect on Kate came closer to insult. She didn't *want* to be like her mother!

They elected to eat in the courtyard outside the restaurant, but it was a glorious day and the place crowded, so while Laura stood guard over their table, Kate queued for lunch, covertly watching through the window while Laura fished in her bag, repaired her make-up, patted her hair. Appearances were everything to her. Smithy had said something similar about Pamela, yet Kate had found more than one argument to prove him wrong and had a nasty feeling that, if she allowed herself to recall them, the same arguments would apply to Laura.

She didn't allow herself to recall them. She pushed them away. But in the same instant she conjured a picture of her feelings for her mother: an arm reaching frantically from the smothering depths of a quicksand. The arm was love, the quicksand a deep, seething hatred in which Kate was already drowning ...

'Hi!' The girl behind the counter smiled a

welcome. 'Haven't seen you for ages. Been away?'

Kate jumped as if awaking from a nightmare. 'Yes,' she agreed ruefully. 'Miles away.'

Did she really hate her mother? Yes, oh, *yes*. And yet she was still seeing her, still reaching out that frantic hand ...

'So how are you, darling?' Laura took her lunch from the tray and made a performance of stirring a quarter of a teaspoon of sugar into her coffee.

'Spoil yourself,' Kate said coolly. 'Have another grain.'

'Oh, no, I—! *Oh*, you're joking. You have such a weird sense of humour, darling. You always sound so serious.'

'That's just insurance, in case no one laughs.'

Laura laughed. 'And how is your poor Cour—er, Smithy?'

Kate grinned. Smithy had spoken to Laura when she rang the other day. Kate hadn't been around to eavesdrop but dearly wished she had. Afterwards, Smithy had said grimly, 'You must ask her to call in one day. *I'll* give her Courteney.' But it seemed he'd already given her Courteney ...

'He's fine,' Kate said. 'But he's not mine. He's married, remember?'

'But you're living with him.'

'Only for his money, Mother.'

Laura laughed again, turning her face to the sky, 'Isn't it a lovely day?' she said.

Kate ate. Laura moved onions to the side of her plate. She always had the chef's salad—a

170

decorative arrangement of everything green, yellow, red and purple—which she took the best part of an hour to rearrange. She talked too much to make eating possible and now launched straight into a monologue about a new friend: 'Who just happens,' she said gleefully, 'to be an *interior decorator!* Isn't that marvellous? Just what you need, darling!'

'Is it?'

'Well, of course it is. The way Mrs Fitzwarren neglected that place ... I was saying to Smithy only the other day what a dreadful shame it is. It's Georgian, isn't it? Honestly, darling, you don't know how lucky you are. You can get all these wonderful paints and wallpapers now, you know, based on the original Georgian designs.'

Kate's eyes narrowed, partly in an attempt to concentrate on what her mother was saying, partly in an attempt to understand why she was saying it. Georgian wallpaper? What had that to do with anything? Smithy had had some windows replaced and the roof repaired and that, so far as home improvements were concerned, was as far as they needed—or could afford—to go. Georgian wallpaper, indeed!

'A sort of primrose yellow,' her mother said. 'No, more of a cream, I suppose. A cross between the two ...'

Kate's mind drifted away. She'd been up until nearly midnight, feeding Smithy plant definitions for his computer. They were hoping to get a booklet printed in time for the June plants (which were legion), but he, the idiot, had turned it into a game—'Who knows most

171

Latin?'—and she'd gone to bed with a headache from laughing so much. She'd been up again at six this morning to do the laundry, clean the kitchen and race around the supermarket before the crowds came in. By the time she was putting the groceries away, Smithy was just getting up, asking her if she'd slept well. 'I've forgotten,' she'd said. 'It was so long ago.'

'And *he* said,' Laura continued excitedly, 'that an interior decorator was just what you need. Well, you're so busy, darling! You can't be expected to do everything, can you?'

'*Who* said?'

'Smithy!'

Kate wrinkled her nose to demand scornfully, 'He actually *said* that? "We need an interior decorator"?'

'Well, perhaps not exactly those words, but he certainly *agreed* with me, darling. And why shouldn't he? These Army officers live in the lap of luxury, you know: everything provided, everything done for them. He must be missing all that, mustn't he? And in his present state of health he needs a comfortable home—clean, pretty, easy to run—and with his poor legs ... Well, I don't suppose he's much use with the hoover, is he, darling?'

Kate sighed. They didn't have a hoover. When she cleaned (which was quite rarely by Laura's standards) she did it all with a broom and mop. No need for more. There'd never been anything as lavish as a carpet at Whitsun Gate and the few rugs Mags had managed to acquire were now going mouldy in the attic, having proved too dangerous a snare for Smithy's dragging feet. Bare boards, bare walls ... Even the furniture was of the rare and strange variety found only on 1950s rubbish dumps. At least, that was where Billy had found most of it. God, Laura would die!

The thought made Kate laugh and, before she'd had time to think again, she said, 'You'd better come over one day and show us where to start.'

Laura laughed too, but her gaze—which never quite made contact with Kate's—now slid hastily away to bestow a smile on a pair of moth-eaten pigeons patrolling the courtyard for crumbs. 'Ahh,' she said. 'Aren't they sweet?'

It didn't hurt. Kate was numb to such rejections and, anyway, had gone past caring. She didn't care, *didn't* care.

'We've had a good spring,' she said calmly. 'Good weather, lots of visitors.'

'Yes, it's been the same in the shop. The sunshine brings everyone out, looking for new clothes. But you'd be amazed—'

'And I'm writing a book,' Kate said.

'—at the kind of people we get in. Rich as Croesus, some of them, and picking up polyester frocks for a couple of pounds. I was saying to Dorothy Peters only the other day ... Oh! Did I tell you her daughter was getting married?'

'No.' Kate looked at her watch. They'd been here an hour and a half, throwing words at each other and watching them bounce back again. Hoover, interior decorator, polyester frocks ... They spoke different languages: all noise, no meaning. Dear God, what was the point?

'I should go,' she lied. 'I'm due at the dentist in twenty minutes.'

She'd have been all right if they hadn't parked their cars in the same place. The tension of being on public display in the restaurant seemed to drain away as they walked back to their cars, so that the usual 'social' kiss on parting no longer seemed appropriate.

They hugged. Rather stiffly, it was true, and Kate was pulling out of it almost before her mother's arms had taken hold. But then Laura kissed her and whispered, 'Remember I love you, Kate,' before turning away.

Remember I love you. It seemed to imply that Kate had forgotten it, let it slip her mind somehow, when in fact ... Her heart thudding with the old rage (six years old, yet still as good as new), Kate drove away, as fast as an ante-deluvian Land Rover could take her.

Remember I love you. Yet Laura had ignored Kate's invitation to visit Whitsun Gate, ignored her news concerning it, ignored even her latest triumph, that she was writing a book! Not much of a book, certainly—its first edition would barely cover ten pages—but Laura hadn't even asked about it! What kind of love was *that?* And who the hell cared? Kate didn't. She wished now she'd said so, wished it with all her heart. Why hadn't she?

Remember I love you.

'I couldn't care less,' Kate said aloud. 'I couldn't care less!'

Then she pulled in at the side of the road and wept.

Smithy and Inky were taking their leave. They'd shaken hands three times, clapped each other's shoulders, wished each other luck (Inky was off on a course for a month) and now were cursing the linden tree, which had coated Inky's car with a haze of sugary glue.

'I told Kate we should fell it,' Smithy grinned.

'And?'

'And she said she'd fell me, so I'm leaving it until I can keep my feet in a fight.'

She arrived home at that moment, cornered too fast at the coach house and, with more faith in the Land Rover's brakes than was remotely justifiable, aimed at a stone wall on the far side of the yard, stopping with barely an inch to spare.

'I don't fancy your chances,' Inky said. 'If she fights the way she drives, you can consider yourself dead.'

Both men smiled in her direction and then more doubtfully at each other as she jumped out and, without sparing them a glance, raced into the public loo, slamming the door.

'Hmm,' Inky said. 'Well, give her my love.' He started the car, reversed a few yards and then leaned out of the window to add, 'Think about that divorce,' before driving away.

The prompt had been unnecessary. Smithy had thought of little else since Inky had reminded him that he had an insurance settlement coming up and that if he made Tess wait she might well lay claim to a share in it. Compensation for his injuries was not a thing Smithy had thought much about—the process could take years—but it was high time he did. His father had given him the London house for a wedding present and Smithy had already guessed he'd lose *that* to Tess, but he was damned if she'd have any more!

Still fuming at the thought (thinking, too, that if only he could stop being angry, he could stop grieving), he stomped into the house and put the kettle on, quite forgetting about Kate until he heard her running upstairs some time later without first shouting hello. It wasn't like her to leave out the basic civilities. Something was wrong. Her mother, of course. Bloody stupid woman.

He waited an hour before she came down again. She'd showered, washed her hair and scrubbed her face to a glow which had failed to diminish the deeper glow of red nose and swollen eyelids.

Smithy said nothing about it. Tears were one of the things he'd never learned to deal with—his own included—and he thought it safer to let Kate dry out a bit before he asked what was wrong.

He spent most of the afternoon drafting a letter to his solicitor, the rest of it preparing supper. He'd realised just before Christmas that he'd have to learn to cook before Kate grasped her opportunity to poison him with half-cooked turkey. He'd made pretty good progress and could now turn out a different (if simple) meal for every night of the week. Tonight it was just steak, salad and new potatoes and—he shut one eye to think it over—a bottle of wine? Yes.

He had only very recently—and very sparingly —begun to drink again and the difference it had made was extraordinary. A glass of wine made a meal so much more civilised and he'd missed that part of his life—the little refinements—without having realised it. After five years of roughing it with Mags, Kate wasn't accustomed to 'little refinements', of course. All she knew about food and drink was that if you didn't shove some of them down occasionally you wasted and died. But she was learning ... slowly.

He laid the table with care and some satisfaction, having bought in new stocks of cutlery and glasses for their (otherwise bleak) Christmas festivities. In the physical sense he'd had many bleaker Christmasses, but none so long or so lonely. In retrospect, the best thing he could say about it was that he'd beaten Kate at Scrabble.

Having learned through bitter experience that she was never punctual for meals, he called, 'Supper, Kate! Five minutes!' before he put the potatoes on to boil. As predicted, she turned up twenty minutes later, still a little puffy around the eyes but otherwise quite cheerful.

'Oh,' she said, after noticing the table. 'Is it Christmas again? Doesn't time fly?'

'Less of your impudence,' he growled. 'I works an' slaves, I ruins me 'ands, (he was quoting Mavis, the day Jeff forgot their wedding

177

anniversary) and all I gets for it is—'

' "Oh, shut thy bloody moanin', woman," ' Kate supplied promptly. ' "You'm always on!" '

While they ate he told her about Inky's visit in some detail, including his advice about the divorce.

'Oh? I thought you wanted to wait.'

He sighed. 'I wanted to *keep* her waiting.'

'For spite?'

Smithy's eyes widened. Spite? He'd called it vengeance: a more 'grown-up' word, having its stem in a few other grown-up words: adultery first among them. But no. Adultery wasn't the first among them. He might have forgiven her that. But when there are things you can't forgive and can't avenge, your feelings turn sour, they wizen and shrink, until all that you're left with is ...

'Yes,' he said softly. 'Spite.' He laughed and poured himself more wine. (Kate, as usual, had barely touched hers.) 'Oh, God, Kate, what awful things love does to us.'

'Yes.' She'd been eating as she usually did—as if there was no tomorrow. Now she stopped and laid down her fork, with a potato and three lettuce leaves still to go. 'They say, don't they, that love is akin to hate? I wonder why?'

'Because they're both passions, I suppose, having too many things in common.'

Kate stared at him, her face puckered with bewilderment. 'But they're supposed to be opposites! Black and white!'

'Hmm.'

He guessed she was talking about herself,

about the tears she'd shed today for love—and hatred. Did he dare develop the discussion? His own feelings about Tess were still too close to the surface for safety and Kate's would make her cry again if he wasn't very careful. But what the hell? She needed help. So did he. And what were a few tears, after all? You couldn't die of weeping.

'Maybe that's our mistake,' he said. 'I don't know whose idea it was that love is akin to hate—probably Shakespeare's; he seemed to think of everything—but whoever said it ... We've never listened, have we? Because we *want* love to be absolute and incorruptible, we *believe* it is and then are torn apart when it proves otherwise. You don't discuss your hurts, Kate, but I'd guess that if you condensed their description to a single word it would be the same word that describes mine: betrayal.'

She pressed her lips together and looked at the ceiling.

'Have some cheese,' he said. 'Drink your wine.'

Without looking at him, she plucked a digestive biscuit from the cheese-board and nibbled it, delicately, like a mouse, swallowing tears with the crumbs.

'You're right so far,' she murmured.

'But perhaps ...' He frowned, searching his mind for a grain of truth among the chaos. 'Perhaps we've only been betrayed by ourselves, by our belief in what love is, rather than by love itself.'

'Meaning?'

179

'Meaning that if we'd seen at the outset that love is flawed—akin to hate—we might not have had such high expectations of it. Our lovers—and mothers—are human, after all. They aren't—and can't be—perfect, so why should we expect their love to be perfect? It's asking too much, isn't it?'

He knew this was so, yet even as he said it, he thought something else, which Kate seemed to read from his mind, word for word. 'I don't want it to be perfect! I only want it to be *there!* And it isn't,' she added grimly. 'She's my mother and she doesn't give a damn about me!'

She drained her glass at a gulp and poured some more, slamming the bottle down with a thud. 'And what's this about our needing an interior decorator?' she demanded.

Smithy laughed. 'A what?'

'She said *you* said—' Kate paused, frowned, shook her head. 'But you didn't say it, did you?'

'No,' he said. 'When would I get a chance? She barely stops to take breath—'

'Or to eat!'

She spilled out the story of her lunch in a series of frustrated gasps, lubricated by further gulps of wine which led to yet another generous refill. Smithy watched this with some amusement, tinged with anxiety. Kate didn't drink. She'd claimed she didn't like wine and had never done more than toy with the half-glass he usually gave her. It was going to her head, loosening her tongue. And her tears.

'I never cry!' she sobbed. 'Hardly ever!'

'You're not crying now,' he said. 'It's just the wine.'

'I never whine, either!'

He bit back a grin. ' 'Course you don't. You're a little ray of sunshine. Happy as the day.'

She laughed, wept some more, blew her nose and whispered, 'Thanks. Sorry. I'd have been all right if she hadn't said she loved me, but ...' She heaved a deep, shuddering sigh. 'It's not true. She doesn't listen to me, Smithy. She doesn't care.'

Although he'd seen it entirely from Kate's point of view while she was telling the story, he now began to see it from Laura's and suspected she might, at this very moment, be telling precisely the same tale. *She doesn't listen to me. She doesn't care.* Neither of them was listening. But, by God, they cared. Too much.

'This new friend of hers,' he asked softly, 'the interior decorator—what sort of age is she?'

'Age?'

'Does she run her own business or work for someone else?'

'I don't know. Why?'

'Didn't you ask?'

'No. Why should I? We don't *want* an interior decorator, for God's sake! *Do* we?'

'That's not the point. But if it were ...'

'What?'

'If it were, if it answered your need, you'd have asked a few questions, wouldn't you?

181

You'd have taken an interest. Cared.'

Kate stared at him, her face paling.

'Love isn't a one-way street, Kate. It has to flow in both directions.' He scratched his cheek. 'You and your mother,' he said, 'are in a traffic jam. Neither of you is giving way—'

'I asked her to come over!'

'But you were joking. At least, you were until she ignored it. But why did she ignore it? Because you were joking. You might also ask yourself *why* you were joking. You said she'd die if she saw this place. Her home is immaculate and yours is a tip, but you don't care: the whole subject of domesticity is beneath you.'

Kate had frozen. Her blue eyes were glaring, her mouth set tight. Smithy felt rather scared, but guessed he'd gone too far to retreat.

'Without actually saying so, maybe you were telling your mother that *she* is beneath you—'

Smithy was proceeding cautiously, making sure that every hint of criticism had its 'balance' of support and reassurance. She had good reason to think her mother beneath her and he was about to say so when Kate leapt to her feet, trembling from head to heel, her eyes blazing with an unholy rage.

'So it's all *my* fault, is it?' she demanded, her voice low, her teeth bared in a smile that was no smile at all.

'No—' Smithy began. But it was too late. And there was no time to duck before she hit him.

182

Chapter Eleven

The human mind is a wonderful thing. This was Kate's last thought before she fell asleep that night: that the human mind is a *wonderful* thing. Even under the influence of three glasses of wine it works fast enough to live a lifetime in a fraction of a second.

A fraction of a second was all the time it took to raise her hand in anger and let it fall again in rage. Yet somewhere between the two she'd run through her entire history and a few bits of Smithy's.

She was five and it was Christmas Eve. Robert had come in for drinks, bearing gifts. He'd said he was Santa Claus, and Kate had believed him. A colleague of her father's rather than a friend, he'd nevertheless been there often enough throughout her childhood for his presence to be unremarkable, natural and pleasant. Few children dislike being noticed and Robert had always noticed her, talked to her, made her laugh. He'd kissed her hair or her cheek, like one of the family. He hadn't kissed her mouth until the day he'd actually *become* one of the family: on the day he'd married her mother. But she'd thought it was because he'd been drinking. It hadn't occurred to her that it could mean anything else.

'Love me, Kate?' he'd asked woozily. And

she'd said yes, all unsuspecting. All unsuspecting, but not *ignorant,* damn it! She'd *known* about sex. She'd learned about it in biology classes, talked about it with her friends. She should have known better!

And that was why, in a moment of blind fury, she raised her arm, wanting to knock Smithy into the middle of next week for saying it was her fault, her fault, *her* fault from beginning to end!

Somehow, she'd thought of all this in the split second it had taken to raise her arm, before it even began its descent, slicing the air, as straight as a die. 'Straight as a die,' she heard Mags saying. 'Honest as the day.'

Do you hit a man for telling the truth? Do you hit a man who can't defend himself, a man who, without your knowledge or intent, has become so dear to you, you'd rather die than hurt him? She remembered Mavis telling her that when his mother had died he'd lost his best friend. She remembered Joanna saying that Tess had visited him just once after the accident and never come near him again.

'What did he say to her?'

'Nothing, presumably, with a broken jaw—'

Broken jaw!

He closed his eyes and, in the same instant, Kate somehow pulled her punch, the muscles in her shoulder absorbing the force so that her hand met his cheek as soft as feathers on the breeze. The human mind is a wonderful thing ...

'Oh, God, Smithy, I'm so sorry!'

184

He laughed. 'Why? It didn't hurt.' He prodded his cheek where her hand had touched. 'I think I must be numb on that side. I didn't feel a thing.'

She sat down, covering her face with her hands.

'And it was my fault, Kate, not yours.'

'No, no!'

'Yes, yes. But I can't say I'm sorry. It's made me see something I should have seen before.'

Unable to look at him, not wanting to ask what he'd seen (which couldn't possibly be pleasant), Kate fixed her gaze on the wine bottle. She noticed there were still a few inches left and, just for something to do, poured them into her glass.

'Is that wise?' Smithy smiled. 'You were tee-total yesterday.'

'Yes,' she murmured. 'I'm only drinking it to save you the trouble.'

'Thanks. What would I do without you?'

'Get drunk. Fall over. Break your leg.' She sighed deeply. 'And here I am, doing it all for you.' She wanted to keep talking, if only to keep Smithy quiet and herself from wondering what he'd seen in her that he should (if he'd had any sense) have seen long ago. 'Doing it all for you,' she added airily. 'Regardlice of the sacrifess.'

'I'm grateful,' Srnithy said. 'But I'll be a lot more grateful when you make the coffee. If you still can.'

'Oh, *I'm* not drunk!' She crossed the kitchen, put the kettle on and reached down the cups without a tremor. 'I've got a cast-iron whatsisname,' she said. 'Thingummybob. Runs in the family.'

'Yes,' Smithy said. 'We had one of those, too. It had brass knobs on, as I recall.'

'Met-ab-olism,' Kate said with care.

'Oh, is that what they're called?'

She reached for the coffee pot, stole a glance at his face and found him watching her, smiling, his chin resting thoughtfully in the heel of his hand. She went hot all over and felt so light of limb and sweet of heart she could have floated away, like thistledown, and not thought it strange.

'You're nuts,' she said softly.

'So are you. You've just put three spoonfuls of oatmeal in the coffee pot.'

'*Have* I?' She came down to earth with a bump and burst out laughing. 'Oh, well, in *that* case, maybe the cast-iron metas—metam—'

'Brass knobs,' Smithy supplied helpfully.

'—passed me by.' She was aware that she was smiling a wide, Cheshire-cat smile that would not go away. And there were thoughts in her mind just as tenacious and strange. The wine; just the wine. She shouldn't have drunk it. Nice as it was, she'd always known it would set things free that should remain all her life behind bars.

I love him.

'At Her Majesty's pleasure,' she murmured.

'What?'

But only because he doesn't love me.

'I ought to be locked up,' she said.

Five minutes had passed since she'd touched

his face, yet she could still feel the texture of his skin on her palm, cool and firm, like close-grained silk. She wanted to touch him again.

Smithy drank his coffee black and un-sweetened, with a single square of dark chocolate from a bar he kept in the fridge. He had expensive tastes. The grocery bill had trebled since Mags had died, although they still hadn't eaten tiger prawns in chilli.

He sat a little way back from the table, turned slightly away from her, with one hand resting beside his coffee cup. Long fingers, clean fingernails, a dusting of golden hairs on his wrist that always tangled in his watchstrap. He'd suffered more pain than Kate could imagine, but still hissed, *'Ouch,* damn it!' when he took off his watch.

He ate his one square of chocolate and slid the remains of the bar towards her.

'When Fiona was small,' he said, 'she was a chocolate buttons junkie. I used to ask her to give me some, and she'd go all ferrety and clutch the neck of that bag as if it were her last hold on life. Pamela worried about her teeth, so she rarely had more than six sweets a day, but I always made her give me one.'

'Beast,' Kate said.

'No, wait. I don't know how old she was—five, six—old enough to know her manners, but not old enough to understand why she'd been taught them. All she knew was that if she wanted to keep in with the grown-ups, she had to be polite. So she'd offer me the bag of sweets. I never took one. I just pretended I had.'

He laughed. 'But she was always just as mean the next time. I suppose if you're that way inclined, the idea of giving something away is just as bad as actually giving it ... But that's not the point, is it?'

Although she'd heard every word he'd said, Kate had never liked Fiona (as ferrety now as when she was six) and had been more interested in watching the shadows Smithy's eyelashes cast on his cheekbones, the glint of his teeth when he smiled, the way his mouth turned down at the corner. She'd thought he'd been talking about chocolate, not making a *point.*

'Er—what point?'

'Fiona was greedy,' he said. 'Fiona was mean. But she was just a little kid, so she had no choice but to do as I asked: offer me a chocolate. But she had so few ... and she treasured every one of them. So which one of us would have been wrong—*truly* wrong, *knowingly* wrong—if I'd really taken them?'

Kate wrinkled her nose. She was inclined to say, 'Serve her right,' but guessed that wasn't what he wanted to hear. And anyway, you couldn't judge a child—even Fiona—in the same way you'd judge an adult.

'Oh,' Smithy said. 'I should add that the sweets were hers, *strictly* hers. She'd bought them with her own pocket money. So? What's the verdict?'

'Well,' Kate sighed, 'I suppose you'd have been wrong. You were ... um ...' She totted it up on her fingers, frowning. 'You were seventeen when Siona was fix. Six, I mean. You could have bought your own chocolate buttons.'

Smithy drummed his fingers on the table, watching them with fierce concentration before saying firmly, 'Morally and mathematically spot on, madam. You win this week's grand prize.'

Kate giggled. Considering what a bad day she'd had, she felt very happy, but strangely tired. Her eyes kept sliding in and out of focus and her elbows felt like cotton wool. As did the inside of her head.

'Clever me,' she said. 'What's the prize?'

'A clear conscience.'

'Oh.' She widened her eyes. 'What a disappointment. I was hoping for a screw on the QEII.'

'I mean, a cruise on the QEII.'

Smithy had been struggling against laughter for some time and now lost the struggle. He'd seen more than a few women getting plastered, but never one who'd done it quite like this. 'Squiffy' was the precise word to describe Kate's condition. She wasn't quite drunk; her *mind* was still with her, but a few other bits had gone AWOL and he wasn't sure—not at all sure—that he wanted any of them to come back. She looked radiant—'lit up' in the physical sense as well as the metaphorical—and so soft, so warm, it was hard not to touch her, to cuddle her, like a puppy.

But he also knew that this was the worst possible time to try it. Her defences were completely shot. Although she knew she was getting her tongue in a knot, she wasn't in the least self-conscious about it. She looked surprised when the words came out the wrong way round but didn't seem to realise quite *how* wrong they were. Oh, dear ...

'Kate,' he said. 'Concentrate, will you?'

'I am! Morally'n mafickly creck, madam. I won a prize!'

He smiled. 'What prize? And don't even *mention* a cruise on the QEII, because that wasn't it.'

Kate frowned. She nodded. 'A clear conscience,' she said slowly. 'Because I don't like chocolate buttons.' She waved her hand dismissively. 'Fiona can keep 'em.'

'I was talking about you,' he said. 'And your stepfather.'

She closed her eyes.

'You blame yourself for it, don't you?'

She nodded.

'But you were just a little girl, Kate.'

'No.' She shook her head, slowly. 'Firteen, fourteen ... fixteen. And Siotio ... Fiona was only fix. There's a big difference, you know.'

'The difference between sex and chocolate buttons is just as big. But the principle is the same. You might have behaved in ways that you *now* think were wrong, but you were too young *then* to make such judgements. He was taking sweets from a baby, Kate.'

'I know.' She opened her eyes, rested her chin on her hands and gazed at him wistfully. 'I know it with the part of my brain that understan's facts. Unforp ... Unfortul ... *Sadly,* there are

190

other parts of my brain that have no use for facts. Just feelings. And I feel, Smiffy ... I feel that it's *my* fault and I've no one to blame but myself.'

'But don't you see that you had no choice, Kate? The point of my telling you about Fiona was to explain that she had no *choice*. She'd been taught to keep on the right side of the grown-ups and could do nothing else. Doesn't that ring a bell? No matter how wrong you think your adults are, you can't do anything about it, because they have all the power. Even if they choose to beat, starve or rape you—'

'He didn't rape me.' she whispered. 'He might never have raped me, but I didn't dare wait to find out. Maybe that's why it's so hard to ...' She pressed her thumb into the table. 'To keep the blame where I *know* it belongs. *He* did it. *He* did it. But when I'm not blaming myself ...'

'You blame your mother?'

She nodded.

'But you love her just the same.'

'I don't know, Smithy. I don't know if I love her or only think I should.'

'Both, I suspect. But I doubt whether it matters very much. The important thing is that you think *she* should love *you*. Love you, that is, according to your *idea* of what love is, regardless of human frailty.'

'I don't know what you mean,' Kate wailed. 'She's my mother! Shouldn't my own mother love me? Regardless?'

Smithy saw that they had come full circle and that he could say nothing more without offending her again. But this time ... yes, he'd quit while he was ahead, for once.

'I think she does love you,' he said. 'She wouldn't pursue you if she didn't, would she?'

'I don't *know!*' A tear slid down her nose and she stroked it away with her thumb, heaving a sigh.

'I know what you're getting at,' she said wearily. 'It's ... it's something about forgiveness, isn't it?'

'Yes, it does seem to be, Kate, but I can't advise you to do what I can't do myself. It's hard. It's *hard* to forgive. But that's the answer, I'm certain.'

She was silent, watching him for a moment before lowering her eyes. 'Are you ... talking about ... Tess?'

He nodded.

'Do you think you'll ever forgive her?'

'No. I think I'll just forget. Eventually.'

'Forget that you loved her?'

That didn't seem possible. Loving Tess had been the best thing that had ever happened to him—and the worst thing he'd ever done. It was a combination one couldn't forget. Like the scars of his accident, he'd carry the marks of it all his life.

'No,' he said. 'But I'd like to forget I hated her, for not loving me.'

Kate bit her lip. She reached out and touched the tips of his fingers. '*I* love you, Smithy. I know it's not worth much, but ... Well, I *do* love you. Don't forget that, will you?'

He smiled, knowing that this was the wine

talking, not Kate. He'd thought for a moment she was sobering up, but evidently not ...

'No,' he said. 'Thanks, Kate. I won't forget.'

But I bet *you* will, he added silently.

In the first grey light of dawn, Kate woke up and blushed, remembering everything, his smile most of all. She turned over, groaning, squeezing her eyes shut to banish the image, but it was printed on the inside of her eyelids: a gentle, derisive, you've-got-to-be-joking smile that seemed to assess her love and dismiss it for the worthless thing it was. Love and hatred were both passions, he'd said, and there was no passion in her love for him. Maybe it was real enough, but shallow and one-sided: not just because he didn't love her, but because she'd run a mile if he did. She didn't *want* him to love her; the very thought was terrifying. But the thought that he didn't—couldn't—was even worse. God, what a state to get into ...

Again she turned over, found the hard edge of the bed, looked at her alarm clock and groaned for a second time. It was half-past four and she was wide awake. If she lay here for another hour, she'd dissolve in her own embarrassment.

At five o'clock she was walking through the gardens with a pail on her arm, picking up the litter she should have collected last night. The sun had risen but the air was still cold, cloaking the ground with a pearly mist which had a soft, mysterious beauty of its own. The dawn chorus was in full swing. She'd heard the first blackbird at daybreak; now his song was

193

joined by every voice in the garden: starlings, rooks and jackdaws included. A hell of a row.

Pat Herald turned up at ten-past six. Although only a few years older than Kate, she already had four children and bags under her eyes from the strain of feeding and clothing them and paying the mortgage. Her husband worked in the council offices at Trowbridge. He looked after the kids until eight o'clock each morning and from six o'clock each night, while Pat put in her four hours' work at Whitsun Gate. She also did eight hours a day at weekends, yet still took home barely enough money to pay the electricity bill. But she liked the work. She liked the peace and simplicity of pulling weeds and dead-heading the flowers. She nearly always arrived late and out of breath, having run from the far end of the village: tense, tired and often near tears if one (or all) of the kids had kept her awake half the night. Yet within a few minutes of starting work, she was calm again and actually said she dreaded the time when, with the children all old enough to go to school, she'd have to get 'a proper job'.

Kate dreaded it, too. Pat was good: quick, strong and efficient, unlike the other part-timers, who used Whitsun Gate as a social club and thought work was something they could do—if they felt so inclined—when they weren't chatting to the visitors. It would be good to be able to offer Pat a full-time job when the time came ... but they'd never be rich enough. It was hard to make enough money even to keep Kate and Smithy on the right side of debt and Kate had an idea that he wouldn't put up with poverty any longer than he had to. Two more years ...

The sun was high in the sky and the day as warm as milk by the time Pat ran home again to send her husband off to do his own stint at bread-winning. They scarcely saw each other and even on the rare occasions when they did, they were too exhausted to care. It was a rotten life. Pat never ceased telling Kate how hard it was and Kate believed her. But she envied her, too, especially at moments like this when, alone, she paused between one phase of the day and the next, knowing she'd be alone for the rest of her life. At least Pat would never have *that* problem ...

' 'Morning, Kate.'

She jumped and blushed, but Smithy was already walking away, admiring the bearded irises, whose first blooms had broken their buds just as the last of the tulips had shed their petals. She'd been dreading their first meeting, dreading having to look at him and know that he was looking at her. Instead he was looking at the irises, asking their names, as if nothing had happened last night. Nothing had, of course, for him. He still loved Tess. Kate's little offering, by comparison, would be scarcely more noticeable to him than a midge-bite.

And yet he seemed different, somehow. Maybe it was her imagination, but he looked better this morning than he'd looked for ages. He was moving more easily, not leaning on his stick quite as heavily. And—she looked at her watch—yes, he was up and about a whole hour earlier than usual.

'You're up early,' she said.

'Yep. Crack of dawn.'

'That was four hours ago.'

'You mean I missed it? *Damn.*'

She laughed, watching his scowl of fake disappointment break into a smile. 'I feel good,' he said, sounding surprised at the idea. 'I think I've turned a corner. If only I had some breakfast to keep my momentum going, I could be mowing the lawns by next Saturday.'

In fact, he confided while they ate, it was his letter to his solicitor that had done the trick. 'Don't ask me why,' he said. 'If you'd told me last week I actually *wanted* a divorce, I wouldn't have believed you. Divorce is an admission of defeat, you see, and I ...' He laughed. 'Ridiculous, I know. I've been staring defeat in the face, where Tess is concerned, since I came off that bloody bike. And for most of the time I've *known* it was defeat. But as you said last night, there are parts of one's brain that have no use for facts. Just feelings. And sometimes there are so many feelings, you can't identify one from another: love and hate, hope and despair ... It's like a tangle of string. There comes a time when you give up the effort to disentangle it and just ... *cut.* I didn't realise it at the time, but writing that letter was like taking a knife to the tangle. I was all tied up with Tess and now ... Now I'm free.'

'To find someone else?' Kate suggested, forcing a smile, because the thought of it was not a smiling matter, except for Smithy, perhaps. A new life. He needed that. Kate didn't.

'Good God, no,' Smithy said scathingly. 'I'm never going to put myself through *that* again. What kind of idiot do you think I am?'

She shrugged. 'I don't think you're any kind of idiot.'

'Good.' He smiled.

'Just a bit dim,' she added. 'You aren't the type to live your life all alone.'

'Are you thinking of leaving, then?'

Kate piled up their dirty plates and carried them to the sink. 'I don't count,' she said. She paused for a moment before she turned on the hot-water tap, hoping that Smithy would take the opportunity to tell her she *did* count and that the idea of spending the rest of his life in a state of celibacy, with her, was not half as bad a prospect as getting his heart broken by someone else.

But he didn't.

Chapter Twelve

The southern boundary of Whitsun Gate was a ha-ha, commanding one of the finest views of England any tourist could wish for. The towns of Frome, Westbury and Warminster were located in it, as too were a few dozen villages and the great houses and parks of Longleat and Stourhead. Yet from the ha-ha, only one farmhouse, two church towers and a tall industrial chimney could be seen. Soft green hills and dense, misty woodlands had covered everything else, folding the evidence away, like a moth between cupped hands. But there was one thing created by man that the land couldn't hide: the Westbury White Horse, carved into its chalky hillside to shine across the miles: ghostly in the moonlight, radiant in the sun. A shred of remembered history informed Smithy that it represented a god, of ancient Celtic origin, but he didn't need to know more than that. Gods are always what one wants them to be and for Smithy the White Horse represented strength and power, the freedom to run: everything he'd had, and lost, and wanted to have again.

Well, he was getting there. He'd turned a corner and now could see another view, in his mind's eye, which—although it was very like the view from the ha-ha—was different in one respect. Summer had come, but the view in his mind's eye was of an autumnal landscape, filled with a sea of mists, as if the place where he stood had broken free of the world and floated away.

Whitsun Gate had become a kind of island, detached from everything he knew. And that was what was wrong with him, still. That was what he must change, before like Kate he found himself saying, 'I don't count,' instead of only thinking it.

She was mowing the lawn, wrestling Billy's huge old petrol-driven mower into the near-perfect straight lines only physical strength could maintain. Every muscle in her body was tuned to the task and she didn't look his way. He watched her to the turn, envying—as always—her fitness and beauty, which was so unlike the beauty of other women. She was grubby and sweaty after a long day's work, blonde hair darkly damp at the roots, cheeks glowing with exertion. He doubted she'd ever anointed her skin with anything softer or more perfumed than soap and a loofah, yet it was flawless and as smooth as the proverbial rose petal. At least, it *looked* smooth, and that—he'd only just realised it—was what good looks were all about: the first suggestion of something more, the need to touch, to check it out, to make certain for oneself that it wasn't really sandpaper. Sometimes he wanted to touch her so desperately he had to clench his fists to stop himself, and that was dangerous, *dangerous!* He *didn't* want her. He just *thought* he did.

She turned, her hips going left, the mower going right, her spine twisting, snake-like, to pull it all together again for the long walk back. He'd often wondered if her aversion to men indicated something deeper than the obvious, that maybe her stepfather's attentions would have been less repellent had they not gone against her natural grain. But she was as buttoned up with women as she was with men and, until yesterday, he'd had no real clue as to which way (if any) her 'grain' truly ran. But yesterday they'd had a film actor in: a big, handsome, red-haired brute who'd asked for a private tour. Kate had gone to pieces and refused to do it, her eyes like blue dinner plates, her face the colour of strawberry juice. 'You'll have to do it,' she told Smithy. 'I can't. I won't be able to speak. I fancy him too much.'

'You *what?*'

She'd swallowed, wringing her hands. 'Well?' she'd wailed. 'I'm perfectly normal underneath! At a distance, I can fancy anyone reasonably good-looking!'

She'd said something else to explain herself, but Smithy had been too stunned to listen. He'd thought, and had to stop himself from saying, 'That leaves *me* out, then,' and the thought had rankled ever since, especially when he'd discovered that, to add insult to injury, the actor had turned out to be intelligent, well-mannered and a fairly knowledgeable gardener.

He'd bought an Elizabethan manor house, just down the road, and wanted to make a knot garden, but he'd asked so many questions, done so much back-tracking, he'd worn Smithy out, leaving him fit for nothing more rigorous than an afternoon's snooze.

He'd contented himself with a long hot shower and then tormented himself with a long cool look in the mirror. Stark naked and dripping wet (but still leaning on his stick), he'd made a pathetic sight.

Although no taller than Smithy, the actor guy had been as fit as a flea: broad shoulders, straight spine, both legs *exactly* the same length ... Stripped off, he'd have been worth the sacrifice even of Kate's precious virtue (always assuming he could catch her), while Smithy ... He looked like a child's first attempt at knitting

200

a scarf: long, thin and full of holes. There was a large, lilac-coloured dent just behind his ribs where they'd drained a collapsed lung, scars on his abdomen where they'd repaired a ruptured gut, a spaghetti junction of wounds and swellings on both legs, half of them acquired on the Great West Road and the other half in an operating theatre. The scar on his face didn't matter so much, if only because it made him look tough—tough with his clothes on, sitting down. But you don't make love with your clothes on, sitting down.

'*You* don't make love,' he'd told his reflection grimly.

So it really didn't matter if he wanted Kate or only thought he did. Either way, it was a dead loss. But she'd been right when she'd said he wasn't the type to live his life all alone. Floating on an island, in a mist. That was for mystics, misfits and poets, and he wasn't any of those. He was a ... He was a ... Oh, God, what the hell *was* he? A husband without a wife, a soldier without a regiment, a sociable man without friends ... Nothing.

Kate made another turn, blowing a loose strand of hair from the end of her nose as she began the last straight run. She had to pass within a few feet of him and, as she approached, darted him a quick, cautious little smile. He'd been unjustifiably snappy with her last night. Partly tiredness. Mainly pique. But pique had flared into temper when she'd asked if he was in pain. 'Yes!' he'd said. 'It took me three bloody hours to show your fancy man around and you could have done it yourself if you'd had any guts!'

'Oh, well,' she'd said lightly. 'Thank God you've got some, or we'd be out of business.'

And then she'd gone to bed, leaving him feeling lonely and deeply ashamed of himself. There was no excuse for self-pity, however hard it was to fight off. Even when you managed to keep it under wraps it got at you from the inside, but when you inflicted it on someone else it nearly always back-fired. He'd been spoiling for a fight, of course—just to clear the tubes—but Kate wouldn't fight. And she'd kept out of his way all day today, making him think they were back where they'd started: *two* sad little islands floating in the mist.

She killed the lawn-mower's engine and leaned over it for a minute, getting her breath back. It was gone nine; the sun had set and she'd probably seen it rise without taking breath since then.

'Kate?'

'Yes?'

'Fancy a drink? I can walk as far as the Seven Stars ... If you can.'

She straightened up, pressing a hand to the small of her back. A drink was the last thing she needed. He saw it in her face, in the sleepy droop of her eyelids. She needed her bed, pronto.

But she surprised him. 'Okay.' She brushed grass-mowings from the legs of her jeans. 'Will you take me as I am, or shall I put my party frock on?'

He smiled. 'Oh, the frock, certainly.'

'Right. I'll just run one up on my sewing machine. Ten minutes?'

'Right.'

It took twenty. She showered, changed into a clean pair of jeans and a fresh white shirt and came downstairs singing the verse of an old Peggy Lee song that had been a favourite with Mags and Billy: something about being able to make a dress out of a feedbag.

She didn't sing the title refrain, *'Cos I'm a woman!* although Smithy knew the lyric well enough to fill the gap, even while he laughed and, for a moment, loved her. She was laughing at herself, wanting him to share the joke: a lovely quality in any human being, man, woman or ... Kate.

Halfway down the stairs she paused and drew the shape of her 'frock' with a descriptive downsweep of both hands. 'What d'you think?'

'Mmm,' he said. 'Very nice. A bit short, perhaps. You're showing an awful lot of leg.'

'So? What's wrong with my legs?'

'They're blue.'

'Tch! A slight circulatory problem, that's all.'

'And frayed around the ankles.'

She let out a wicked little chortle and bent one leg to inspect the frayed hem of her jeans. 'Yes,' she said. 'Worrying, isn't it?'

'Perhaps,' Smithy suggested as he locked the door, 'there's another layer underneath. You ever checked?'

'A normal layer, you mean?' She sent him a sideways smile.

'Mmm.'

They walked in silence to the gate. Then, 'Forget it,' she said gently. 'I'm incurable.'

'But you *fancied* that guy. Doesn't that mean ...?'

'It means he's great on the television screen, that's all. He can't get out; he can't get near me. Or, at least, I thought he couldn't.'

I can, Smithy thought. He imagined cupping her face with his hands, touching her lips with his tongue. He imagined her knee in his groin and abandoned the thought, sighing.

There were a few tables set out on the pub's forecourt, all occupied by the *crème de la crème* of village youth. Brassy lasses with rings through their noses, oily lads with tattoos on their arms. Kate, who never walked close enough to Smithy to allow any accidental contact, was suddenly *very* close, almost touching, her arm only a hair's breadth clear of his own.

They'd been to the Seven Stars only a few times before but had always entered at the side-door, from the car park, so they'd never run this particular gauntlet until now. The kids looked up at Kate, leering and smirking. Smithy looked down at her, smiling, the thought barely formed—but certain for all that—that she was huddling close to seem to belong to him, to be in the circle of his protection. He expected her face to look pinched, for her eyes to be cast down. Instead, her chin was up and she was smiling, her eyes bright, scanning the faces as if to find one she recognised.

'K-K-Katy!' one of the lads called out. 'Ow's yer garden growin', darlin'?'

Beside Smithy—but on the wrong side for safety—Kate took a long stride forward, leaning into it while leaving her back foot behind. Eyes wide and mischievous, smile wide and teasing, she reached out a hand as though to tousle the boy's hair. 'It's a lot prettier than you,' she said.

The girls shrieked with laughter. Kate brought her feet together and opened the door for Smithy. He knew then what she'd done. His stick had been within kicking distance of the group (and they were the type to kick it) and Kate had put her own leg in the way. She'd created a diversion. She'd protected *him!*

Fury hit him so hard he thought for a moment he'd pass out with the force of it. With jaw clenched, heart pounding, he limped to the nearest bar stool and perched there, shaking with a rage that—in such circumstances—could find no outlet at all. How dare she? How *dare* she?

'Evenin' Smithy. Kate.'

He dragged his eyes to the barman, but saw him only with difficulty, through a boiling mist.

'Kate,' he snapped. 'What would you like to drink?'

The barman talked about the weather. Smithy managed to point to his favourite brew. His heartbeat slowed to an ominous thud, but his fists stayed clenched, as did his teeth. He couldn't get over it. He couldn't believe it.

He couldn't even drink until he was sure his hands had stopped shaking.

A ferocious glance under his brows told him that Kate knew something was wrong, but not exactly what it was. She was staring at the floor, chewing her lip, her apple-blossom complexion fading to pallor. But she felt his eyes on her and turned to meet them. Smithy turned away.

'Well, this is fun,' she said dryly. 'We must do it again some time.'

'You know those louts?' he hissed.

'Yes, I watched them grow up. I also watched them set fire to Mrs Whittle's cat. Lovely lads. Do anything for a laugh.'

'I am *not* Mrs Whittle's cat!'

He went to an empty table in the corner and sat there for some minutes before she brought their drinks and sat opposite him, her eyes blank, registering nothing.

He imagined one of those booted feet shooting out to kick his stick from under him. He was still a soldier at heart, but that didn't mean he could defend himself any more. Kate had known that. He hadn't. The danger hadn't even crossed his mind. A few young lads? He could tear them apart with his bare hands.

'I'm sorry,' Kate said.

He covered his eyes. 'No,' he said quietly. '*I'm* sorry. I didn't think.'

'Neither did I.'

'Yes, you did.' He sighed. 'God, it's hard to be a man when you're only half a man!'

Self-pity again. But how—when it kept

cropping up with such monotonous regularity—could he beat it? A sense of humour had its limits, and those limits were always bounded by pride! He'd thought he'd been protecting *her*. Stupid sod.

'Mmm,' she said. 'I know what you mean. But you'll get over it. This time next year you'll be banging their heads together.'

'I had something more interesting in mind.'

He entertained himself with this thought before remembering another. 'Weren't *you* scared, Kate?'

She smiled. 'Only of you.'

'For me,' he corrected.

'No. *Of* you. If you'd snarled at them they'd have turned nasty, so I thought it best to look as if I was enjoying it. They don't know the difference.'

'I wouldn't have snarled. I never snarl.'

'Snap, then.'

'I never snap.

Her eyes widened. 'Lie through your teeth, then.'

'Ah, well, that's different. I do that all the time.'

They laughed and it was over; she'd taken his pride and given it back again, with words he'd hoped never to hear from her: 'I was afraid of you'.

'But you aren't really afraid of me?' he asked. 'Are you?'

'No. Why should I be?'

Because I want you, he thought. Just to see, to touch, to taste, to know how you'd be. You have every reason to be afraid ... Except that I'm too afraid to try it.

'Well,' he said, 'because I *am* a man. Mostly.'

Kate almost laughed. She stopped herself just in time, aware that although he was joking about it now, the idea of being only 'half a man' had hurt him badly just a few minutes ago.

'Then it's a woman you need,' she said. 'Mostly. And I'm mostly not one.'

'Rubbish. What he did to you ... it's only skin deep, Kate! Why don't you do something about it? Have you ever thought of seeing a shrink?'

Yes, she'd thought of it. Quite often, during the past few months. To be normal, to give herself an outside chance of ... of keeping Smithy for herself. But to keep him she'd have to give herself up to him, let him touch her as Robert had touched her. Touch him, the way Robert had made her touch. And she'd rather die.

'Kate?'

He wanted an answer. In his view, he'd thrown her a lifeline, the hope of salvation, and she was meant to catch it and thank him for caring. Well, it wasn't as easy as that. People who are saved are then obliged to live like other people and if that meant being mauled by some man, men, even a man like Smithy, she didn't *want* to be saved!

'Yes?' she said coolly.

He stared at her. Although she'd learned to meet his eyes, she looked now at the scar on his face, detaching herself from his thoughts, denying him access to hers.

He sighed. 'Okay,' he said. 'Forget it. We'll change the subject. What do you think of the weather?'

'I think it'll hold for a few days.'

'Well, that's a mercy. You've studied meteorology in some depth, I take it?'

Kate winced. He'd lost his rag twice in two days and was about to lose it again. And it was all her fault. She should never have told him she was 'normal underneath', if only because it wasn't strictly true. She could think a man delicious without *ever* wanting to eat him. The furthest her 'fancying' ever went was a warm hug, a platonic kiss (on the eyes, usually), and a few loving words. She often imagined going that far with Smithy, and it was lovely—until she imagined him going further. And then, like him, she changed the subject.

'I'm thinking of buying a car,' he said flatly.

'Oh! Can you drive yet?'

He sucked his cheek and watched his fingers drumming on the table. 'An automatic,' he said. 'No clutch control. My right leg's strong enough to cope with the brake and throttle. And I need the freedom. I'm beginning to feel caged.'

Kate immediately envisaged him breaking free. Maybe just taking off on little jaunts at first, but then ... A terrible grief clutched at her heart. Two years. Then he'd be gone.

'Oh,' she said.

'But it's not just that. We need to get moving, Kate. We need to look at other gardens, see what *they're* doing to make a decent living. We don't want to turn ourselves into a fairground, obviously, but if we're to make a go of it in the long-term, we *do* need to make the best of what we have. Right?'

'Do you think there'll be a long term?' she asked faintly.

Smithy drew back in his chair, squaring his shoulders. 'Not at our present rate of progress, no. We're breaking even, that's all. And that's not good enough. I need to be firing on all cylinders, Kate, going for it, feeling ... feeling that I'm taking an active part in the world, not isolating myself from it, as you do.' He narrowed his eyes and leaned towards her, adding passionately, 'I'm *young*, Kate! I've still got some fire in my belly and I'm damned if I want—'

He withdrew, drank a little of his beer and went on softly, 'That's what *you* want though, isn't it? To shut yourself away, to live on an island, as if no one else exists.'

He looked at his hands. 'It's a kind of death, Kate. Can't you see that? You're strong and healthy and beautiful, yet you're living exactly the way Mags lived when she was sixty. It was all right for her. She'd done everything she needed to do before she even arrived here. But you—'

'I'm doing all I can,' Kate said.

Smithy groaned with frustration. 'You're missing the point! I'm not saying you don't do enough for the business. I'm saying you don't do enough for *you*. You're not—'

He halted, took a deep breath and looked away.

'Trying?' Kate suggested innocently.

'Oh, you're very trying.' He laughed grimly. 'But you're doing something I'd always thought an impossibility: you're teaching me patience.' He finished his drink and thumped the glass down on the table. 'Come on. You're tired. Let's go home.'

Kate had the idea she'd failed an important test, but just before she fell asleep (a scant half-hour later) the thought came to her that she hadn't failed at all. She'd succeeded in doing precisely what she wanted to do: shutting him up, shutting him out, making him leave her to her own devices, however sad and circuitous those devices might be. And that was worse than failing. It was suicide.

She rarely remembered such thoughts. Although the last thought of the day was often some kind of revelation, when she woke up the next morning she'd forgotten everything—except that it had been important. But this thought stayed. It was the first thing she thought of the next morning. She woke with sinking heart, wondering what was wrong with her. And then she remembered. She was losing him. She *must* lose him. This was no kind of life for such a man. As he came back to health he'd realise that he could do anything—anything not too punishingly physical, at least—and, with the sale of Whitsun Gate, he'd be rich enough to take his chances elsewhere. But what would happen to Kate? She'd be rich, too, of course ... But that didn't matter. Without her 'island', without Smithy, she'd be lost!

Shoals of car manufacturers' brochures began to arrive with the mail, but after a while Smithy stopped remarking on them and said, when she enquired, that he intended to wait until Phil and Inky were there to help him. 'It's a big decision,' he muttered. 'I need a second opinion.'

Kate was aware that he also needed some encouragement. He needed to feel that some progress was being made. 'So,' she said, 'we'll visit some gardens in the meantime, shall we? How about East Lambrook? We can get there in less than an hour.'

'How?'

'In the Land Rover. How else?'

Smithy shook his head. Kate knew he'd never liked the Land Rover. It was old and uncomfortable; the seats didn't hold him firmly enough and the shock absorbers absorbed only those shocks that might have snapped the spine of an elephant. But he was strong enough now to cope with it. Wasn't he?

'Come on,' she encouraged. 'The summer will be over if we wait any longer.'

Smithy scowled. Kate scowled back, bewildered, noticing a sudden reddening of the skin around his eyes before he turned away to stare at the wall.

'I thought it was what you wanted,' she murmured helplessly.

'Yes,' Smithy said.

'So?'

He opened his mouth and shut it again. 'I don't want to go in the Land Rover,' he said abruptly. 'For one thing, you drive like a bat out of hell—'

'I do not!'

'You do.'

'Rubbish! Top speed in that crate is fifty!'

'It *feels* like eighty.'

'So I'll drive slower!'

'No.'

Kate turned on her heel and walked away before she could lose her temper. She *never* lost her temper. She *refused* to lose it. But that didn't mean it didn't lose her. The next few hours passed without her notice. She welcomed the visitors, sold them their tickets and the Latin booklet (which was going like hot cakes in its July edition), but even while she was being nice to them, she was cursing Smithy in the roundest terms she could think of. What was the point of trying to please him?

And yet, when the two hours had passed and he came to relieve her at the gate, she suddenly understood what was bothering him. After barely surviving one road accident, he was scared of everyone's driving, not just hers. He needed a car of his own because he needed to be in control, taking the wheel, holding his life in his *own* hands, rather than trusting it to anyone else's. Frome and Radstock were as far as he'd travelled since he'd come here and, beyond thinking a longer journey might be uncomfortable for him, she hadn't wondered why. Which was stupid of her, because the first

213

thing he'd said to her after Mags had died was in answer to her question, 'Good journey down?'

'I don't know,' he'd said. 'I took knock-out drops before we left.'

'Look,' he said now. 'I didn't mean—'

'I know.' She smiled, handed him the roll of tickets and walked backwards down the drive. 'Take no notice. I'm just stupid.'

She didn't give him time to deny it, so thought it rather perverse of her to be peeved when he didn't. It was true, anyway. She was as thick as a plank and cowardly to boot. Or perhaps just cowardly. After all, she could think; she could work things out and, as Smithy had said in one of his more kindly moments, she was young, strong and (not that it mattered) beautiful. It *was* in her power to change things, but she was too scared to try it. Changes were frightening. If she could face them with a guarantee that everything would be better afterwards ...

But life wasn't like that. For things to get better you had to risk the possibility of their getting worse, and that was a risk she couldn't take.

'*Won't* take,' she whispered firmly, almost as if someone had put up an argument. Whoever that someone was (and she had an idea it was Smithy), he now said, 'Why not? What choice do you have? If you take a risk, things *might* get better. And if you don't ...'

If she didn't, he'd go. He'd sell Whitsun Gate. What could be worse than that?

Chapter Thirteen

'Oh, no!' Mavis shrieked. 'I can't stand shellfish! I only got to look at a shrimp and me bowels turns to—'

'I'm not asking you to eat it!' Smithy said hurriedly. 'Just cook it!'

'I had scampi and chips once. Sick? Cor, I fought I was dyin'! Our Jeff fought I was, too, 'cos I got a cast-iron stomach, usually, and he'd never seen me like it before. Well, we'd known each other since we was twelve, see, and I musta been twenty-free ... No, I tell a lie. Twenty-four, I musta been, 'cos I'd just had our Nigel. I remember that, because he had this terrible colic ...'

Smithy could take a lively interest in no one's digestive processes. Even his own bored him silly, so Mavis's and Nigel's stood no chance. But when one was asking special favours, one had to make an effort. 'Good Lord,' he said. 'Poor old Nigel.'

'Kep' me awake three night on the trot, he did ...'

Smithy had asked Phil and Jane to lunch on Monday—Mavis's day off—intending to give them bread and cheese in the kitchen. Inky had rung him soon afterwards demanding to know why he and Joanna hadn't been invited and then Phil had rung again to say his parents were coming, too. Phil's people weren't the sort to eat bread and cheese in a kitchen that looked like a bomb-site, so Smithy had asked Mavis to do the honours. He'd thought she'd be pleased with the extra money he'd offered, but she was never pleased with anything unless she'd had a good shout about it first.

'I'm not sayin' I'm allergic,' she went on. 'The scampi might just have been off, but I ain't never tried it again and I don't mean to, neither. Straight through me it went: in one end, out the—'

'Mavis!'

She took a step backwards. ' 'Ere,' she said. 'You been a bit tetchy just lately, my love. Anyfing wrong?'

'No.' He dragged a smile to his face. Then, as inspiration struck, he switched off the smile to heave a pathetic sigh. 'I'm just a bit worried, that's all, Mavis. Eight people to lunch and they're the sort of people who ...' He shrugged. 'Well, you know. I'd like to make a decent impression, and how can I do it if you won't help me?'

'Aww!' She slung her arm around his shoulders and followed through with a neck-breaking hug. ' 'Course I'll 'elp you, my love!'

Smithy hadn't realised how strong he'd become until then. Weighed down by love—and the hard-packed fat she always called 'big bones'—her arm felt like a sack of coal dumped from a great height, and he hadn't even staggered!

'Thanks.' He planted a smacking kiss on her

cheek. 'You're a brick.' He could have added, 'A ton of bricks,' if she hadn't at that moment gone all weak and helpless, clutching her throat to whisper, 'Ooh, you kissed me ...' She cupped her palm, very gently, over the place where his lips had touched. 'Ooh.'

It was rather touching, in a way. Kate had once said that Mavis was tragic: 'a sleeping beauty without a prince', and although she hadn't (at least he thought she hadn't) been joking at the time, he'd replied, 'She doesn't need a prince! If she's asleep, the last thing we want is to wake her up!'

And yet, awakened, Mavis looked as if she was sleeping. Her hard, dark eyes had grown misty and she seemed blissfully disinclined ever to speak again.

'Tell you what,' he said gently, 'if you'll make the chilli sauce, I'll cook the prawns.'

'No need,' she breathed. 'I'll do it, my love.'

That was on Friday. She was still in a daze on Saturday, but was back to normal on Sunday, when she confided to Kate (at full volume) that she'd never been kissed before.

'My God,' Smithy laughed. 'What the hell's Jeff been doing all this time?'

Kate frowned. 'I don't think she meant she'd *never* been kissed. Just that she'd never been kissed by ...'

'Me?'

'No, I don't think it's that ...'

She seemed to think it mattered, as if he'd ravished the woman instead of just kissing her.

217

'It was just a kiss on the cheek, Kate! What on earth's all the fuss about?'

'Nothing.' She'd wandered off, in as much of a daze as the Sleeping Mavis, but it was beyond Smithy's patience to spare it much thought. Kate and her hang-ups were as much as he could handle. He couldn't cope with Mavis's, too.

Not that he was quite *handling* Kate's hang-ups. He was just letting them hang, having realised, a month or so back, that he was pushing her too hard. A remark of his own had taught him wisdom: 'It's only skin-deep.' Afterwards it had come back to him, like a ghost in the night, and called him a bloody fool. After all, *skin* is only skin-deep, but—as he knew to his cost—it's also the thing that keeps body and soul together. Try tearing it off with a few masterful words and the whole person falls apart.

Masterful. That was Smithy's hang-up, of course, thinking he could *master* something that needed delicacy, gentleness and patience. Although delicacy was not his best suit, gentleness he could manage. Manage it beautifully, too, given the chance. But patience was hard and getting harder. As his strength returned, a bit at a time, he wanted more than ever to be acting, moving, making things happen.

And yet his hard-won patience seemed to be paying off. Kate was making a real effort to think 'business' rather than just 'garden' and had visited a few other places on her own to see what was happening elsewhere. She hadn't said a great deal about these visits and the little she'd said had been negative. No teas in one place, a tacky gift shop in another, more weeds than flowers or rigid planting schemes that left no room for nature to work its magic. He didn't doubt her judgement in reaching such conclusions, but experience had taught him that nothing was ever *entirely* negative. However bad a situation, something positive can usually arise from it, but Kate hadn't looked at it with that thought in mind. All she'd wanted to know was that Whitsun Gate was as good as it could get, that no change was necessary, no change allowed.

Still, they'd had a good summer. Decent weather, for one thing, and a steady stream of visitors that usually swelled to a crowd from Friday to Sunday. Mavis—toned down by her conscience and the occasional raised eyebrow—had managed to offend hardly anyone this season and Kate's Latin booklet (revised again to describe the principal plants of August) had sold very well. Smithy's own work in taking cuttings had paid off, too. He'd begun it just to feel he was doing something to help, without even guessing how helpful it would be. Taking cuttings was time-consuming work, something Kate and Mags had always 'fitted in' to an otherwise punishing work-load. But it had been all Smithy could do, so they'd ended up with more plants for sale than ever before.

It didn't seem to amount to much—his puny efforts, Kate's booklet, Mavis's marginally improved manners—and perhaps, after all, none of it had mattered so much as the weather. But the profits had gone up. And now, with Kate representing the only important fly in the ointment, Smithy was fairly certain he wanted to stay. He'd spent most of the summer out of doors, soaking up sunshine and fresh air, and when he thought of living another kind of life—especially a London kind of life—it seemed inappropriate to the way he was now. But he still needed more. A *lot* more.

Monday's post brought something he hadn't expected. A shock? A surprise? London ... His stomach swooped with terror, a terror he'd felt for a long time, ignoring it as much as possible in the hope that it would wear off. But such terrors did not wear off. They had to be wrestled with, subdued ... Damn it, he should have been braver sooner! He should have bought a car!

Kate came home with the shopping a few minutes later and his fears were somehow swamped by the business of unloading groceries and taking those she needed to Mavis in the tearooms. She'd already been busy, laying tables on the terrace and baking pastry shells for the fresh raspberries which (minus the pastry shells) had been Smithy's only suggestion for a pudding. The prawns would be served with French bread and a salad and Kate had bought four kinds of cheese. Clean, pretty and simple—just as long as it was only Mavis who couldn't stand shellfish!

When he went back to the house, Kate had disappeared and was still not in evidence when

Inky and Joanna turned up, almost an hour later. He'd ordered, rather than invited her to join them: to eat, drink, talk and relax for a few hours, instead of always muttering, 'They're *your* friends,' and sloping off by herself. She seemed more shy of the women than of the men, although Smithy couldn't imagine why this should be. Jane and Jo were lovely girls: bright, pretty, modern and intelligent. He'd have thought Kate would jump at the chance to make them *her* friends. But no. He'd ended up telling her she'd have to be there because they'd be talking business, making decisions. 'And we can't do anything without you, can we?'

'What sort of decisions?'

'I won't know until we've discussed all the possibilities.'

'What possibilities?' She'd looked as ferrety, at that moment, as Fiona with her bag of chocolate buttons, holding hard to the things that were hers.

'Nothing is possible,' he'd said gently, 'unless you say so, Kate. I can't do anything without you.'

It was true. She must know it was true. Yet although she'd said nothing more, something in her eyes had called him a liar.

'It's a sort of business lunch,' Kate had said, blushing, as the saleswoman looked askance at her usual outfit and uttered a silent, but resounding, 'Oh, yeah?'

At fifteen and sixteen, Kate had done most of her clothes shopping with Laura in tow and, since then, mostly from market stalls in Frome. In short, she had no idea. The only way to buy the right outfit for Smithy's lunch was to throw herself on this woman's mercy, and since throwing herself on *anyone's* mercy was not Kate's style, she had no option but to put up a fight.

'Have you heard of the gardens at Whitsun Gate?' she'd demanded aloofly. 'I own them.' Then, indicating her jeans and chunky leather boots, 'I also work in them, as you can see.'

The woman had understood and changed her attitude, but the process had still taken three hours and cost a fortune. Now, lurking in one of the empty bedrooms at Whitsun Gate (the only one which boasted a full-length mirror), Kate was certain she'd wasted her money. She looked silly in a skirt and even sillier wearing make-up. Although she'd barely touched her lashes with mascara, she somehow looked all eyes: half-starved and terrified, Oliver Twist in a frock.

She should have checked it out with Smithy; *he* wouldn't have minced his words if he thought she looked an idiot! And there was no excuse for not asking him; she'd bought it all last week. But she'd wanted to surprise him. Bloody fool!

'Take it off,' she told herself angrily. 'Take it *off.*'

She was tip-toeing back to her own room when she heard car doors slamming outside and tip-toed back again to peer down into the yard. Inky and Joanna ... Joanna looked gorgeous, damn her. Clingy pink top, floaty summer skirt, a thin gold chain at her throat to set off her tan. She'd grown her hair since the last time Kate had seen her and had either lost weight or grown a few inches taller. No, she was wearing high-heeled shoes; white canvas espadrilles, very like the ones Kate had almost bought before deciding she'd probably fall off them and break her ankle. A girl needed practice at that sort of thing ...

She turned to stare once more at her own reflection. Clingy white top, floaty summer skirt, bare feet. She chewed her thumbnail and scowled at herself critically. Colours, shoes and jewellery aside, there wasn't much to choose between Joanna's get-up and her own, and maybe the shoes (she hadn't a 'jewel' to her name) *would* make a difference.

'Come on,' she whispered. 'You can do it.'

'Smithy!'

Kate stood behind the curtain, to peer again into the yard, where Smithy had now appeared to welcome his friends.

'My God, what a hunk!' Joanna laughed. 'You look marvellous!'

Kate chewed her lip, watching the exchange of hugs and kisses. Smithy was dressed up, too. Cream chinos, red polo shirt, loafers. He'd had his hair cut again—at the first sign that a curl might be sprouting he had it shorn off at the roots—but otherwise ... Yes, he was a hunk. Whatever that was.

Inky clapped him on the shoulder. 'Hey, what have you been up to? Weight-training?'

'No.' Smithy grinned and indicated his stick.

'Just letting my shoulders do the walking.'

They shook hands. Inky said something that Kate didn't catch, but promptly understood as Smithy laughed, 'God only knows. Hiding somewhere.' They turned towards the arch that led to the terrace. 'Bet you a tenner she doesn't show up,' he added dryly.

Kate felt sick. His tone of voice hadn't been unpleasant. Just resigned, as if he'd written her off, *shrugged* her off, as being beyond hope of improvement. And that wasn't fair. She'd just improved herself into an overdraft, for God's sake!

She'd go down *now*. She wouldn't think about it any more. She'd just go! But she had first to find her shoes, and the delay, short as it was, was more than long enough to make her hesitate again.

'He'll go,' she told herself. 'If you don't come up to scratch, he'll go, Kate.'

For perhaps the hundredth time she imagined his going, and found herself in darkness without him, as if the sun couldn't shine if he wasn't near, as if the flowers couldn't bloom ...

'Oh, *stop* it!' she hissed. 'You sound like a bloody love song!'

Was she in love? It certainly felt like it, but love meant so much more than the things she felt. Maybe she'd just adopted him, as a big brother. A girl could love a big brother, without wanting him to ...

She stood up, gazed at herself in the small mirror over her dressing table and found after all that she had nothing much to complain of.

Nice figure, pretty hair, eyes, nose and mouth in roughly the right places. Something impelled her to wrap her arms around her ribs, pretending that it was Smithy who held her. And to rock herself, very gently, as though it was Smithy who rocked her. She closed her eyes, turned her face up for his kiss. She heard him whisper, 'Oh, Kate ...' and felt her body yearn toward his, as if he was really there.

She opened her eyes. 'There,' she said to her reflection, 'that wasn't so bad, was it?'

'I never been kissed before,' Mavis had told her. 'Not by a man I really *fancied*, if you know what I mean, Kate.'

'What? Not even Jeff?'

'Oh, our Jeff's all right ... but I've known him since I was a little kid, Kate, before I even knew what it was all about. I never 'ad another boyfriend, see, so I never really knew what I was missin' until I was married to him and it was too late. Oh, don't get me wrong! I *loves* our Jeff! It's just ...' After a brief pause for thought, 'He's got very short legs,' she'd concluded glumly. 'Puts me right off, that do.'

'Have you ever thought of leaving him?'

Mavis laughed. 'Fousands of times! In me dreams. But I'm not as green as I'm cabbage-looking, Kate. Our Jeff ...' She closed one eye to think it over. 'He's like a good, solid fruit cake, our Jeff is, the kinda cake what *keeps*, if you know what I mean. Only trouble is, he got no icin' on the top. Not a lot of hair, neither, come to think ... But you can't live on just icin', see, can you, Kate? An' that's all I'd get if I married one of my ear-oles. Smiffy, for instance—'

'He's not just icing!'

Mavis looked at her thoughtfully. 'No, not for you, maybe. But people've gotta match *up*, Kate, that's the point. Smiffy's a lovely man, but ... well, even if I was twenty years younger. Even if ...' She sighed. 'Even if he fancied me, I couldn't *match* 'im, Kate. He'd go over me like a bloody steam roller. I'd feel ... Well, take this for a f'rinstance. He comes in yer sometimes when I'm shouting me mouth off and—know what he does? He *looks*. That's all. He don't say a word, he don't scowl or complain, yet he makes me feel like a worm, 'cos I'm not as nice as 'im, not as polite as 'im, not as clever. That's why I loves him, o' course, 'cos he's nice and polite and clever, but I couldn't *live* with it, Kate. Our Jeff never makes me feel like that, see. An' Smithy never makes *you* feel like that. You're his equal. The same. And that's all that matters.'

'What if I don't fancy him?'

'Puh!' Mavis had said. 'Pull the other leg.'

Kate had often suspected that Mavis wasn't as green as she was cabbage-looking. But she'd never suspected she had X-ray vision.

As guests so often do, Smithy's guests messed up his lunch schedule by asking for a tour of the gardens before they ate. It was Phil's idea. His parents were like Kate—buttoned up so tight they could scarcely breathe—and although Smithy had met them a few times before, they seemed to have forgotten him, or else found him so changed they couldn't make the connection.

So lunch was an hour late. The old folk (barely into their sixties, but that was old enough!) loosened up as they admired the place, oohing and aahing over the Bride's Garden in a manner which should have been balm to Smithy's soul. And yet, as everyone else began to relax and enjoy the visit, he became increasingly tense and distracted. He thought at first it was hunger; he'd had breakfast an hour earlier than usual and was now having lunch an hour later. His 'brass-knobs metabolism', still struggling after two years of drugs, poor appetite and depression, was sensitive to such breaks in routine. He'd feel better when he'd eaten.

'You fretting about Kate?' Inky asked as they strolled back to the terrace.

'I could wallop her,' Smithy said, and only then understood that the tension he felt was anger. He'd kept his eyes skinned throughout the walk for a glimpse of his elusive partner, but if she was anywhere in the gardens she was hiding in a tree. Silly, *silly* girl. If only she'd ... If only ...

'How intriguing,' Inky teased. 'I hadn't taken you for that type. Think she'd like it?'

Although Smithy laughed, he wasn't greatly amused. In spite of his chosen profession he never *had* been the violent type and, having suffered so much violence (albeit accidental) on his own account, would have said he hated the idea now more than ever before. But when patience was forced upon a man who didn't have any, strange things could happen. And there were times ... Yes, there were times when he could cheerfully wallop Kate. The only thing he doubted was that he'd feel so cheerful when the deed was done.

'No,' he said. 'That'd put the tin lid on it. *Nobody* meddles with Kate.'

By the time they joined the others, Mavis had brought out the champagne (Phil's gift) and the conversation was dedicated to Kate, Kate, Kate. Kate was wonderful, Kate was a genius, Kate worked like a horse while Smithy just lay around and ate grapes ...

'I do not,' he said haughtily. 'I'm the propagation specialist.'

'Well, we know *that,* old son, but do you do any *work?*'

'Smiffy,' Mavis hissed from the tearoom door. 'Did you lock up the house?'

'I ... No, I don't think I did. Why?'

'Better go and see to it, my love. There's some woman been hangin' about out there, and I didn't like to go and shoo her off in case you lot come back, wantin' yer dinner.'

Smithy wanted his 'dinner'. He also wanted his possessions to be waiting for him when his guests had gone, and that might be a problem if 'some woman' was turning the house over while he ate. Mags had been robbed several times—it was one of the natural consequences of inviting the public in—but she had never had much to steal. She'd certainly never had a computer, a stereo, a state-of-the-art camera ...

Aware that Inky was just a few steps behind

him, he walked back to the house and found the culprit trying the door. Nice-looking girl. Pity about her morals.

'What do you think you're doing?' he demanded icily.

'Locking the door. Why?' Even as she turned her head to look at him, he wasn't quite certain it was Kate. She had Kate's voice, Kate's hair, Kate's wry little smile. But everything else was different and he could only stare at her, open-mouthed, as he might have stared at a map that had brought him to the wrong destination. *Was it Kate?*

'I was just about to join you,' she said, 'when you all walked off.'

'You should have—' he breathed '—come with us.'

'Why? I've seen it all before.'

He couldn't think of anything else to say and wished he'd had the presence of mind to try Inky's quip: 'My God, Miss Jones, you're beautiful without your glasses!'

Kate laughed, blushed and swished a hand through her skirt, striking a coy little pose to say, 'Really? You like it?'

Rather to his consternation, Smithy found himself blushing too, although he was by no means the blushing type. Sheer confusion, he guessed. A kind of embarrassment, such as a man might feel when the dancer's sixth veil hits the deck and there's only one left to fall. So it was Inky who paid the compliments, led her to join the others and introduced her to Phil's parents. Smithy couldn't find the words.

He couldn't find his thoughts. For the next ten minutes, he couldn't even find his appetite, although it came back, luckily, before the others had scoffed his share of the tiger prawns.

As in her absence, Kate was the centre of attention, which gave Smithy space to regain his equilibrium. The gardens were scarcely mentioned, he noticed. The girls did the usual girly things: 'Kate! You look wonderful! Where'd you get that skirt?' while the men gently teased and—even more gently—flirted, seeing her as Smithy was seeing her, for the first time as a woman. But, oh, such a young one ... on her mettle, like a girl on her first date: laughing a little too brightly, talking a little too much. It wouldn't have taken much more to have made Smithy weep, but whether for her, or for something quite other ... No, he couldn't have said.

Except in and out of Kate's glass, the wine was flowing like water. He saw her raise her glass often enough, but she took barely a sip each time. And every time she drank she looked at him, as if to say, 'This is me, not the wine, talking.'

Yes, hard as it was to believe, this was Kate talking. She'd put a little paint around her eyes, set her hair loose from the ratty rubber band that usually confined it and, of course, was wearing something new, something feminine. But she was the same Kate. Nothing in *her* had changed. It was something in him.

As often happens when everyone is talking at once, everyone suddenly *stopped* talking and

230

there was a moment's silence before Phil said, from the far side of the table, 'How are the legs coming along, Smithy? You're looking pretty good.'

'Damn! I need to look pale and interesting for a few weeks yet. I've been called for a medical.'

'Oh! Your compensation? When? Where?'

'September the third. London.' His heart squeezed with the panic he'd felt when he'd opened the letter. He could travel up by train, of course, but then he'd have to get around town by taxi and you can't tell a London cabbie to stick to twenty all the way. (It didn't go down too well with the Frome cabbies, either.)

'Oh!' Joanna laughed. 'We're going up on the first! You can drive up with us, Smithy!'

'Oh ... I—er. Thanks, but—'

No one seemed to hear him. They bounced his travel arrangements around like a tennis ball, making decisions as if he weren't there. All of his friends were the same in this respect (*he* was the same, now he came to think of it) and he'd always appreciated it, until now. It wasn't interference so much as generosity: 'You've got a problem, we'll solve it for you,' and all he had to do, if he didn't like it, was to shout out 'No', loud and clear. But if he did that, they'd want to know why. He imagined himself admitting—loud and clear—that he was scared of motor-travel, telling them that he still had to take tranquillisers for a ten-minute drive into Frome and even then suffered panic attacks when a blind bend loomed or a car on the

231

far side of the road whizzed by. He'd worked out that he might feel a lot safer if *he* did the driving, but even that wasn't certain and the only reason he hadn't bought a car, so far, was that he was scared of that, too. He'd tell them later. Get Inky on his own and just ... *tell* him.

He'd been eating one of Mavis's raspberry tarts while all this was going on and now stared at his empty plate, realising that he hadn't tasted a crumb of it. Thanks to Kate's big transformation, the prawns had gone down in much the same way. Best meal of the summer, and he'd been in too much of a fog to appreciate it!

When the fog cleared slightly he saw that Kate was now deep in conversation with Phil's mother, talking about the gardens at last. She clearly hadn't noticed (neither had anyone else!) the state he'd been in and although she'd done everything he'd wanted of her, he found he didn't like it as much as he'd expected. No longer on her mettle, relaxed and at ease, she looked as like Jane and Joanna as made no difference at all. 'Fitting in' in the physical sense, merely by dressing as they did, seemed to have spliced her into the group in the social sense, too. There was no sign left of defensiveness, nothing to indicate that a wrong word or move from one of the others—or from him—would send her hackles up and drive her into hiding again. So what was bothering him? He should be delighted, not feeling like this—well and truly peeved! She'd knocked him sideways and he was still reeling from the shock.

Still on the subject of the garden, Phil's mother said, 'It's perfect, Kate,' and on impulse (a malicious impulse, he realised later), Smithy interjected coolly, 'Oh, no. It's far from perfect yet. We have a lot of changes to make, don't we, Kate?'

She should have jumped, stiffened, turned pale. Or at least averted her eyes. Instead, she threw him a teasing grin. 'Oh, *finally*,' she said. 'I was beginning to think you'd forgotten!'

Chapter Fourteen

Smithy's eyebrows went up. Apart from that, he 'just looked'. But Mavis had been right: it didn't bother Kate. Whatever he was thinking he'd change his mind ... any minute now.

'Forgotten what?' he asked.

She laughed. 'I'll give you a clue: will you call the meeting to order or shall I?'

'A meeting!' Jane and Phil spoke at the same moment and since they'd made no attempt to keep their voices down, everyone else sat up and took notice without further effort on the 'chair-woman's' part.

'What's it about?' Joanna demanded excitedly. 'Come on, Kate. Tell all.'

'Well, perhaps Smithy—'

'No,' he said wonderingly. 'Please. Feel free.'

233

It was a good choice of words. She *did* feel free. As small as it had now proved, her effort to 'come up to scratch' had seemed—in anticipation—an enormous risk. When you've spent six years of your life trying to merge with woodwork, it takes a fair amount of nerve suddenly to shout 'Notice me!' without falling apart at the seams.

Yet all of her fears had proved groundless. At first, she'd thought Smithy's friends had welcomed her into the group 'as if' they really liked her. But as the lunch had progressed and she hadn't been ignored, criticised, or taken out of her depth, she'd gradually deleted 'as if' and realised that they really *did* like her and had accepted her as one of their own.

It was a lovely feeling. The best thing about it was that (satisfaction aside) it was no feeling at all. She'd heard their initial compliments in a blind panic, aware only of herself, thinking only of the impression she was making. Was her skirt too short, her neckline too low? *Should* she have worn the eye make-up or washed it off as soon as she'd thought how silly it looked? Since then, however, she'd completely forgotten herself, flown free of herself, simply *known* that everything was all right.

Smithy had helped just by leaving her to find her own level, not pushing her, scarcely speaking to her, although whenever she looked at him she found him looking at her and seeming to like what he saw. Yes, it had been worth the risk. Being noticed was nice.

Just as well, too, because everyone was looking

at her now, expecting her to say something clever. She decided funny would be better. 'Well,' she said, 'it's about all these changes Smithy keeps rabbiting on about.'

They grinned. Inky muttered, 'Rabbit-rabbit-rabbit,' and Smithy sucked in his cheeks and pretended to look hurt.

'In fact we've already made changes and—though it pains me to admit it—Smithy's contributions have made the most profit.'

'What contributions?' Phil demanded with a snort. '*He* doesn't do anything!'

'Oh, he does. This year's profits on plant sales are forty per cent up on last year's and that's entirely Smithy's doing. He's raised all the new plants.'

'Except roses,' Smithy said, 'wisteria, clematis, paeonies and just about everything else an idiot couldn't propagate with his eyes closed.'

'But we've never done many of those, anyway,' Kate added firmly, 'so the difference is still the same.' She heard the tone of her voice with a thrill of amazement. She sounded so confident! So alive! And that was exactly how she felt. She'd grabbed herself by the scruff of the neck and kicked herself into action and now she was enjoying the game, controlling *it,* rather than letting her fear of it control *her.* God, why hadn't she done this before? It was easy!

'But that's as far as we're likely to go on plant sales,' she continued brightly, 'unless we have more over-wintering cover. At the moment we have only a small heated greenhouse and if we want better sales—especially in the spring—we'll need more room and more heat, which costs money.'

'How much money?' Inky asked.

'A few thousand for the house; a few hundred a year to heat it. But we might raise that amount with Smithy's other work. His computer.'

If Kate had waited until Smithy had invited her to this lunch, she wouldn't have been able to work it all out. But she'd been visiting other gardens, nurseries and garden centres for the past six weeks and now had all the details at her fingertips.

'We've been selling a monthly booklet, which explains Latin plant names—'

'That's *your* work,' Smithy said.

'No, that's my knowledge. It's your work.' She glanced around the table. 'Smithy feeds all the information into his computer and prints out the booklet, which we've been selling at the gate. Nearly everyone buys it, and no one has ever quibbled about the price, so we could probably charge more. And ...'

She explained that all the gardens she'd seen had sold books of some kind, mostly written and produced by the gardeners themselves. 'It'll cost money, of course, but it might be worth producing a properly published book of Latin names. People have been very interested in the booklets and quite a few ask for the previous months' lists when they're on their way out. If we could offer them a book of the whole year's plants, I think they'd buy it.'

Everyone looked anxious as they totted up the figures she'd given and she decided that this was

236

the right time to pin Smithy down.

'But none of it's worth doing,' she said, 'unless Smithy decides to stay.'

'Stay?' Jane gasped. 'Why shouldn't he stay?'

'Well, we're only committed for three years and almost half of that's already gone.'

She threw a sideways glance at him, but he 'just looked' and said nothing.

'Well, Smithy?' Jane demanded. 'Are you planning to stay?'

He laughed. 'We'll see. Any other ideas, Kate?'

'Yes. The important thing about a garden like this is its character. We can't spoil it by introducing tacky gimmicks, but we can certainly do more to enhance it. I've noticed, for example, that most of the gardens I've seen have nicer houses than ours.'

'Also open to the public?'

'Not always. But the ones that aren't make the visitors wish they were. And ours just makes them thank God it isn't. We can smarten it up on the outside. That wouldn't cost too much. Get the woodwork painted, take down the worst of the old curtains and keep the windows clean. Billy would never let Mags put climbers on the house—he said they were bad for the stonework—but I don't see that a few climbing roses would hurt. Would they?'

'No,' Smithy said. 'They wouldn't hurt.' He smiled and poured more coffee into her cup. 'Go on,' he said. 'There's more, isn't there?'

'Only another book, for some time in the future, perhaps. Mags kept a diary when she first came here, describing how she and Billy put the garden together. I read a bit of it ages ago and it's good—I don't know where it is, or even if it still exists, but if we could find it and edit it—' She shrugged. 'Something to do in the winter months, maybe?' Smithy nodded, but with a shrug that mimicked her own, seeming to indicate he wasn't keen.

'That's it?'

'Yes. Oh ... no. There's something else. People spend a fortune in garden centres on the sort of plants we've never bothered with: alyssum, lobelia, petunias. The only real reason we don't do it is because we're plant snobs, but it's also because we haven't enough room to raise them from seed.'

She snapped her notebook shut and sank back in her chair, not knowing, until that moment, how tense she'd become. Everyone—except herself and Smithy—had begun talking as soon as she'd stopped and she was happy to let them get on with it; she'd done her bit.

'How are you off for capital, Smithy?'

He pulled a face and rocked his hand, doubtfully. 'Not good. But there's my medical. Even if they aren't generous with the payout, I'm bound to be better off when it finally comes through. I think I could risk a few thousand.'

Kate blinked, knowing something else she hadn't known before: that she hadn't expected anyone—especially Smithy—to take her ideas seriously. She'd pulled them together seriously enough, knowing that if she didn't appear to be making the right kind of effort, he would lose

238

hope of their partnership ever 'going anywhere'. But she'd seen it all as a bluff, a ploy, a carrot to lead him along with. She'd been saying, in effect, 'Okay, so maybe these ideas are no good, but I'm going in the right direction, aren't I?'

She certainly hadn't expected to arrive anywhere. And she hadn't for a moment thought that Smithy was fool enough to be led quite so far up the garden path. Risk a few thousand? He couldn't! He couldn't put his money into a bluff!

'You can't!' she gasped. 'What about your car?'

It was gone six. Not exactly a record for a 'lunch' that had begun at eleven—in better days, Smithy had known a few that had run through to midnight—but seven hours had been more than enough for him. He was exhausted. Pleasantly so, but still enough to watch his friends' departure with relief.

Kate was being kissed: quite soundly by the women, who hugged her, thanked her for a lovely day, told her she was wonderful (yet again) and planted fresh pink roses on her cheeks from their recently renewed lipstick.

She stood up to it very well, considering. But when Phil attempted the same procedure, she laughed and took one step backwards, averting her face so that his lips just grazed her ear.

'Hey!' he said. 'That's not fair!' And before Kate could retreat further, he caught her under the arms and lifted her off her feet. 'Nice kiss for your Uncle Phil,' he commanded sternly.

'Anywhere you like, but make it a smacker.'

In the instant of going aloft, Kate's smile faltered, before—amazingly—it broke out again in a cheeky grin.

'Should I take that literally, or do you like having all your own teeth?'

'Huh! You don't scare me! Give us a kiss, quick, before the wife catches us.'

Jane was actually standing right next to them, rolling her eyes in mock despair. It was all a joke and, at least in intention, completely harmless, yet Smithy saw the connection between this and Kate's real trauma. In a sense, Jane was like Kate's mother, watching the torment without doing a single thing to stop it.

He opened his mouth to say, 'Put her down,' but Kate was one step ahead of him. She'd braced her arms against Phil's shoulders to keep what distance she could. Now she groaned, 'Ohh!' and leaned forward to deposit the required kiss on his cheek. 'There. Satisfied?'

As Phil laughed and put her down, Smithy took a protective step towards her just in case Inky should get the same idea. But Kate foxed him again, actually standing on her toes and beckoning Inky to bend his head for his share of the action.

So she kissed everyone, in the end, including Phil's father. Everyone except Smithy.

'My, my,' he said, as they watched the cars disappear up the drive. 'Weren't we brave?'

'We were,' she said. 'Think we'll get a medal?'

He didn't realise his hand had strayed to her

shoulder until she tipped back her head and leaned wearily against his arm. He held his breath. His thumb was situated on the very edge of her blouse. A few millimetres to the right and he could actually touch her neck. He lifted his thumb, moved it the required few millimetres and stroked it once across her skin. Immediately she stepped away, muttering, 'Right, that's that, then. Back to work.'

He'd expected nothing else. He wasn't disappointed. But the pain of rejection was as bad as it had always been. His problem, not hers. But hers didn't make laughing it off any easier.

'Work? Are you mad?'

She smiled. 'Not as mad as some people I could mention.'

'Meaning?'

She shrugged. 'Were you drunk, or do you really mean to invest a few thousand pounds in my crackpot ideas?'

'They aren't crackpot ideas. They're all worth thinking about. We'll have to discuss it further, of course, decide which is the best move, but yes ... I'll risk a few thousand.' He laughed again. 'And, no, I wasn't drunk! How dare you suggest such a thing?'

'I thought you'd have to be to volunteer for a long drive up the M4 with Inky and Jo. Wouldn't a train be more comfortable?'

It was sweet of her to phrase it in terms of comfort. He'd never actually told her he was afraid of cars (although, having been minced by a few, he had every reason to be), but he knew she'd sussed it some time ago, when he'd declined her offer of a long drive in the Land Rover.

Well, she'd faced up to so many of her own fears today—and come through smiling—he'd decided he'd better try for the same result.

'And how would I get around London?' he asked wryly. 'On a flying carpet?'

She laughed. 'You could borrow Pamela's.'

'What? At the rental *she* charges? No. I'm going to be an ear-ole, for once.' He assumed a superior smirk. 'Damned if I'll be beaten by a dame.'

Kate blushed, turned away, jumped in the air and skedaddled into the house. As he followed her into the hall, he heard her running upstairs. She was singing again; this time a song from 'South Pacific', *There is Nothing Like a Dame*. When she came down again, she'd changed back into her jeans and looked exactly as the song said: 'nothing like a dame'. But Smithy had noticed that, when she sang, it was always to assert her femininity, even if she laughed it off at the same time. And that was a good sign. Today had been even better: the pretty skirt, the subtle make up ... the legs. Nice legs. Dainty ankles. Small, high breasts: rounded and firm, like ripe little—

Oh, God, how did he come to be thinking about *that* again?

Because he wanted a woman. He *didn't* want Kate! He wanted a *woman!*

For Kate, seeing Smithy off to London was like

sending her only child off to his first term at boarding school. Now that the moment had come he was fine, looking forward to it, glad to see the back of her: 'Stop fussing, will you? Of course I'll be all right!' It was just his poor old 'mum' who was going to pieces. How on earth would he manage without her?

She watched Inky's car to the end of the drive and then ran after it, to watch it out of the car park. She'd have run to the car-park entrance, too, to watch it out of the village, but common sense prevailed and she trailed back to the yard, listening to the silence, feeling it all around her, like a wall of glass.

He's only gone to London, she told herself. He hasn't died, you fool. But the silence was the same as on the day Mags had died: not quite real—yet worse than real.

She'd have been all right if he'd gone for three days, as he'd originally planned, but somehow it had stretched to a week. He'd rung Pamela and asked if he could 'pop in' for five minutes, not expecting much more than a muted, 'How nice.' But she'd been thrilled silly. 'Pop in?' she'd said. 'Certainly not! Come and stay with us, for heaven's sake!'

Smithy had been thrilled, too. He hadn't admitted it, but when he'd hung up at the end of the call, he'd closed his eyes and heaved a sigh of relief, as if his rift with Pamela had really hurt him. Well, why not? His father aside, she was the only family he had left and it didn't seem to matter that he didn't actually like her.

The worst thing for Kate was that, although she knew where he'd be staying, she had no idea *why* he'd be staying so long. He'd have his medical on the third. That aside, she hadn't a clue what he'd be doing, who he'd be seeing ... Would he see Tess? Would he (after seeming to forget it) discover that he still loved her? The very thought was enough to make Kate shudder. Worse was the fact that he hadn't told her anything of his plans. She wouldn't even have known about his medical if he hadn't told the others while she was there to hear. Not that it mattered, except to confirm what she'd known all along: that *she* didn't matter, that she didn't count. As she had once said of herself, Smithy was just parking with her until something better came along. He hadn't even said he'd ring her. Just told her to ring him 'if there's an emergency'.

'Aw! 'Ave he gone?'

Mavis, red in the face and gasping for breath, galloped in at the gate and paused, hanging on to the gatepost for support.

'Aw,' she said. 'I wanted to see 'im off, but our Nigel got his zip stuck in his underpants and I couldn't just go off an' leave him, could I?'

'I don't see why not,' Kate said. 'I would have.'

'You wouldn't! He was in bloody agony, poor dab, where our Kirsty had tried to get him out and jammed him in worse! Ooh, she'm a cack-'anded madam, that one, and the *dinners* she gives 'im! Thank Gawd he still comes to us Mondays, or he'd waste away.'

She hurried along to the tearooms, recounting her daughter-in-law's failings in the sing-song style of a child reciting a poem. Like everyone else in the village (except, perhaps, Kirsty), Kate had heard it all before and had no desire to hear it again. Yet she followed at Mavis's heels like a hungry cat, just to hear someone talking, just to drive the silence away.

But it was amazing how quiet Mavis could be when you weren't listening to her. She clacked on for a good ten minutes without Kate hearing a word, until she said, 'You'll be all right, will you, Kate? You won't be scared in the nights, on yer own?'

This possibility hadn't crossed Kate's mind. Now that it did, she remembered the nights she'd spent alone in the house when Mags had died: the mysterious drippings and creakings that had kept her staring into the darkness for hours at a stretch, wondering if this noise or that was a door opening, or someone sneaking up the stairs ...

'No,' she lied. 'Why should I be? Smithy's no Superman. He couldn't fight off a mouse, let alone a burglar.'

'Yeah,' Mavis conceded thoughtfully. 'That's not the point, though, is it, my love? Our Jeff's no Superman neither, pertickly when his back's playin' him up. But it's nice to know he's there.'

Kate shrugged. 'That's different. You sleep right next to him; you can't help knowing he's there.'

But sometimes, when she woke in the night, it was a comfort like no other to know that Smithy was there. He'd recently weaned himself off his sleeping pills and sometimes woke up in the early hours to make a pot of tea. The tap of his walking stick, the sighing thud of the fridge door, even the tinny rasp of the tea-caddy opening and closing: although these sounds echoed through the house as loudly as any other, they were as soothing to Kate as if he'd whispered, 'Hush, go back to sleep; it's only me.'

She shrugged off the thought and went to work, sternly resolving to forget all about him. She succeeded. For ten minutes at a time. But then she'd think of something she wanted to tell him, or she'd hear a hesitant step on the gravel and look up, expecting to see him—and instead seeing a stranger. 'Oh, look at those delphiniums. How *do* they get them to flower so late? Mine never do.'

Kate rarely heard such questions without wanting to supply the answer, but this time she let the answer run through her mind unspoken: 'A plant's main purpose in life is to reproduce, so if you cut down the first flowers before the seeds ripen ...'

That's what had happened to her, she realised. Robert had cut her down before she was 'ripe' enough, either to understand why he should do such a thing or to protect herself from it. Well, she understood it now, that yearning to touch and be touched. She was like the delphiniums: if you cut down the first flowers before the seeds ripen, the plant will make new flowers, try again.

The only difference was, flowers weren't afraid to try again and Kate was. She still was. And yet ... When Smithy had put his arm around her, it had felt so easy, so natural and good ... Good, like the smell of baking bread, or the caress of a warm bath when you ache in every muscle and want nothing more than to rest, to float away. She could have stayed there forever—and perhaps even convinced herself that 'a warm bath' was all there was to it—if he hadn't moved his hand to stroke her neck.

Even now she could feel an echo of the feeling she'd had then: as if the skin on her neck were one end of an electric wire that ran right through her body—not to earth, but to a warm spot in the pit of her stomach that had suddenly grown warmer. She hadn't liked it. She didn't like it now. Just because she needed Smithy didn't mean she *wanted* to need him!

'Why?' she said out loud. She was pulling weeds under the base of Mags' beloved dove tree, and a man on the path nearby looked at her strangely and turned away, evidently thinking she was crazy. Maybe she was. Because that warm spot was sex. Her body wanted it and her brain didn't. *Why?*

Jammed into a corner of the landing, with Robert's mouth filling hers like a gag, his hand grinding her breast and her mother just downstairs, cooking supper, the strongest feeling Kate had had, revulsion aside, was helplessness.

247

No, not quite that, because she'd known she could bite him, kick him, push him downstairs. The worst thing was harder to identify. The worst thing was ... Oh, what *was* it?

The day seemed endless. She went back to the house for lunch, took the loaf of bread from its bin, stared at it for a moment and put it away again, her appetite gone. The house was empty, its emptiness like buzzing midges in the air, irritating her to madness. She went into Smithy's room and curled up on his bed. She hadn't made it and there was still a dent in his pillow where his head had been, only six hours ago. And already it felt like a fortnight. How would *he* manage without *her?* Ho-ho.

His bed was high and hard and weighed a ton, as she knew to her cost, because she'd had to turn the mattress every week for the first three months after he'd bought it. 'Why a king-size?' she'd demanded irritably. 'You expecting company?'

'Sorry, Kate. I need to move around a lot.'

'So sleep on the lawn! This isn't any softer!'

She didn't say things like that, any more. The hedgehog prickles turned inwards now, hurting her more than they hurt anyone else. There was a reason for that, too. She was inuring herself to the pain, controlling it, before it went out of her control, when Smithy ...

She'd been stroking his pillow, wishing it was his hair, when her hand stilled and her eyes widened with horror as she completed the thought. When Smithy *didn't* touch her!

'Oh!' She sat up, jumped off the bed and ran

248

back to the kitchen, her heart thudding with confusion. She wanted him to touch her? Yes, but she dreaded it, too. Having hated the idea for so long, she couldn't trust herself suddenly to like it, just step over all the walls she'd been building and behave as if ... live as if ...

Oh, God, walls were safe! No matter how small or how lonely the space they enclosed, walls were safe and when you stepped out from their protection, you weren't safe any more. *Anything* could hurt you. It couldn't hurt her now.

Yet as that long week dragged by she found that anything could. Even working hurt. She found muscles aching in her back and shoulders that hadn't ached since she'd first come to Whitsun Gate. She drove the garden fork into her foot, hit the back of her head on the underside of the sun-dial (a consequence of straightening up too suddenly while clipping the box hedge underneath) and was stung by a wasp. But the worst agony was waiting for the phone to ring, which it did only once while she was within earshot.

'Oh, you're there!' Laura laughed. 'I'd almost given up expecting *you* to answer the 'phone, darling. Where's Smithy today?'

'Gone to London. For a week.' She was aware that her tone was as flat as a pancake. In this case, its flatness was the result of acute disappointment, rather than the chronic variety which had made it flatter by the day. Even Mavis had noticed it and said, 'Aw, you're missin' 'im, ain't you, my love?' But the last

249

thing she'd expected was that Laura would notice. Laura didn't notice anything. Laura didn't care.

'Oh, you must be so lonely, in that big house, all by yourself! I know how that feels, darling. Never mind, keep your chin up. He'll be back.'

Kate smiled wearily. 'I suppose you're ringing to—'

'I remember when your father died. I sent you to Grandma—do you remember?—and the house was so empty ...' She laughed nervously. 'It was alive, that emptiness, as if swarms of little insects were crawling all over me. I couldn't bear it.'

Kate swallowed. She'd never thought of that, and had certainly never been told it before. Laura was the kind of woman who never talked about her feelings, or about anything else that might—or might not—make her feel uncomfortable. 'Don't mention it,' was her policy, 'and it might go away.'

'Was that why you married Robert?' Kate asked now, dragging the words out by force, for even his name sickened her, as did the reply she expected to hear: *No! I married him because I loved him!*

'Yes,' Laura said, surprisingly. 'I suppose it was. It's so nice to have a man around the house, isn't it?'

'Any man, Mother?'

There was a brief pause. 'But he wasn't just any man, darling! I'd known him so long! I thought ...'

But whatever she'd thought was blown away on a gasp of nervous laughter. 'Well, I mustn't keep you. I know how busy you are. I was just ringing to check ... All right for Monday?'

As usually happened when Laura dodged the issue like this, Kate's heart leapt with a rage which—usually—took hours to wear off. But this time it didn't. Even as she put down the phone she felt calm again, as if something essential had slipped into place.

I'd known him so long! I thought ...

What had she thought? That she could trust him? She knew otherwise now. Yes, she *did* know it, for even if she hadn't believed a single word Kate had told her about him, such words cannot be spoken without creating a doubt. And it was a doubt Laura couldn't handle, didn't care to confront, for if she did, her marriage would be over and she'd be alone again. Kate's father's death had given her an idea of what it was like to stand alone in the world—and it was an idea that terrified her witless.

It didn't terrify Kate. She certainly didn't like it, but—having never expected anything more—had learned to accept it as an inevitable consequence of the thing she *was* terrified of. *Men.* And that included Smithy. Because she knew ... yes, she knew that if the absent-minded touch of his finger had set her jumping, there was no hope of anything more. She understood enough about sex to know that it was surrender, a loss of control in every sense of the word. And that was what terrified her. Not sex itself, but the feeling of being taken hostage to someone

251

else's needs. Not Robert's ... she'd never cared about *his* filthy needs! Bite him, kick him, throw him downstairs ...

And then explain it all to Laura. Poor frightened little Laura. That she'd been thirty-seven when Kate was sixteen: an adult, a mother, a (supposedly) responsible woman, was the reason Kate had been angry with her for so long. Yet she hadn't been angry with her *then;* she'd been angry with Robert, not just for molesting her, but for blackmailing her into silence in her mother's defence.

Her anger hadn't changed direction until, with rape the next most likely development, she'd finally told her mother what was happening.

'You're lying! You're lying! If it's been going on all this time, as you claim, why have you never told me before?'

Her face as white now as it had been then, her hands shaking just as violently, Kate whispered, 'Because I didn't want to hurt you!'

That had been her downfall. To think that Laura could be protected from hurt, to think that she *should* be protected when her task, as a mother, had been to protect Kate. But why had Kate then taken all the blame for it? Why, even now, did her conscience keep murmuring its dreadful dirge: My fault, all my fault?

It was because she'd always thought herself stronger than Laura, had thought she should shoulder all the burdens her mother couldn't bear. And it wasn't true. It wasn't true! Kate couldn't bear the loneliness, either. Not for the rest of her life!

Not even for the rest of this week, unless she took a grip on herself pretty sharpish ...

Was she just lonely? Or was she in love?

Chapter Fifteen

It was on the way back, his fears all forgotten, that Smithy confessed to Inky that he'd been 'a little nervous' of the journey up.

'But a decent car makes all the difference,' he said. 'Being comfortable, not getting thrown around on the corners. That bloody Land Rover!'

'It's probably just because you're not driving it,' Inky said. 'I'm the same with Jo. She's a good driver—'

'Huh!' Joanna said.

'But when she's in the driving seat, I'm biting my nails.'

'Huh,' she said again. 'Biting my head off, you mean!'

'When in fear for my life,' Inky said haughtily, 'I think that's excusable.'

'*I* don't! Before we got married, you said you'd happily die for me.'

Smithy laughed. Inky and Jo were of that special breed of people who never quarrel in public (or perhaps not at all), and if they did seem to be quarrelling it was always a joke. This joke, he was sure, was intended to tell him it was normal to be scared. Nice of them, even if it was untrue.

'Nearly home, Smithy,' Joanna said now. 'How's it feel?'

'I'm not sure. I think I'd feel better if Kate had rung. I'm not sure what to expect. She's such a ...'

'Puzzle,' Joanna said. 'You rang this morning, did you?'

'Yep. No answer.' He'd rung twice during the week too, choosing the times when she was most likely to be indoors. No answer. Not that he was worried. Kate could look after herself.

'I'm usually quite good at summing up women,' Joanna said. 'But I can't seem to make her out.'

'Join the club,' Inky and Smithy said in unison.

'So what is it? Anyone know?'

'How do you mean?' Inky said. 'Beyond being brought up by wolves? Or have you taken that into account?'

'Oh, that's what it is! So if I just throw back my head and howl?'

'Spot on,' Inky assured her. 'You try that, Jo.'

'And see where it'll get you,' Smithy added dryly.

There was a short silence before she asked thoughtfully, 'Do you like her, Smithy?'

He was aware that she was being mildly euphemistic, using 'like her', to mean 'love her', or 'fancy her rotten'. To a degree, all those things were true. The difficulty was only to know *how* true and, more to the point, *why*. Social isolation, sexual deprivation, the need he'd always had (but never confessed) to love and be loved: all these things were enough to deceive him into thinking that less was more. As for 'fancying her rotten', her sheer unavailability could be responsible for that: lusting after forbidden fruits was a part of the human condition. Still, he could admit to *liking* her. That much was true.

'Yes, of course,' he said blandly. 'She's a nice girl.'

Joanna sighed. 'God, how incredibly revealing. You could sell that to the Sunday papers, you know.'

'There's nothing more to tell, Jo. As you said, Kate's a puzzle. Shy. Lacks confidence. All that.'

All that. And more.

'No, it's more than that,' Joanna said. 'She's like a chameleon, always changing. Look at the way she took that meeting! She wasn't shy then, was she?'

No, not then. And not for the best part of a week afterwards, when she'd talked herself hoarse (as had he) about her ideas for the business. In fact he'd already thought of most of them—the greenhouse, the books (no; to be fair, the books had been her idea in the first place)—but he hadn't thought of doing spring bedding and he certainly hadn't thought of smartening up the house on the outside. (The inside, yes.) But there had been no point in suggesting any of them until she was ready to make changes. And now ... Now that she *was* ready, *he* wasn't certain that any changes would be worthwhile.

'Oh, the meeting,' Inky said. 'Did you decide which one to go for? If any?'

'The greenhouse. It'll be another year, at least, before I'm likely to be able to help with the heavy work, so it seems the best thing to keep me busy. Kate wants to go halves with the initial outlay, but I'm not sure. She's only got the money Mags left her and I don't want ... Well, we'll see.'

'You're still thinking you might sell up, then? When you're served the three years, I mean?'

Smithy heaved a sigh. 'I don't know, Inky. I can't think of anything else I *want* to do, but on the other hand ...'

'Yes?'

'If I stay, I'll need to make a pretty huge investment. In the house, I mean. It's uncomfortable, dirty, freezing in winter. And Kate doesn't give a tuppenny cuss. She's about as interested in domestic comforts as Pamela is in gardening. So I've got to be certain. I've got to be sure. First, that we can make a living on profit alone ...'

'And second?'

Smithy hesitated. 'And, second, that we can make a go of the partnership on a long-term basis. I'm not sure of that, yet. While Kate remains a puzzle, I'll remain undecided.'

A puzzle, a puzzle ...

She'd said, 'I'll miss you,' and had looked

very much as if she meant it. So why hadn't she *rung?*

His week in London had been exhausting. Good, on the whole, but the pace of life, the noise and the constant press of too many people had stretched his nerves and made him ache for his own company, for the peace of the gardens and the gentle relief of Kate's comings and goings. He hadn't realised how gentle she was until he'd returned to the bosom of Pamela's family. The constant carping between Fiona and her mother, the explosive arrivals and departures of the two boys and their girlfriends, the way everyone yelled to (or at) each other and Michael's pre-prandial need to whine—passionately—about every 'bloody stupid' person who'd crossed him since he'd eaten breakfast ... It had struck Smithy that it was all an exercise in attention-seeking; as if, in spite of their apparent self-importance, they felt they lacked any importance at all. It was galling to think that he'd once lived like that, that he'd once picked arguments with them just to announce, 'I'm here, too.' Oh, dear.

Still, he hadn't picked any arguments this time. He'd been too tired, for one thing, and for another ... Well, he hadn't seen any point. What was he to them, after all? A mere second-cousin: not so much a part of the family as one of its satellites, cleaving to them only for want of anyone nearer and dearer. He didn't seem to need them now. These last few years—boring, lonely and depressing as they had been—had nevertheless taught him a few things and the best of them was that he *could* stand alone. In fact, all he wanted at the moment was to *be* alone! With Kate, of course. But she didn't count ...

They'd planned to arrive home at about six, when the visitors (and Mavis) had gone, but they were ten minutes early, had to wait for the last two visitors' cars to leave the car park and then met Mavis on her way out. Inky's Volvo was no match for the HGV. She hurled herself at it with a howl of joy and took Smithy's head in an embrace that almost broke his neck. 'Cor!' she said. 'Am I glad to see you!'

She'd already punched a hole in his brow with what she'd probably call a 'motherly' kiss. Now she went all gooey and pink about the gills and demanded coyly, 'Gissa kiss, then, my 'andsome.'

'Not before witnesses,' Smithy muttered, pretending shyness. 'What will people say?'

'Puh! Bugger that!'

She puckered her mouth. Afraid she might faint if he took the invitation as offered, Smithy aimed for her cheek and followed up with a whispered, 'Brazen hussy,' which he instantly regretted. Her mouth was now only an inch from his ear, her laughter a deafening shriek which was still scrambling his brain ten minutes later. She whirled away, to yell down the drive, 'He's 'ome, Kate! Kisses all round! Come an' get it!'

Kate was nowhere in sight, but just to hear her name spoken in such 'healthy' terms, was a relief that knocked the breath from Smithy's lungs. He

258

hadn't realised he'd been as worried as all that. If he'd had to say anything about it, he'd have said, 'a bit anxious'. Now, to his surprise, he found he was also a bit annoyed. If she was all right, why the hell hadn't she rung?

She was tidying up the plant-sales trestles as Inky pulled in under the linden tree. Standing with her back to them, as if she'd heard neither the car nor Mavis's yells, whose echoes even now were reaching the far shores of Madagascar. Smithy scowled.

Inky walked round the car to help him out. 'Hey, Kate, we're back!' he called. 'Did you miss me?'

She turned then. 'No,' she said wonderingly. 'I didn't throw anything at you.'

Inky laughed. Even Smithy managed a smile. Her wit was rarely out of action. Unlike her feet, which seemed to have been dipped in glue and left to harden. Rather like his legs, in fact. The right wouldn't bend and the left wouldn't straighten—but it had been the same when they'd arrived in London. Inky knew what to do.

'I'm stuck.' said Smithy. 'Just lift my—'

'Stuck?' Inky demanded with a laugh. 'Whadjya mean, stuck? You've *had* your medical. No need to lay it on so thick now, you know!'

'S'okay. I'll do it.' Kate darted under Inky's arm to lift the offending legs over the door-sill and haul Smithy to his feet. Firm, brisk, no smile, no eye-contact—except with Jo, who passed out his stick from the back seat and kissed Kate's cheek.

'Hi, Joanna. Good trip?'

Inky, now laden with Smithy's bags, dropped another kiss on the top of her head, but Smithy turned away, annoyed with himself for not taking the same liberties. The ridiculous thing was that she'd actually *trained* him not to and now he was almost as scared of her as she was of him!

Slowly (it would take a while for his legs to loosen up after the drive), he made his way towards the house, hearing Joanna telling Kate about her week in London. Then Kate said, 'Whoops, the door's locked,' and ran past him to unlock it, so she was waiting on the step when he arrived. A pale loop of her hair had escaped its usual pony-tail to frame her face like a caressing hand. She took a deep breath and smiled. 'Welcome home.'

'Thanks. You all right?'

She seemed almost to flinch, but he realised when she spoke that she'd actually been nerving herself to say, 'A lot better for seeing *you*. I hadn't realised you made so much noise until you stopped!'

He *could* have kissed her then, quite easily, but she took a step backwards to let him pass, and the moment passed, too. He didn't notice how clean the hall was until, a few moments later, he saw how clean the kitchen was, although he failed to notice even this until he came face to face with a jug of flowers on the table. *Flowers?* In the *house?* In *Kate's* house? And the table had been scrubbed, the floor and windows polished to a shine. Now this was what he *called* a welcome!

But how to thank her for it without reducing himself to tears? He reversed back into the hall, pretending shock. 'Oh,' he stammered. 'I'm so sorry, madam. I seem to have come to the wrong house.'

She laughed, blushed and told him to shut up, which was easy enough to do, because Inky and Joanna had followed them in, both talking at once to complete various discussions they'd begun in the car. Minutes passed before a lull allowed Kate to ask, 'How was your medical, Smithy?'

Assuming she knew what its purpose had been, he said. 'Fine. It's all decided. I'm mentally and physically scarred for life, permanently disabled, virtually unemployable and—'

And then he saw the appalled look on her face. Inky saw it too and came to the rescue. 'No,' he laughed. 'That's what Smithy told *them*, you dope!' He narrowed his eyes. 'And they seemed to swallow most of it, didn't they, Smithy?'

Kate still looked bewildered.

'The worse it sounds,' Smithy explained, 'the more compensation I'm likely to get.'

'But ... weren't they doctors? Couldn't they tell?'

'Yes. And there's a measure of truth in it all, of course. Just not the *full* measure.'

He hoped.

He also hoped the look on her face had been concern for him, rather than the (quite understandable) fear that she'd always have to take the lion's share of the work. In fact, unless the insurance paid up a sizeable fortune, the chances were that she always would take the lion's share—which gave him yet another reason for doubting they had any sort of future here.

He was never going to be strong enough to do the kind of work Billy had done. Building walls, mixing concrete, ripping out tree roots: all that sort of thing would have to be paid for, with money they didn't have and were never likely to earn. Optimise their profits all they liked, the only way Whitsun Gate could make them rich was if they sold it.

As soon as Jo and Inky had gone, he went to his room to unpack, have a shower and change his clothes. He noticed at once that Kate had cleaned his room, too. *And* put a rosebud in a vase on his dressing table. So much effort, just to welcome him home.

He sat on the edge of his bed for a while, wondering what it could mean. That she'd missed him, yes. That she was glad he was home. But it didn't prove anything, except that she was as lonely as he was. God, how confusing.

He was severely tempted to rush back to the kitchen, grab her in his arms and kiss her, just to see how she'd react. But he couldn't. And it wasn't just because he was afraid of being punched in the teeth. Even if she left his dentistry intact, even if she only went rigid and told him to leave her alone ... No, he couldn't bear that.

His medical had included an interview with a shrink. It was not the first such interview, but it was the first in which Smithy had deemed it necessary to speak about Tess. The accident, after all, had *ended* his marriage, even if, to all intents and purposes, it had been over before ... Before it had begun. Love was dead, but his pride was alive and still bleeding from its wounds. The only trouble was that until he'd actually said it out loud, he hadn't realised how deep those wounds had gone.

So there was only one way he'd ever get around to checking Kate's 'reactions': the day she came into his room, found him stark naked and announced (without flinching), 'I love you. Do what you like with me.'

Pigs would fly sooner.

'So what have I got?' he asked himself while he showered. 'A girl I can't touch, a body I can't stomach and an itch I can't scratch.'

Still, in the fullness of time, he might just have some money.

He also discovered that he was about to have some supper. When he returned to the kitchen, he found the table laid with a bottle of wine, a cold roast chicken, a crusty loaf and a bowl of salad.

'*Kate?*' he teased. 'Is this *you?*'

'No, it's Mavis.'

He nodded. 'Oh, right" he said. 'I thought you looked different. Does Jeff know you're out?'

'Mavis did the food, you idiot. So if you have any complaints—'

'Who me?' He sat down. 'Now when have you ever heard *me* complain? You've forgotten the wine glasses, by the way.'

'Hmph.' Kate said, as if to herself. 'He's back.' The glasses were in the cupboard just behind his chair. Kate reached them down, set one beside his plate and, as she withdrew her hand, allowed it to brush the side of his arm before coming to rest on his shoulder.

'There,' she said. 'Anything else, your lordship?'

It was just an experiment. The opportunity to touch him arose and Kate took it, just to see how she would feel. There hadn't been time to wonder how *he* might feel, although as soon as she felt him stiffen, she knew she'd feared such a thing all along. It was a horrible sensation, like a thousand tiny needles piercing her heart. When she thought of it later, she was amazed to think that so subtle a rejection could hurt so much, for he hadn't exactly flinched, just gone rigid for a moment. And he'd recovered immediately, patting her hand before she could withdraw it, saying, 'Thanks, Kate,' and, 'Come on, let's eat, before the food gets cold.'

'It's cold already.' She tried to sound natural, but her voice failed her and the only thing she could be grateful for was that she was standing behind him, that he couldn't see her face. She was accustomed to blush when things took her by surprise, but this was different: a scalding stain of humiliation she thought would never fade.

Why hadn't she kept her own counsel? Why hadn't she believed (and God knew she'd told herself often enough!) that she didn't matter to him? That she didn't *count!*

'Tell me about your week,' she said. 'How was Pamela?' She walked across the kitchen and ran herself a glass of water, keeping her face averted from him and hearing his reply as if he was still in London, far away. She'd never touch him again.

She forced herself to be calm, to listen—if only distantly—to what he was saying about Pamela, who'd welcomed him like the Prodigal and had then only gradually bored him to tears. 'No spontaneity,' he said. 'That's her trouble.'

Kate hated him then, for a moment. He didn't like spontaneity, either! She'd just tried it, hadn't she?

'She plans everything down to the last word, the last little detail. You were right about her home. It *is* a work of art, in a way. Comfortable, clean, everything just so. It was bliss for a while, after this place. But there's something missing from it, Kate. I don't know what.'

'Dirt?' she suggested grimly.

He laughed. 'There's not much of that here at the moment, is there? Thanks, Kate. It was a lovely welcome home.' He blinked and banged the side of his head as if to clear his ears. *'Almost* better than Mavis's,' he added, wincing.

'At least you can't accuse *her* of lacking spontaneity,' Kate murmured. 'Maybe you're just difficult to please.'

Smithy's eyes widened.

Kate pretended not to notice and helped herself to more salad, deliberately clattering the salad-servers to cover a too lengthy silence.

'Yes,' Smithy said at last, 'maybe I am. I'm a bit ... confused, to tell the truth, Kate. I'm getting so much stronger physically, but it seems ... Well, when I was fighting a purely physical battle I had no energy left to deal with the ... emotional things. That's what depression is, I suppose. When you have too many problems to resolve, you have to put them in a stack and work through them in order: life-threatening things first, life-enhancing things last. Getting my head straight was fairly far down the stack and I think I'm just reaching it.'

Angry as it had made her, Kate realised now that she preferred to think of him as being 'hard to please' (which was positive, at least) rather than confused. She had enough trouble with her own emotions. She couldn't deal with Smithy's, too.

A typically trite remark, 'Well, let me know when you've got past it!' was already forming in her mind when she noticed that she was pushing her food around her plate, arranging little islands of lettuce, celery and green peppers, exactly as her mother always did. So *that* was what it meant! It meant: I can't sort out your feelings when my own are driving me crazy. So I'll just sort out this helpless little salad instead ...

She smiled. It wasn't an especially pleasant smile, so it was no great surprise when Smithy asked faintly, 'Are you laughing at me, Kate?'

'No,' she said. 'At myself. Look what I've just done.'

She tilted her plate to show him. 'This is what my mother does. She's afraid to sort out our differences, so she sorts out her food, instead. And I've done the same thing.'

'Why?'

'Because I'm afraid of your feelings, I suppose. I don't want you to be confused—'

'Neither do I, Kate.'

'No, but that's not the point. You've tried so hard to sort me out, and I'm refusing to do the same for you. It's pure cowardice, Smithy. The salad was easier. It couldn't fight back.'

He grinned and seemed about to say something, but Kate wanted to keep going while her courage was up.

'So what's the worst difficulty?' she demanded quickly. 'Tess?'

Smithy ignored that to ask a question of his own. 'And *have* I sorted you out?'

It was the last thing Kate had expected him to say. And what the hell was the answer? Yes, I'm a normal woman, fully wired to your touch, but if you touch me again I'll scream my head off, because *you* don't love *me*, damn you!

'No,' she said bluntly. 'But I've shown this salad who's boss, so that's progress. I couldn't have done that a year ago, could I?'

Smithy smiled and looked at his hands. 'Hmm,' he said. 'That's the trouble with emotions. They're not mixed like a salad; they're woven together and we have to unravel the whole lot to find the one we're after.

That's why they're so frightening, I suppose. We're afraid that after we've unravelled them all, there'll be nothing left.'

Kate noticed that he'd said 'we', and hoped for a moment that he'd meant his emotions were woven together with her own. But he didn't mean that. All he meant was that he was as lost as she was and as helpless to fight his way clear. It was an idea she hated. She wanted Smithy to be strong so that, when she needed him ...

But if that was the case, what did he really mean to her? No more than the pergola meant to the wisteria: something large and wooden to lean on? Well, wood had to be cared for, too. And since the wisteria didn't care about such things, she supposed the poor, stupid gardener would have to do it.

'It's not even that easy,' she said. 'Because our own emotions are woven into other people's. For instance, I can't unravel myself from my mother unless she unravels herself from Robert. And you, presumably, have to unravel yourself from Tess?'

'No, not really. I think I've done most of that. I didn't love her, you see, Kate. I was infatuated, besotted ... And that's an exercise in fantasy, not love. I saw my solicitor when I was in Town—about the divorce I mean—and it's all over now, bar the formalities. It was a relief.' He covered his eyes as if to soothe a headache. 'But it's left me ...'

Free? Kate asked silently. To love *me?*

He looked up. 'It's left me with a few

problems. First, I don't trust myself not to make the same mistake again. And second, whether I loved her or I didn't, she hurt me, Kate, very badly. So how am I ever going to trust someone else not to do the same?'

Kate smiled wryly. 'I thought that was *my* problem.'

'Hmm,' he sighed. 'It's catching.'

Kate conjured an image of Robert's face, and, as she'd done with every man she'd met since then, laid that image over Smithy's face and told herself, 'He's the same.' But it didn't work. Smithy was *not* the same. And she was not the same as Tess, but how was she to convince him of that?

She'd lived with him for more than a year now and at some time during the past few months had almost ceased to 'see' him as a physical presence and begun instead simply to 'feel' that he was there (or, during the past week, feel that he wasn't). His short-cropped hair, his limp, his walking stick, the scar on his face ... Yes, she'd been aware of them all, but they'd slipped into the background somehow, ceased to matter. It was as if his body was ... well, just a pergola, supporting the twining branches of his personality and the blossoms of his soul. He was beautiful. No matter how damaged the supporting woodwork, *he* was beautiful.

But did she love him? She didn't know.

'But if you know how it feels to be infatuated, you'll recognise it again,' she said, 'and know it isn't love.'

'Maybe,' he smiled. 'But how will I know if

it is? *That's* the question.'

Kate sighed and looked at her hands. Yes, that was the question. But how did one know anything one hadn't seen before? There were reference books for most things: rare plants, birds and insects, strange words one found in a novel. But you had to take love on trust, and that, it seemed, was a thing neither of them could do.

She heard a small—but remarkably unpleasant —voice in the back of her mind, saying, 'Good! I don't want him to trust anyone else! I don't want him to love anyone! I want him to stay with me!'

And if that was love, she was Lady Godiva. Yet did any woman who loved a man want to see him happy with someone else? No. Love was jealous, love was selfish, love *was* akin to hate.

'Perhaps you're forgetting your own advice,' she said. 'About having too many expectations of love, I mean. And maybe it's nothing like your expectations. Mags loved Billy, after all, but you'd never have known it, would you?'

'They knew it,' Smithy said. 'They were like—'

'Two sides of the same coin. That's what Mags told me once. We were talking about feminism, not love, but ... She said feminism would never get anywhere until it accepted that men and women were two sides of the same coin: different motifs, same value. And she said they hadn't any value at all if they were divided from each other.'

Smithy's eyes widened. 'Did she say that?'

Kate smiled. 'Mmm. I think she was trying to tell me something.'

'But you didn't believe her?'

I believe her now, Kate thought. But she couldn't say it. She couldn't tell him. She was a different kind of coin. She didn't count.

Chapter Sixteen

Smithy bought his car the following week. It was a carefully informed choice: large, solid, safe and second-hand. He'd visited a few dealers while he was in London, had asked all the relevant questions, done all the appropriate worrying and now (with a little help from Phil), had simply chosen the one he wanted and put his money down. He'd driven automatics before. He knew how it was done. The only thing he was still not certain of was that he dared to do it.

It didn't matter. He could try it out in the car park for a few days before risking life and limb on the roads. And, if he didn't get the hang of it, he could sell it again without losing much money. Pride was another matter, but he deemed even that worth the risk of buying—or trying to buy—his freedom. To go out on his own, on a whim. To drive a few miles down the road to buy himself a pair of socks, or to call in at the Royal Oak for a drink. That was all he needed.

He did not need Kate to turn pale and

whisper, 'What d'you mean, you've bought it?' as if, instead of buying a car, he'd sold Whitsun Gate and rendered her homeless.

'They're delivering on Monday,' he said, lifting a questioning eyebrow for a clue to the source of her dismay.

She attempted a smile. 'Oh ... nice.'

'Oh, nuts,' he mimicked flatly. 'What's wrong?'

'Nothing.'

She attempted to leave, as in days of yore, but Smithy was quicker on his pins than he'd been in days of yore and he managed to fill the doorway before she reached it.

'Give,' he said.

Kate scowled at him under her eyebrows. 'There's nothing wrong,' she said. 'Why should there be? It's your money; you can buy what you like with it.'

'Quite. And it hasn't broken the bank. We won't have to starve. So what's—?' He laughed suddenly, remembering one of the many unfinished conversations they'd had at that meeting of hers. He'd offered to pay for the new greenhouse and she'd said, 'You can't! What about your car?' But the car had scarcely been mentioned since then and the greenhouse had. So what was she saying now? *You can't! What about my greenhouse?*

Except in regard to the little they mutually earned and mutually spent, Smithy had always been loath to discuss money with her. It was one of the mistakes he'd made with Tess (probably one of the reasons she'd married him) and had vowed never to make again. It wasn't only that, however. Until he'd agreed, last week, to surrender the London house to Tess, he hadn't been certain that his capital (which was a fair bit more than Mags had left him) was safe. He hadn't been able to depend on it. But in fact the house was 'all' he would lose and he might well have recouped some of that had he been prepared to put up a fight. But fighting took time and if he'd waited he might have lost a hell of a lot more.

'Don't worry,' he teased Kate now. 'I can still afford the greenhouse.'

Kate's eyes flashed. 'Half the greenhouse,' she corrected him stubbornly. 'We're partners, remember? And that wasn't what ...' Her face reddening, she turned away. 'Oh, let me out of here, will you? I've got work to do.'

'Right.' He cleared the doorway and Kate marched out with her nose in the air.

So if the greenhouse wasn't worrying her, what was? The fear that he'd kill himself in the car? Or kill someone else? Or go off joy-riding while she did all the work? Whatever, she wasn't going to tell him about it, so the best thing he could do was try to reassure her on all points and hope she'd get over it.

He still wasn't happy to let her contribute to the greenhouse, however. He'd already told her that, but she didn't want to know. She kept insisting they were partners. *Equal* partners. Nothing he could say would convince her that if he paid for the greenhouse, he'd merely be balancing what he saw (and she refused to see)

273

as a gross inequality of labour.

'Tell you what,' he said, the next time he saw her. 'I'll loan you your half of the greenhouse—'

'No need. I can—'

'Listen, will you? I'll loan you your half and you can pay me back from your salary over the next two years. That'll leave your capital intact, so that if a disaster happens in the meantime—'

'What disaster?'

'Any disaster. That's the whole point, Kate. *Any* disaster can happen. I'm the proof of it, aren't I?'

She smiled. 'And what if another disaster happens to you? Won't you need the money you've loaned me?'

'Maybe,' he laughed. 'But then I'll just call in *your* capital, of which there'll be a whole lot more, because it'll be earning interest on the full amount rather than just half of it! See? Safer all round!'

She stood with a hand on her hip, looking straight at him, her eyes narrowed thoroughly. It was an unusual stance for her, although he didn't notice it at the time except, subliminally, to appreciate her figure and the way her jeans fitted at the crotch: not well enough to reveal anything, just well enough to hint that there was something worth revealing.

'No, it's too neat,' she concluded at last. 'But thanks, Smithy. I'll think about it.'

'Too neat for *what?*' he gasped. 'Are you suggesting I'm ripping you off?'

'No. I'm suggesting you're being too generous.' She slanted him a coy, almost lecherous
little smile. 'It hadn't occurred to me that you
might be ripping me off, but that's something
to think about, too, now you mention it.'

The sheer cheek of it was a delight. He
growled, 'Aaargh!' and aimed his stick in the
direction of her behind, but it wasn't until she
laughed and ran off that he realised quite *why*
it was a delight. She'd actually been flirting
with him!

She'd done it very prettily, too. Not so much
thrusting herself at him as setting herself out for
his inspection.

'Like it? You can have it. No, you can't. Well,
maybe you can, but only if you can catch it.'

Little monkey! He knew that game. He knew
how to win it, too. Next time she came near
him, he'd ignore her.

The pleasure of this new development stayed
with him as he made his way to the ticket office:
an antiquated garden shed, heavily wreathed
with a Clematis 'Lasustern', its radiant blue
flowers reflecting a late-summer sky. But the
pleasure faded. He was too old for this kind
of lark, too sad and too jaded. She needed
someone young and whole, as innocent and
beautiful as she was. Not him.

'Cheer up, young man!'

The woman was a retired nursing officer (he
could tell by her sensible shoes, her starched
frock and her jolly, no-nonsense voice, which
had been 'cheering up' the terminal cases for
time out of mind). 'It's a beautiful day,' she

informed him briskly, 'and you have a wonderful job.'

'The pay's terrible.' He smiled.

'Hooh!' She slapped his arm. 'Come on, come on! Life is what you make it!'

He sold her a ticket and a booklet of plant names, told her where to find the ladies' loo and the tearooms. But as she marched down the drive, busily looking for someone else to cheer up, he saw in her the living proof that she was wrong. Life isn't what you make it. You are what life makes you.

Kate didn't know what was happening to her. She never *had* known; her life had always seemed to be a shifting sand of confusions and insecurities in which the garden was her only solid base, the only thing she was sure of. But this was different. This was worse.

It had begun on the day Smithy returned from London. Or maybe the night before when, knowing that he was due home (but not sure that he'd actually come), her nerves, stretched to their limits by an eternal week of waiting for him, had torn into feathery little atoms, like a dandelion clock, and blown away on the wind. She wasn't herself any more.

She could remember what kind of person she'd been and how she'd behaved, but being that person and (more importantly) behaving like her, didn't seem to come naturally any more. She had to keep asking herself, 'How does Kate do this? What does she say? How does she walk, talk, eat, read the newspaper?

How does she get through the day?'

And, when she knew the answers to these questions (which wasn't often), she then had to *mimic* herself—her old self—and only hope to do it convincingly enough to make her seem the same. But it hardly ever worked. The first time it had happened, when Smithy had come home, she'd wanted to run to him (as Mavis had done; lucky Mavis) and grab him in her arms and kiss him all over. But Kate didn't do that kind of thing. Kate was cool. Kate was dry. Kate didn't even like touching, let alone hugging, kissing and going crazy with joy. No, Kate would just turn, smile and say, 'Hi, Smithy. Had a good week?'

Hi, Smithy. Had a good week? That was easy enough. But what did she do with her hands while she said it? How did she move? Did she walk towards him or hang back? And how was she to smile, when she wanted to laugh and cry and tell him she'd missed him so much she'd thought she'd die of it? The conflict between these two extremes had so paralysed her, she'd probably have stood there a week had not Inky helped her out. But poor old Smithy had had a lousy welcome home. She hadn't even said hello until it was too late to matter.

Things had improved a bit after that. She'd gathered herself together, held herself very tightly and determined never to let go again. But something had loosened her hold. His smile, his voice, his hands, the tilt of his head ... Fragments. Tumbling and reforming, like the tiny coloured scraps in a kaleidoscope, whose every movement made a new pattern: beautiful and mysterious—and utterly bewildering.

She felt so *happy!* She felt so sad and afraid. But the worst thing of all was her energy. Drained to its dregs while he was away, it had come back with such force she felt she could do anything: dig the entire seven acres in a day, paint the house, clean the drains ... Yet at the same time she seemed unable to do anything very much; dig a bit, weed a bit, prune something, stake something, weed a bit more. With a garden as large and as complex as Whitsun Gate, you needed a system to keep it all at its best. Kate had had a system. Where had it gone?

She wasn't sleeping too well, either. She had no appetite. If she didn't know what was wrong, she'd think she was ill. But she did know. She did know. And in those few sane moments when she could think straight, she knew she'd much rather be ill. There was no future in loving Smithy. Mavis had been wrong about their being equals. He was beautiful, free, a normal and increasingly healthy young man. Just give him that bloody car of his and he'd be off. A bit at a time, perhaps, but *off.*

'Going to a party, tonight, Kate. Don't wait up.'

'I'll be away for the weekend, Kate. Sure you can manage?'

Sod him. And sod *her:* the bitch with the dangly earrings he was sure to meet pretty soon ...

'I'm bringing a friend home for dinner,

Kate. Name of Jezebel. Make yourself scarce, will you?'

While she would rather be asleep, these imagined things he said became lengthy imagined conversations, showdowns, fights. She'd actually found herself crying once or twice, as if they'd really happened. Then, when she finally fell asleep (and woke up late and befuddled), she'd think they *had* happened, that she'd completely lost her grip and told Smithy she loved him. And that *he'd* said, 'Oh, come on! Who are you trying to kid? You'll never be any good for that kind of thing!'

It wore off ... as soon as she laid eyes on him it wore off, when he smiled, when he reached for his coffee and stroked his finger, idly, along the rim of the cup.

'You're looking tired, Kate. Anything I can do to help?'

Yep! Tell me you're crazy about me. That's all! I'll take it from there!

'No, I'm fine.'

She actually resented the gardens now, just for keeping her away from him. They lived almost their entire lives on the same patch of ground, yet none of their various duties brought them together. When he was walking the gardens, she was stuck in plant sales. When she was at the gate, he was in the greenhouse, multiplying plants. She found herself stretching breakfast and supper to their outer limits, just to be with him, to watch him and listen. She hadn't collected the litter for the best part of a week and had now actually heard the dread

279

words, 'What's that little red flower? Oh ... it's a chocolate wrapper.'

It was like being possessed by devils: wicked, grinning little fiends who'd taken away all she knew or cared about (her own pride first among them) and put chaos in their place. Pride in an immaculate garden, for example, made her decide, there and then, to collect up the litter. She needed only a plastic bucket and a rubber glove, both of which were in their usual place in the toolshed. But the devils made her take only the bucket. They told her she couldn't find the glove and that, if she tried hard enough, she *might* find she'd left it in the ticket office, where Smithy was.

The sheer childishness of such a ploy made her blush, for what was the use of it? How would it help? 'Have I left my glove in there, Smithy?'

'No.'

'Oh.'

But it might be more than that, mightn't it? He might be having a quiet half hour and want to chat. Or she could *make* him chat; discuss his offer of a loan, tease him a little, make him laugh, test him, challenge him, find out—somehow—how he *really* felt about her. Sometimes he seemed to like her more than she dared to hope. Sometimes his eyes were so warm when he looked at her, his smile so sweet ... *Sweet?* God, that proved she was going mad! Smithy's smile was *never* sweet: his scar made sure of that! And yet she loved even his scar. She could see beyond it, to the sweetness of his soul.

But she couldn't see that glove ... Now what had she been doing the last time she had it? Picking up litter in the drive? Ah! Maybe she'd left it in the ticket office!

'Good!' the little devils laughed. 'Go for it, kid!'

She went for it by the quickest route possible, which meant breaking one more of her long-held rules: never walk where you don't want the visitors to walk. The wrong way around the one-way system, through the gate marked 'No Entry', up and over the daffodil bank and (worse yet) through the gap in the eleagnus hedge which years of careful pruning and training had almost managed to close. She paused before forcing her way through it, listening for the sound of voices, hearing none and knowing (oh, bliss!) that Smithy was alone.

In fact he wasn't there. He'd walked up to the top of the drive and was leaning on the gate, doing his exercises. He was standing on his weaker leg, stretching the other, flexing his knee and his ankle as if—Kate recognised the motion—he was operating the brake-pedal of a car.

She called out, 'I hope you're wearing your seat-belt!' and took a businesslike step towards the ticket office to begin the 'search' for her glove.

'Seat belt?' Smithy grinned. 'I'm wearing my crash-helmet!'

She laughed and, on the same breath, whispered a curse as a young couple crossed the car park towards him. There wouldn't be time to talk. She couldn't hang around while he sold them their tickets; it would be too obvious when all she needed to do was dive into the ticket office, look for her glove and dive out again.

Although she had never consciously assessed the visitors the way Smithy did, guessing their ages and occupations, the size of their bank-balances and of their gardens, it was something she'd been *unconsciously* doing for the past six years. Even without seeing them except from the corner of her eye, Kate knew everything worth knowing about the approaching couple. They were smart, well-off, thirty-ish and in love (she could tell from the way they were walking, hand in hand, he looking down at her, she up at him). For this latter fact alone, Kate hated their guts and, as Smithy turned to greet them, she darted the man a resentful glance and whispered, 'Oh, clear off, damn you.'

A second later she was inside the ticket office, crouching under the bench, shuddering with horror. *Thirty-ish?* He was fifty, the bastard, and in lust, not in love with his adulterous companion! Teeth chattering, eyes squeezed shut to ease the sting of tears, Kate curled herself up as tight as she would go, leaving only her ears exposed to the obscenity that was her stepfather.

'No,' he replied to Smithy's usual question. 'No, we've never been here before, have we, darling? Heard of it, of course. Live just up the road, actually, in Bath ...'

They seemed to stand there for hours.

282

Robert asked if Smithy owned the place (almost everyone asked him the same question, although no one had ever asked Kate) and, when Smithy said that he did, 'with my partner', Kate was reminded of yet another loathsome element of her stepfather's character. He made judgements about people of the 'better or worse than me' variety and, depending on the way his decision went, he either patronised or sucked up, changing his voice and his attitude to suit.

As shocked, sick and helpless as she felt, Kate was nevertheless amazed when, in a voice clearly intended to mimic Smithy's, Robert said, 'Beautiful old house you've got. Georgian, isn't it?' and went on paying compliments until another group of visitors arrived and his voice, at last, was displaced by others.

Long minutes passed before Kate dared to move. She didn't even think, except of the pain in her chest as her heart-beat eased from racing panic to a hard, squelching thud. She straightened her legs and attempted to straighten her spine, but she had no strength, no will to find her feet again. Had she been given a choice, she would have stayed there forever and quietly died.

A shadow fell across her. Smithy gasped, 'What the—? What the *hell* are you doing?'

He both looked and sounded outraged, as if hiding on the floor of the ticket office was something she did every day and he had long grown weary of.

'What's the *matter* with you? What are you *doing* there?'

'I'm—I'm ...' But explaining herself was more than Kate could bear to do. She hid her face in her hands and wept.

He thought at first ... he didn't think at first. The shock of finding anyone—let alone Kate—lying helpless on the floor of the ticket office had driven all sense from his mind. A tramp, a drunk, a drug addict? No, it was Kate; and Kate was ill, Kate was dying, Kate was lying on the floor of the ticket office, too weak to stand.

It was sheer terror that had made him swear at her. Her face was so white, her eyes so dazed, her body as limp-jointed as a doll's. It was almost a relief when she started to cry: if she had strength enough for that, it couldn't be too critical.

'Kate,' he urged more gently. 'What's wrong? Are you ill?'

'No!' She curled up on herself and sobbed.

Smithy was suddenly angry. Angry with her for scaring him so badly; angry with himself for being helpless to help her. He couldn't even pick her up. He certainly couldn't get down there with her. And—damn it—now there were more visitors to deal with! He stepped outside and slammed the door, meeting the newcomers at the gate, talking and walking with them to the foot of the drive, for fear they might hear her crying.

What the hell was wrong with her? She'd been fine five minutes ago, *laughing*, for Christ's sake! Come to think of it, she'd disappeared straight afterwards: one minute there, the next minute gone. He'd thought she'd been quicker on her feet than usual, but it hadn't occurred to him ...

He opened the door. She was standing up now, thank God, and had dried her tears. But she wouldn't look at him. Without actually turning her face to the wall, she'd turned as far from him as she could go. She was in trouble, certainly. But what trouble?

'Kate? What's going on, here? You can tell me in your own time, but I ... insist you tell me.'

'My stepfather just came in,' she said flatly.

Smithy did a rapid re-shuffle of the most recent visitors. A mother and daughter. An ancient married couple who looked as if they might die before they reached the Herb Garden. A middle-aged Romeo with a girl young enough to be his ... daughter.

'Dark guy?' he said. 'Polo-necked sweater, tweed jacket?' He'd summed *him* up. He'd known the woman on his arm was not his wife; he'd noticed how the faint Midlands accent (scarcely noticeable, but Smithy was hard to fool) had subtly switched to Old School Tie; he'd noticed the rather less subtle way his manner had changed, from being all over his girlfriend to being all over Smithy. Not an uncommon type; Smithy had met hundreds like him and knew one thing that was common to them all: they could be knocked down with the prod of a fingertip. Any fingertip. Kate's included. And she'd let *him* ruin her life? Shit, it was like drowning in a puddle!

285

He felt like shaking her, but was too furious to try it. Instead—and very quietly, for fear another group of visitors should arrive—he said, 'Do you know why vicious, odious little men like your stepfather manage to do so much damage, Kate? Because stupid, craven little people like you and your mother *let* them, that's why!'

She closed her eyes.

'This is *your* property, Kate! If you don't want him here—' He threw a handful of coins on the counter '—give him his money back and tell him to get out!'

'I can't!' she wailed. 'I can't bear to look at him!'

Had anyone asked, Smithy would have said his temper had snapped some minutes ago, but he would have been wrong. It snapped now.

'And I can't bear to look at *you*,' he said. 'For God's sake, Kate, grow up. Before you make yourself as contemptible as he is!'

Again he slammed the door shut and hurried to the top of the drive, where he could lean on the gate to get a grip on his temper. It was true that he couldn't bear to look at her, although not for the reasons he'd implied. She was such a *lovely* girl; not just in the physical sense (that too, of course) but ... well, for all her failings, she was ... God, he could kick her from here to kingdom come! She was worth ten of that slimy little bastard!

He swallowed, filled his lungs and exhaled very slowly, aware that he'd just done something very wrong, very cruel. He wasn't angry with Kate. He wasn't even angry with her stepfather.

286

He was angry with himself, aware that if he'd had half the courage he'd told Kate she lacked, he'd have chased after the guy himself and kicked *him* from here to kingdom come!

But you needed two good legs for that sort of thing and, lacking them, you had to use your sense instead. Set Mavis on him then?

He shrugged, smiled and turned back down the drive to apologise to Kate. But the ticket office was empty. She had gone.

Chapter Seventeen

Kate hadn't known she'd been in a state of hysteria until Smithy had cured her of it. He'd used the usual method—in its metaphorical version, at least—a good, hard slap in the face and one more for luck. The truth. The absolute truth. Painful and shocking as it had been, it had been a relief on a par with extracting a splinter from a festering wound. There. All better. All cold and quiet and strong inside. She could do anything now.

She crept out of the ticket office and went back the way she had come: through the gap in the eleagnus, down the daffodil bank. Ignoring the entrance to the Herb Garden—the first part of the visitors' route—she jumped over the box hedge to wait for Robert on the lawn. She knew almost to the minute how long he would take to reach her. Herb Garden, topiary lawn, the

287

woods, the rockery and the Rose Walk. A keen gardener might take an hour to get through it. Robert, fifteen minutes at most.

She wanted a good, long view of him; time to steel herself for the confrontation before he saw her. Laura had told her, years ago, that she'd never told Robert where Kate was living, and although Kate hadn't believed it, she believed it now. He wouldn't be here if he knew. What would he do when he saw her? What would he say? Bluff. That was the answer to both questions. He'd bluff his way out of it. If she'd *let* him.

'Because stupid, craven little people like you and your mother *let* him ...'

True. True on all points.

'I can't bear to look at you ...'

Kate smiled and lifted her chin, recalling just why she'd gone to the ticket office in the first place. Something to do with finding out how Smithy *really* felt about her? Well, she'd succeeded in that, at least. It didn't hurt too badly at the moment, although she knew it would, later, when she'd dealt with Robert. Once she'd dealt with him, she could deal with anything.

Robert and his floozy ... holding hands in the Rose Walk, he leaning over her, smiling into her eyes, fashioning himself on one of Mavis's famous ear-oles: the big, handsome strong guy rendered helpless by love. He was only five foot seven, so if his girlfriend was taking the bait, she was a whole lot dafter than Kate had ever been!

But Kate had been daft enough. Stupid, in fact. Stupid *and* craven; she mustn't forget that. Or let it happen again, although her heart rate had resumed its 'squelching thud' mode of action, leaping into her throat, depriving her of air. Breathe, she told herself. Deep and slow ... If you let him beat you now, you're lost forever.

He laughed, tossing back his head at something the woman had said. Then he saw Kate, stared at her for a moment and turned away. But she hadn't changed *too* much since he'd seen her last. He looked again.

Although almost the full length of the lawn divided them, Kate's eyesight was quite good enough to inform her that his face turned red ... grey ... and red again before he laughed and shouted, 'Kate!' hurrying towards her with his arms outstretched, as if meeting her from the airport after a long trip abroad. Bluff ...

'Kate! Kate, is it you? What are—?'

'What am *I* doing here?'

Although she'd brought 'blood chilling' down to a fine art, it was not an art she'd practised just recently and she was relieved to know it still worked. Something in the eyes, something in the voice? Whatever, it stopped Robert in his tracks. It didn't quite wipe the smile from his face, but that would go soon.

'I live here,' she said icily. 'This is my property—'

'*Yours?*'

'—and I want you and your girlfriend out of here, before your breath blights the roses.' She pointed to a small wicket gate, clearly marked 'No Entry'.

'That's the way out.'

'*Girlfriend?*' He laughed, implying—as he always had—that Kate was a silly little thing, too young and innocent to realise how very lucky she was to know him, to have the mark of his hands on her body and the taste of his tongue in her mouth. He shepherded the woman to his side. She was scarcely much older than Kate, *and* as stupid, *and* as craven. But she had more sense than Robert had: she was scared.

'Allow me to introduce my secretary,' he said. 'My *secretary*, Kate—Hannah Kenny.' He shook his head, gently chiding. 'Your mother knows—'

'My mother knows what she wants to know,' Kate said, her voice so icy it could have frozen a charging bull elephant. 'But I'm sure your *secretary* is more perceptive.' She darted a poisoned smile in that lady's direction. 'Robert is my stepfather,' she said pleasantly. 'When I was fourteen, he—'

'Let's get out of here!'

Vicious ... The word hadn't meant very much to her when Smithy had said it. 'Odious' had seemed nearer the mark. But vicious was precisely how Robert looked in the second before he turned away, grabbing the woman's arm to return the way he had come.

Kate darted around them, baring her teeth to point again at the gate. '*That* way.'

The latch on the gate had a tendency to stick and it gave Kate a certain pleasure to see

290

Robert fumbling with it, his hands shaking in his haste to get away. She'd meant to give him his money back, but it didn't seem appropriate now, and it was beneath her dignity to make the melodramatic gesture and throw it in his face.

She gave them a good start before following them. The girl had silly shoes on and could barely keep up with Robert's pace, but Kate could. Her stride outpaced each one of theirs so that, although she never advanced within spitting distance (which was also beneath her dignity), she knew Robert was afraid she'd overtake them and finish what she'd begun. *It's called child abuse now, but I didn't know that, then ...*

Now all that was left was to get them past Smithy without involving him further. It was not beyond Robert to call him to his aid, to protest his innocence, to call Kate a liar. And she knew she couldn't bear that. Smithy despised her ...

For God's sake, grow up. Before you make yourself as contemptible as he is!

Before? Oh, well, there was hope in that ... of a kind.

It was almost four o'clock. A small crowd of the afternoon's visitors was milling around in plant sales where another of the part-timers, a retired doctor's wife, was holding the fort. Two of her satisfied customers, their arms full of plants, decided to leave the premises just as Robert turned into the drive, coming between him and Kate and giving her a sudden jolt of real fear. If Robert decided on a showdown with Smithy now, he'd have witnesses, damn him!

As Robert came level with him, Smithy was looking up the drive, not down it, but suddenly he turned, smiled over Robert's head and said to the following couple, 'Good Lord, you've bought us out!'

It was masterly. Not necessarily deliberate (he hadn't *seemed* to know what was happening), but masterly just the same. He'd robbed Robert of his audience and left him with no option but to keep going. When Kate walked by a moment later, Smithy had his back to her and was deep in conversation: 'Oh, you'll love that one. It'll take a year or two to settle, but give it a good, sunny spot ...'

Had he needed to turn his back? Could he still not bear to look at her? And what the hell did it matter? She'd been kidding herself anyway. She was worse than Mavis, or at best exactly the same: wanting something she couldn't have, if only because—even if she could get it—she wouldn't have a clue what to do with it.

She stood at the gate to watch Robert to his car. The girl, clearly in a hurry to make herself scarce, dived in on the passenger's side, but Robert turned and sent Kate a look she did not, for a moment, understand. His eyes were wide, his mouth sagging with ... fear, yes, but more than that, worse than that. He looked utterly bewildered.

He reversed the car at speed, turned at speed and fled, spitting gravel, leaving Kate to frown at the space where he'd been. He'd looked *bewildered*, as if ... as if he hadn't known what he'd done to her. Or forgotten it ...

She felt the blood leave her face as if someone had pulled the plug, leaving her cold, weak and trembling for the second time in an hour. Forgotten it? She ran through their meeting in her mind, putting new interpretations on everything that had happened. His face had changed colour when he'd recognised her, but not for the reasons she'd imagined. He'd thought his *girlfriend* was the issue! Until she'd enlightened him.

He'd *forgotten!* He'd given her all these years of agony and forgotten all about it! It would have been funny; she could have laughed ... if it hadn't been such a tragedy. He'd ruined her life. And *forgotten* it? Yes, why not? Because she wasn't the only one. Ruining people's lives was something he did for fun, like a joyrider squashing hedgehogs, knowing nothing and caring less for the carnage he left behind him. 'Oh, come *on!* What's your problem, Kate? It's only a bit of fun!'

The visitors were leaving, passing her at the gate without seeming to notice her. 'Best chocolate cake I've ever tasted—'

'Only one pound fifty! I'd have paid twice that at the garden centre!'

'God, I wish it was mine! Fancy *living* here, Mum, waking up every morning and seeing ...'

'*Such* a nice man. I wonder what happened to his leg?'

Smithy.

The colour returned to Kate's face in a deep flush of shame. *For God's sake, grow up!*

Yes, it was high time she did. But how?

Smithy could scarcely believe she'd done it. Even when she'd disappeared from the ticket office, he hadn't for a moment suspected she'd been taking his advice. He'd thought she'd run into the house to hide under the bed, or maybe to watch her unwanted visitor from the upstairs windows until the coast was clear and he had gone.

But she'd thrown the bugger out! Scared the life out of him, too. Boy, the look on his *face!* And the look on hers ... so calm, so cold and dignified. A queen couldn't have done it better.

She was falling apart a bit now, poor kid, holding on to the gate as if her legs had given out. But that was just the after-shock. Give her a few minutes ...

Smithy needed a few minutes, too. He'd said some pretty harsh things to her and would have to choose the right way to smooth them over. He wouldn't apologise. Harsh as he'd been, he clearly hadn't been wrong. People were always much stronger than they imagined, but they usually needed to be challenged into proving it, recognising it. And if he'd done that for Kate, he had nothing to apologise for. But he did have some 'smoothing over' to do and, short of kissing her ('Get your dirty mitts off me!'), or calling her a brave girl (Patronising bastard!'), he hadn't a clue how to do it.

Kate turned around at last. She stared at him for a moment, yawned, hooked her elbows over the gate and said, 'I'm starving. What's for supper?'

'Chicken.' He smiled, knowing from the exaggerated ease of her pose (did she know how it pushed her breasts forward?) and the languor of her tone that she'd been planning the entire move for the past five minutes. 'If you'll finish up here, I'll get started on it, shall I?'

'Okay.' She unhooked her elbows and held out her hand for the cash-belt without meeting his eyes. 'I don't seem to have done anything useful today.'

'Oh, I dunno ...'

'I meant to clear up the litter, but—'

'I thought you'd cleared up a pretty large chunk of it.'

She looked at her feet and went on looking at them. Guessing that it was a choice between a foot-inspection or crying her eyes out, Smithy made a tactful departure, returning to the house via the tearooms to see if Mavis had any cake left that might do duty as a pudding. Fresh fruit and dark chocolate aside, he had no taste for sweet things, but Kate could eat anything and, since he couldn't give her the cuddle she needed (or did he mean the cuddle *he* needed?), the least he could do was feed her.

'Got any chocolate cake left, Mavis?'

'Ooh!' she squealed. 'What'll you give me for it?'

A quick scan of the counter had already informed him that there was nothing left, save a sad-looking triangle of treacle tart.

'A dirty weekend in Minehead?' he suggested idly.

She laughed and pretended to search the cupboards for the required cake. 'Oh, bugger,' she hissed. 'Outa bloody luck!' She performed a lewd wink. 'Tell you what, ask me again tomorrow and I'll make one special and keep it by!'

He took the treacle tart, reflecting, as he carried it back to the house, that Mavis had changed a bit since their 'first kiss'. She seemed less overwhelming somehow. Softer, less aggressive. But as he reviewed their most recent exchange, the shrieks and the curses were much the same as they'd ever been, so maybe *he'd* changed. Become more tolerant, perhaps? More perceptive of her well-padded vulnerabilities? Or ... He threw back his head and heaved a sigh. Or so bloody hungry for love even Mavis would do?

'More tolerant,' he told himself. But he had a nasty suspicion he was lying.

He didn't see Kate again until she came down from her shower, almost two hours later. 'I've picked up the litter,' she said. 'At last.'

'Find anything interesting?'

'A pork pie with maggots, a screwdriver, a white lace glove, and about thirty toffee wrappers, all dropped in the same place.'

'What place?'

'The woods.'

Smithy laughed. 'Someone cheating on a diet?' He emptied the vegetables into a serving dish, turned to put it on the table and caught

Kate with a look in her eyes he'd never seen before. It reminded him of something, but she looked away before he could place it. 'Pity' was the first word to come to mind, but it couldn't have been that. He still had a few pitying looks from the visitors when they saw him hobbling about with his stick, but Kate had seen him on two sticks—and in agony—and had never seemed to pity him. So ...?

'How are you feeling now?' he asked, hoping for a clue.

'Still starving.'

He ate a little. Kate ate a lot and at a speed which made him think she'd jump up and go before he could announce the treacle tart.

'Manners,' he chided dryly. 'You're not in the Workhouse now, you know.'

'Don't be so bossy. You're not in the Army now, you know.' Her smile, though it scarcely lifted the corners of her mouth, had a radiance which almost brought tears to his eyes. Was she cured?

'I know that's not as good as my not being in the Workhouse, but—'

'What's not?'

'I mean you *liked* the Army; it was your life and you've lost it. But this needn't be so bad, need it? Most people live on housing estates, or in narrow little streets with no trees. We've got so much, Smithy. I've always loved the—no, I haven't. I do *now*, of course, but I never really knew ... Well, yes, I *did*, I suppose ...'

Smithy recalled that he'd never liked women who yak, but it suddenly seemed quite pleasant.

Intriguing. She'd get to the point if he let her run on.

Kate sighed. 'When I was at school—after Robert, this was, not before—I wanted to go to University. I didn't want anything else, not instead or beyond it. I wanted to do History, or maybe English ... But really, I suppose, I just wanted to get away without actually *running* away.'

She stopped, stared at the remains of her meal and forked up a small sliver of chicken, which she chewed as if it was the whole bird, plus feathers.

Smithy didn't say a word, so it was a shock when she added gruffly, 'Don't *rush* me. I'll *get* there.'

But pride ever goeth before a fall. She began to cry, silently, like a soldier, gritting her teeth while the tears slid down her cheeks, checked only by a stroking finger.

'Sorry,' she whispered.

'Don't be. I cry too, sometimes.'

'Not into your chicken, though.'

'No. Too much salt ruins it. It's better with peanuts.'

She laughed and blew her nose. 'Where was I?'

'Wanting to go to University.'

'Ah, yes. Well, I ran away instead and came here because I couldn't think of anyone else who might have me. I didn't know Mags all that well, but of all the people I knew, she seemed the most likely to ... believe me.'

'And she did?'

Kate nodded. 'At least, she never said she didn't. But she was pretty frank about wanting help in the garden and I wanted a home, so—' She shrugged. 'That was that. Education over.'

Smithy said nothing.

Kate added impatiently, 'And don't tell me it *wasn't* over! I know that now. I didn't then. I thought he'd ruined my life, taken *everything* from me!'

She glared at him. Smithy smiled, wondering why—without a scrap of help from his side—she was turning it into an argument.

'And then,' Kate went on, 'today, when he ...'

She bit her lip to keep back the tears.

'Turned up here?' Smithy prompted quietly.

'No. When he went. I felt very calm. Things slipped into place. I thought, "You've ruined my life," but it didn't ring true any more. I was quite peeved about it, to tell the truth. I *wanted* to be angry, so I tried to think where I'd be now if I'd taken my degree. And do you know where I was?'

'No. Where?'

'In a little flat in Birmingham. In a street without any trees.'

Smithy laughed. With surprise at first, but that changed to an almost searing joy which, even as he laughed, made him want to weep. She'd never said anything so positive, so deep, so aware. She was thinking! She was learning! At last!

'Why Birmingham?' he demanded, still laughing.

'Oh, that doesn't matter. It could be London or Manchester, anywhere really. The important thing is my *age*, you see. I'm twenty-two, only a year out of college and in my first job. I don't know what it is—teacher, banker, librarian—but I know it's the bottom rung of the ladder, because your first job always is, isn't it?'

He watched her. She had been smiling, but now her face tightened into a shy, defensive mask. It wasn't an expression she'd ever assumed before. When Kate was on the defensive, her eyes blanked out so that she seemed to be saying nothing beyond, 'Closed for lunch'. Her eyes were saying a hell of a lot more than that now: 'I'm desperate; I'm afraid; *please* don't hurt me!'

As if he would.

'Go on,' he said. 'You're in a flat in Birmingham, in your first job ...'

'And I have a boyfriend,' she whispered. 'The same as me. Just starting out and ... and dreaming. Of where we might end up in ten or twenty years' time.'

Her expression changed again. She was stern now, her eyes hard and challenging. 'And do you know where we end up? In our dreams?'

The challenge was real. He couldn't just say, 'No. Where?' as before. She wanted him to think about it, although thinking wasn't strictly necessary. She'd given him enough clues, as had quite a few of their visitors, as did the Sunday newspapers week after week, not to mention the countless glossy magazines one saw stacked in the newsagent's. In short, a large proportion of

300

the population of Britain dreamed of 'ending up' at Whitsun Gate, or somewhere like it. An old country house, a lovely garden ...

Smithy had never dreamed of ending up anywhere. For him, 'ending up' had been more of a nightmare than a dream; something he'd prefer not to think about. His dreams had mostly been about travelling—either through the world in the physical sense or through his mind: putting his weaknesses behind him as he marched forward into his strengths.

Nevertheless, he *had* 'ended up'. With a hell of a bump, too, against something that had often felt like a stone wall. No way over, no way under ... no way out. True, he *had* travelled, through his mind. He was travelling now, although the road was a little bumpy and there was much more to think about than his own destination. Kate's journey was the important one. He had to see *her* safely home.

'Here?' he suggested cautiously.

'Yes.' Kate nodded. She sighed. She looked at her plate and began to chase a grain of rice from one side of her plate to the other. 'So ...' she said. 'He didn't take everything, did he? He gave me at least half of everything I might have dreamed of, *if* ...'

'If you'd done what you dreamed of in the first place?'

'Yes.' She smiled again, that strange, almost pitying smile he'd seen on her face before. What the hell *was* it?

'So it isn't so bad, is it, Smithy? We could have done worse, couldn't we?'

She stood up and rushed across the kitchen to put the kettle on, escaping not just him but the answer to her question, which (had he provided one) would have been drowned by the drumming of water against metal.

He reviewed their conversation so far. Her stepfather had chased her to Whitsun Gate, Mags had given it to her and thus ...

It was the same for him, of course. Tess had chased him to Whitsun Gate, Mags had given it to him and thus ... Hmm. Where would *he* be now, if she hadn't?

Could he have survived the past year if he'd spent it all with Pamela? Yes, probably, he was the type who survived. But what would he have been like at the end of it? Not as he was now, certainly. Whitsun Gate had given him time to think and to heal, space to work and make plans ... His entire life had seemed to be passing in this bloody awful kitchen, but he'd been growing out of it all the time, changing, adapting, finding things inside himself he'd never known were there.

He smiled. 'Yes,' he said. 'We could do a lot worse.'

Kate braced her arms against the sink to gaze up into the fading leaves of the linden tree.

'But you think you could do better,' she said. 'Don't you?'

Smithy frowned. He was beginning to see where she was leading. At least, he thought he was, but he could be wrong. *Did* he think he could do better? Yes, he had thought—felt, rather—that Whitsun Gate was a sort of halfway

302

house, a bridge between the life he had lost and the one he had still to find ...

A bridge. In a soldier's estimation a bridge is a powerful thing: a way forward, a way out, a short-cut, an escape. But maybe ... Maybe ...

Hard as it was to concentrate on his own journey when Kate's was still in progress, he knew suddenly that he had reached an important turning in the road. He'd been crossing bridges all his life: always trying to find something on the other side. But what if it was here?

He tried to fix her gaze with his own. 'Yes,' he said. 'I think I can do better.'

Kate caught her breath. Her eyes whirled to his face, and then away.

'But not necessarily elsewhere,' he said.

The conversation had not gone as Kate had planned. She'd said, 'He gave me at least half of what I might have dreamed of,' and then had paused. waiting for Smithy to ask the obvious: 'What about the other half?'

But he hadn't. And now she was up a gum tree, vaguely suspecting that they were talking about different things. Why did he never keep to the script, damn him? And what was she supposed to do with *her* lines if he didn't cue her in?

'I'm still hungry,' she said gloomily.

It was true: she'd spent the past few weeks with scarcely any appetite at all and now suddenly was ravenous, mentally turning out the cupboards in search of a non-existent hoard of jammy dodgers.

'Oh, God!' Smithy came as near as he could to jumping to his feet. 'I forgot your treacle tart!'

The treacle tart had clearly suffered a good deal since it had come out of Mavis's oven, some time this morning. The middle had dissolved and the crust turned to a powder, but Smithy was clearly very proud of having acquired it for her. 'There,' he said. 'Will that keep body and soul together?'

'Mmm,' she said. 'Nice. Did you knit it yourself?'

'Hey, show a little gratitude! I had to offer Mavis a dirty weekend to get you that!'

Kate laughed, ate and was grateful; but the mood had changed, her chance had gone and might never come again. She'd had it all worked out. No revealing confessions, nothing soppy, nothing threatening. Just, 'I think the other half's all right now,' and leave the rest to him. He wouldn't ask more if he didn't want to know.

But maybe he knew already ... and really *didn't* want to know.

The evenings were beginning to shorten and she spent the next few hours in the garden, working—and thinking—until dusk closed around her. All manner of strange things had happened today and although she'd thought most of them through and drawn—she was certain—the right conclusions from them, she knew the repercussions would run for a long time yet.

The one thing she hadn't thought about was her mother. An image of Laura kept popping up in her mind like a jack-in-the-box, squealing. 'What about me?' before Kate could press the lid down and lock her in again.

My mother knows what she wants to know. That was true. There was no point in telling her anything else unless you wanted to be called a liar again (and Kate didn't). So what was the use of thinking about her? None at all.

There wasn't much point in thinking about Smithy, either, but Kate wanted to think about him; she wanted to understand him, to get him sorted out in her mind so that, perhaps for the first time ever, she'd know precisely what kind of person she was dealing with. She was aware now that she'd only ever seen him in two dimensions: first as that dreaded cardboard cut-out, 'the man', and then as another cardboard cut-out, 'the romantic ear-ole'.

In spite of her efforts to do so, she'd never quite managed to put the two together. They didn't seem to *fit* together. The man was ... The man was a hyena: obscene in his ugliness, violent in his greed, beneath contempt, yet too dangerous to be beneath her notice. And the romantic ear-ole? He was a teddy-bear: a soft, fluffy, cuddly thing, harmlessly inanimate. You could stuff him up your nightie and he'd do nothing worse than keep you warm. Put the two together and you found yourself with a different kind of animal entirely: a lion, perhaps. Just as dangerous as the first, just as warm and furry as the second, but far more complicated than either of them. A lion was beautiful, noble ...

and terrifying. Unless, of course, one happened to be a lioness.

Could Kate be a lioness? It was what Smithy wanted her to be; he'd said as much this morning. 'If you don't want him here, throw him out!' as if Robert were nothing. Yet that was what he'd turned out to be. Nothing. It was almost as if he'd been a figment of her imagination all this time: a monster *she'd* created from something so small and puny, it could be frightened away with a few words: 'When I was fourteen, he—'

For God's sake, grow up!

As cures for hysterics go, that one had been a lulu—she could still feel the sting of it—but it had cured her of more than hysterics.

She wasn't fourteen any more. She'd grown up.

Chapter Eighteen

They delivered the car while Smithy was in the shower: just left it under the linden tree and posted the keys and documents through the letter-box. He saw the bulky white envelope lying there and thought, 'More bloody junk-mail.' before going through to the kitchen to make the day's first pot of coffee. And then he saw it: gleaming in the shadows under the linden tree, like a basking shark in a green lagoon.

He filled the kettle. He drew himself up to

his full height, squared his jaw and addressed the assembled company (himself) in the clear, confident tones of one who has done it all, seen it all, and fears nothing any more.

'Keep absolutely calm. Take one step at a time. Coffee first.'

He switched on the kettle, reached down the coffee, found a spoon, stared at it for a moment and threw it back in the drawer. Five minutes later he was executing a perfect three-point turn and was on his way out.

It was easy! A hell of a lot easier than falling off a log (which he'd done quite a lot of, too, in his time). He'd been told, many times over, that you never forget how to drive. It's a skill—like walking and talking—that gets imprinted on your brain and stays forever more. But having had such a terrible time learning to walk again, he hadn't really believed it.

It didn't even hurt! The movement in his right ankle and knee was more than sufficient to the task and the power steering was a joy: he cruised around the car park in ever-decreasing circles, smiling, unable to stop smiling, smiling until his jaw ached.

He'd meant to restrict himself to the car park for a day or two, a week or two, for however long it took to get the hang of it. But he'd done that, seen that, been there. He tried out the radio, the lights and windscreen-wipers, played with the electric windows, then drove slowly towards the outer gate and turned into the village.

He suffered a slight tremor of fear as he waited at the junction with the main Frome road. He had no memory at all of the accident that had nearly killed him, but he'd been given a detailed account of it which now passed before his eyes in glorious Technicolor, reminding him (rather horribly) that his own driving had never been at fault. It was the *other* guy you had to be scared of!

A lorry's brakes had failed at a red light just as Smithy had come through on the green. The impact had thrown him up (witnesses had claimed between twelve and fifteen feet high) and back on to the bonnet of the car behind, which had swerved and thrown him sideways, under the wheels of the oncoming traffic. It was a miracle he'd survived. Did he *really* want to risk all that again?

Yes, he did. Fear was fear only until you'd faced it out. Then it was freedom.

He turned into the Frome road, put his foot down to keep up with the traffic, drove a few miles towards Radstock and turned into the lane towards Kilmersdon, on his way home. Pretty lanes, lovely villages, rabbits browsing by the roadside, cows lumbering to their fields. Hardly a strange adventure. But he was alone. He was travelling under his own steam. He was a man again.

Hoping that Kate didn't know the car had been delivered, he left it in the car park and went back to the house on foot, thinking—yet again—that he'd get the linden tree felled before it could ruin his paintwork. But he'd have to sort it out with Kate first. She loved that tree, damn her.

She was browsing through the latest bulb catalogue, drinking the coffee he hadn't made.

'Oh! I thought you were still in bed!'

'At this time of day? It's gone eight o'clock!'

'It *has* been known.' Kate grinned. 'Anyway, it's our day off.'

He pursed his mouth: Mavis being sanctimonious. 'Hoo! It may be a day off for *some!*'

Dumping Mavis, he became himself again. Or tried to. The car had made him new. He wasn't entirely sure he could find 'himself' in the shape he'd been an hour ago. He'd been older, then. Slower. About thirty miles an hour slower.

'Are you going to Frome today?' he asked.

'Mmm. Want something?'

'You're not seeing your mother?'

'No.'

He kept wondering about her mother, but not daring to ask until Kate brought up the subject again. He had strong feelings about the infidelity question and in normal circumstances would have said no one should tell anyone, even if they were mother and daughter. But Kate's case was different; her own betrayal was so tangled up with her mother's, he thought she probably *should* tell. But he wasn't certain. So unless she directly asked his advice, he was going to keep his mouth shut.

'In that case,' he said, 'I'll come with you. There are a few things I want that I'd rather do for myself.' Drive his own car, for example.

'What about your car?'

309

'What about it?'

'Didn't you say they were delivering today?'

He shrugged. 'Oh, they'll drop the keys through the letterbox if I'm not here.'

'I thought you'd be excited about it. Want to see it, I mean.'

'What on earth for? I'm not a *teenager*, Kate!'

He felt like a teenager.

Smithy parked where Kate usually parked when she was meeting her mother, at the bottom of town, near the river. He turned off the engine and leaned forward slightly, turning his head to look at her. 'Well? How was it for you?'

Kate took the inference, tried not to blush and failed, which left her with nothing to do but laugh. 'The earth moved,' she said. 'I think I left it about five miles back.'

'That was your stomach.'

'No. No, you—er ...' She swallowed her next line (You were wonderful), to say instead, 'You coped very well. Weren't you scared?'

'Not a bit. Were you?'

Yes, she'd been scared, although not of the car and not of Smithy's driving. Just of the *fact* that he was driving, which had made him different, somehow. She'd said scarcely a word to him since they'd left home and although that had been partly due to other factors, she'd been as shy of him as if they'd only just met. Which they hadn't. So maybe it *was* the car. When he'd told her it was second-hand, she'd expected something more elderly, but this was like Michael's car or Inky's: gleaming, luxurious and smelling faintly of leather.

'No,' she said, 'I wasn't scared. It's very smooth without the gear-changes. It almost seems to drive itself ... Although I realise it doesn't,' she added hastily.

She realised something else a minute or two later, when Smithy prised himself out of the car, reached for his walking stick and became himself again. *Disabled.*

It was a horrible thought. It was horrible because she knew she liked him *better* this way, knew him better, trusted him more. She remembered the hottest days of last summer when she'd lain naked and safe in her bed, gleefully aware that she could be naked because *he* couldn't get upstairs. God, what a bitch she was. What a selfish, cruel ...

'Hey, come on!' Smithy was waiting for her on the bridge. 'What's wrong? Got a bone in your leg?'

He looked so happy ... The car had freed him and she'd dreaded it, as if he were a pet rabbit who had no *right* to be free because he was hers! But Smithy wasn't hers. He could escape any time he liked and there was nothing she could do about it.

She ran to join him and then slowed her stride to match his, keeping a tactful half-step ahead to protect him from people barging by in the opposite direction. Her instinct was to walk directly in front, with guarding arms outstretched, shouting, 'Knock him down and you're dead!' But she knew better. He was a *wild* rabbit and apt to turn vicious (as she knew to her cost) if you dared to call him a bunny.

'I love this town,' Smithy said. 'Especially when the sun's shining. It's beautiful, isn't it?'

'Is it?' She looked around, eyes widening with amazement, but she was too familiar with the place to see any beauty in it. 'I've always thought it a bit of a dump,' she said. 'There's nothing *here*, is there?'

He laughed. 'How about history? You took a dream-degree in History, didn't you?'

Kate pulled a face and said hurriedly, 'No, it was in English. Anything you want to know about Jane Austen?'

'I did mine in engineering, but I still managed to find out that Frome was founded in the seventh century by a guy called St Aldhelm, that it had a thriving market listed in the Domesday Book—'

'Oh, shut up,' Kate muttered.

'—and that in the sixteenth and seventeenth centuries it had one of the largest cloth-making industries in England. It's also got more ancient buildings than most small towns—'

'Watch out for that truck,' Kate warned, indicating one a few hundred yards up the road. 'Someone might push you under it.'

Smithy stopped walking. 'What's *wrong* with you?' he laughed. 'What's wrong with looking around you? Have you *no* sense of curiosity?'

They'd reached the bank, which was to be Kate's first port of call. She jumped up on the step to meet Smithy eye-to-eye. 'Yes,' she said. 'I'm curious to know how my bank-balance stands, and why, if you want an argument, you have to pick one in the middle of the street!'

He was still laughing at her.

'And why you never let your hair grow.' she added bravely. 'Have you *no* sense of vanity? You look like Ivan Denisovitch, starving in Siberia!'

'Ha! That's a whole lot better than looking like Little Lord Fauntleroy, poncing around in ringlets!'

Kate smirked suddenly. '*Ringlets?* Really?'

'Oh, shut up,' he muttered.

She could have kissed him. She almost did. Her hands flew up to catch his face before changing direction to cover her mouth and a sudden fit of the giggles.

They arranged to meet back at the car in an hour, although Kate finished her shopping in half that time, thinking throughout about her alleged lack of curiosity. It wasn't true, but she knew what he meant. She was like her mother, afraid of asking questions for fear that she wouldn't like the answers. But why? Whether you asked or not, the answers still came to you, eventually. You couldn't escape the truth.

Her way back to the car took her through St John's churchyard and, with time in hand, she paused on the steps to look down over the rooftops of the town, an interlocking maze of of old terracotta tiles, crooked chimneys, gables and ancient timbers. The warm, muted colours set up a shimmering contrast against a clear September sky, reminding Kate of the illustrated fairy tales she'd read as a child: *Hansel and Gretel, The Pied Piper of Hamelin.* Yes, it was beautiful. Why hadn't she noticed it before? Because every time she left the safety of Whitsun Gate, she'd closed her mind to everything except the necessities that had brought her out; closed her mind to everything but the need she felt to go home again.

That had gone. She was in love. Nowhere was safe any more—except where he was. And he was here.

Smithy got back to the car ten minutes early, his trip into town having proved almost entirely fruitless. He'd meant to buy some music for the tape-deck, but had been unable to find anything he wanted. He'd meant to buy a service manual for his car, but Halford's hadn't had one. And he'd meant to get his hair cut, but something had stopped him—an icy wind, whistling in from Siberia. Ivan Denisovitch, indeed.

He saw Kate, breezing down from the market place, walking jauntily over the bridge. She had on her skinny white jeans and a bright yellow sweatshirt. Her hair was loose, framing her face in a moving cloud of gold. He looked beyond her, picking out every woman he could find, but finding none prettier—and certainly none healthier! The glow in her cheeks and the spring in her heels was like a metaphor for life itself. Yet she hadn't even *begun* living, yet. She was like a September daffodil, still in the bulb. And he couldn't bend low enough to plant her, damn it.

She jumped into the car. 'All done? Did you get what you wanted?'

'Nope. This place is a dump. I don't know what you see in it.'

Kate looked at him, her eyes full of laughter, her cheeks full of a derisive, 'Pooh!' which she swallowed, to say instead: 'Oh, come on, look around you. It's beautiful! Did you know it was founded in the seventh century, by the way?'

'Hmph! Hasn't progressed much since then, has it?'

She laughed and fastened her seat-belt. 'Home, James.'

'How about going out for lunch?'

'It isn't lunchtime. It's only eleven o'clock.'

'Hmm. So it is.' He started the car, turned obediently for home and then, with a laugh, took the wrong turning at the crossroads and aimed towards Longleat, or Shaftesbury, or Poole Harbour and the sea.

Kate giggled or, rather, gasped, 'Where are you *going?*'

'I don't know. I don't care. Do you?'

She took a moment to reply, very softly, 'No.'

It was enough. It was more than enough.

'I'm sick to death of sitting in that bloody kitchen,' he said. 'We'll have to do something about it, Kate. We'll have to do something about the entire house.'

She was silent.

'I'm not criticising,' he said hurriedly.

'Oh. That makes a change.'

'I *never* criticise!'

315

'No, of course not. Neither do I. Watch out for that cyclist. And check your rear-view mirror. Don't you *want* to see what's behind you? Have you *no* sense of curiosity?'

'Whoops,' he laughed. 'But I'm better than I used to be, Kate. Honest.'

'So am I,' she said.

Smithy smiled, knowing it was true. She was not the girl she'd been a year ago. There was a constant light in her eyes now, a softness, a sweetness that hadn't been there before. Had he played a part in changing her, or would she have changed regardless, just because so many other things had changed?

'Did you criticise Tess very much?' she asked now. 'Is that why ... it didn't work out?'

'No, I didn't criticise her. I could see no wrong in her. Even when I *knew* she was wrong, I used to tell myself I'd made a mistake.'

'That's what went wrong, then. You *should* have criticised her.' She turned to him, grinning impishly. 'It's done *me* the world of good.'

'Has it? Why? Has no one criticised you before?'

'Oh, yes. But no one's told me the truth before. If you criticised me for being too fat, for instance—'

'You're not fat!'

'Quite. So if you told me I was, I'd hate you for it, not just because it's not true ...'

'Go on.'

'But because I'd begin to think it was.'

'*What?*'

'You know what I mean.'

316

Did he? No, he didn't. But it didn't really matter. What mattered was that he had made a difference to her. And, considering some of the rotten things he'd said to her just lately, it was sweet of her to tell him so.

He turned into a pub and parked with his nose to the view. The White Horse. The god of freedom. It was much closer now: perhaps only a few miles away as the crow flew.

He took a deep breath. He closed his eyes, aware that the car was his white horse, his galloping steed, his strength and virility. He might never run up the Brecon Beacons again, but while he could drive ...

'Come on,' he said. 'Lunch is on me.'

Had anyone told Kate yesterday that she'd actually be celebrating Smithy's car today, she wouldn't have believed it, but it was amazing how quickly she'd changed her mind. No, not changed it; just adapted it to suit. Smithy looked so happy. She couldn't grudge him his happiness. And *she* felt ... Not happy, exactly, but light and fizzy, rendered almost transparent by hope. It had been so lovely when he'd driven off with her into the blue! But it hadn't been that that had put champagne bubbles in her blood. It had been what he'd said about the kitchen. The entire house! He was planning to stay!

He was studying the menu now, jiggling his eyebrows in a manner that seemed more pleased than otherwise. He liked 'clean' food: fresh and expensive, simple and pretty. Kate

317

liked anything, just as long as it filled the gap, although she doubted that she could still eat one of Mags's slithery stews.

When he went to the bar to place their orders, she watched him, remembering the first time they'd had a pub lunch at the Seven Stars, seeing the changes in him as if they'd happened overnight. He was like another man. He'd been so thin, so pale, doubled over his sticks like a man of eighty. Did he look older than his years now? Yes, just a bit. He'd suffered too much for it to have left no mark on him and, in repose, his face still looked a little grim. But he'd gained weight and built enough muscles in his back and shoulders to pull his spine almost straight again. He would always have a limp (his left leg was slightly shorter than his right), but he wouldn't always need a stick and even now could manage without it except, as he put it, 'for cornering'. He was suntanned, too, and the barmaid, who could see him only from the waist up, was probably thinking him a fine figure of a man. Which he was. All through.

'What are you smirking at?' he asked as he resumed his seat.

'Actually, I was thinking about the kitchen.'

He glanced behind him.

'*Our* kitchen. What do you want to do with it?'

'Oh! Gut it and refit it, of course. What else?'

'Won't that cost a lot?'

He nodded. 'Yes. But you needn't worry about that. I realise you'd be quite happy living

318

in a garden shed and, that being so ...'

'You're moving me into the shed?' she suggested glumly.

He laughed. 'No. But since I'm the one who wants rather more than a garden shed, I should pay for it, and you—most certainly—should not.' He frowned and looked at his hands. 'I need a home, Kate.' He looked up again, his smile rueful. 'Come back, Pamela, all is forgiven. Actually, it was staying at her place that finished me off. A spot of comfort makes everything easier, somehow. I don't need luxury. A little warmth, a little cleanliness ... And I'm really not criticising; just stating facts.'

'So the kitchen isn't everything?'

'No. We won't be able to tackle it all at once, of course, but I thought the kitchen, the sitting room and your bedroom would do for a start. Maybe the hall, too.'

'My bedroom's all right.'

'Your bedroom's a garden shed, Kate.'

She laughed. 'How would you know?'

'You left the door open.' Registering her shock, he added indignantly, 'I didn't go *in!* What kind of creep do you take me for?'

She was amazed. 'You've been upstairs?'

'Yes, I wanted to get an idea of how much needs to be—'

'My God, what if you'd fallen?'

'Don't be silly. I wouldn't have gone if there'd been any danger of that.'

'What do you mean—' Kate gasped '—*if* there'd been any danger? Of course there was danger! *Any* idiot can fall downstairs!'

319

'I am *not*—' Their lunch arrived just as Kate registered that Smithy was furious and about to remind her that he 'was *not* Mrs Whittle's cat!'

'Sorry,' she said. 'I only meant—'

'I know what you meant.' He was smiling, but his eyes were not. 'Your sanctuary's been invaded. You aren't safe any more.'

'No! That's not—'

'Do you have any idea how insulting that is?'

'I didn't *mean* that.' She stared at her plate, aware that he was staring at her and, she hoped, counting to ten. But he wasn't.

'You did mean that,' he said coldly.

'Oh, don't be so stupid! If you'd wanted to mess with me you'd have done it ages ago!'

Although they'd both been keeping their voices down, Kate was angry, close to tears and deeply embarrassed. Of all the places, of all the *times,* to have a row! And she wasn't the fighting type! She couldn't even fight him in private, let alone in the middle of a crowded pub!

'If I'd wanted you months ago,' he said, 'do you imagine I wouldn't have had the decency to keep it to myself? Do you imagine *I'd* conduct myself like—'

'I imagined you'd fall downstairs,' she said grimly. 'That's *all* I imagined and I've already apologised for that!'

Smithy glared at her briefly and began to eat. But Kate had lost her appetite. She wanted to weep. To run away. *If I'd wanted you* ... Oh, God. That meant he hadn't!

'Kate?' he said.

'Yes?'

'Eat your lunch.' He waited until she'd begun to eat before asking softly, 'When do you see your mother again?'

She shrugged. 'I don't know. Have you thought that if we improve the house, we'll increase its value? And, if you pay for it all on your own, you'll give me an unfair advantage if we sell up. So—'

'Oh! We're selling up, are we?'

'I don't know. We might. Or you might want to buy me out one day, or—'

'Might I? Why?'

She gritted her teeth. Why did he have to make an argument out of everything? 'You might want to get married again, for instance. And your wife won't want me around, will she?'

Smithy blinked. 'I don't see why not. You're no trouble.'

'Really?' she murmured. 'You do surprise me.'

He laughed. 'The house is big enough, surely?'

'Only until the kids come along.'

'So? You can baby-sit. There, it's all arranged. Any more problems?'

'Twit,' Kate said. 'I'm *trying* to be realistic.'

'You're being ridiculous.' His voice had grown chill again. 'Who'd *have* me?'

She didn't understand him for a moment. And then, suddenly, she did. Barely half an hour ago she'd been assessing his physical condition and—give or take a few rough spots—finding it good. But she'd been comparing it with the state he'd been in a year ago, while he must always be comparing it with the man he'd been before. But she hadn't even liked him then, hadn't given a damn for him, hadn't known then that he was beautiful.

He pushed his plate aside and leaned his elbow on the table to finger his mouth; the corner of his mouth where the scar had spoiled it.

She went on eating, hoping he'd relax and follow suit, but he just sat there, fingering his mouth.

'I'd have you,' she whispered.

He appeared at first not to have heard her. Then, slowly, he raised his eyes to gaze wonderingly into her face, a faint smile twisting his mouth. Twisting his mouth so that she didn't know what it meant. Pleasure? Pity? Amusement?

'Would you, Kate?' His smile broadened and became ... very kind, leaving her with no course but to pretend she'd meant something else.

'If I thought I'd be any use to you, yes,' she said. 'You're a good man, Smithy. A beautiful man. Beautiful on the inside, where it matters.'

She pushed her plate away. Smithy reached for her hand and gently stroked it. 'Oh, Kate,' he sighed. 'I could say that you are beautiful on the outside, where it matters, and be as wrong as you are. What matters is not how others perceive us, but how we perceive ourselves. I could tell you—and once have been certain—that if I took you to bed with me, you'd melt. But you know otherwise and, because you know it, it's *true.*' He laughed softly. 'I can see by the look in your eyes that you're appalled at the very thought, and it's the thought—as the actress said to the bishop—that counts.'

He reached for his stick, leaving her hand naked and all alone on the table. 'Come on,' he said. 'Let's get out of here, shall we?'

He reached the door before Kate could get her breath back, let alone tell him he was wrong.

'I ruined your lunch.' he said as she joined him in the car.

'It was my fault. All you wanted was a few rolls of wallpaper and I landed you with a wife and six kids.'

He laughed. 'And a baby-sitter.'

'Yes, well, I'm not so sure about that. Let's take it one step at a time, shall we? Wallpaper first. They do some lovely ones now, you know, in the original Georgian designs.'

'Isn't that a bit pretentious for the likes of us?'

'Think so? *I* thought so. Just because it's a Georgian house ... I mean, you wouldn't have a Georgian lavatory, would you, so why should you have their wallpaper?'

Smithy threw her a sideways glance which seemed to be some kind of comment.

'Go on,' he said.

'Go on with what?'

'Well, if you don't want Georgian wallpaper, what do you want? Chintz? Chrome and leather?

323

Art bloody *Nouveau?*'

Kate gathered he wasn't too keen on *Art Nouveau.* She also gathered that he expected her to have opinions and ideas and come up with them, pronto. She didn't have any. She didn't want any. If he needed a home, she wanted him to have the home *he* wanted, a place where he could be happy and comfortable for as long as ... Forever.

The way he'd decorated his bedroom might give her a clue. It was very plain, simple and immaculately tidy. Every time she went in to make his bed or sweep the floor she compared it not with the way it had been before but with her mother's bedroom as she'd last seen it: a suffocating pink softness of cushions and frills ...

'I can't stand frills,' she said. 'And I can't stand pink.'

He laughed. 'Did you ever mention that to Mags?'

'What? Oh! No, it's different in the garden. Yellows are a problem in the garden.'

They talked all the way home. Just as they came through Maiden Bradley, Smithy said, 'So you want a complete contrast with the garden?'

She laughed ruefully. 'No, I'm just being spiteful.'

'Spiteful? What does that mean?'

'It means I want my mother to hate it. But I want you to love it, so take no notice of me.'

Smithy was quiet for a while. Then, rather

324

warily, he asked, 'Are you going to tell her, Kate? About—er—'

'Seeing Robert? No.'

He smiled. 'Not even for spite?'

'Huh! It would be like cutting off my nose to spite my face! When you tell my mother something she doesn't want to know, she calls you a liar; and even though you know she's wrong, you believe her. *You* take the blame, just because she's left you with nowhere else to put it.'

'That's ridiculous, Kate.'

'Is it? Weren't you the one who told yourself you were mistaken when all the facts said *Tess* was wrong? It's exactly the same thing. You were mistaken without making a mistake and I'm a liar who told no lies. I didn't even exaggerate, Smithy! If anything, I played it down, because I didn't—*I didn't*—want to hurt her! So are we really what we perceive ourselves to be, or only what they *tell* us we are?'

Smithy was silent. She'd half expected him to argue the point, to tell her she was being ridiculous again and to tell her why. She'd almost hoped he would, if only to say the one thing—that small, mysterious thing—that would take the blame away from her and make everything right again.

But Smithy was silent. Even when they arrived back at Whitsun Gate, he was silent, staring straight ahead, as if in a trance, at the blank back wall of the tearooms beyond the linden tree.

Kate glanced at him warily and, when he

still made no sound, she looked again. A trance, yes. His eyes were wide, the expression on his face a curious mixture of pain and bewilderment. She couldn't see the scar on his face, but saw his fingers gently tracing it from cheekbone to jaw. He covered his mouth. Then, raising his hand, he covered the entire side of his face, as if to say, 'Don't look.'

Are we really what we perceive ourselves to be, or only what they tell us we are?

'Smithy?'

'Hmm?' He still didn't look at her.

'Did Tess tell you you were ugly?'

He closed his eyes. 'No.' He turned to her, smiling. 'She threw up. Not quite literally, but near enough.'

'Did she say anything?'

'Yes. She said, "Oh, well. That's that, then." '

'That's *all?*'

He laughed. 'You had to be there.'

'It's lucky I wasn't. I'd have killed her.'

'Would you, Kate?' He sounded sad and disbelieving. And he was right, of course.

'No,' she admitted. 'I hardly knew you and didn't like you, anyway, so—'

'Didn't you? Why? Just because I was a man?'

'No, because you were an arrogant little sod.'

His eyebrows shot up. His eyes filled with laughter.

'So I haven't changed at all, then?'

Kate could have thrown herself into his arms

right then, forgetting everything except that she loved him.

But something stopped her. She'd forgotten to unfasten her seat belt.

Chapter Nineteen

Smithy couldn't sleep. He'd had a phase, after giving up his sleeping pills, of sleeping two hours on and two hours off, but he'd beaten that. He'd slept like a baby for a while. And now he couldn't sleep at all. He was tired: too tired to sit up, too sleepy to read, yet the minute he switched off the light and closed his eyes, a little devil with a pitchfork prodded him into wakefulness again.

He knew what was wrong with him. Inflammation of the heart and the brain and the lower abdomen, inflammation of the thighs. Kate-itis.

Yet sweet as she was, Kate wasn't sweet enough for Smithy's liking. Kate was cold and dry and ...

No, she wasn't. But she'd changed so much, recently, he no longer knew *what* she was. A body. Lithe and strong and supple (if just a touch on the thin side), although he rarely saw her now as the sum of her parts. Just the parts. There was something about the way her throat moved when she laughed, something about the way her hips moved when she walked

... and those dinky little biceps of hers drove him crackers! He could watch them for hours (given the chance) and not get weary of the sight. Breasts? Yes, two; just the same as other women, *normal* women. He'd prefer them a little fuller. He also wished she'd buy a decent bra, without a bloody silly seam just where no seam had any right to be!

She wasn't perfect. By no means perfect.

'So go to sleep,' he said aloud.

She wore plain, white, stretchy briefs, so tiny on the clothesline they looked like little old ladies' handkerchiefs ...

He groaned and turned over, thumping his pillow.

... with a narrow lace edging which, in his dreams, was always nipped between his finger and thumb ...

Oh, God, this was ridiculous! Clothes-line sex! How had he been reduced to this?

He liked her hands, too. He hadn't expected to like her hands, but there was something rather touching about them: the squared off fingernails, the rough skin on the offside of her index finger where the trowel rubbed ... Too bony, though.

She wasn't perfect. Not by any means. So why couldn't he forget her and go to sleep?

He didn't love her. He didn't. The only trouble with him was that he'd got himself stuck with a woman who didn't damn well *work*. It was like being in love with a mermaid. Certain essentials were missing. There was no future in it. Only drowning.

It wasn't fair. He'd had enough trouble,

surely? And what had he done to deserve any of it, except—'

You were an arrogant little sod.

He wasn't certain how he'd managed to laugh that one off. Probably because, like Kate, he recognised the truth when he tripped over it. But it had hurt. He'd wished with all his heart that he was still an arrogant sod, still strong and confident enough to make his play without a thought for the consequences. It was one thing to be rejected when you knew you were up to scratch; you could (and did) tell yourself that the silly girl didn't know what she was missing. But he couldn't hack it, now. There was too much riding on it: not just his pride, but the house and the business and, more importantly, what was fast becoming a precious—if very peculiar—friendship.

She'd said some sweet things to him just lately and he'd thought for a minute or two that her mermaid-tail didn't matter, that sweetness and affection might be enough. But a man couldn't live that way. Women might be able to separate the two, but for a man, love wasn't love without ...

'Let's call it sex, shall we?' he whispered. 'Let's be honest. She likes that. She's not the sort of girl to take offence.'

Like hell she wasn't! Say 'sex' to Kate and she'd take offence so fast, you wouldn't know what had hit you until you woke up in Casualty with a spade through your skull!

Love, then? He loved her eyes. Sometimes he wondered if he'd imagined the way they'd used

329

to go dead on him: cold, flat and blank, like a blackboard on which no one had written. It never happened now. The board was covered with curious equations; but if you didn't know what any of them meant, it might just as well be blank for all the use it was. There were times ...

What *was* the time? Christ, ten to three! And he'd been here since eleven! Right, that was it, he'd had enough. He'd get up for an hour, make a pot of tea ...

He woke, barely three hours later, to a series of ear-splitting clangs and crashes which brought an image to his mind of a large gang of burglars lobbing bricks through every window in the house. He didn't give a damn. Let them take what they wanted. Just so long as they let him *sleep*.

He slipped away, swooping blissfully down the long slide to oblivion without quite reaching the bottom. A stair creaked—and suddenly he was wide awake and fighting mad. They could have his bloody stereo; he was damned if they'd have Kate!

Even wide awake and fighting mad, Smithy made slow enough progress (as he perceived it) for Kate to be on her third rapist before he managed to exit his room. Stark naked under his bathrobe and with no time to put on his slippers, he felt almost exquisitely vulnerable, but not afraid. He was conscious enough now to guess that the gang of marauders had been a figment of his dreams, but that *noise* certainly hadn't been! What was it?

330

The hall was only faintly lit by the dim, grey twilight of dawn, but there was quite enough fight to allow him to identify the culprits. One of them was a large, galvanised pail. The other—whom he caught in the act of picking it up after its fall down the stairs—was Kate.

'Oh, *thanks!*' he said. 'I'd just gone to sleep, damn you!'

'Sorry.' Without retrieving the pail, she sat on the bottom step of the stairs, huddling against the newel post as if his next move would be to break his stick across her shoulders. Except to pick her out from the identity parade as the guilty party, Smithy hadn't actually looked at her until now. He hadn't noticed anything except that she'd woken him up. Rather weird, considering what had kept him awake half the night, because she was almost as naked as he was: bare feet, bare legs and arms, the bit in the middle scantily covered by a ragged little shift of washed-out cotton, which he could only suppose was her nightdress. There was something wrong ...

'What's the matter?'

'I don't know. I keep being sick. I think it's stopped now, but I feel ...'

'Have you eaten anything you shouldn't?' Her pub lunch had gone through her system days ago, but you never knew with Kate. When she was hungry, she could eat any damn thing!

Seething with barely suppressed fury, he fetched the First Aid box and took her temperature. It was well up, which rather shocked him. He hadn't expected it. Kate was never ill! But she was ill now and looked set to remain that way for a while ...

Partly because he was so tired and partly because nothing like it had happened before, the world at that moment seemed to tip sideways and fall on his head. How were they to manage without Kate? She did everything! The gardening, the gate, plant sales, the part-time rotas! He could, at a pinch, fill a few of the gaps, but who would look after Kate while he was doing it? He hadn't told her (well, she'd made such a fuss!) that he'd decided his first trip up the stairs was likely to be his last. It was all right going up, but coming down was both painful *and* dangerous, and the danger would be threefold if he was wearing himself out elsewhere.

And now her teeth were chattering. Great! The first real challenge he'd faced in years, and he couldn't damn well hack it!

'You'd better go back to bed.'

'No, I ...' Her voice was very faint. 'I'll be all right in a minute.'

Smithy sighed. A minute? She could be sick for a week! And he could barely stand up, let alone climb—

He widened his eyes. There was no need for him to go upstairs. He could look after her down here!

'You can crash out in my bed,' he said wearily. 'It doesn't look as if I'm going to need it for a while.'

She sat bolt upright and stared at him. '*Your* bed?' she gasped. 'No, I can't, you might—'

Smithy didn't wait for more. He was angry enough already; he didn't need this!

'I thought I was the arrogant one!' he snapped. 'But just how desirable do you think you are at this moment? And just how desperate do you think *I* am?'

Kate collapsed again, wailing, 'Oh, *no!*'

'Get into my bed!' he roared. 'Use your bloody sense, will you?'

He limped into the kitchen, not bothering to check which way she went. He filled the kettle and slammed it down. He opened the cupboard and drawers and slammed them shut. But when his coffee was prepared and there was nothing left to do but wait for the kettle to boil, a sad little silence fell and he heard Kate, weakly weeping in his room across the hall.

He sighed. He pressed shaking fingers to hot, aching eyes. 'Oh, well done, Smithy,' he whispered. 'Now shoot yourself, why don't you?'

Kate woke at one in the afternoon, with a crashing headache. The headache was all she could think about for a while, but then she remembered where she was and how she'd got there and let out a groan of horror. He'd got it all wrong!

Her stomach was all right, though. A bit sore and hollow, but hollow felt very good, in the circumstances. She'd never been sick before. At least, if she had, it had happened so long ago she'd forgotten all about it. Some people threw up all the time and thought nothing of it, but

Kate had been convinced she was dying. And she'd been so brave, so considerate, so *unselfish*. Even while she was praying she'd survive the night, she'd prayed just as hard she wouldn't wake Smithy.

God, she hated him! Selfish, nasty, cruel ... Twice he'd seen her in a state of collapse, needing nothing more than a few kind words and a shoulder to cry on, and on both occasions he'd taken her to pieces! It wasn't fair, it wasn't fair! He'd got it all wrong!

She wept. But crying made her headache worse and she didn't have a hanky. She turned her head to look for one and found a box of tissues on the table, a jug of water and, on the floor beside the bed, the galvanised bucket that had caused all the trouble.

So he'd been in ... He'd brought the tissues and the water (and the bucket) and watched her sleeping in his bed. It was a very comforting thought until she imagined the look on his face. Just how desirable did she think she was?

Oh, God ...

She poured some water and carefully sipped it, rejoicing in the relief it gave to her mouth and throat, fearing the effect it might have on her stomach. But it was all right. If she had the terminal disease she'd dreaded in the early hours, it wasn't going to kill her yet.

She slept again and woke to the touch of Smithy's hand on her forehead. She opened her eyes, blushing with humiliation as he took three steps backwards. She wanted to scream, 'All right, there's no need to rub it in!' but knew she'd burst into tears if she said a word.

'It's all right,' he said. 'Just taking your temperature.'

Kate glanced at his face to take his. Cool.

'Seems to have gone down,' he said. 'How are you feeling now?'

'Fine. A headache, that's all.'

'You've probably dehydrated. Drink some water. Mavis says there's a twenty-four-hour bug going the rounds. You'll be all right tomorrow.'

'Oh ... good.'

He turned to go out. 'Let him go,' Kate told herself sadly. 'He doesn't love you, he doesn't care.'

But loving him was like having a ventriloquist pulling her strings and she murmured his name just as he said, more loudly, 'Kate?'

'Yes?'

He didn't turn around. 'I'm sorry I was so ...' He ran his fingers through the half-inch pile of his hair. 'I'm sorry.'

'Smithy?'

'Yes?'

'You got it all wrong. I thought if I had your bed, you'd probably end up in mine. And—and—' She searched for a polite alternative for the highly undesirable phrase, I was sick all over it.

'Owing to the events of the night,' she said, 'all the bedding's in the bath.'

Smithy scratched the back of his head. He turned to face her, smiling. 'So where are *we* going to sleep tonight?'

This was Kate's chance! All she had to say was, 'Here!' and ... No, he'd rather sleep on the roof.

Smithy laughed. 'All right,' he said. 'Don't panic. I'll see to it.'

She worried for a while about how he would see to it. Then she worried about what would have happened if she'd said they could share his bed—and thanked God she hadn't. She'd taken enough insults for one day. She was arrogant and ugly and he'd have to be desperate! Pig.

Her headache eased a little. She imagined Smithy getting into bed beside her and every muscle in her body clenched: stomach, jaw, eyes ... Even her knees snapped together.

Oh, for God's sake, he sneered. *Just how desperate do you think I am?*

He was getting back to normal, that was the trouble. He'd needed to keep on the right side of her because he'd needed her help; he'd needed her to care for him. And now he didn't. He had his car, he could shop and cook for himself, run the gardens without her. All he needed was an experienced, full-time gardener and a wife with enough guts and intelligence to answer back when he wanted to 'clear his tubes'. Exit Kate. And when she'd gone and his wife asked him about her, he'd laugh and say, 'Oh, she had her uses.'

His new wife had red hair, like the old one. They said the victims of broken marriages tended to fall for the same type, make the same mistake again. Well, good for him. He deserved to be miserable!

She narrowed her eyes, trying to call Tess to mind. Very tall. Straight red hair, beautiful make-up, wonderful clothes. Kate hadn't taken much notice at the time, partly because Tess hadn't seemed to notice her; but she remembered thinking that it was like having a priest in the house when you weren't religious. You knew he was holy and deserving of respect, but hadn't a clue what to say to him. The red hair aside, Tess had even looked like a priest. She'd worn black all the time, sharply tailored, with oddly shaped seams and pleats just where you least expected them. She'd looked ... carved. Carved out of copper, ivory and ebony, a thing so out of keeping with the dust and junk of Whitsun Gate, it was as if it weren't real.

The house was silent. Kate slid out of bed to visit Smithy's bathroom and caught sight of her own reflection in his wardrobe mirror. With the sculpted image of Tess still in her mind, the shock was devastating. She was hideous! Blinking with horror, she looked down at the rag of a nightdress she'd found at the back of a drawer. Every other garment she possessed had gone in the bath with her sheets, but she'd forgotten ... She'd been too ill to care what she looked like! She hadn't even *thought* ...

But what *would* she have thought, had she cared? That she was pretty enough for it not to matter?

I thought I was the arrogant one!

He was right again, damn him! It had never crossed her mind, but he was right; it was arrogant to think that every man who looked at you wanted to drag you into the bushes. Why they hell should they? She *looked* like the bushes!

It was almost five o'clock. He'd be home soon … And she was better. She didn't need to stay here any longer. He didn't have to see her like this again.

Oh, damn him. He'd cured her of *everything*, now! Fear of Robert, fear of sex, childishness, cowardice, arrogance … She closed her eyes.

'Dear God,' she whispered. 'What's left?'

In spite of her claims to have thrown off a twenty-four-hour bug in half the normal time, Kate wasn't as tough as she thought. The aftermath dragged on, day after day. She had no energy, no appetite, no interest in anything. She'd even lost interest in getting herself raped, although the first time Smithy found her mooching around the kitchen in her pyjamas it had felt more like the end of the world than a hopeful development. They were nice pyjamas, too—Doris Day crossed with Frome Market—but Kate wasn't flaunting anything. She just didn't care.

Viruses were like that. They took it out of you. But it was all a bit worrying. They'd ordered the new greenhouse and located a site for it in the private garden, but the site had to be cleared and, whatever else Smithy could do, he couldn't do *that*. Even for Kate in peak condition it was a big job, for the site was home to some of her most precious stock-plants, none of which (for fear of theft) could be moved to the public gardens. So they had to be moved into the homes of less precious plants, which first had to be moved to the kitchen garden, which first had to be cleared to receive them. Difficult.

'Do you think Pat Herald could give us a few extra hours, Kate?'

She shrugged. 'I don't know.'

'Well ... shall I ask her?'

'If you like.'

Smithy asked her. She said there was no point, that she'd be working for nothing when all she earned would go straight to the child-minder.

Smithy asked Kate if they should pay extra for the child-minder. She shrugged. 'Fine by me.'

And that wasn't like her. She wasn't nearly as tight-fisted as Mags had been, but she'd been trained by Mags (and by poverty) never to spend money without first thinking it through. She might eventually say, 'Fine by me,' but she sure as hell didn't begin with it!

A week passed before he began to suspect that something more than a virus was to blame. He advised her to see her doctor. She smiled, raised an eyebrow and said wryly, 'Why should I need a doctor? I've got you.'

He thought she was paying him a compliment at first, but when she walked out immediately afterwards he knew it hadn't been a compliment. The wry little smile, the dry little joke (if it had been a joke) and the sudden exit ... Yes, this was how she'd been when he'd first moved in. And it was having the same effect on him. He felt helpless and lonely, left out in the cold. But how had it happened? What the hell had changed?

No, he was just being paranoid. She was feeling a bit low, that was all. He'd buy her some vitamins.

Pat Herald and the rain began doing overtime at virtually the same moment, making the work even harder. And slower. Yet the timing was critical. If the greenhouse wasn't in place before the first frosts, it would have to wait until spring—and lose them yet another year's profits.

'Never mind,' he said, hoping to sound reassuring. 'We'll do it, I'm sure.'

'Hmm,' Kate murmured. 'I suppose *we* will.' The emphasis wasn't great, but it was discernible and—under the circumstances—unfair in the extreme. He was doing everything he could to help! He'd taken all her gate duties to free her! What more did she want? Blood?

He almost said all this, but buttoned his lip at the last moment contenting himself with an angry glare, which Kate, who was on her way out again, failed to notice.

Smithy felt sick. They'd gone back to the beginning ... And he didn't know why. Had he done something.? Not done something? What was *wrong* with her?

Their little outing to Frome seemed like a distant dream now. Kate, the happy daffodil, dancing over the bridge; Kate arguing with him, laughing at him, telling him he was beautiful 'inside'. He'd stroked her hand ...

He hadn't thought about it at the time and now was surprised she'd let him do it. But he hadn't touched anything else. She couldn't possibly have thought ...

No, no. She'd been fine after that! So what had he *done?*

A wet Wednesday on unrelieved gate-duty was unrelieved hell. He spent most of it in the ticket office, flicking through gardening magazines, but still managed to get bored, damp and bone-numbingly cold. They had just two people in between two and four o'clock and, as soon as they'd gone, Smithy shut up shop and went home for a hot shower, dry clothes and a coffee.

While he was waiting for the kettle to boil, he wandered through to the dining room to see what progress Kate had made in the private garden. It was like Flanders Field out there: mud, mud and more mud. But then the mud moved. A Kate-sized streak of it, hefting a dustbin-sized lump of it to a pram-sized heap of it, which turned out to be a wheelbarrow.

Had it been anyone else it might have been funny. But it wasn't funny; it was horrible. Pat had gone home an hour ago and although she'd said she'd had to hose herself down before she could leave, Smithy had thought she'd meant her boots, not her entire body! He knew for a fact that Kate's waterproof suit was luminous orange, but except for a few patches on her shoulders, there was no orange to be seen.

Having been caked in mud more than once on his own account, Smithy knew how it felt. It weighed a ton, it pinned you down, made every move ten times the effort. Bad enough when you were six foot two and in training, but when you were Kate? Undersized and under par ...

He opened the window. 'Kate! It's time to come in! You've done enough!'

She didn't turn. She picked up another load, dumped it in the barrow, fell flat on her back and got up again as if nothing had happened.

'Kate!'

She took up the handles of the barrow and went slithering off down the path, lurching and sliding like a drunk on a skating rink.

There had scarcely been a day during the past two years when Smithy hadn't thought, 'I wish I could run,' but he'd never wished it as much. He wished he could run after her and catch her in his arms and tell her ... Tell her ...

Oh, God, he loved her!

But he couldn't tell her that!

He went round by the back way and through the copse at the top of the kitchen garden. Without risking the mud it was the shortest way, but he still moved slowly enough to think he'd miss her.

He didn't, quite. As he emerged from the trees, she was putting the last of her barrow-load of plants in the ground, down on her knees, scooping soil around the roots with her hands. He knew why: a spade was worse than useless in these conditions. But she looked so pitiful ...

'Kate!'

She ignored him. She stood up, scraped her

342

hands down the front of her coat (which made no difference at all) and clumped away with her wheelbarrow.

'*Kate!*' It was a parade-ground yell, dragged from so deep in Smithy's lungs, its force almost knocked him down. But it stopped Kate.

They met halfway down the path, she making even slower progress than Smithy, hampered as she was by a few kilos of mud under, over and probably inside her boots.

'Yes?' she demanded irritably.

'It's time to come in. You've done enough.'

'What?' She dragged off her hood. 'I can't hear you!'

He sighed. Now she had mud in her hair, too.

'It's time to come in,' he said again. 'What are you trying to do? Kill yourself?'

She stared at him. He couldn't read the expression on her face, but a barely perceptible movement of her shoulders warned him that she was about to shrug and turn away. He caught her wrist. In fact all he caught was a handful of mud, but her wrist was in there somewhere. Squeeze hard enough ... And there it was: caught.

'Now,' he said. 'Are you going to drag me along with you, or let me take you home?'

'For God's sake,' she snapped. 'I've almost finished!'

'You *have* finished.'

She stared at his hand, willing him to remove it, but only a few seconds passed before she

343

sighed and fell into step beside him.

They didn't speak again until she came down from her bath: clean and relatively dry, but still not quite recognisable, still not quite ... Kate.

He gave her a glass of wine and swallowed a mouthful of his own, steeling himself to tell her that the greenhouse could go on hold, that it didn't matter, that he'd realised at last that 'we' were not doing all the work: *she* was. But he'd have to be tactful ... for once.

'I'll explain this as simply as I can,' he said. 'I mean as truthfully as I—'

'Oh, shit,' Kate muttered. 'Not *more?*'

The shock made him blink. Kate didn't use foul language. 'Sod' was her favourite expletive, with the occasional 'bloody' thrown in if she was really cross; but this ... what was *wrong* with her?

'More what?' he asked stiffly.

'More truth!' she snapped angrily. 'I'm sick to death of the truth! Tell me a few lies, will you? Just to make a change?'

He'd been scanning his mind for the best part of a fortnight for the error he'd made. Now he tried again, but still found no answer. It had begun when she was ill. He'd lain awake half the night, lusting after her underwear ... Then *she'd* woken him up and *he'd* told her to get into his bed. He had not been polite; he *had* made her cry. But he'd apologised! And she'd seemed to accept ... Or had something happened *after* that? He didn't know.

344

Lies. He hated lies and confusions, dishonest games. Why couldn't she just *tell* him what had hurt her?

'Okay,' he said. 'I'll tell you a few lies. Your hair is black, your nose is green, your hands are blue and I hate you.'

Her face, which had been a picture of misery, changed as he recited his litany, first to blink and look away: *You're boring me;* and then to scowl at him under her eyebrows: *Did I hear what I thought I heard?*

'My hands aren't blue.' She turned them over, as if to make sure.

'No, I was lying.' He smiled, but Kate didn't look at him. She traced the grain of the table and watched her finger tracing it, six inches to the right, a few turns around a wood-knot and six inches back again.

'So you don't hate me?' she concluded at last.

'No, I don't.'

He'd hoped, when he'd said it, that she might think in terms of opposites rather than negatives, but now he was glad she hadn't. Kate didn't want him to love her. That was the last thing she wanted.

'I didn't mean to hurt you,' he said, 'or make you unhappy. And that, I'm afraid, *is* the truth, whether you like it or not.'

Her eyes filled with tears. She examined her fingernails, turned in her chair to examine the floor, scratched her neck and at last (to the wine bottle) said, 'I'm starving. What's for supper?'

Chapter Twenty

Kate had been thinking in terms of opposites, not negatives. She'd also been writing the script again, the one Smithy was determined now to follow. According to the script, she said, 'You don't hate me?' He said, 'No, I love you,' and they lived happily ever after. But he kept missing his cue, plunging her into a state of labyrinthine embarrassment from which there seemed no escape, except through the humdrum, 'What's for supper?'

'Steak, salad and baked potatoes,' he said. 'The potatoes aren't done yet.' He smiled. 'And the truth I was attempting to tell you was about myself. I didn't realise, until I saw you up to your eyes in mud this afternoon, how hard I'd been pushing you.'

'Pushing me?'

'To get the greenhouse organised.'

'You haven't been pushing me. *I* want the greenhouse organised.'

Smithy sat back in his chair. 'So where have I gone wrong? What truth, exactly, are you sick of hearing?'

Kate blushed and looked elsewhere. How could she answer *that* without making a bloody fool of herself?

'I don't know,' she said, playing for time. 'You're hard to please, that's all.'

'I don't understand,' he said. 'Hard to please in what respect? You're a wonderful gardener, you work like a slave, you're—'

'Arrogant" she murmured, addressing a dent at the corner of the table which had suddenly become the most interesting thing in the room.

'What?' He looked at her as if she'd gone mad. 'Arrogant? For God's sake, Kate, that's the last thing you are! What on earth put that idea in your head?'

'You did.'

'*When?*' His eyes widened suddenly and without turning his head he looked away, the penny dropping so violently Kate almost heard it clang.

'Ah,' he said. 'I'd forgotten that. I was ...' He smiled, touching his fingers to his mouth as if to suppress laughter. 'I was barely conscious at the time, Kate, and ...' He screwed his mouth to one side and directed his gaze at the wine bottle. 'I was—er—trying to be tactful.'

'Tactful,' she repeated flatly. 'Oh, well, thank God *you're* not the United Nations Ambassador to Moscow.'

Smithy laughed, a joyous whoop which lit his eyes and made Kate blush, simply because he looked so happy.

'All I was *trying* to say,' he said, 'is that I don't—er ... that is, that I wouldn't impose on you while you were ...' He laughed again. 'You're right. I could start World War Three this way, couldn't I?'

He stood up and busied himself making the salad before adding thoughtfully, 'Maybe it's

347

you who's difficult to please, Kate. Having erected your barriers, you know precisely where they are ... and I don't. Look at it from my point of view, will you? I do my best to keep on the right side of your—er ... special sensitivities, but I can't always get it right, can I?'

He began slicing a pepper and then stopped and looked down at it with a frown. 'I'm a man and you're a woman. Even leaving out the development you fear—'

'I *don't* fear it,' she said. 'That's the whole point!'

'You don't?' he asked softly. 'I thought the whole point was that you did.'

'Yes, but ...' Kate sighed. She couldn't just blurt it out without first knowing that there was more to it than man and woman! She and Robert had been no more than that and she'd rather die than give herself up to *that* again!

'But you're different,' she said.

'Am I, Kate? In what way?'

'Well, for one thing, I'm not afraid of you. I know you; I trust you and—'

And then the doorbell rang. They both jumped and stared at each other (no one ever came to the front door; no one ever came at all after dark), and Smithy sighed and said, 'I'll go.'

Kate could have wept. She'd been almost there! And so, in a way, had he. Maybe he didn't love her, but she knew he felt more than he dared to say. Her 'special sensitivities' were getting in *his* way, as well as hers, and yet the way he'd hauled her in from the garden was

348

surely an expression of some kind of love? If he didn't care—'

Smithy had closed the kitchen door but now she heard him shout, 'Good lord!' as if he'd had the happy surprise of his life. Then his voice faded and another—a woman's—filtered through from the hall. Kate couldn't distinguish what was being said, but knew it was bad news. None of his friends ever used the front door. Pamela and her family never used the front door. Was it Tess?

Her heart thudding, she crept to the kitchen door and opened it, one inch at a time. 'I've no idea,' she heard Smithy say. 'She's around here, somewhere, but—'

Why was he saying that? He knew exactly where she was!

And then she heard her mother's voice. 'Well, it's lovely to see *you* at last. After all this time! But you aren't at all as I imagined! So tall, so ... Goodness, isn't it a dreadful evening? So this is where you live! I've never been inside this house before, you know, and ... Well, I wonder where she is? She wouldn't be gardening at this time of ... Absolutely bucketing down now, and so dark, the headlights don't seem to penetrate ...'

Kate tiptoed along the passageway, biting her lip. What was her mother doing here? They were meant to be having lunch tomorrow, which meant—she didn't know what it meant, except that it meant trouble; and there was trouble by the barrow-load in her mother's voice, her unfinished sentences and the breathless, little-girl giggles that punctuated every phrase. She was doing it because she didn't want Smithy to get a word in, even to ask why she was here.

She was pacing the hall like a tiger, talking her head off; Smithy standing with one arm outstretched to indicate the sitting-room door, watching her as if she were some kind of weird insect he'd found on the lettuce.

'Hello, Mother,' Kate said. 'What are you doing here?'

Laura laughed. 'Ah, there you are, darling! Smithy said you'd ... Well, I've met him at last, but why didn't you tell me he was so ... Isn't he gorgeous? And so tall! I didn't expect—'

He sent Kate a look which managed to say both, 'Save me,' and, 'What *did* you tell her?' but apart from 'crippled' Kate couldn't recall telling Laura anything about him. He was private. He was Kate's. She hadn't wanted Laura to get anywhere near him. Yet here she was.

'What are you doing here?' she asked again.

Laura laughed again. 'Well, you did say I could come, darling, and I just happened to—'

'Just happened to be passing?' Kate smiled cynically. 'You're a liar, Mother.'

A great shudder rippled through Laura's body. Her smile fell into shards, making her look old for a moment before she pulled it all together and laughed again. 'Oh, it's nothing to worry about, darling. You'll be pleased, I know you will!'

She turned her head to stare at the wall, her eyes filling with tears. 'I've left Robert,' she whispered.

Smithy had been almost there. He'd uttered the dread phrase, 'I'm a man and you're a woman,' and Kate—he was sure—had understood its implications, even if she hadn't quite grasped where it might be leading. *I trust you,* wasn't—in the circumstances—an especially encouraging sentiment, but it was a beginning. If she trusted him and if he was careful not to hurry her, he might just be able to tell her how he felt. But he hadn't got that far before the doorbell rang and now he had an idea he would never speak, that the choice had been taken from him, its death-knell the doorbell and the manic jangle of Laura's laughter.

Although he'd never, to his knowledge, seen her before, he'd recognised her instantly. Older, smarter and more overtly feminine, she was nevertheless Kate's spitting image. Yet he'd hated her on sight and, had the rules of courtesy not prevented it, he'd have slammed the door in her face rather than let her in.

He didn't understand it at first. He hadn't felt the same about her husband, the one who'd actually *done* all the damage. But as she paced and prattled, loitered and laughed, it all became perfectly clear. Robert *hadn't* done all the damage. He was nothing; a contemptible, jumped up little toad whom Kate could flatten (in fact, *had* flattened) in a moment. No, it was Laura who was the real culprit. It was she who'd betrayed Kate, she who'd damaged her beyond repair. Skin deep? Yes, what Robert had done might well have been only skin deep had Laura

351

then not driven it through Kate's heart with the point of a knife.

He wondered why he hadn't seen it before ... But then, you had to see Laura to believe she was real. She had a physical fragility that Kate didn't share, a brittle, almost manic quality that made you feel a word could shatter her, let alone the no-holds-barred pasting Smithy felt she deserved. And now she was here, invading Kate's territory, her last safe haven. He had no right to ask her to leave, but guessed that if she stayed she would destroy everything, just because Kate loved her and would suffer—had suffered—anything, rather than tell her what she could not bear to hear.

Yet as soon as Kate spoke to her mother, he understood something new about her. She wasn't like Laura at all! She was *strong*. You could knock her down as many times as you liked and she'd bounce straight back, every time. But it hadn't always been true, surely? When he'd first known her she'd been as brittle as her mother, albeit in a different way. But she'd softened, warmed, grown ...

Yes, she had changed. But what had changed her?

He caught his breath and looked at her just as she looked at him with a warmth in her eyes that gave him the answer he needed. She'd said she trusted him. And for a girl like Kate, who'd never trusted anyone, trust and love were the same.

He smiled. He almost laughed. He could cope with anything now!

'I've left Robert.'

Kate had waited years for her mother to say those words, but now ... It was too late. She didn't care any more, except to feel sad that she didn't care.

'Why?' she said, and had deliberately to make her voice soft, deliberately to express a concern she did not feel.

'Some woman.' Laura laughed, like a mother whose little boy has been getting into mischief again. 'Oh, she's not the first!'

Kate resisted the urge to say, 'But you've known that for a long time, haven't you?'

Being cruel and not caring were different things. She couldn't make herself care. She could only make herself seem to care. And it looked as if she would have to, anyway. If Laura had left Robert, where else could she turn but to Kate?

'Come on,' she said gently. 'Let's get a cup of tea, shall we?'

'I think I'd rather have a drink, darling. I need something with a little strength in it.'

Smithy went off to the kitchen to fetch some wine. Kate took Laura into the sitting room and tried to guide her to a chair, but her mother had other ideas. 'So this is Whitsun Gate! Oh, you *do* need a decorator, don't you, darling? Good Lord, what happened to the carpet?'

'It was a magic one,' Kate said. 'It flew away.'

She stooped to put some logs on the dying fire. 'No,' she said. 'we had some rugs in here,

353

but they were dangerous for Smithy, so—'

'He's fine now, though, isn't he? And so—oh! Not at all what I expected!' She threw Kate a bewildered glance, almost a frightened glance, as if Smithy's unexpectedness (what *had* she expected?) had suddenly made Kate rather unexpected, too. But then, she thought they were lovers, tied up with each other, absorbing each other, like husband and wife.

'I'll fetch the glasses,' Kate said.

She ran to the kitchen, to Smithy, as if to a private place where she could be herself again. And Smithy greeted her as if he understood that, his smile warmly rueful as he asked softly, 'All right?'

Kate shrugged. 'She hasn't said any—'

'And this is your kitchen!' Laura said brightly. 'Well! It's quite ... large, isn't it?'

Large as it was, Kate felt herself holding her breath, drawing her elbows close to her ribs, as if they were all jammed inside a tiny lift-cubicle, going down. She also guessed that for as long as Laura stayed (dear God, how long?) she was likely to follow Kate everywhere, just so that she could keep talking. Talking about anything, everything and nothing at all, rather than have to think about Robert.

She talked for the next hour and never mentioned him again. Smithy took a polite interest in her suggestions for decorating the house, but when he found he couldn't divert her from her 'original Georgian wallpapers', and she wouldn't let him answer her questions or forward his own ideas without interruption, he stopped trying and 'just looked'.

Kate looked too, but didn't listen. Her mind was too busy with other things. Where, for example, was Laura going to sleep? The best spare room was piled up with junk, as well as with the dust and cobwebs that had gathered since she'd last attacked it with a broom and mop. The bed was probably damp, the bedding lurking somewhere in the bowels of the airing cupboard ...

While Laura was examining the curtains, guessing their age (about the same as her own) and measuring up for new ones, Kate caught Smithy's eye and whispered, 'I'm going upstairs to make the bed.'

But Laura heard. 'Oh, I'll come up and help you, darling!'

Kate's heart had barely time to sink before Smithy volunteered to drown instead. 'I was hoping you'd help me get supper, Laura.' He smiled invitingly enough, but there was a commanding edge to his voice which provoked a panicky acquiescence in Laura, 'Oh—oh, yes, of course I'll help, if that's—' and a surge of gratitude in Kate which made her want to kiss him.

'Right,' she said, 'see you,' and hurtled from the room before another word could be said. She stripped the electric blanket from Smithy's bed, put it on Laura's, heaved all the junk into the next room, upended a broom to sweep the ceiling and curtain rails, swept the floor, dusted the furniture and swizzled a wet mop over the lino. At intervals during all this, Laura came to the foot of the stairs to call, 'Sure I can't help, darling?'

Panic and irritation aside, the only thoughts to pass through Kate's mind while she worked were surprising ones. She was ashamed of her home and sorry it offered Laura such cold comfort. She also recognised that her failure to take an interest in anything domestic was only in small part the result of Mags's influence. It was mostly an act of defiance, a determination to be as unlike her mother as she could possibly contrive. It hadn't worked. She'd give her eyes, at this moment, for a few acres of fitted carpet and a *hoover!*

Although by no means the longest evening Smithy had endured, his evening with Laura was certainly one of the longest. The loathing he'd felt for her at first sight did not so much diminish as get buried under rock-falls of other emotions: pity for her, anxiety for Kate, a growing conviction that, if she was allowed, Laura would talk for a million years rather than entertain a serious thought for her own predicament.

She talked about decorating the house. She talked about food—cooking it, serving it, eating it, buying it. She compared the merits and failings of various supermarket chains, bemoaned the demise of small, specialist foodshops and described the locations of the various butchers, bakers and greengrocers she'd patronised in Bath when Kate was small. 'All gone now, of course. And there used to be a wonderful fishmonger, but that's gone now. There used to be a marvellous cheese shop, but that's gone too.'

Smithy was tempted to add, 'I used to be sane, but that's gone too.' Luckily, he couldn't get a word in.

The best thing she said all evening (part of a detailed recital of Kate's childhood: colic and teething problems, chickenpox and measles, what the doctor had said and how wrong he'd been), was 'She's not a bit like me, of course, except in looks. She's got her father's mind, her father's ways. Drives me mad, sometimes—'

Smithy doubted that Laura's emotional state had much to do with her genetic make-up, but he was glad Kate was like her father, just the same.

'He was a very quiet man,' Laura went on briskly. 'Very self-contained, just like Kate. I'd talk to him for hours and all he'd ever say was, "Hmm," but he was as solid as a rock. I always knew I could depend on him.'

This was the nearest she came to saying anything about Robert's being as solid and dependable as slime, but she changed the subject immediately afterwards, sending Smithy into a state verging on coma as she told him about her charity work: the shop she helped to run and the minute details of her colleagues' lives, loves, clothes, hairstyles, skin blemishes and ingrowing toenails.

She talked all through supper, coffee and the washing up. Kate's eyes had blanked out. She said, 'Hmm,' and, 'Oh,' and, 'Oh, did she?' and at half-past nine began to yawn. Even at dead of winter she rarely got up later than six or stayed up later than ten. Her energy, between times, seemed inexhaustible, but once she started yawning she was finished. And she'd had a harder day than usual, today. If she didn't go to bed pretty soon, she wouldn't make it off the sofa, let alone up the stairs.

Laura was describing someone's wedding photographs. 'I'm not saying it wasn't a lovely *dress*, but honestly, Kate, I can't say the same for the—'

No sense waiting for her to draw breath. She never did. Smithy said, 'Come on, Kate, you've had it for today. Show Laura to her room and—'

'Oh!' Laura laughed. 'It's only half-past nine! Isn't he bossy, darling? I'm not even tired, let alone—'

'Kate,' Smithy said firmly, '*is* tired.'

Laura's smile slipped away like snow from a sunny roof. It was the saddest thing he had ever seen. She was clearly terrified of going to bed, of lying awake all night in a strange house, alone, with no one to hear her screams. And that was all she was doing, really. Screaming.

But until she stopped screaming, who could help her?

'Take my radio with you,' he offered. 'And Kate will find you something to read. I'll make you a flask of tea in case you wake in the night.'

'Oh ...' Her eyes filled with tears and as Kate shepherded her into the hall, she began weakly to cry. 'Oh, Kate, oh, Kate! Oh, what a beautiful man! Oh, I do envy you, darling!'

He supposed she meant 'beautiful inside', which, in the circumstances, was very perceptive of her! But why should she envy Kate? He'd barely uttered a kind word all night, and then sent the pair of them to bed as if they were children! Oh, well, maybe she liked the strong, silent type ...

Kate came down again within a few minutes to fetch the radio from his room and ten minutes after that was back again to fetch the flask. She looked harassed and close to tears and although he felt he was pushing her too far, he couldn't resist asking, 'What did she mean, she envies you? Envies you what?'

Kate's eyes had the propped-up-with-match-sticks look which went with being over-tired, but perhaps because she was tired she didn't even hesitate before she said, 'She thinks we're lovers.'

'What?'

She smiled wanly. 'You heard.'

Smithy had, but didn't entirely believe he had. 'Why should she think that?'

'Because we're living together, and two and two makes five, as everyone knows.'

'You mean you've never *told* her?'

'Told her what? Oh, about ...'

'Your little problem! The one *she* landed you with!'

She smiled and shrugged. 'What would be the point? She can't hear me, Smithy.'

'No.' He rolled his eyes. 'She can't hear anyone, can she?' He moved his fingertips to indicate 'yak-yak-yak'. 'Is she always like this?'

Kate sighed and looked at the floor. 'Not as bad. She's panicking ... and I don't know how to ...'

She reached for the flask and ran her finger in a circle over the upturned cup. 'I was watching her tonight, pretending I was you, seeing her for the first time. I was watching you, too. You think she's only ninety pence to the pound, don't you?'

He smiled. 'Panic takes people that way, Kate. Give her a day or two—'

'No. That's what I was trying to say. It won't work, because I've just realised ... she's been in a panic ever since my father died. And I think the thing that frightens her most is the idea that she's alone.'

Smithy had a nightmare vision of Laura moving in on a permanent basis rather than be alone, but he pushed it aside. 'You mean that's why she married Ratface? Just for his *company?*'

Kate managed a choked little laugh. 'No, not quite. The trouble is ... she's never had to do anything for herself, Smithy. Apart from voluntary work, she's never had a job, never had to take any responsibility for anything. My father looked after everything: house, money, cars, insurance, all the big decisions. I asked her once why she'd married Robert and she said it was nice to have a man around the house. She needed someone to look after her, that's all.'

Chapter Twenty-one

'You needed looking after, too,' Smithy said. 'Remember that, Kate. What you've just said describes a spoiled and very selfish woman—'

'I know!' She'd watched Smithy watching her mother tonight and although a disinterested observer would have said he'd been kind and fairly welcoming, Kate knew otherwise. 'Ninety pence to the pound' wasn't all he'd thought about Laura. She'd bored and infuriated him. He couldn't stand her.

Kate sympathised. She couldn't stand Laura, either, but it wasn't as simple as that; she loved her, too, and wanted—no, *needed*—to help her. But how *could* she help? This was Smithy's home, Smithy's life. She couldn't—daren't—assume he'd put up with a woman he hated (or at best despised) for any longer than basic courtesy dictated. Two days? A week? Then he'd dump a lorry load of rocks on her: the truth, the whole truth ... Kate had found those rocks devastating enough, but she'd been trained by necessity to bounce back into shape when she was flattened, and Laura hadn't. It would kill her!

'Oh, Smithy, please be patient with her! Just for a day or two. I'll—I'll do what I can—'

'Hey ...' He caught her hand. 'Calm down, will you?'

'Yes, but you see ... I've never really looked

361

at it from her point of view, Smithy. All I could think about was what it had done to *me*, so I've been selfish, too, and—'

'Don't be silly. Kate. If you'd looked at it from her point of view, would you have stayed? Got yourself raped just to save *her* precious feelings? Too great a sacrifice, I think, don't you, darling?'

Kate's jaw dropped with amazement. He'd never called her darling! And he was holding her hand, which meant ...

He laughed. 'Just practising,' he explained. 'We're lovers, remember?'

Kate could have wept. She wanted him to hold her, hold her tight, love her and comfort her, not play stupid games! But, since that was what he *was* doing ...

'Ah, yes, darling" she said dryly. 'How could I forget, darling?' She batted her eyelashes at him and turned away. 'I'm going to bed, darling. Don't keep me waiting too long, will you?'

Her exit, though swift, was beautifully executed. She imagined him staring after her, admiring her for her coolness if nothing else. But just as she reached the foot of the stairs, he called sweetly, 'You forgot Laura's flask, darling,' which meant she had to go back and do it all over again.

The next few days were hell. It had stopped raining, which meant that Kate could have put in some useful work had her mother not been there. But Laura was everywhere, not merely following Kate wherever she went but trying to get her to walk in another direction entirely. 'Since I'm here, darling, we might as well get some spring-cleaning under way.'

'You're joking, Mother! I've got a few hundred plants to move—to name but a few.'

But Laura didn't give up. She wanted to be busy and have company while she was doing it. She began to clean out the kitchen cupboards while Smithy was still eating breakfast, heaping the table with tins of beans and sticky jampots, telling him merrily that he lived in a slum, poor soul, and that Kate should be ashamed of herself for 'letting things go'. While he clamped his teeth together and put padlocks on them for extra security, Kate swallowed a scream and walked out, fast.

Not so fast, however, that she couldn't snatch up the telephone when it rang. Owing to the recent bad weather, she was told, the new greenhouse would not be delivered for another week—and that was only if the rain held off in the meantime. Compared with many of the things that had happened to her, this was not a disaster; in fact, it missed the disaster slot by miles. But when she thought of her desperate race to clear the site, and of Pat's nine hours' extra work at double the money, it felt like a disaster—or at least a very good reason for swearing, kicking something and bursting into tears. In the event, she only swore. As she stormed back to the kitchen to report the news to Smithy, he met her in the doorway and had to grab the lintel to keep her from knocking him down.

'Hey!'

'The bloody *greenhouse* isn't coming! They're behind with deliveries because of the bloody *rain!*'

His arm fell to her shoulder. He pressed her head to his chest and gently stroked her hair. 'Shhh,' he murmured. 'It doesn't matter.'

For a moment, if only to support him, Kate had stiffened. Now, suspecting that he was playing the 'lover game' for Laura's benefit, she relaxed, sighed and let her arms do what came naturally: folding around him, holding him close. It felt wonderful. Like flying through a storm into sudden sunshine; like falling contentedly asleep and at the same time waking up, refreshed and ready for anything, because nothing mattered except the scent of his body and the touch of his hand in her hair.

And then Laura laughed. 'Hey, you two! It's no wonder no work gets done if this is how you spend all your time!'

Smithy withdrew, smiling the chill, sadistic smile which, formerly, Kate had seen only in films about psychopathic axe-murderers. 'I think I'll go out,' he murmured. 'Anything I can fetch you from Aberdeen, darling?'

As soon as he'd gone (only to fetch the groceries, with any luck), Laura announced that he was too old for Kate, too cool and sophisticated, too accustomed to better things. 'You'll see what I mean when the romance wears off, darling. He's the demanding sort. I can see it in his eyes. Your father was the same. He didn't want a wife; he wanted a handmaiden.'

'And what did Robert want?' Kate snapped angrily.

'*Every* man wants a decent home,' her mother said. 'Oh, you might have Smithy doing the cooking *now*, but that won't last. Men are all the same—'

'If that's true.' Kate said, 'it's also true of women! And I'd rather—' But she walked out with the sentence unfinished, except in her thoughts. She'd rather die than be like her mother: blind and deaf, terrified of everything but the sound of her own voice!

Like Mavis, though, Laura wasn't as green as she was cabbage-looking. 'Cool' didn't quite describe Smithy, who was too hot to handle more often than not. But 'too old and sophisticated' had rung horribly true; and he *did* want a decent home, which he was most unlikely to get if he depended on Kate to supply it. Even *with* fitted carpets and a hoover, she'd never be housekeeper. She didn't want to be. If that was all a woman was good for once the romance wore off ... Not that it had worn *on*, yet. Not that it would.

In three days of reasonable weather, she managed less than half the work she'd intended to do, and even that half depended on leaving Smithy alone with her mother. She overheard the tail-end of several of their 'little chats', each time doubting that Smithy's patience could last the course. Although he was polite enough, his voice was different when he spoke to Laura: not soft and lazy as it was in ordinary conversation and not rasping as it was when he was being argumentative. It was hard, cold and clipped: the sort of voice he'd never used with Kate, even to tell her she was blood-chilling, craven and undesirable. He kept asking what Laura was planning to do about Robert, told her she should see a solicitor, find out where she stood, do something positive to protect her interests. He was right, but Laura wouldn't listen. She wasn't daft. She knew he was just trying to get rid of her.

The worst thing for Kate was having no chance to talk to him alone, either to reassure him or to find some reassurance for herself. A minute or two was the limit of Laura's tolerance of her own company. If Smithy left her to find Kate in the garden, Laura followed. If Kate left her to join Smithy, wherever he was, Laura followed. They nipped into Smithy's bedroom on one occasion. He closed the door, hissed, 'Are *you* getting any sense out of her?' and before Kate had said more than, 'No, but—' Laura was at the door, saying, 'I thought I'd start on the dining room, darling. All right if I move the computer?'

'I think you'd better sort her out,' Smithy whispered, 'before I kill her.'

At first, Smithy had thought it was worth having Laura there just for the excuse it gave him to play at being Kate's lover. But that lost its charm after their first clinch. He'd expected her to cooperate to the point of not actually kicking him. He hadn't expected her to settle in, like a cat on a velvet cushion, moulding herself to his shape, moulding him to her own. It had very nearly killed him. Her hands stroking his back, his hand stroking her hair ... It was the Victorian ankle syndrome again. You ache to see it. You *see* it! And suddenly you want the whole leg, *both* legs, the lot.

He'd wondered, at the time, if she'd been able to relax just because her mother was there as chaperone, or because she thought it a game, or ... Or because, in spite of everything, it was what she really wanted. It had certainly seemed that way. He'd held her for half a minute at most, yet he'd felt as if she'd always been there, been born there in the moment he had been born and never been parted from him since.

But a man could believe anything if he wanted it enough. Wanting it didn't make it true. Yet he believed it, he believed it! All he needed now was the proof—and he couldn't get that while Laura stayed.

He couldn't get anything while Laura stayed. Peace, privacy, a sensible conversation, a decent meal. He'd surrendered the cooking on the second day, just to give her something useful to do that didn't involve turning the house inside out. On the third day she told him gleefully that she'd made him (*him,* not Kate) a 'lovely treacle pudding'.

He laughed. 'I'm afraid I don't like puddings, but—'

'Oh, what rubbish!' Laura laughed. 'There's not a man alive who doesn't like puddings!'

The rage he felt was out of all proportion to what she'd actually said, but not to her true meaning. She was saying she knew *everything* about men, and he was the same as all the others, a clone, a robot, programmed to respond not as he deemed fit, but as she deemed appropriate to the pattern.

He listened to her more carefully after that and found (without surprise) that he disliked almost everything about her. She was a nervous wreck and maybe that merited some sympathy, but her attitudes were all wrong. She kept putting Kate down, usually when Kate wasn't there to defend herself, and always with that merry, jangling little laugh that said, 'Take no notice; I'm only joking,' but Smithy could allow only one joke of that sort. Perhaps it was just a trick to boost her own confidence, or maybe she was getting in the first strike before Kate could put *her* down, or maybe, if she'd really fallen for the 'lover game' (which was doubtful), she was trying to nudge Smithy out of the picture by directing his attention to Kate's faults.

If that was her game she was on a hiding to nothing. He'd been compiling a ledger of Kate's faults since he'd first laid eyes on her and although he'd since revised most of them, there were a few still outstanding ...

'One-track mind, that's Kate's trouble,' Laura said. 'All she ever thinks of is her silly garden.'

'Her silly garden is her living,' Smithy replied coolly.

'Well, yes. Yes, of course, but there's more to life than work, and she's got—'

'Nothing else? I wonder why.'

'Still, now I'm here, perhaps I can sort her

out a bit. Get this house straight, for one thing.
I can't abide a messy house. I'm sure you can't
either, but we'll soon—'

'Oh, *we'll* manage,' Smithy said quietly. 'It's
you we're worried about. You can't hope to
solve other people's problems if you can't
solve your own, so yours really must come
first. What are you going to do about your
husband, Laura?'

'Oh, he can wait!'

'Maybe he can. But that's not the way to deal
with it.'

'Nonsense! He'll come to his senses! He'll
find out which side his bread's buttered!' She
laughed again, her face twitching with the effort
of not screaming at him to shut up, but Smithy
had begun and knew now that he wouldn't
stop until it was over. Kate couldn't do it;
she could barely look at her mother, let alone
speak to her as she needed to be spoken to.
Needed? Yes. But Laura's needs were of little
importance except as they served Kate's. He
had to pull them clear of one another, sever
the emotional noose that was strangling them
both ... And strangling him.

He pitied Laura, yes; but pity alone dim-
inished giver and receiver alike and did no
one any good. Neither did hatred, of course,
and he *did* hate her, not just for all the harm
she'd done to Kate, but for the harm she could
still do. He loved Kate; he had no doubt of it
now; but, as he knew to his cost, love *wasn't*
a oneway street. It had to run both ways and,
until he cleared the traffic-jam that was Laura,

Kate would be trapped in the middle of it: immovable, unreachable.

So ... he was going to play traffic cop to Laura's double-decker bus. He had no idea which way it would go, but was well aware that his notion of 'truth' was on rocky ground with a woman he scarcely knew. He could tip her over the edge of madness and gain nothing, destroy everything. Kate loved her ... And would hate him if he did anything to hurt her. But he wasn't planning to tell Laura the truth. Just planning to make her tell him. And if she wouldn't ...? Tough!

'Which side his bread's buttered?' he echoed coldly. 'How sad. I hadn't realised he depended on you for money.'

'I don't mean that! I mean ... Well, men are like children, aren't they? They just want—' She met his eyes and must have seen murder in them, because she took one step backwards before continuing brightly, 'Present company excepted, of course.'

Most of the pleasure went out of gardening when you had to do it flat out. Hard work was a thing Kate enjoyed more often than not, but only when she could pause occasionally to ponder what she'd done and was about to do; only when there was time to think out the long-term effects of her planting schemes, anticipate possible problems—in short, do it properly. There was nothing 'proper' about planting tulips like a dog burying a bone, racing against time lest some other dog (Laura) should catch her at it and snatch the prize away. Not that Laura wanted Kate's tulips; she just didn't want Kate to have them, didn't want Kate to care about them, to care about anything, in fact, that wasn't labelled, 'Mother'.

A spoiled and very selfish woman? Yes, Smithy was right. He wasn't *always* right, which was a mercy, because he'd be damn near perfect otherwise. He wasn't even as impatient as Kate had once thought. Given a totally insoluble problem, like Mavis, he could be as patient as the grave (except when she wasn't around to hear him plotting to gag her), but when he could *solve* a problem, he did it fast, cutting through all the irrelevancies like so much bindweed and getting straight to the answer that really mattered. A spoiled and very selfish woman ...

Yes, that was at the heart of it. If Laura was hurt, unhappy, lonely and afraid, if she was too bewildered to cope with the way her life had worked out, she had no one to blame but herself. She'd made the choices. No one had forced her. So pitying her was not merely irrelevant, but useless and destructive. And letting her play her stupid housekeeping games at Whitsun Gate was just adding insult to injury. She couldn't stay. She was making Smithy miserable, and he'd had enough misery; he didn't deserve more. He wouldn't *tolerate* more. If Kate didn't sort Laura out—and do it soon—she'd drive him away and be as bad as her mother. All it would take was a little determination, a little intelligence, a little

371

courage. And she had a little of all those things. Just a little.

She walked back to the house, stopped to wash her boots at the hosepipe outside the kitchen window and heard Smithy's voice, as hard as nails, saying, 'So he's just a child, is he? What does that mean? If it means he's incapable of taking responsibility for his actions, then *you* are a child. And if it means being unable to think, plan, calculate and decide—'

Kate groaned. He'd beaten her to it!

'—then *you* are no more adult than a babe in arms. You turned Kate out to fend for herself—'

'I did not! She left of her own accord!'

'You turned her *away*, Laura, when she really *was* a child! If she'd waited for you to come to your senses, she'd still be waiting, wouldn't she? How long is it now? Six years, seven?'

'Oh, Kate's all right,' Laura said blithely. 'She's got you.'

There was a long, breathless silence. Breathless, at least, on Kate's side of the window, where she tried to imagine the look on Smithy's face—and then wished she hadn't. She was accustomed to Laura's methods of conducting a dialogue—she didn't so much *miss* the point as nip smartly around to the other side—but it was the sort of game Smithy couldn't stand. He was going to blow his top. Any minute ... now.

'Now that's where you're wrong,' he said quietly. 'Kate's on her own and always will be, because—'

'No!' Kate screamed. 'No, Smithy, don't! Don't tell her!'

Her boots still unwashed, she skidded around the corner and in through the back door. 'Don't tell her!' she yelled again. 'It's not *true!*'

Before she was halfway along the passage, Smithy came out to meet her, blocking the doorway, his eyes blazing, his mouth set in a line so savage, she stopped running and simply stared at him.

'What's not true?' Laura cried sharply from inside the kitchen. 'Don't tell me what?'

'Say that again,' Smithy demanded coldly.

'*What's* not true?' Laura wailed.

Afterwards, Kate couldn't decide whether it was the sound of her mother's voice or the look on Smithy's face that had confused her into silence. But the confusion was great: an avalanche of memories and impressions, questions and more questions, with no answers to guide her.

Why was Smithy looking at her like that? He'd been angry with her mother and now he was angry with her. But what had she done? There was anger in her mother's voice, too; anger and tears. And 'What's not true?' sounded so much like, *That's not true! You're lying!*

'Say that again!' Smithy repeated, and her face turned cold as the answer came. He thought she'd been lying all along! Either that, or he thought she was lying now. But how could she explain? What was she supposed to say with her mother here, listening to every word? It was so complicated, so private, so ... desperate! Did he expect her to shout it out loud? *I want to have sex with you!*

And how the hell could she? She had no idea how he felt about her! Fond? What did *that* mean? And if he could look at her like this—as if he hated her guts—how could she say even, 'I love you,' with any hope of keeping her dignity?

Hopelessly searching for something she *could* say, she averted her eyes.

'Oh, go to hell!' Smithy said, and turned away.

But as he cleared the kitchen doorway, Laura came hurtling out, sobbing, 'Kate! Oh, Kate, what's happening? *What's* not true? What did you mean?'

Smithy went to his bedroom and slammed the door.

Laura jumped, looked after him for a moment and then turned again to Kate. 'Well!' she said. 'What a ridiculous fuss to make over a treacle pudding! And *he* has the nerve to tell me *I'm* childish!'

The avalanche of confusion began again, coupled by a wild surge of physical energy which seemed to be centred in Kate's right arm. She wanted to slap her mother's face, knock her down, jump up and down on her and run to Smithy. She wanted to scream at him, beg him to explain. But the only thought to crystallise into speech was, 'Treacle *pudding?* Are you crazy?'

374

Only marginally containing the strength of her rage, she took Laura by the elbow, steered her into the kitchen, shut the door and leaned against it, staring grimly into her mother's eyes. 'Don't speak,' she commanded shakily. 'Don't say one more word, Mother, or I'll—' She swallowed, heaved a deep, calming breath which had no effect at all and then another. And three more.

I'll kill you, I'll kill you, she thought.

But even while she thought this, she heard Smithy saying, *Go to hell,* his voice so cold, so weary, he couldn't possibly have meant anything else. But why? What had she done?

The answer was standing right in front of her, her face streaked with tears, her mouth opening and closing as if the effort to keep quiet was testing her to the limit of her strength. Yes, having Laura for a mother was all she'd done to offend him, but by God, that was enough! Well, she couldn't *stop* having Laura for a mother, but she could certainly get her out of this house, Smithy's home. Laura had a home of her own, and if she didn't want to share it with Robert, she could damn well kick *him* out! And about time, too!

The timing clock on the stove went 'ping!' Laura took the lid off a pot at the back of the stove and hauled out a china pudding basin which she slammed down on the table, saying, 'There! *That's* what all this fuss—'

'Shut up!' Kate snapped. 'Do you think we're all as demented as you are, Mother? Do you

375

imagine—' She paused, took yet another deep breath and went on softly, 'But, no, you aren't demented, are you? You're just selfish, manipulative and dishonest. You want your own way—'

'No!' Laura wailed. 'How can you say that? I've done everything I could to help you since the minute I arrived. Cooking, cleaning ... I've never seen such a mess! And *you've* never raised a hand to help me! All you can think about is greenhouses and tulips and—'

Her voice was like a drug, one of the nasty, punitive drugs notoriously used by the KGB to numb the mind, sap the will and leave one hanging in limbo, deprived of all sense, all feeling.

'—leaving me alone with—'

She'd ruined everything. Again.

'—you should have heard how he—'

It was like being possessed, crushed, sucked dry.

'—scrubbed this floor on my hands and knees and *now* look at it! And you call *me* selfish? How dare you? You're just like your father! You never think of anyone but yourself!'

Kate laughed suddenly, remembering the few thousand times she'd heard that before without ever believing it: *She's just like her father.*

She supposed she'd been too young, when he was alive, to think in terms of resemblances other than the physical. She'd looked like her mother and so had thought she was the same. Yet, 'She's just like her father' referred to other things: his quietness, his disinclination to

376

argue, his love of books and trees and peaceful places. He, too, had been accused of thinking of nothing but his work and, to an extent, Kate had thought it true, for he'd rarely been at home and, even when he was, he'd been 'absent' in his own thoughts, or in a book of someone else's. As different from Laura as chalk from cheese ... And Kate was the same! She *wasn't* like her mother!

'But you loved him, didn't you?' she asked softly now.

Laura's mouth snapped shut. Her eyes filled with tears. *'Yes!'* she sobbed. And that was all she said. It was the only thing in her world that needed no excuses, no pretences. The only thing that was true.

'Then you'll understand when I tell you that I love Smithy and that I won't let—'

It had grown dark outside and all she'd seen in the window was her own reflection, but now she saw something moving beyond it, dimly lit by the lamp over the back door. She ran across the kitchen, leaning over the sink to cup her hands against the glass. Smithy, carrying a bag! Smithy, going away!

'Smithy, no! *Wait!'*

He turned his head to look at her. Then opened the car door and threw the bag inside.

She ran. The kitchen door stuck; the back door stuck; she tripped over the step, slipped on the path—and arrived under the linden tree just in time to see the tail-lights of his car disappearing beyond the gate.

Kate turned to see her mother at the back

door, following, always following, *never* letting go.

'There!' Kate screamed. 'He's gone! *Now* are you satisfied?'

Chapter Twenty-two

Kate cried for hours, huddling under Smithy's duvet, soaking his pillow. At first she felt nothing but grief and rage, so tightly enmeshed she hardly knew one from the other. All she knew was that it wasn't *fair!* He was *always* talking, damn him! Telling her this, explaining that, asking, probing, analysing, criticising; yet the one time she'd needed an explanation ... Oh, how could he go off without saying a word of why, or where, or when he'd come back?

He'd never come back. She knew it as well as she knew her own name. 'Go to hell,' he'd said; and he'd meant it! But what had she done? What had she said?

Don't tell her! It's not true!

'Say that again.'

She should have said it again. Why hadn't she? Why had she supposed he was asking for explanations? If she'd said it again, maybe he wouldn't have looked at her that way: so angry, so cold ...

She wept until she was sick of weeping. And then went back to the beginning again. Why had he been so angry? What had she *done?*

Lied? Lied about Robert? Lied about everything? He'd been reminding Laura that she'd thrown Kate out, and Laura had said: 'I did not! She left of her own accord!' and that, in a way, *was* true. Laura wasn't the type actually to *throw* anyone out. But she'd given Kate no option! She *hadn't* left of her own accord. She'd been driven!

Her head ached, her eyes burned. She slept and was suddenly wide awake again, staring into the darkness as the circle began anew.

Why had he been so angry?

And where was he now? He'd have gone to Inky or Phil and would be telling them everything about her. Even without her bloody mother she was bad enough, he'd say. Cold? She was blood-chilling. Craven, arrogant, unattractive ... She couldn't even cook!

Kate wept again, slept again, and dreamed of being crushed by an avalanche of her mother's treacle puddings.

'I've brought you some tea,' Laura said softly. 'I've packed. I'll go in a minute, but ...'

'What time is it?' Kate croaked.

'Half-past ten.'

Kate sat up, groaning. Her eyes were so swollen she could scarcely see and the room was lit only by the light from the hall. Yet she knew that her mother had been crying, too.

'I just want to tell you that I ...' Laura sighed. 'Every word you—and Smithy—said about me was true. And I'm sorry, Kate. Sorry for everything.' She sighed again. 'I should never have married Robert.'

Kate swallowed her tea, not caring. 'Why did you?' she murmured hopelessly.

'Oh, because I couldn't bear to live alone. Because I couldn't—' She sat on the bed, tipping back her head to stare at the ceiling. 'I couldn't fill in my tax returns,' she said bleakly.

'What?'

'I didn't even know how to pay the gas bills. Your father had done all that sort of thing and I ...' She shrugged. 'I took it all for granted. I didn't understand any of the mechanics of living and I didn't want to *learn*, Kate. It scared me. I flew into a panic every time a buff envelope hit the doormat. I wasn't short of money—far from it—but I used to lie awake nights, thinking the electricity would be cut off, that the car would break down ... And don't tell me I was pathetic. I know.'

None of this was new to Kate—she'd worked most of it out for herself—but it was new to hear Laura admitting it. Her voice, like Kate's, had been changed by too much weeping, but that wasn't the only change. She wasn't just hoarse, she was calm. Calm and sad, accepting sadness as she'd never before accepted it.

'And then there was you,' she added gently. 'Twelve years old and growing up fast. When I wasn't lying awake worrying about buff envelopes, I was lying awake worrying about teenagers. Boyfriends and sex, illegitimate babies, drugs and drink, men loitering on street corners waiting to ...'

'Rape me,' Kate supplied wearily.

Laura bowed her head.

'You knew it was true, didn't you, Mother? You knew I wasn't lying.'

'Yes.' Her voice was barely audible. 'And I know what it did to you, Kate. Mrs Fitzwarren told me.'

'What?' Kate whispered.

'She wrote to me. She said—this was a few weeks before your eighteenth birthday—that I'd ruined you; that you were terrified of men and would never ... never have the chance to be the kind of mother I *should* have been. And, of course, she told me what kind of mother I really was. Selfish, stupid, irresponsible ... All true. I knew it was true, but I told myself it wasn't. I believed her, Kate, but I didn't *want* to believe her. I couldn't bear to think I'd done you so much harm.'

If only in the name of charity, Kate knew that this was the time to absolve her: to say, 'No, it was Robert who did the harm.' But it wasn't true. Robert had only knocked her down. It was Laura who'd then driven a steam-roller over her.

'I meant ... Oh, Kate, when I first wrote and asked you to meet me for lunch, I *meant*, I really meant to ... talk to you, to tell you that I'd been wrong!' Laura shook her head. 'But I couldn't do it.'

'You're doing it now, Mother. Why not then?'

There was a long silence before Laura spoke again, her voice softer than ever. 'Well,' she

381

said, 'I've nothing to lose now, have I? I've lost you; I've lost Robert ... not that he was worth much.' She took Kate's hand. 'But at least he dealt with the little buff envelopes.'

Kate sighed. She knew Laura was being ironic, but knew too that she was voicing a *real* fear, however minor it might seem to anyone else. Some people were afraid of spiders, some of snakes or—even stranger—of butterflies or birds. Buff envelopes were no more ridiculous. But she'd never heard of anyone actually *marrying* a man to fend such things off.

'Did you ever love him?' she asked.

'I *told* myself I did. I'd known him so long, Kate. And I knew he wanted me. What I didn't know was that he wanted everything in a skirt, my own daughter included.'

She turned to face Kate, grabbing her other hand, as if she thought that holding them both might complete some kind of circuit of forgiveness.

'My only excuse is that he ... he's a *fool*, Kate. He didn't know what he was doing to you. He thought he was just playing! He didn't realise you couldn't defend yourself, that you didn't understand, weren't *old* enough to know how to deal with it. Any grown woman would have told him to get lost—many women have—but you never said a word. And he thought ... He thought you liked it.'

Her heart thudding with rage—not with Laura, not even with Robert, but with herself—Kate slumped back against the pillows. She knew now why Smithy had gone; she knew why she hadn't said again, 'It's not true'. Because it *was* true. Still true! She was afraid of him. No, she was afraid of any man who might make her feel as helpless, as powerless and ashamed ...

'No!' she wailed. 'He *did* know! Oh, *you're* the fool, Mother, not him! He knew precisely what he was doing! He knew I couldn't do anything to defend myself without hurting you! That's what he depended on!'

She began to weep, the tears running down her face unchecked. 'And you weren't *worth* it!' she sobbed. 'You sold me down the river just to get your bloody gas bills paid!'

Laura sat in silence for a long time, her hand gently patting Kate's leg under the duvet until she stopped crying and blew her nose.

'You didn't even tell him *why* I'd left home, did you, Mother?'

'No. We didn't talk about it at all until this year, last summer, when he saw you here.'

'He *told* you?'

Laura smiled wanly. 'He didn't have much choice. He was afraid you'd tell me first. But that was why I said he didn't know what he was doing. He said you'd ... mentioned it, but he was genuinely bewildered, Kate. He actually *asked* me what he'd done.'

Kate laughed bitterly. 'And you said you hadn't a clue?'

'No. I told him what he'd done. And he said, "Oh, that! That was nothing!" And then I knew ...'

'Knew?'

'That I'd sold you down the river for nothing,

Kate. That's what *I* am; and that's what *he* is. Nothing.'

'And ... is that why you left him?'

Laura pushed a hand through her hair. 'I didn't leave him. He left me. You've seen the state I've been in, Kate—partly because of Smithy—'

'Smithy?'

'But mostly because I ... I haven't been able to live with myself, Kate. Not for years. And when I told Robert what he'd done, it was the first time I'd faced what *I* had done. It drove me crazy. I hated myself so much I couldn't bear it, but I ...' She laughed softly. 'Well, *naturally*, I dumped all the blame on him. I made his life a misery—not before time, but nevertheless, it wasn't *all* his fault; most of it was mine—so he packed up and left. I managed three days on my own. And then ... then I met Smithy.'

He hadn't been at all what she'd expected. The last time she'd seen him had been when long hair was in fashion. He'd been about sixteen, not yet fully grown except for his hair, which had hung to his shoulders in a mane of blond curls.

'Ringlets?' Kate asked wistfully.

'No ...' Laura frowned, trying to remember. 'More like bubbles, I think, but blond, very blond. He's quite dark now, isn't he? That was the first shock. No, the first shock was his height. No ...'

She'd been shocked by everything, in fact: the complete Smithy. Although she'd made some logical adjustments to the remembered image—aged him a few years, cut his hair—he'd remained much the same in her mind.

'He ... *matched* you,' she said thoughtfully. 'Actually, he looked a lot like you when he was a boy—looked as you do now, I mean—and that's what I expected to find: a matched pair of young, innocent ...'

'Gullible?' Kate whispered.

'No, not gullible. But I came to make my peace with you, Kate—as I'm trying to do now—and although I expected you to judge me as harshly as I deserve, I didn't expect *him* ...'

She'd thought they were lovers, *young* lovers, with love to spare for the penitent mother whose faults, however great, had been erased by their love.

'But it was like meeting the avenging angel,' she said. 'I said who I was, and he looked straight through me—and loathed me—and I didn't know where I was after that. You've changed so much over the past year, Kate. You've blossomed, relaxed, grown prettier, even dressed differently. And I thought ... Well, it did seem strange that you were using the bathroom upstairs when there's a bathroom down here, but I honestly thought you were sleeping with him, darling. I thought *that* injury, at least, had been healed. And then he said you were alone ...'

She rubbed her eyes. 'Well', she added softly, 'young and innocent he ain't.'

'So you hate him,' Kate sighed.

'No! I can't say I *like* him, exactly ... He terrified me from first to last, but only because

... Because he's the first man I've respected after knowing him for *half* a day, let alone three.'

'Didn't you respect Daddy?'

'No. At least, I *would* have, if I'd bothered to get to know him—to understand him, I mean—but I didn't do that until it was too late. He was a gentle man.' She carefully separated the two words, making certain Kate understood her. 'And although Smithy is most certainly a *gentleman*—'

'Gentle he ain't,' Kate concluded wryly.

And yet he *was* gentle. When you were being what he wanted you to be. And all he wanted you to be was—

'Honest,' she whispered. 'That's all he wants people to be. Just to be honest and—and brave enough to look for the truth and face up to it.'

'And that's why he left? Because you'd called him a liar?'

'I didn't call him a liar!'

But maybe she had. He'd been telling Laura the truth, as far as he knew it at least, and when she'd said it wasn't true maybe that *was* how he interpreted it: that in telling him only half the truth, she'd *made* him a liar.

'It's complicated,' she said hopelessly. 'Mags told him I was afraid of men and he's respected that completely. He's never touched me, never said anything suggestive, never looked at me the way men look when they're giving you the come-on ...'

And because of that, she'd trusted him. Because of that, she'd loved him and imagined—

386

for some ridiculous reason—that if it ever came to *making* love, she'd go into a trance and know nothing more until it was over. It would be just like Mavis's romantic novels, where he takes her in his arms, breathes, 'Oh, my darling, come to me ...'

And suddenly they're having breakfast in their bathrobes on the terrace.

'What I mean is, I thought I wasn't afraid. I really *believed* I wasn't afraid, but when he told me to say it again, I was! I couldn't say it again, because then he'd say, "Prove it," and I couldn't!'

Laura smiled. 'I was afraid, too,' she said, 'the first time. Most women are, Kate, the first time. Do you ever want to touch him?'

'All the time.'

'Do you watch him? Do you think he's beautiful?'

Kate nodded miserably, feeling his absence from the house like a lead weight on her shoulders.

'He made everything beautiful,' she said. 'I love even the scar on his face and I suppose that's not beautiful, but it seems so to me ...'

With a huge effort of will, she swallowed tears.

'Know what I think?' Laura said gently. 'I think you're just a virgin: ready and willing, but too much in the habit of being scared to believe it. And there's nothing to it, really. All you have to do is ...' She smiled. 'Tell him you want him, but tell him you're shy. He'll see to the rest.'

387

Kate smiled sadly. 'You're probably right,' she said. 'But he's *gone*, Mum! I can't tell him now, can I?'

Laura burst into tears and, since this was precisely what Kate needed to do, she wept, too. She pulled Laura into her arms and rocked her, back and forth, like a child.

'It's not your fault, Mum!' she wailed. 'It's mine!'

Laura blew her nose. 'Nonsense" she said. *'Everything's* my bloody fault. But that wasn't why I was crying; I was just being selfish again. You called me Mum! You haven't done that since you left home!'

It was strange ... a little word that had escaped without Kate's notice, yet it meant everything, it forgave everything.

'Oh, well,' she smiled. 'You weren't my mum after that, were you? You were my bloody mother.'

They stared at each other blearily for a moment and, in the same instant, said, 'God, my head's *splitting!*' and laughed.

Kate's headache lasted for five days. This was partly because she refused to take aspirins, preferring Mags's favourite remedy: 'Hard work and fresh air.' But it was mostly because, every time she stopped crying and announced to her mother (who'd unpacked), 'I think I've dried up, finally,' something always started her off again. It was usually the telephone.

Her conscious mind kept telling her, 'He won't ring; it won't be him.' Yet when she heard another voice—trying to sell her double glazing or confirming her order for beech hedging—her heart sank, her eyes filled with tears and her head was splitting again.

And yet, paradoxically, she was aware that those five days were some of the happiest of her life. She talked endlessly with her mother, not merely catching up on the 'missing' years, but learning things about Laura she'd never known before. That she'd been brought up in poverty was the most surprising—and the most revealing—for it explained almost everything Kate had never understood: Laura's passion for cleanliness, her obsession with 'appearances' *and* her terror of little buff envelopes!

Her father had died when she was very young; she and her mother had lived in dread not only of the arrival of the gas bills, but of certain days in the week when the rent had to be paid, or the butcher, or the grocer. They hadn't quite worn rags, but one of Laura's most painful memories was of wearing her school coat until it was four inches shorter than her skirt and wouldn't do up.

'It wouldn't have mattered,' she said, 'if we'd just been poor. We weren't the only ones, after all. But my mother was accustomed to better things. She was ashamed of being poor and passed that on to me. I told myself lies about it: that my good coat was at the cleaner's, for instance ...'

For her first—in fact, only—salaried job, as a clerk at the Admiralty in Bath, she'd bought her first good suit, on credit, from a mail-order catalogue. She'd made the last payment on it three years later: 'A week before I married your father.'

Laura's mother had died when she was eighteen and afterwards she'd reinvented herself as a smart young thing temporarily down on her luck. 'I almost believed it myself,' she said. 'I was careful not to tell any *actual* lies because, having tried that at school, I knew I'd get found out. But you can lie by implication, by omission, by seeming to misunderstand the questions people ask ... The important thing was to convince *myself* I'd been brought up in the manor house, because if I could believe it, who could doubt it?' She smiled ruefully. 'No one did. Your father didn't.'

'Did you *never* tell him?' Kate asked incredulously.

'No. I've never told anyone, until now.'

It was clearly a relief to her, but not nearly as great a relief as it was for Kate to talk to her about Smithy. On one occasion, she spent the best part of ten minutes just describing his hands. And the best part of an hour describing his smile and his laughter, the way his eyes lit up when he was picking an argument ... all beautiful!

'But he thinks he's ugly, Mum. I suppose it's because he was so good-looking before. He was vain about it, too—it's one of the things I didn't like about him when I first knew him. He thought he was God's gift. And now he thinks he's ugly.'

'*Really?* Is that what he told you?'

390

'Not exactly; but he thinks his wife left him because of how he looked after the accident, and I think it was just because he was crippled. She didn't want him when he was well, so why should she want him when he was an invalid? Invalids don't go away on Army exercises, do they? She'd have been stuck with him. No freedom to play around with other men.' She shrugged. 'She was like that, apparently.'

Laura smiled. 'We should have introduced her to Robert. But hasn't it occurred to you, Kate, that if Smithy thinks he's ugly, he's probably as shy of you as you are of him? If he's ashamed of his looks—and let's face it, "looks" don't end at the neck—maybe he's just shy of taking his clothes off?'

Kate hadn't thought of that. She worried about it for the rest of the afternoon and then almost kicked herself for bothering. Because they'd never got that far. He'd held her hand, he'd stroked her hair, he'd said he was fond of her. He'd also said he'd have to be desperate ... *and* that he wasn't!

So she was just going around in circles, playing games with what might have been, or could be one day, if only he were here. But he wasn't here. His computer was here. His stereo was here. His camera and most of his clothes ... She'd looked at these things, stroked them—as if by one remove to touch Smithy—telling herself that he must come back, if only to fetch them. But he'd ditched a whole house rather than see Tess again and even his mail could be claimed by a solicitor.

He'd never come back.

While Kate worked in the garden, Laura went on cleaning the house and finally arrived in the attic where she found a cardboard carton full of Mags's diaries. They covered a period of ten years: from the day she and Billy had bought Whitsun Gate to three days after they'd opened to the public. The last entry, on 10 March 1964, concluded, 'Oh, bugger it! I haven't got time for this!'

'Hmph!' Laura said. 'Typical!'

And then the phone rang.

Chapter Twenty-three

Smithy had no right to feel elated to be going home; he kept telling himself he had no right, forcing himself into another state of mind, reminding himself of the cool, the calm, the sensible decisions he'd made while he was away. It had been Kate's idea—the first she'd ever voiced—to turn the house into two separate flats, and this, he was certain, was the right thing to do now. They'd be colleagues, neighbours. Friends, if he could bear it. But they'd live separate lives. As soon as his insurance money came through.

Grimly he drove across the wild, misty wastes of Salisbury Plain, imagining what Kate would say when he told her he was 'moving her into the shed'. He wanted her to be pleased. He wanted her to breathe a sigh of relief and start planning how they might arrange it. But he couldn't imagine that. He could only imagine her looking shocked, asking him to reconsider ... And then he'd find his hand tapping to the music on the radio and feel a similar rhythm catching at his heart.

But he'd get over that. He'd worked it all out. All he needed to do was keep himself detached until he could make the pair of them *semi*-detached. It wasn't impossible; he just had to imagine she was married to someone else. Even if it was only a metaphorical marriage—like a nun's—it would put her beyond the moral pale.

She'd sounded so strange on the phone. He'd thought she had a cold at first and he still wasn't certain she hadn't been crying. But if she had, there was nothing he could do about it. A man couldn't love a woman without making love to her; and she *couldn't* make love. He'd seen it in her eyes. The entire sorry story:

It isn't true!

Oh, yes, it is ...

Few things were more hurtful than to see that kind of fear in a woman's eyes. But he'd get over it. And it was a comfort to know that he'd never deceived himself where she was concerned. She had faults. Her mother was one of them.

'Is Laura still with you, Kate?'

'She's just leaving. In a few hours, that is. We've—er—sorted it out, Smithy. She's all right now.'

Hmm.

'And she's found a box in the attic, full of Mags's diaries. Gardening diaries, I mean. I haven't had a chance to read them properly yet, but they look good.'

Warminster. He hadn't spoken to his friends on his way out and he wouldn't do so now. Talking about it wouldn't help if he couldn't tell the truth, and the truth was Kate's business alone. But that wasn't the reason he hadn't called in. He'd still been thinking—no, feeling, wishing—that Kate might be his wife one day, and he did *not* discuss his wife's sexual hang-ups with his friends.

But he was over that. He'd thought it all through. He couldn't live with her; he couldn't live without her; but he could live by the rules. Be calm, be kind. And *detached!* The first thing he'd tell her was that he'd be going away for a while ...

Pamela had been unusually sweet to him this time round. He'd thought—for a split second—that she'd sussed his problem, when in fact she'd just been angling for a decent holiday on the cheap. 'You look a bit down, Smithy. Why don't you give yourself a break, darling? Whitsun Gate is always so *freezing* in winter—'

True.

'And you haven't seen your father for ages. Hey, why don't we *all* go to Kenya?'

Bless her little cotton socks. Still, she at least *knew* she was as transparent as cling-film. Unlike Kate's mother, who was as obvious as a charging buffalo, yet somehow managed to

394

convince herself she was being subtle!

So he was going to Kenya. He and his father had never got on—inevitable, really; his father was a diplomat of the first water—never spoke a true word if a polite lie would serve instead—but blood is thicker than water and the old guy had wept when Smithy had asked, 'What's the weather like out there? Fancy a few visitors?' So that was all arranged ...

Frome, and suddenly he was scared. Ten minutes more. And what would he find when he arrived? Kate had never been predictable. There wasn't one word that would sum her up. 'Dull' did it for Pamela, 'sparky' for Joanna, 'peaceful' for Jane and 'loud' for darling Mavis. But Kate was an enigma; just when you thought you'd pinned her down, she moved, she changed, she became something else.

Treacle pudding? Are you crazy?

God, if he hadn't been so furious, he'd have laughed like a drain. Three days of virtual silence, patience and passivity, and suddenly *that!* Had she really sorted Laura out? It seemed about as unlikely as Pamela doing the can-can; Laura needed three years in a clinic to sort her out, not—

He shrugged. No, maybe all she'd needed was to get her daughter back; all the more reason for Smithy to remove himself from the action. He was getting stronger by the day and another three days with Laura might well give him strength enough to strangle her. Sorted out or not sorted out, she was always going to *yak.*

He drove through the car park at Whitsun Gate, his heart thudding. He parked under the linden tree and made another sensible decision. He'd get it felled and damn Kate's opinion on the subject. It was a bloody nuisance. All it did was make work. Even now, with the honeydew problem at an end for the year, it had filled the yard with fallen leaves: slippery and dangerous in the wet, blowing everywhere in the wind. It could go.

He slammed the car door, fished out his bags from the back of the car and slammed the tail-gate shut, expecting the sound to bring Kate out to meet him.

He hadn't allowed himself to be elated at the thought of seeing her again, yet in spite of himself had been so. Now, as if all the lights had gone out, his elation died. In spite of everything he had thought, decided and planned, nothing meant anything without Kate. But he couldn't have her; she didn't want him.

She was standing at the far end of the hall, her stance reminding him of a game he'd played as a small child, where everyone skipped and jumped until the one who was 'It' cried, 'Statues!' and everyone turned to stone. He could only suppose Kate had seen his car from the landing window, run downstairs just as he opened the back door and, as their eyes met, turned to stone. Only a moment passed before she moved again, but it seemed like an hour to Smithy.

There was time for him to imagine Tess standing beside her: tall, pale and immaculate with shining red hair. The contrast was extraordinary. Even in suspended animation, Kate was full of life. Full of light, of warmth and colour, and so many feelings, so many aspects to her nature, you'd need a lifetime to get to know half of them. It had taken him just three years to know Tess; to know her to her bones and find that there was nothing worth knowing.

She'd been hot in bed; red-hot, like her hair, but in the end all she'd done was burn him. Maybe it was true that love was no good without sex; but not nearly as true as that sex was no good without love. It was love he needed. The love of a woman's heart and soul and mind. But, oh, he wanted her body, too!

He sighed, and all his sensible decisions withered and blew away, like linden leaves on the wind.

And then Kate moved.

'Hi,' she said. 'Good journey down?'

It was like going back to the beginning, when Pamela had brought him down for Mags's funeral. But Kate hadn't been shy of him, then. She'd never been shy until now. 'Shy' wasn't when you kept people at arm's length; it was when you wanted to run into their arms and stay there forever—but didn't dare move for fear of making a mistake.

'Fine,' he said. 'No problems.'

He looked and sounded only marginally less angry than when he'd left and although he'd given no hint of it when he'd telephoned, she now had the idea that really he had come home only to get his things. But she mustn't panic. Make him feel welcome. Make him change his mind ... That was all she could do.

She smiled. 'I'll take your bag, shall I?'

'Thanks.' It was of the carpet-bag variety, scarcely big enough to carry a single change of clothes, but it seemed to be weighing him down; he couldn't even lift it towards her. She stooped to take it and, as she straightened up, felt his lips brush her cheek before he turned to close the door.

'Well?' he said, when she made no move to clear the gangway. 'Aren't you going to scream?'

'No. Why should I? You missed.'

'I never miss.' He still looked angry. And yet he'd kissed her, which meant ... She didn't know what it meant. A tease, a taunt? Perhaps, taking that he knew—or thought he knew—everything about her, he'd meant it only to hurt her.

She carried his bag to his room, calling over her shoulder, 'I'm glad you're back. The house rattles when you're not here.'

'That was your mother,' he said.

Kate slumped at the foot of his bed, grinding her teeth on a yell of frustration. Then, 'Yes,' she called dryly. 'Sorry about that. Want some coffee?'

'Yes.'

But he was standing with his back to the sink when she returned to the kitchen, standing with his hands in his pockets as if deliberately to thwart her pretence of carrying on as normal.

She paused, smiled, tried to read his face,

his eyes, the cynical half-smile which could be—probably was—just the scar twisting his mouth to one side. But there was something in his eyes ...

'Oh, before I forget,' he said, 'I'm going away. To Kenya.'

She'd seen slugs do what she did then. When you sprinkle salt on them, they shrivel up: just turn inside out and slowly die. They can't help it. Neither could Kate. The only thing that surprised her, when the first agony passed, was that she was still standing more or less upright. She couldn't see. She couldn't speak. But at least she was still standing.

'Kate?'

She shook her head, closed her eyes and leaned against the door jamb, trying not to cry. She knew nothing else until his hand touched her hair. 'What's the matter?' he asked softly. 'I was talking about a holiday, Kate, not emigration.'

The relief was wonderful, but it lasted scarcely a moment before rage took its place.

'Why?' she screamed. 'Why don't you emigrate? You're no damn good to *me!*'

'No,' Smithy sighed. 'I don't suppose I am.'

She was sorry on the instant. Two minutes ago, she'd been frantic to welcome him home; now she was telling him to emigrate. Telling him he was no good!

He put the kettle on. She sat at the table with her head in her hands, trying to find her way back to where she'd been, but having little idea of where that was. Fearing he'd leave her, yes. That was why his little bombshell had blown her apart, because she'd been expecting nothing better. But it *was* better. A holiday wasn't forever.

'I'm sorry.' she said.

He passed her a cup of coffee and sat opposite her, rubbing his eyes, stroking his cup, waiting.

'It wasn't true,' she added, sighing. 'You're every damn good, as I'm sure you know.'

'No, I didn't know.'

'I can't think why. It's true.'

He smiled. 'Well, that's a comfort.' He seemed disinclined to say more, but when Kate looked up again, he was watching her, as if still wondering what her 'tantrum' had been about.

'You looked angry,' she explained miserably. 'When you came in, I mean. I thought you'd decided to leave. After ... last week.'

'I wasn't angry, Kate. A little apprehensive, perhaps.' He grinned suddenly. 'I was afraid you'd shout at me.'

It was all right, after that. All right, but not the same as before her mother's visit. Smithy seemed quieter, less inclined to argue and, strangely, Kate missed all those little explosions of his, aware for the first time that they'd always been *little:* blow up, cool down, laugh and begin afresh. He didn't sulk, bear grudges, or keep harping back to unresolved questions. He'd just been 'clearing his tubes'.

His quietness, by comparison, seemed very big. It meant something, and she didn't know what. Depression? Decisions made and not discussed, like his bloody holiday, but worse? Not that she could bear to think of anything worse than his holiday. He'd be away for three whole weeks, at Christmas of all times! That was bad enough. If there was anything worse in the offing, she didn't want to know.

There were two hopeful signs: he supervised the construction of the new greenhouse with sufficient enthusiasm to indicate that he would make use of it in the spring, and he read Mags's diaries (one volume behind Kate) with an interest which almost matched her own: laughing every now and then, murmuring, 'Well, fancy that,' when something new caught his attention. The diaries were unlike any gardening book Kate had ever read; they were hilariously funny in places, expressing Mags's character as well as that of her garden, and with a little editing (or maybe a lot), Kate was convinced they would make a book that would sell. As usual, Smithy poured cold water on the idea: 'It'll be difficult to condense them without losing their spirit.'

'I could try, couldn't I?'

'Yes,' he said, with as much enthusiasm as if she'd offered to invent a solar-powered helicopter, 'you could try.'

But he was mostly out, disappearing for hours at a time and usually coming home laden with shopping. She guessed from the carrier bags he brought back that he'd been buying new clothes for the trip to Kenya, although the only thing he showed her was a pair of shorts.

He held them in front of him, over his jeans, baring gritted teeth to ask, 'What d'you think?'

They were fashionably long, pleated at the waist and in a colour halfway between cream and safari brown. Smart, typically expensive, perfectly appropriate.

'Nice,' she said.

'If I wear tennis socks halfway up the calf?'

She pulled a face. 'What on earth for? You'll get a brown stripe through the middle.'

He smiled pityingly and turned away. 'You haven't seen my legs.'

'Yes, I have.'

He turned again. 'When? How could you?'

He looked so amazed the chance of teasing him seemed too good to resist. Kate shrugged and assumed an expression of off-handed guilt. 'Oh, you know. Keyholes.'

'*What?*'

She laughed. 'When I was ill, you fool. You had your bathrobe on.'

'Oh!' He blinked and thought it over. 'I'd forgotten that.' Then he frowned and repeated warily, 'Socks?'

Kate knew it was important. He was afraid of what other people would think, which was crazy, because other people would scarcely notice. They'd just think, 'Nasty accident,' and forget it. Women might be more bothered, of course ... A stranger, attracted to his top half ... But if Kate hadn't been shocked, why should anyone else be?

Because no one else loved him, no one else

knew him, no one else cared enough *not* to care that he wasn't perfectly symmetrical.

'I read somewhere that women are mostly attracted to faces and—and bums.' She blushed and laughed, craning her neck as if to get a better view of his nether regions. 'And you're all right in both departments. I'd forget it, if I were you. Just smile—and twitch your hips a lot.'

Smithy pulled a disgusted face. 'They'll think I'm gay, you daft bat!'

Kate shrugged, deciding privately that this might not be such a bad thing. 'Okay,' she conceded. *'Don't* smile.'

He laughed then. But that was the last time he laughed and he barely smiled in the week before he left, although he talked a good deal and appeared to be having a crisis of conscience about leaving her alone for Christmas.

'I'll be all right,' she said. 'My mother's coming.'

'Wouldn't it be more comfortable for you to go to her?'

'No.'

He didn't ask why. Although she'd mentioned Laura to him more than once, he wasn't interested, didn't want to know. In some ways Kate felt the same. Robert had asked for a truce (his girlfriend had ditched him) and although Laura had resisted so far, there was no guarantee she'd last the course. She'd discovered direct debit for paying the bills, but she still hated being alone. As did Kate.

She was so dreading Smithy's departure, it

didn't cross her mind that he could be dreading it too until he was about to leave. He'd spend the night at Pamela's, leave his car there and then travel to Heathrow in Michael's car. With Michael to see to the luggage and Pamela to wait on him in the departure lounge, it looked like being a trouble-free journey, so it seemed strange when he said, 'Wish me luck, Kate?'

'Yes, of course. Have a lovely time.'

He tipped his head to one side, waiting for more.

'And good luck,' she added obligingly.

Smithy's shoulders slumped. His mouth tightened with exasperation. 'Not like that, you fool. A kiss wouldn't exactly hurt you, would it? You've got three weeks to get over it!'

'Oh!' She was amazed and would have been delighted had he not spoiled it with that 'three weeks' jibe. She wouldn't need to get over it. She *wanted* it.

Laughing, she stepped forward, looking down to hide a deepening blush. She'd have stayed there a month, just waiting for the blush to fade, but he'd miss his plane if she did—the plane coming back as well as the one going out—so waiting wasn't an option. She tipped up her face and found him gazing at the wall, inclining his cheek towards her as if she were a child.

Kate had no wish to kiss him like a child. If ever she was to become a woman in his eyes, this was her chance to prove she could do it. But his cheek was close, his mouth far away.

'In your own time,' she murmured. 'I can wait.'

She didn't wait long. Surprise brought his head around and, insofar as she'd deliberately surprised him, Kate at *that* point was in charge. But Smithy took over, his mouth covering hers before she could draw breath. Instinct made her wince; not so much with fear as with resignation. She knew what would happen next.

But her expectations did not materialise. His arm around her waist was soft and warm, his mouth on hers like velvet: stroking, rather than crushing; tasting, not consuming. She knew it wasn't the real thing, knew there was more; and the resigned part of her mind seemed to shrug and mutter, 'Oh, get on with it, will you?'

But Smithy withdrew. He set a child's kiss at the corner of her mouth, another on her cheek, another on her hair, and then just stood, looking furious again.

He took a deep breath, produced an approximation of a smile and said briskly, 'Right, I'm off.'

He opened the door. 'Don't come out.'

She stood in the doorway and watched him go, walking more briskly than usual, scarcely using his stick. He was in a hurry now. He'd found her wanting and couldn't wait to see the back of her. He reversed at speed, turned at speed and drove away fast. He didn't even wave.

Although Christmas was all they'd arranged, Kate had fully expected Laura to join her at Whitsun Gate as soon as Smithy left it. She discovered, when she telephoned, that her mother had other ideas. 'Oh, no, darling. I haven't finished my Christmas shopping yet. And I'm going to a party on Wednesday, there's a sherry do at the shop on Friday and I'm having the neighbours in on Saturday, so it'll have to be Sunday. No, it's the carol service on Sunday. It'll have to be Monday.'

'That's Christmas Eve!'

'Yes, and guess what I'm doing *after* Christmas?'

Kate had hoped she'd be seeing in the New Year with her only daughter, but now guessed otherwise. Scowling into the telephone, she muttered glumly, 'Surprise me.'

'I'm going on a cruise! With Georgie Marchant!'

'*Who?*'

'Georgie Marchant. You know, darling. I've told you about her thousands of times, but you never listen, do you?'

'No,' Kate agreed weakly. 'He's a transvestite, is she?'

'Georgina, you idiot. Interior decorator. She's left her husband, too, but they'd booked the cruise months ago, so we're going together. Won't that be marvellous? A holiday in the sun while everyone here freezes!'

Kate began to think she was the only one who'd be left to freeze. Even Mavis and Jeff were going to Tenerife ...

Well, she wasn't going to spend the entire three weeks moping. She'd work in the garden when the weather allowed and, when it didn't, she'd work on Mags's diaries. Difficult they might be, but they were too good to waste.

She didn't go into Smithy's room until two days before Christmas and then only to get his electric blanket to air Laura's bed. His good luck kiss had proved something of a torment, not for the reasons he'd assumed, but because—as with everything else where Smithy was concerned—it had been so inconclusive. He'd kissed her as if he loved her, looked as if he loathed her ...

But he'd left a Christmas card on his pillow, her name on the envelope written large and very upright, with no loops or decorations save a long, slashing stroke at the end, which seemed to indicate he'd written it in a hurry.

The picture on the card was a botanical drawing of a Christmas rose; the message—under the printed greetings—just said, 'With love, CFS'.

Not even 'Smithy'. And *that* kind of love didn't mean anything; it was just a polite alternative to 'Yours sincerely'. Better than nothing, she supposed, but she had doubts, even about that. She'd expected nothing and would not have been disappointed if he'd left nothing; but somehow his initials were worse: impersonal, cold, unkind.

She turned the card over and found more writing on the back. 'Look in the bottom of the wardrobe on Christmas Day. It's wired to explode if you open it before.'

Kate laughed. All the strength went from her legs and she sat at the foot of the bed, alternately clutching the card to her chest and kissing it all over.

She'd ceased caring about Christmas presents after her first Christmas with Mags and Billy, who'd given her a pair of heavy-duty gardening gloves and a hot-water bottle. But the mysterious contents of Smithy's wardrobe drove her almost crazy with excitement. She'd bought him a new wallet, having noticed that the stitching on his old one was coming apart. She'd chosen it to match the old one as closely as possible, hoping he'd notice the care she'd taken and think (perhaps with pleasure) that it meant she cared for *him*. His gift would convey the same kind of message: 'He loves me ... he loves me not.'

She opened the wardrobe at six o'clock on Christmas morning and found three parcels: a flat rectangle directed to Laura (maybe this was the bomb he'd wired up!), a large box shape for Kate and a smaller one, which could be a reference book. She carried them through to the sitting room and left them there unopened, but the rest of the morning was a torment of suspense. She lit the fire, cleaned the sprouts, prepared breakfast, ran Laura's bath and woke her with a tray of tea and biscuits. 'Hurry up, Mum. Father Christmas came. He left something for you, too.'

'For me? *Smithy* did?'

When the time at last came, they both stared at his gifts as if they really *might* blow up, although Laura's exploded only with laughter. It was a glossy cookery book called Just Desserts, with a bookmark strategically placed beside the recipe for treacle pudding. A kind of apology? Neither of them was sure. It was certainly a joke, but even the title was ambiguous. A joke against Laura, or a joke against Smithy?

Her hands trembling, terrified of another joke, Kate opened the smaller of her parcels and found only a box of typing paper. Bewildered, she opened the larger parcel. It was an electronic typewriter, with a sheet of paper inserted on which he'd typed, 'Since you're determined to be a writer ... Go for it, and good luck. CFS'.

Kate laughed and immediately burst into tears. 'Oh, Mum!' she wailed. 'What does it *mean?*'

Laura stroked the typewriter with a reverential finger. 'I think it mean's he's loaded,' she said. 'These things cost a bomb.'

Chapter Twenty-four

Laura departed the day after Boxing Day. She'd talked a good deal: not meaninglessly, as before, but still paying more attention to herself than to Kate. There were moments when Kate resented this, but she reasoned that since they were both in a state of uncertainty, a degree of selfishness —on both sides—was more or less inevitable.

The good news was that Laura seemed to have made up her mind about Robert. Their marriage was over. She was still nervous about living alone, but had taken courage—and some wisdom—from her friendship with Georgie Marchant, who sounded like a woman whose head was screwed on properly. The only trouble was, she'd persuaded Laura that *all* men were closely related to bulls and baboons and, having thought precisely that for the past ten years, it was something Kate no longer wanted to hear. Smithy was different.

'You said yourself he was the only man you'd respected,' she reminded her mother irritably.

'Yes, but that doesn't mean I'd want to live with him! He's too tough for you, Kate. You'll never mange him. You'll be waiting on him hand, foot and finger—'

Kate gave up after that. Laura was talking about herself again. She'd always waited on men 'hand, foot and finger', and in fact knew no other way to relate to them—perhaps simply *because* she'd never respected them.

Maybe, Kate thought, the whole relationship between men and women depended on self-respect more than any other kind. Laura had deemed her only talent to be that of 'handmaiden' and had played the role to the hilt, asking and giving nothing more, expecting to be loved just for her treacle puddings, her perfect housekeeping and pretty face. She'd certainly never asked to be loved for what she was inside. She hadn't liked what she was; she'd been ashamed of it.

The same wasn't true of Kate. In a way, she'd had too much respect for herself, put herself

410

above the rest of her sex, or at least very firmly outside it. But 'firmly' was the word. She'd told Smithy who she was and he'd never asked her to be different from the way she was—just better.

He'd made her better. Not to serve *him,* but to increase her self-respect and thus—hopefully— his respect for her. Even on the subject of Mags's diaries, he hadn't so much discouraged her as pointed out the difficulties she would face. Then he'd given her the typewriter and told her to go for it.

But the house seemed unnaturally silent when Laura had gone and there were twelve days of it to get through before Smithy would come home. It was difficult even to concentrate on reading the typewriter's instruction manual, and a grey, wet dusk had fallen before Kate actually began to type.

'The quick brown fox jumps over the lazy dog.'

A page of that, a page of half-remembered poetry, a love letter to Smithy, which began, 'Yoy werd right; it will take threw eeks? and mor eto get over kisssinb—'

'Oh, very romantic!' She tore the page out, reached for a clean sheet of paper and gazed in amazement at the next sheet in the box, where Smithy had written her name in his large, upright hand. She caught her breath, peeled that sheet away and found a letter beneath it.

I hope you reach this page long before my return and will send your reply to meet me at Pamela's address in London. Please think before you write, Kate. One's instinctive fears—as you discovered recently with your stepfather—are not always the best guide, although this is a case of the pot calling the kettle black: I'm writing this because I'm afraid to speak to you, for reasons which I hope will gradually become clear.

For all my faults—and I realise I have many—the past eighteen months should have taught you that men are not all the same. For some of us—I hope most—the act of physical love is an expression of spiritual love; the animal need is so linked with the emotional it cannot be separated. For example, there are men (I am one) who would find it impossible to employ the services of a prostitute, simply because there is neither time nor inclination to form an emotional bond with such a woman.

The opposite is also true; once an emotional bond is formed, the physical need becomes greater, and that is my present—and increasingly unbearable—predicament. I love you, Kate, and therefore I want you.

She gasped, her heart swelling with so much joy—and so much terror—she hardly knew one from the other. He loved her! But his tone was so cold, so formal. What was he trying to tell her? That she'd ruined it? That he wouldn't be coming back?

Forgive the formality of this declaration. It's my fourth attempt and I'm trying to keep us both as calm as possible. You need fear nothing, Kate. Loving you, in a sense, is like loving myself: because I need you to love me, I'll do nothing to hurt you, or turn your feelings against me.

For this reason, I have done everything to fight off my own feelings, but I lost the fight when I returned from London. You said I seemed angry. I wasn't angry; I was desperate, and have been so ever since, wanting to tell you, fearing to tell you, afraid of the look in your eyes when you understood what I was asking.

You said once that you trusted me. Trust me a little further; give me a chance to teach you that physical love need be no less generous and gentle than the emotional kind. It is an expression of that love, not—as your experience has indicated—its antithesis.

You were forced into that situation and will not be forced by me. You have nothing to lose, Kate. Say no and I will take nothing from you. Say yes, and I'll give you the world.

Think before you reply. Even if the answer you wish to give is in my favour, think it over very carefully. I will never again be entirely fit and if I reach old age—ten years ahead of you—am likely to do so in poorer health than is usual. In the study of patience, tolerance and diplomacy, I think I've learned all I'm ever likely to learn and can't, with any honesty, promise you a quiet life should you choose to spend it with me.

You, by contrast, are young, strong and beautiful, and should you choose to love me now, might one day think you've cast your pearls before swine. That would break my heart, Kate, and so it's in my own defence that I say again, think. Love *is* a bed of roses, after all. Beautiful, I promise you, but still full of thorns.

He signed himself again 'CFS', but it seemed quite different to Kate now. He hated his name, but nevertheless it was his true name and, like every other truth, he would not deny it. Honest as the day ...

Kate was amazed at how calm she felt, how quiet and at ease. She read the letter over and over, finding explanations for everything she'd worried about: his quietness, his anger, his 'good luck' kiss. Although she still feared his 'expression of love' and knew she'd go on fearing it until (God willing) he'd proved such fears groundless, she was aware that the balance had changed. Her happiness had depended on Smithy; now his was depending on her.

Abandoning the typewriter, she spent the rest of the evening writing to him in biro: page after page, explaining everything she'd ever thought and ever felt about him. It was a beautiful letter. She wept while she wrote it, wept while she read it. Then she threw it on the fire and watched it burn.

'Correct me if I'm wrong,' Pamela said, 'but isn't that Kate?'

Smithy's heart was too tired to leap. It just jounced a little as he scanned the waiting faces at the barrier. Their flight had come in two hours late and, although wide awake, he was exhausted enough to think that everything—including Pamela—was a delusion. Even the girl she pointed out at the barrier only looked like Kate because he wanted her to. Anyway, she was looking beyond him, waiting for someone else, and her expensive red coat was like no garment *his* Kate had ever possessed.

'It is!' Pamela gave him a sharp dig with her elbow (she was always forgetting) and he staggered and grasped the handrail, just as the girl in the red coat looked up at him and laughed. 'Oh,' she said. 'I didn't recognise you! You're so brown!'

'It *is* Kate!' Pamela said. 'I told you it was Kate! Kate, what are you doing here?'

'Push off, Pamela,' Smithy said dreamily.

'I was looking for your walking stick,' Kate said. 'Where is it?'

'I left it in a restaurant ...'

'I love you,' she said.

'And I'd walked a hundred yards before I missed it, so I thought—'

She took his hand to guide him to the right side of the barrier. 'I love you,' she said again.

Smithy closed his eyes for a moment, the better to understand her, to believe her and know that it was real. He gazed into her face and knew that she'd loved him for a long time. He'd seen that smile before—a melting smile;

415

he'd taken it for pity!—but never so clear, never so true. She'd always been afraid before. Now she wasn't.

He took her in his arms and kissed her hair. He kissed her eyes, her cheeks, and the tip of her nose. His arms tightened to crush her, to press her body against his as though to fuse them together for ever more.

'You knew about this?' he heard Michael saying irritably. 'Great! Why am I always the last to know?'

'I didn't. I swear! Why d'you think I spent all that time trying to fix him up with Cheryl?'

'Who's Cheryl?' Kate murmured.

Smithy laughed and kissed her mouth, briefly but decisively. 'I haven't a clue. Will you marry me?'

'Yes. Oh, yes.'

'She told *me* she wasn't interested in men,' Pamela said. 'And I believed her!'

'You'd believe anything,' Michael said.

Smithy's exhaustion left him. He felt strong enough to run up the Brecon Beacons. 'Let's go home,' he said.

Long before it was over, Kate knew that if her love could survive the journey home, it could survive anything. The last time Smithy had felt fresh air on his skin it had been thirty degrees in the shade. A 'mild' English January was twenty-five degrees colder and, to bridge the gap, he had the car heater going like a blast furnace. Kate took off her coat—her mother's Christmas present—her sweater, her shoes, her

416

socks. By the time they reached Salisbury Plain, in a howling gale, she was ready to strip to the skin and walk the rest of the way stark naked.

Smithy turned the heater down a notch. Just the one notch. 'I'm getting tired now,' he said, apparently surprised by the phenomenon. 'I could sleep for a week.'

'With me?'

He grinned. 'I think that might keep me awake, don't you? And anyway, I'm not planning to sleep with you for a while yet.'

'You aren't?' She wasn't certain whether this was bad news or good. 'Why not?'

'It's not the way it's done.'

'Oh ...' she said. 'I thought it was.'

'You've been reading the wrong books. He sweeps her up in his arms, right? And all her fears melt away on a hot tide of passion. But it doesn't work that way, Kate. If I sweep you up in my arms, you'll freeze solid—'

'Gosh,' she said, with a wistful glance at the heater control. 'Sounds lovely.'

'And I might never thaw you again. So it has to be a gradual procedure. It'll probably take weeks. Months, if I can bear it. I've been reading about it. I have to build your trust, first.'

'You've done that.'

'Not enough. For me, emotional love and sexual love are virtually the same thing. For you, they're different. One is good, the other bad. You don't believe they can exist together.'

'I do. You told me all that in your letter.'

He laughed. 'But your unconscious mind

can't read, Kate. It's informed by instinct and habit. No matter what your intellect tells it, it still goes its own way. We have to teach it some new habits, that's all.'

Kate threw him a sideways glance. 'Dirty habits?' she suggested mischievously.

'No; it's already got those. It thinks every man is a potential rapist, every touch an assault, every compliment an insult—'

Smiling, she watched him and listened, knowing that he was talking a load of junk, but too happy to put up an argument. It didn't matter. Rendered virtually comatose by the heat, all she could think of was how wonderful he was, how beautiful he was. She hadn't recognised him at the airport. Her unconscious mind had been looking for a pale, haggard Smithy with a convict haircut and a walking stick. A strong, blond, suntanned ear-ole had turned up instead—with curls. They were still very young curls, little half-hoops of tarnished gold, and she had an idea they'd never grow to maturity—but they were lovely while they lasted. He looked fitter, too; not just brown. He'd been swimming every day, sometimes in his father's pool, sometimes in the Indian Ocean. He hadn't spared more than a passing thought for his scarred body. A perfect body, he'd said, was important only for pulling the girls, and the only girl he'd wanted had been thousands of miles away, reading his letter. Answering yes. Reading it again and not answering at all.

'The trick is,' he said, 'to keep touching each other safely for a while. Hands, arms, shoulders, hair. Nothing intimate. Then, when you've grown accustomed to that idea, we'll move a little closer.'

'Closer to each other?' She was teasing him. She knew precisely what he meant and loved him for it, but knew it wasn't necessary. Her unconscious mind was more literate than he imagined. It was a slow reader, admittedly, but it had had twelve whole days to match his letter with the conclusions it had reached long before. When you love a man, when you trust a man and—at long last—when you know he loves you, he can do what he likes with you. Even keep you waiting for weeks on end.

'Closer to the erogenous zones,' he explained crossly.

Kate suppressed a grin, widened her eyes and asked innocently, 'How do we know where they are?'

Smithy glared at her. 'If you're pulling my leg—'

'Oh! Is that an erogenous zone? Am I rushing you?'

He chewed his lip for a while before saying calmly, 'One of yours will get itself walloped if you don't behave. We're doing this my way, Kate. I don't dare do it any other way. It's too important.' He reached for her hand and squeezed it tightly. 'I couldn't bear to lose you now.'

They went to their separate beds before nine o'clock and, for both of them, that was a few hours too late.

But Kate was still too excited to sleep. Over-wound, over-wrought, over-awed ... They'd spent the evening on the sofa, holding hands, which was as far as Smithy would go on Day One. He'd said that if she was very good he might reach her elbows tomorrow. It sounded lovely. Too lovely. Her elbows weren't hugely excited at the prospect, but other parts of her anatomy (the ones near the end of the queue) fairly ached with longing.

It didn't help to have a howling wind at the window, sucking the curtains in and out, like the sound of heavy breathing. Kate usually enjoyed stormy nights; they made her feel safe and warm, grateful for the roof over her head and the soft pillows under it, but tonight—even if she couldn't touch him—she wanted to be in Smithy's bed. That was the safest place.

She got up to close the window and stood there for a while, watching the branches of the linden tree whipping the clouds and the clouds racing the moon. The window didn't fit too well and as soon as she closed it, it set up a moan which recalled to her mind the lines of a poem she'd learned at school and never remembered since.

A savage place! as holy and enchanted
As e're beneath a waning moon was haunted
By woman wailing for her demon lover.

How strange ... She'd been sixteen when she'd learned those lines and had hated them, thinking they referred to Robert. Robert, a demon? No, the demon was downstairs, already asleep, and sleeping all by himself, the demon ...

She shivered, laughed and ran back to bed, to cuddle her pillow and pretend it was Smithy.

'These new aircraft are marvellous,' Smithy's father said. 'Made of the finest porcelain, you know, and virtually indestructible as long as they don't hit anything.'

Smithy hadn't been afraid of flying before. Now he was terrified, partly because the porcelain aeroplane wasn't as quiet as the ordinary sort. It rattled and howled and shuddered, throwing him from side to side until his fist hit the bulkhead, smashing it to fragments just where the wing joined the fuselage.

He woke with a yell and subsided, gasping, realising that—as so often happened—a few seconds of reality had created a dream that had seemed to last an eternity. The rattling and howling was the wind; the crash of broken china just a flowerpot falling (there went another) to smash into fragments on the path.

He felt very rested and wide awake. Although it was still dark outside, this was January, so it might be time to get up. He'd left his watch in the bathroom and lay in bed for a while longer, listening for Kate's early-morning movements to give him an idea of the time. But the gale was too fierce ...

He closed his eyes and thought about Kate. Lovely Kate, adorable Kate ... And about his father, who wasn't so bad after all. Very quiet man, one of the still-waters-run-deep type, not Smithy's type at all. But they'd seemed ... they'd grown more alike, somehow or other.

'Forgive me,' his father had said, 'and try not to misunderstand me when I say ...'

'Hmm?'

'You needed a spot of trouble. Something to throw you back against the wall. It's made you, you know.'

He hadn't said any more, which was a blessing, because Smithy might have wept if he had. 'It's made you,' was not only the first unsolicited praise his father had given him, but also the truest. He'd needed his accident, he'd needed his troubles with Tess to teach him not only his own vulnerability but that of other people. The whole experience had taught him humility: an understanding of pain he'd never before suffered, humiliations he'd never before endured. Fear, loneliness, the crushing weight of depression ... Add it all up, and what did he have? He had Kate, who wouldn't have touched him with a bargepole before his troubles had 'made him'.

He'd told his father about her, too. Everything about her. And his father had said, 'Got a book, somewhere ...'

He had ten thousand books. History, science, medicine, architecture, English, French and German literature, botany, zoology. And sex: how to do it, how to do it better, how to do without it and what to do when it all goes wrong.

The first thing you have to do when it all goes

wrong is toughen up. It's one thing to keep your hands off a woman who might knock you down if you do. It's quite another to keep your hands off a woman who declares herself ready and willing! Silly girl. She *wasn't* ready. She couldn't possibly be. That sort of trauma didn't just go away. It needed patience and gentleness, a slow acclimatisation to touch and feel and ... And to how people looked when they were naked. Oh, God. What if she couldn't hack it? What if the very sight of him revolted her?

He sighed. Deal with it when the time came. Elbows today. Legs next week.

He turned on the light, went to the bathroom and retrieved his watch. It was only half-past three! But he was awake, wide awake. He'd make a pot of tea. He reached for his dressing gown and paused, eyes widening as the force of the storm increased, its growls and screams now taking on another, deeper note, a continuous roar which he supposed could only be the woods taking a hammering. Was Kate sleeping through it? It was really quite scary; worrying at least. He hadn't yet heard anything that sounded like breaking glass, but it would be ironic to lose the greenhouse just as they'd finished building the bloody thing.

And then there was another sound. A terrible rumbling from overhead, as if the roof—

Kate screamed, 'Smithy!' and he dropped his dressing gown and tore out of the room just as she leapt down the stairs, still screaming, 'The linden tree! It's coming down!'

He had no idea how tall that tree was, but had

thought more than once that its height might be greater than its distance from the house ... A catalogue of his many decisions riffled before his eyes like a calendar of wasted days. He'd meant to get the house decorated; thank God he hadn't. He'd meant to fell the linden tree; why hadn't he?

He caught Kate by the waist and tried to steer her under the stairs, but she was terrified, sobbing, clinging to him so hard, he couldn't move.

It was as if the bowels of the earth had burst open. The tree shrieked as it fell. The house shuddered and all the lights went out. Smithy held Kate's head against his chest and cradled her in his arms, aware that if the roof caved in, he'd break like a twig.

There was a rain of hail against the kitchen window and then a strange, breathless silence, as if the storm had paused to view the ruin of its rage before it took breath to rage anew. The house was still standing. Smithy and Kate only just.

'It's all right,' he breathed. 'It's all right, sweetheart, it's over. Don't cry.'

'Did it miss us?'

'I think so,' he smiled. '*I'm* not dead anyway. Are you?'

'No.' She laughed and wept in the same breath. 'But I can't see you. It's brought the power lines down!'

'Hmm,' he murmured.

'Smithy!'

'Hmm?'

'What about the beech tree on the daffodil bank?'

The gale was a westerly. The beech, if it fell, would hit the car park, not the house.

'Smithy!' she wailed. 'If the beech tree comes down it'll kill us!'

He smiled and held her closer, burying his lips in her hair. The lights were out, her pyjamas at half mast ...

'Let's die happy,' he whispered.

Shocked as she was by the fall of the linden tree, Kate was yet more shocked that Smithy had 'fallen' for the beech tree trick. His sense of direction was unerring, which meant he should know that a westerly gale pushes everything eastwards: the linden tree towards the house (its topmost twigs had actually brushed the kitchen window), the beech tree towards the car park. But he was scared, she'd felt him trembling in her arms, clinging to her as hard as she'd clung to him, and only a fear that he'd remember the 'rules' and send her away again kept her from telling him that this was a westerly gale, that he was safe.

He took her into his room and closed the door, holding her gently, kissing her gently, although he shook as if the gale were at his back and only his own strength sheltered her from its force.

'It's all right,' he whispered. 'It's all right, sweetheart, I won't hurt you.'

'I know,' she said, and was amazed to discover that she wanted him to hurt her, to kiss her hard and hold her hard, to push his body into hers until they fused into one.

He sat at the foot of the bed, holding her between his knees, stroking her face like a blind man, as though to learn who she was through the touch of his fingers. She wanted to discover the same mysteries in the same way: learn everything she needed to know by touch alone; but the fury of the gale had invaded her blood, driving her helplessly against him, as if against the only rock in a stormy sea.

'Hold me!' she wailed. 'Smithy!'

Smithy was amazed. It hadn't said anything about this in his father's 'How to do it' manual. Kate was meant to be retreating, not advancing; and he was meant to be coaxing her on, not trying to fight her off!

'Wait, wait!' he breathed frantically. 'We've got all night, sweetheart, as long as it takes.'

He doubted that. If she didn't start behaving by the book, he'd lose his grip and forget everything except how much he wanted her.

'Stand still,' he said gently. 'Let me touch you.'

But Kate couldn't stand still. She took his head in her hands and began feverishly to kiss him: his eyes, his cheeks, his mouth, his throat.

'I love you!' she whispered. 'Oh, Smithy, Smithy, I love you so much!'

It was a wonder he heard her over the noise of the storm, but it was all he wanted to hear, all he'd ever wanted to hear.

'Oh,' he groaned. 'To hell with the book.'

Postscript

Pat Herald's youngest had started school at last and she, new to her status as full-time gardener, had dug the planting hole, flooded it, fertilised it and now stood back to let Kate plant *Tilia Europa,* the only tree—of the dozen they'd lost in the storm—that she hadn't yet replaced. It was barely six feet tall, a mere wand of a tree, but Kate wanted it to get its roots down during the winter and begin to grow just as her baby was born, next spring.

She and Smithy had been married two years. The first had been the worst. They hardly ever quarrelled now, although she had a feeling he'd blow a gasket when he noticed young *Tilia* had taken up residence behind the tearooms. Bossy sod. He'd completely taken over when she'd told him she was pregnant—he'd even planted the tulips this year—but she was already bored with being coddled, and there were six months to go yet!

'Don't worry,' Pat said cynically, 'it'll wear off before you reach your third.' She smiled. 'Graham coddled me when I was expecting James. By the time I got to Miranda, he was too exhausted to care.'

Kate didn't think Smithy was ever likely to reach that stage. Exhausted or not, he noticed *everything*. But there was a chance—just a chance—that he wouldn't notice *Tilia* until it was too late to dig it up.

'Quick,' Pat said, as they heeled in the earth around the roots, 'there's a car coming!'

'It's all right,' Kate said. 'It won't be him. He's gone to do the shopping and that takes—' She turned to see a dark red Volvo turning into the yard. (The grey one had come a cropper when the linden tree had fallen on it.)

'You were saying?' Pat groaned.

Gritting her teeth, Kate snipped off the label and turned, smiling, to greet her husband.

'Hi,' she said. 'I thought you'd be gone for hours yet.'

He grinned. 'Is that what you were hoping? What are you planting? I don't remember ordering another tree.'

'No,' she said. 'But it's all right, I haven't been exerting myself. Pat dug the hole.'

Secreting the *Tilia* label in the palm of her hand, she wrapped her arms around his neck and felt his arms close around her waist, gently, always gently. He was the most gentle man in the world—when he wasn't clearing his tubes—and still the most beautiful. More beautiful by the day.

He loved being loved. So did Kate, and it was a strange thing how love drew love to itself, making everyone sweeter, kinder and more loving than before. They had hardly any time to themselves nowadays, what with Pamela coming down to visit (*and* staying!), and Laura popping in whenever her busy life allowed. She was working for Georgie Marchant now, calling herself an interior decorator (in fact she was only a secretary). But she was an independent woman and happier than she'd ever been as a 'handmaiden', so Kate could forgive her a few little fibs now and then. After all, she wasn't above telling a few herself, now and then ...

'So what is it?' Smithy asked.

'Hmm?'

'The tree.' He detached her arms from his neck, held her hands and discovered the label, which she'd failed to push up her sleeve. *'Tilia Europa,'* he read. 'Common Lime. Why have you cut the label off?' He laughed suddenly. 'Hey! It's a linden tree! You little—'

He grabbed her by the scruff of the neck, turned her into his arms and held her head against his shoulder, stroking her hair. Kate smiled contentedly. He never kept to the script. He'd blow up over nothing just when she least expected it, yet when she gave him good reason to fight—as now—he'd give in like a lamb, making her feel loved and safe, happy beyond words.

His insurance settlement had made him quite well off, given him room to find his dreams. A comfortable home, enough help with the work to make a family possible, and sufficient left over to give the gardens an extra gloss. Books, plants, flower pots ...

'So you don't mind,' she murmured, 'about the linden tree?'

'No. After all it did for us, we owe it a decent home, don't we?'

His hand moved again to the nape of her

neck, tightening to shake her. 'So dig the damn thing up!' he growled. 'And put it somewhere else, where it won't drip on my *car!*'

The publishers hope that this book has given you enjoyable reading. Large Print Books are especially designed to be as easy to see and hold as possible. If you wish a complete list of our books, please ask at your local library or write directly to: Magna Large Print Books, Long Preston, North Yorkshire, BD23 4ND, England.

This Large Print Book for the Partially sighted, who cannot read normal print, is published under the auspices of

THE ULVERSCROFT FOUNDATION

THE ULVERSCROFT FOUNDATION

. . . we hope that you have enjoyed this Large Print Book. Please think for a moment about those people who have worse eyesight problems than you . . . and are unable to even read or enjoy Large Print, without great difficulty.

You can help them by sending a donation, large or small to:

**The Ulverscroft Foundation,
1, The Green, Bradgate Road,
Anstey, Leicestershire, LE7 7FU,
England.**
or request a copy of our brochure for more details.

The Foundation will use all your help to assist those people who are handicapped by various sight problems and need special attention.

Thank you very much for your help.